The angels keep their ancient places;—
Turn but a stone, and start a wing!
'Tis ye, 'tis your estrangèd faces,
That miss the many-splendoured thing.

Francis Thompson

Turn but a Stone

Bernard Bridge

Published by Fisher Press, Post Office Box 41,
Sevenoaks, Kent, TN15 6YN, England

Turn but a Stone was first published in 2011

British Library Cataloguing in Publication Data.
A catalogue record for this book is available from
The British Library

ISBN 978-1-874037-22-4

Printed and bound in Great Britain by
CPI Antony Rowe, Chippenham and Eastbourne

PREFACE

I have given a solemn undertaken not to reveal how what follows came into my possession. But even if I had not done so I believe that some reticence about certain aspects of belief and spiritual matters is desirable. I hope that it will not be held against me that, after much soul searching, I have now agreed to make this public. Further comment might breach the rule that revelation should help create faith, but not impair free will.

The text is based on a manuscript that I have transcribed. The handwriting was at times difficult to decipher, but I have tried to render it as accurately as I could. There was no title or heading of any kind. These are all mine.

Robert Hugh Benson is an historical figure. He was a well-known Roman Catholic priest and best-selling novelist in the early part of the last century. He died at the age of forty-three soon after the outbreak of the First World War. He was buried in the orchard of the large country house that he had purchased at Hare Street, near Buntingford in Hertfordshire. The funds for its purchase were derived in significant part from the proceeds of his success as a novelist. In his will he left this house to the Roman Catholic Archdiocese of Westminster. In his memory a chapel was later erected over his grave. The archbishops of Westminster still use the house and grounds as their country retreat today.

Benson was the youngest son of Edward White Benson, Anglican Archbishop of Canterbury. He had two older brothers. A C Benson was President of Magdalene College, Cambridge and a celebrated diarist—he also wrote the words to 'Land of Hope and Glory', now sung to the tune of one of Sir Edward Elgar's Pomp and Circumstance marches. E F Benson was the second son—his novels on the foibles of Lucia and Miss Mapp capture to perfection certain elements of middle-class village life in the nineteen-twenties and thirties.

Robert Hugh Benson, the third son, was ordained as an Anglican clergyman in the late nineteenth century while still a young man. His first appointment was as curate at the village church of St Mary the Virgin in Kemsing in Kent He remained there for fifteen months during 1897-98. His letters suggest that his Kemsing days were particularly happy.

As the son of an Anglican Archbishop of Canterbury his conversion to Roman Catholicism on 11 September 1902 caused a national sensation. It was again news when he became a Roman Catholic priest in Rome on 12 June 1904. Ten years of skilful defence of the teachings of the Roman Catholic Church followed. Each year also saw the publication of one or sometimes two novels.

It would be vain to seek Bernard Bridge, whose account forms the basis for this book, in Kemsing today. There is a tomb of a Bernard Philip Cyprian Bridge in Kemsing Churchyard. But he died in 1905 when he was just 12 years old. His grave has been at times rather overgrown so that those seeking detailed evidence may need to dirty their hands in order to read the inscription along the flat edge of the grave stone.

Hugh Benson's heraldic device of three trefoils can still be seen in stained glass high up at the west end of the south wall of St Mary's Church, but the motto, 'Fayr bien, crains bien' is now difficult to decipher.

I have managed to establish that there are still today descendants in the male line of the Bridge family who were living in Kemsing in the 1890s. But as far as I have been able to discover there are no recent Bridge connections with the village.

ANTONY MATTHEW

To the Masters of The Keys, past and present,
who will understand,
and with thanks to Geraldine Cutting and
Jock Powell for their help.

CHAPTER ONE

MEETING BY THE CHURCHYARD

AT last I have an opportunity to set down in something approaching chronological order what happened. The notes that I made in the seven Civil Service notebooks, and then took with us for recording what took place on our journey, are before me now on my desk. Their dull, buff-yellow covers look ordinary enough. They were designed for shorthand, and mostly used by typists at the office for this purpose. But given their contents, the two heraldic bars gules on each cover, and what appears as a Government motto above, 'FOR CLASSIFIED INFORMATION ONLY', now seem particularly apt.

The notes within have often proved useful in verifying points of detail or pieces of dialogue to produce this longer account. But there are a few gaps in the notes where I was either too tired, too disturbed, too distracted or too exhilerated to write much. There are also some happenings about which I have thought it prudent to remain reticent.

Many incidents or conversations are recorded at considerable length. Some readers may find some of the intellectual discussions and arguments over long. But they are an integral part of the story. At certain times the notes I made consisted of a few key words or phrases. Nevertheless the events and conversations themselves remain so vividly in my mind that I have no doubt that I could have reconstructed this testimony almost in its entirety without the notebooks. The loss to the account would have been primarily in the charting of my changing states of mind as one startling event followed another.

In the light of my knowledge of the outome, even now I have to be consciously on my guard against any suggestion that as each event took place I had any prior inkling of what might happen next. The evidence that there are people who have something that is commonly understood as second sight seems compelling, even though they may well be only a few in number. I am certain, however, that I have never been one of these. Nor had I previously ever had anything that might be described as a mystical experience.

In order to explain what I was doing on that day when the adventure began I need to say something about myself. My name is Bernard Bridge. I earn my living as a middle ranking Civil Servant in Her Majesty's Treasury. I am not among the Ministry's high flyers. In fact I am rather old for my grade. This was in part because I began my career in Whitehall when I was in my early forties. But also I suspect because my superiors will have marked me down as an incurable dilettante.

There is a large garden at my house in the Kentish village of Kemsing. This occupies me for much of the time at weekends during the summer months. During these long evenings after returning from London I sometimes cut part of the lawn, weed the asparagus bed, summer prune the spurs on the apple trees, or take on other tasks as the need becomes apparent. But in winter, when there is both less to do, or the weather provides an excuse for not working outdoors, I am usually busy with some project of my own.

Recently I had become interested in local history. This had been further inspired by an enthusiast from a neighbouring village. She had given a talk about the information she had been able to glean about members of the families in her village through studying the graves and headstones, or sometimes the very much grander monuments of the village churchyard.

Some rudimentary family trees were able to be constructed where several generations of one family had continued to live and be buried in the village. At times she said it was possible to obtain some insight into the closeness or otherwise of some of the dead's relationships with each other, their profession, even their attitude to death and religion. Their artistic sense or lack of it might be suggested by their headstones and monuments, although without certainty, as these may well have been erected by their heirs without any personal instructions from the deceased.

Since I had already done some work from literary sources on the people who had lived in Kemsing in the late 18th and 19th century I felt inspired to see what additional material I might obtain from examining what I could turn up in the churchyard surrounding St Mary's Church in our village.

So early on a clear Saturday morning on the 5th of March 1983, a little before nine o'clock, I set out from our house in the High Street, and proceeded up Church Lane to St Mary's. It is not much more than a hundred yards from the house to the church. I noticed, as I passed, that there was no sign as yet of any life at the Vicarage. The Vicar and his small family live in this former alehouse. Within, it seems to date from the 16th century, but outside it has an 18th century casing. It is tile-hung on the first storey facing the lane. On that morning I could see that some starlings had already begun investigating a tile gap as a possible nest site.

A little further on I noted that the old people, in their purpose-built modern cottages, laid out on the sides of the two squares around the Church car park, had drawn their curtains. But none had yet ventured outside. The sun was now well up but the experienced would have observed the light north wind which made it still feel chilly. I paused at the lych gate and looked over at the Church.

St Mary's is a typical Kentish very late Saxon or early Norman church. The walls are a quite harmonious mixture of three different materials: rendered and limewashed stone, Kentish ragstone, and flint. The bell tower and short spire are both now shingled in Canadian red cedar. The south face of the steep pitched roof caught the morning sun. Above the grave stones and through the line of trees which form a backdrop to the Church and cordoned it off from the garden beyond, I could just catch a glimpse of the North Downs.

The churchyard of St Mary's is about two acres in area. No complete record of the graves and monuments existed at the time of these events. Anyone like myself wanting to do research had to make his own way. Fortunately the graves are generally grouped roughly into historical periods, although past incumbent vicars have occasionally allowed their parishioners to be buried out of the area which was being developed at the time. At a glance you could tell by the condition and nature of the head stones that the oldest graves were in the South and South Eastern corners of the church.

I wove my way past what I could see were largely 18th and 17th century graves along the east end of the Church. I was looking for some of the 19th century graves to complement my local historical research. I noticed that most graves had been laid out in the traditional East/West axis so that they were facing the right way for the Second Coming, traditionally expected from the East. But I also observed that some of the headstones on the eastern boundary of the churchyard were at the eastern end of the grave, thus blocking the individual's immediate view at the Second Coming.

The gravestones that I was particularly looking for were those of the local squires of the late nineteenth century and early Edwardian period, and of those of an extraordinary 19th century Vicar, and of his immediate family and circle of friends. Kemsing had no more than five hundred souls at that time. I had read some accounts of this period in a village history, and in various letters of those who had lived in Kemsing at that time.

This Vicar was a High Churchman and quite an aesthete. Evidence for this can be seen in the Church: there are some fine monuments on the walls, a reredos and tester in a late mediaeval style, the carved wooden and gilded figures of Christ's Crucifixion on top of the rood screen, and stained glass, most of which date from his time. The subsequent careers of those in the circle and the later literary, artistic and architectural achievements of some, suggested to me that Kemsing must have been passing through a sort of brief Golden Age of culture during his incumbency.

I knelt down in the grass which was still wet from a light frost and began to make copies of some inscriptions and made notes of certain dates. My object was to construct a series of short family trees which would show how those in whom I was interested were related by blood or marriage.

Having done what I could I decided to walk along the edge of the north side of the churchyard looking to see if there were any gravestones which dated from that period but were 'out of place.' I had no success in my quest and soon realized I was now entering the most recently developed part of the graveyard. There was a wall on my right about forty yards long with a concrete path running alongside it. Just off this to the left, about half-way along the wall, was a birdbath in reconstructed stone. I recognised that this was the new site for the burial of cremated remains.

In the interest of conserving space parishioners were now encouraged to have their relations' ashes laid here. Small plaques, after their lettering and text had been vetted by the Vicar, were laid flat in the ground in front of the wall. The flatness, we had been told, was important so that there would be no difficulties in putting a mower over them to cut the surrounding grass.

On impulse I decided to go beyond the end of the long wall to have another glimpse of the 19th century vicarage. This had been built for the Vicar who had presided over Kemsing's flock during its cultural Golden Age. The huge old vicarage was now a Youth Hostel, whereas his latter-day successor now lived in the former ale-house which I had passed on my way up Church Lane.

Despite the sun on its south face the Youth Hostel which I could see through some trees still looked rather forbidding with its three huge gables, dark slate roof and rag stone walls. Nothing was now discernible of what I had read about it in old accounts: its many grass terraces, the Italian garden, the pools and the clipped yew hedges. All the elements of surprise and delight had gone. There were no flower beds or borders, just a huge sloping lawn for ease of mowing.

I was now in a sort of small spinney just inside the Youth Hostel's grounds. I could see no sign of anyone up at the house. Just to my left there was a very small neglected area not far from the wall of the churchyard for cremated remains. Here among some scruffy bushes and stunted saplings the ground rose up into a mound.

I remembered that this was where the old vicarage rubbish dump had been. My wife Angela and several village friends had done a certain amount of excavating here over the years among the stones, clay and other rubble. They had uncovered some interesting 19th century and Edwardian earthenware paste containers, and some old medicine bottles in brightly coloured glass. Occasionally there were fragments of blue or pink china showing just enough of a scene or figures to tantalise but not to enable you to tell what it was all about. Very rarely an old coin was found.

The patch of ground was clearly part of the Youth Hostel Grounds, and it was necessary to cross over a rather broken down wire fence to reach the mound. Would-be excavators generally took the view that the area was a kind of territorial no-man's land where peaceable digging ought to be permitted. In any case the mound was quite well-screened from the Youth Hostel so that the risk of being observed by the youth hostel warden or his staff, if they were to take a proprietorial view of the dump and its contents, was quite small.

I went up to the wire fence. I had no digging instrument with me, but I half-hoped that some interesting treasure might have been brought to the surface of the mound by the winter rains, and had not yet been noticed by village treasure hunters. I looked up through the stunted trees towards the Youth Hostel. No-one still seemed to be about.

I started to clamber over the wire fence. I got over all right, but one trouser leg was caught on a piece of barbed wire. I turned back to face the fence to free myself. It was once I had managed this, and had turned round again to face the dump that I saw him.

He was kneeling on the ground wearing what appeared to be a long black robe. He seemed to be fossicking among some stones and looking for something. I could not see his face which was turned away in the direction of the old vicarage. In my embarassment I began to think of how I could explain what I was doing lurking there when I was noticed, as now seemed inevitable. For a few seconds he did not appear to have heard my approach. Then he turned round, and, looking up, smiled.

"I think I have just lost my pencil here. Be a good chap and help me look for it."

Relieved that he did not appear to be questioning my presence in the hostel's gounds, I walked quickly over to the mound and knelt down beside him. I had only been on all fours at his side for a couple of seconds when he leapt to his feet.

"There it is," he shouted triumphantly. He was holding a small stub of a red pencil between his index finger and thumb.

I got to my feet, brushing the dirt from my trousers. It was only then that I had a chance to look at him. The black robe was clearly some sort of religious dress. The collar was definitely clerical. But it was his face which quickly drew my attention.

He had keen light blue eyes under slightly hooded lids. The eyes were a little prominent. As if in response to my gaze he pushed his butter-coloured hair back from his temples where it had fallen forward when he had been searching for his pencil. It was almost as if he wanted me to have a better view. Despite his aquiline nose, full lips and firm set of the chin, his face seemed remarkably boyish. His two lips were an interesting contrast. The upper lip looked tender and sensitive, the lower lip authoritative, almost aggressive. At first his boyish looks suggested to me that he might be in his mid-twenties. Yet his air of authority made me revise my first impression. I concluded that he was probably in his late thirties.

"Do you live here?" he asked abruptly. I saw that he had slipped a handkerchief back into a slit in the side of his robe. But then he casually wiped his hands on the fabric of the garment.

"If you mean in the village, yes," I said. "I live just below the Church."

He looked at me curiously. I felt that he wanted to ask me a further question, but had decided against it.

I was on the point of asking him what he was doing in Kemsing, or rather, in a discreet way, trying to find out what a cleric was up to scrabbling around in an old rubbish dump at the bottom of the Youth Hostel garden, when quite suddenly I realised that I recognised him.

He was Robert Hugh Benson. The only difficulty was that this Benson had died in 1914.

I stared at him hard. There was a pause while he absorbed my gaze Then he smiled back infectiously, and pulled out a packet of cigarettes from his robe.

"Do you smoke?" he said.

" No," I said, rather too loudly. I rather wished that I did smoke so that I could do something to calm me, for my heart was starting to race.

"Dd....do you mind if I do?" He spoke with unaffected courtesy, stammering slightly on the first 'd'.

"It is so much more enjoyable in the open air," he added. "You can just pretend this new companion of yours is burning aromatic leaves after the winter. Let's find somewhere to sit down, and you can tell me about Kemsing."

He lifted his robe up from the ground, then vaulted athletically over the barbed wire fence and set off in the direction of the churchyard. I followed obediently. My brain seemed to be like that of a telephonist in a busy exchange being flooded with too many incoming calls.

How could this be Benson? Perhaps it was someone just like him. Was someone dressing up as Benson? Was it some sort of Benson anniversary? His death perhaps? But why would anyone want to commemorate that? Was there a Benson Society where people dressed up to impersonate him like members of the Sherlock Holmes Society did? But Benson wasn't really well enough known for that. I thought that there was a literary society for his older brother, E F Benson, but I had never heard of one for Rober Hugh.

Still Britain was a place where there were many little societies of just a few members who kept alive the memory of almost anyone who had ever had some sort of fame in the past. I knew there was a Randolph Caldecott Society that interested itself in this Victorian illustrator. Since Caldecott had lived in Kemsing in the 1880s the village had occasional visits from those keeping his flame alive.

Tramping along behind him I almost bumped into him when he stopped suddenly to light his cigarette. As he slipped the packet back into his robe I noticed they were Benson & Hedges.

"Is there a seat somewhere in the churchyard?"

"There is one near the rose-bed in the southwestern corner."

He strode ahead between the rows of graves. The headstones were modern since we were passing through the latest area for burial. He paused to look at a number of inscriptions.

"Some of the texts seem rather secular for a Christian Churchyard," he observed wryly.

"Both the type of stone and the texts are regulated by the Vicar," I explained. "The overall rules are laid down by the Diocese. The black basalt headstones with gilt lettering date from the time of the last Vicar and have caused much tut-tutting under the new regime because they don't really weather tastefully."

I was amazed to find myself talking quite normally.

"But the Church authorities don't choose the texts surely?"

"Not at present," I replied, "but there are plans to limit the amount of text on the tablets for the cremated remains to the name and dates of the person who has died. That's where the ashes of those who are cremated are deposited," I said, pointing back at the long wall. "The ashes have to be put directly into the ground without an urn or container of any kind, and the tablets have to lie flat so that it is easy to mow around them."

"Are many people cremated in Kemsing?" He seemed to be frowning a little.

"It's probably a little more common than burial now. People think it tidier, and of course it takes up less space."

"Propaganda," he said brusquely. "They are just victims of propaganda. What contempt for the mortal remains of one of God's creatures. Where would we be without the relics of God's saints?" His blue eyes flashed in the sun. "You'll find me a trifle dogmatic." He smiled again.

We walked on side by side. Why not simply ask him who he is? That's the simplest and most straightforward thing to do. We were just coming up to the west corner of the north wall of the Church. I suddenly remembered that when Benson had been a curate at the Church in the 1890s he was said to have presented a small stained-glass window.

It was still there, set rather high up and included some sort of Benson coat of arms with three trefoils. It was really impossible to make anything of the design from the outside in the morning light. I looked across at him. There was no doubt that he too was looking up at the window. But he said nothing.

Why shouldn't I make some comment to suggest that I guessed who he was, or rather whom he was impersonating? At first I thought that the reason I remained silent was for fear of sounding rather odd. If he wanted to explain, he would, I said to myself. The other difficulty was that he just seemed too matter of fact to be playing a role. Could he perhaps be some sort of relation who also happened to be a clergyman?

Why was I, who was normally so inquisitive, so reticent? It was as though I feared that if I asked certain leading questions a spell would be broken, and the opportunity for some important experience would be lost for ever. By the time we had reached the wooden seat I had decided to say nothing yet, but wait for him to volunteer some explanation himself.

Our seat faced the morning sun and the wall near the rose garden reflected some warmth. I began to relax a little. A pair of blackbirds were looking for worms among the primroses which had been planted on a grave. As we sat side by side he turned to me, having just completed a deep draw on his cigarette, and remarked:

"I suppose it was sensible to turn the old vicarage into a Youth Hostel. It must be useful for those on walking tours, or on pilgrimages since Kemsing is on the Pilgrims' Way to Canterbury."

"It is quite full much of the year," I said. "In the summer I see visitors almost every weekend coming down Church Lane, past my house and heading for the public footpath which crosses the field beyond. But they don't seem to need to be young to qualify for the hostel any more. They have their packs on their backs and often have ordinance survey maps in a transparent case hanging from their necks."

"Do some visitors go past your house on bicycles?" he asked with a hint of mischief in his eyes.

The footpath which passes our house was opened in 1897 to commemorate Queen Victoria's Jubilee. I remembered that this event took place when Robert Hugh Benson had been curate to the flamboyant artistic Vicar, Thomas Carleton Skarrat. I dragged something from my memory of reading R H Benson's biography. Benson had learnt to ride a bicycle in Kemsing!

Flustered that I had taken a little too long to make a reply I said quickly:

"Of course the path through to St Edith's Road is now

usually too narrow and overgrown with nettles to bicycle along it comfortably.

"What a pity." He paused, and then added, "Do you have a bicycle?"

I was startled. But managed to reply, "No, the only one we have is away with my son, Cyprian, at boarding school."

"Could you bb..orrow one for me to ride?" He stammered on the b, then turned to face me with a boyish grin. "You must know people in the village who have one."

It was an audacious request, yet made in quite the most winning manner.

I was sitting alongside a complete stranger. For some reason he was impersonating a former Kemsing village curate. This curate, I knew, later became a Roman Catholic priest and a best-selling novelist. He had died before the First World War. And here he was asking me to borrow a bicycle for him!

He stretched back in his seat and clasped his hands behind the back of his head for a moment. In doing so he rucked up his robe so that it came halfway up his legs to reveal well-muscled calves. It was almost as though he was seeking to convince me that he was quite capable of pedalling powerfully.

The gesture and his appealing air of authority seemed to prevent me from saying anything other than that I would try to find him a suitable machine.

"My name is Benson: Hugh Benson." He stammered again ever so slightly on the b. "You will need to tell the owner of the bicycle that."

He said it so simply and quickly that for a second I did not comprehend the significance of the words. After that I realized that it was no longer possible for me to pretend to myself that I was just making a simple mistake. There was no doubt that my new acquaintance, with his winning and outwardly frank manner, was seeking to persuade me that he really was Hugh Benson.

I remembered that Robert Hugh Benson was always

known as Hugh. The more disturbing aspect was that the person now in front of me just did not seem to be of a sort who would get involved in acting out some sort of charade. I had almost screwed up courage to ask him whether he had ever lived in Kemsing when he gripped my arm tightly.

"Listen," he said. "Can you hear them? They must be nesting."

There was a gentle distant cooing.

"It's the white doves on the roof of the Church," he said. "They are like the guardian angels of St Mary's."

He sprung suddenly to his feet.

"Quick we must pick some primroses for St Edith at her well. I think I saw lots in that empty part of the graveyard."

I found myself tagging along behind him as he wove his way rapidly through the headstones. Once in the waste ground he pounced on groups of primroses and soon had gathered a small bunch. I picked one or two flowers myself and gave them to him. He pulled out a piece of string from the pocket of his robe and tied up the stems methodically. Then he looked at me penetratingly.

"When do you think you could let me have the bicycle?"

"Ww... would tomorrow do?" I seemed to have picked up his stammer.

"I had hoped that I might have a ride this afternoon since it's turning out to be such a lovely day. But tomorrow could well be another fine day from the look of the clouds. It would be splendid if you could meet me with the bicycle tomorrow morning at a quarter to ten."

He suddenly pulled a gold pocket watch from the slit in his robe.

"Goodness!. It's nearly half past ten and I haven't said my office. I will just put the primroses on the wall of the well for St Edith, and then I must take the footpath to Otford. I am so pleased that we have met."

He stretched out his hand to me rather formally. His handshake was warm and firm. A moment later all I could see of him was his retreating boyish head above what I had decided was a black cassock, moving away rapidly down the church footpath. He went through the little gate with its tiled roof, on past the Church Hall, then disappeared from view. The path led to St Edith's Well, but it was not possible with the eye to follow the path from the Church.

I need now to record the extraordinary sense of loss that I felt at his departure. It was as if I had just been told that someone very dear to me had died. Its physical manifestation was a nervous emptiness in the stomach. Overwhelmed with this feeling I somehow got myself back to our house. I was quite unconscious of anything outside myself.

I was glad that no-one from the family seemed to be about. I rushed straight to my study and collapsed into the chair at my desk, stretching my hands out before me among all the papers scattered on it. I rested my head and shoulders on my arms. I realised that I was breathing heavily and that my heart was racing.

I don't know how long I stayed in this position. It may have been a quarter of an hour before I summoned up the courage to do what I knew I must do. I struggled up on my feet and went over to the bookshelf on the wall by the window. Martindale's two volume biography of Robert Hugh Benson was there. I picked up the second volume. I knew that it contained a half length photograph of him at the front of this volume. The biography had been published in 1916 just two years after Benson's death.

I opened the book carefully with my right hand. My left hand which was holding the book was shaking slightly. In the manner of books of that time there was a thin piece of tissue paper that lay on top of the photograph. Even before I turned this back I could see through the thin paper film that the person whom I had just met was the person in the photograph. I pulled back the tissue paper carefully with my right hand.

The face scrutinised me from the photograph just as he had been doing when we were talking in the churchyard. The only difference that I could see was that in the photograph he was wearing a jacket with his clerical collar, rather than a cassock.

It was at this point that I made my first notes. I used the Government shorthand booklet that I had taken with me to the churchyard to record the information on the tombstones. These first notes are a little hard to decipher but they seem to be as follow:

Robert Hugh Benson. Born 18 November 1871; died 19 October 1914; son of Edward White Benson, Archbishop of Canterbury; brother of A C Benson and E F Benson. Another brother died and there were one or perhaps two sisters.

The person in the Churchyard must be:

1. a ghost
2. an imposter (but why?)
3. an exact double with the same name (statistical likely hood?)

Am I

1. seeing things?
2. dreaming?
3. involved in some sort of miracle?
4. being drawn into some kind of mysterious prank?

If 3, immediately above, why is he appearing to me? (no previous experience of anything supernatural; myself a middle-of-the-road Anglican; not sure if ghosts are 'orthodox').

I leafed through Benson's biography. I remembered that for a time he had been interested in the supernatural, as was fashionable then—I remembered that Conan Doyle and Oliver Lodge were also involved—but Benson had regarded it as a dangerous world to dabble with. His novel, *The Necromancers*, had included some sort of alleged spiritual appearance to a young man of his dead fiancée during a seance. But my encounter, I concluded, was quite different. It was in bright daylight.

By now I was beginning to feel more rational and in control of myself. Why not go and look for Angela? I walked through the house in search of her. She was not in her usual haunts. The cats, however, were reassuring in the kitchen. They followed me as I went out into the courtyard. The barn door was open and I could see that the car had gone. Angela must have gone shopping.

The house has a large garden to the east, which is partly walled. Some of the garden walls are the remains of the walls of the house from the time when it was partly burned down earlier in the century. These walls formed an attractive backdrop for garden flowers. Over the low wall of the courtyard I could see Angela's mother, who had a small flat in our house. She was gathering early daffodils in a wild part of the garden beyond the large old yew tree in the centre of the lawn. She waved to me. For a moment I thought of confiding in her. Then I had what I thought was a better idea.

It took only a few minutes to walk from the house to St Edith's Well.

I should perhaps say something here about St Edith. She is the patron saint of the village. She was born in Kemsing in the 10th century, but soon after her birth went with her mother, who was a mistress of King Edgar, to Wilton near Salisbury. Her mother became Abbess of a convent there. Edith was well educated there by French chaplains to the convent, and then devoted her life to the service of the poor.

After the death of his legitimate wife King Edgar wanted to marry Edith's mother. But she preferred to remain in her convent. When Edith's half-brother, King Edward the Martyr, was murdered at Corfe Castle, some nobles wanted young Edith to be their Queen. She declined, preferring to continue her life consecrated to God at the convent. She died at the age of 23, and the miracles that subseqently occurred at her tomb helped establish her cult.

Kemsing, as the place of her birth, set up its own shrine to St Edith in St Mary's churchyard This was then destroyed at the Reformation. But the well in front of the Saxon dwelling in which she was born (the building has long since gone) still remains dedicated to her. Its waters have traditionally been said to have healing powers. For many years her feast day on 16 September, or a convenient date near that, has been marked by separate devotions at the Well by the Anglicans and the Roman Catholics of Kemsing and the surrounding towns and villages.

The Well is in the midst of a small triangular village green in the old part of the village. The two village pubs, The Bell and The Wheatsheaf, stand on higher ground overlooking it, seeming to guard it. The village High Street runs along one side of the green, eventually leading on to the village of Otford, a mile and three quarters away. The road along the other side leads to Seal, the other neighbouring village. The third side has as its boundary a footpath which connects to another little path to the Post Office.

I came quickly down this footpath. The green is enclosed by a waist-high ragstone wall. Entry is by a small wooden gate from the road. I pushed this open. The Well itself is outlined above ground with a low stone wall shaped like a large key-hole. A metal grill is fitted on top to deter children from falling in.

There was no doubt. There, on top of the grill, lay a small posy of fresh primroses tied into a bunch with a piece of string. I stared at them for ten seconds or so, half-wondering if I should count them, or try to identify the few that I had picked. But I did not touch them. I looked away. Then I looked back at them suddenly. I half-expected that when I did so they would no longer be there.

I hurried back up to the butcher's shop, which is just beyond The Bell, and went in.

The young butcher was carefully cutting up some fillet steak.

"Lovely morning, Mr Bridge."

"I wonder, Paul, whether you have seen a chap in clerical dress pass by the shop this morning on his way to the Well."

"No, I haven't seen anyone like that."

"Thanks, sorry to have bothered you."

I went out quickly. As soon as I emerged I realised that

Benson would not have passed by the shop on his way to the Well. The footpath he took from the Church would have brought him out beyond the Well. He could then have just walked back a few yards, deposited the posy, then gone on his way to Otford. I must follow his tracks and ask further along the High Street. I ran down the footpath again, crossed St Edith's Road, then continued along the High Street to the grocer's shop.

The shopkeeper was new to the village. He was a plump middle-aged man who wore spectacles. My wife had told me that he intended to improve the choice of cheese available in the village.

Bursting in I found him standing at the counter by the cash till.

"Excuse me, but have you seen a young man in a clergyman's robe walking past your shop recently?"

He paused to reflect.

"Yes, I believe I have. But I could not say how long ago," he added. "He appeared to be reading a small black book as he was walking."

His breviary, I thought to myself. So I am not the only one seeing him. Hugh Benson's double seems to be able to be seen by at least one other person in the village. On reflection my next remark must have seemed a rather odd *non-sequitur*.

"You wouldn't know who in the village might be willing to hire me a bicycle?

He peered at me thoughtfully and rubbed his nose.

"I can't think of anyone off-hand. I'm new to the village. I've given my old one to my married son. Why not try at the garage next door? They might know someone who would lend you one. Are you wanting it for yourself?" he added inquisitively, moving his spectacles back up to the bridge of his nose to focus on me more closely.

" No, it's for a friend."

"Lovely weather for cycling. Would he be going far?"

"I'm not sure."

"Half his luck," the grocer added enigmatically. Suddenly, the drawer in the cash register shot out, apparently unexpectedly, and hit the grocer's hand. This brought the inquisition to an abrupt close.

After expressing an opinion on the cussedness of mechanical things I took my leave.

"What on earth does he want a bicycle for?" I asked myself as I walked slowly to the garage.

The Kemsing garage is much more than a place where cars are repaired and petrol bought. Village boys interested in cars get their first job here: first working the petrol pumps, then after showing some competence and some rapport with customers, graduating to the workshop to act as assistants to the mechanics, and with the task of keeping the workshop reasonably clean and tidy. If they are personable, they are then given the privilege of using the workshop's tools to work on their motor-bikes after hours.

Middle-aged men call in for a chat, using as an opener the need for advice on the mysteries of their lawnmowers. The culture is overwhelmingly masculine: odd bits of iron and steel lie about, as well as various dials whose purposes are hard to determine to the mechanically and electronically illiterate like me There are the great mysterious inspection pits, scattered tools and pieces of rag, little patches of sump oil and grease. The ensemble would make a fine modern art installation. In this inner sanctum, above the work benches with their lathes, where village ladies did not normally penetrate, are the usual calendars of topless girls smiling their pearly white smiles down at the men in their greasy overalls.

Presiding over this male enclave on this morning, as always, was a cheery, rotund, middle-aged man with twinkly eyes and a warm smile. I had always thought that George Wigsell was the embodiment of all that was good in the village: a keen scout master—so of course he knew most of the boys who later aspired to help in the garage—; a regular voluntary helper at the village Old Peoples' Home; well over forty years service in the Church choir; and several periods as a church warden.

Above all he loved his work of repairing motor cars. And this love was infectious. Many young men who began by helping at the petrol pumps went on to acquire a deep love of the internal combustion engine, as well as a real understanding of it. Then, over time, many also learned that acquiring a love of doing things well in the mechanic shop could be applied also to what they later did with their lives.

Wherever a difficulty arose, or the village needed something done or organised, it was a commonplace for people to say that the best thing to do would be to "Ask George."

So I did.

As I entered the garage George emerged from behind a rather rusty Ford Escort. He beamed as he wiped his hands on a piece of paper towel.

"And what can I do for you, Mr Bridge?"

"I'm trying to hire a bicycle, George. Do you have any ideas?"

"Is it you that's needing it?"

"No. Actually it's for a visitor to the village. The only one we ourselves have is away with my lad, Cyprian, at school. The visitor just needs it for tomorrow. I'll take responsibility for it."

I spoke rather too quickly. I could see that George was intrigued, and wanted me to add to my explanation.

"It's for a chap called Benson." I had decided not to mention that he was a Roman Catholic priest.

"Can he ride a bike?"

"Look, George, I wouldn't be wanting to borrow a bike if he couldn't, would I?"

He looked at me quizzically for a moment and then smiled.

"I think that my old one still works. But the tyres are bound to need pumping up."

"May I come around and pick it up tomorrow morning?"

"All right then. How early?"

"I'll come before I go to eight o'clock Communion, say about half-past seven. Would that be too early?"

"We're still hoping to get you back to the 9.30 Parish Communion."

This was a sore point. The combination of the new Alternative Service Book and the Vicar's increased emphasis in his sermons on what I regarded as 'political issues' had led Angela and me to desert this service in favour of the Prayer Book at 8 am, when there was no sermon. I had occasional regrets because we missed the excellent village choir.

"I'm sure you will see us at the 9.30 service sometimes, but the Book of Common Prayer Communion Service suits us on a regular basis. Besides we like an early start."

"I think the choir is now better than it has been for years," George added, as if to entice me.

"I hear the boys sing like seraphim," I said as I turned to go. "I'll be there tomorrow."

"See you at 7.30 then." He finished wiping his hands, deposited the paper towel in a big oil drum, and was walking towards the office as I left.

It was only when I was outside on the footpath that I remembered something. The phrase about the choir singing like seraphim came from one of Hugh Benson's letters.

When I returned to the house I found Angela seated at the kitchen table. Its surface was completely covered with packets of seed. She was busy making lists and notes on a piece of squared paper.

In retrospect I should probably have told her there and then of the mystifying encounter and what was on my mind. But I allowed myself to be drawn in immediately into an involved discussion of vegetable seeds and when and where they should be sown and later planted out.

We agreed we needed to bear in mind where they had been planted in the vegetable plot last year and in the previous year, to ensure proper crop rotation.

My mother-in-law came in, and added her views on these complicated issues. Every decision then had to be recorded in a plan of the beds drawn roughly on the squared paper.

The process took almost an hour. When it was complete I was asked to take some packets of seed out to the green house and prepare trays of Arthur Bowers seed potting compost while Angela got the lunch ready. Somehow I knew then that I had missed a chance to make a clean breast of what was on my mind.

The greenhouse had trapped the warmth of the sun. I started to fill the trays. I am not normally secretive, but somehow my resolve to confide in Angela about my 'Benson' adventure weakened as I scooped the crumbly fine compost into the trays and began soaking it with a watering can.

I rationalised this lack of frankness to myself in this way. The whole story was rather preposterous. Although Angela and her mother had heard me mention Benson they knew almost nothing about him, apart from the fact that he was one of the better known clerical figures in the history of the village. Neither of them had read any of his books, nor his biography. They were bound to say that the priest I had met just happened to have the same name. It was just a coincidence. As they hadn't seen him they would not be able to compare the person I had seen with the picture in his biography. Both of them would be likely to take the view that it was simply my odd romantic streak that had come out because the two names were the same.

But there was clearly another side to my reluctance. Even at this stage I suspected that I might be being drawn into a private adventure, and I wasn't certain that I wanted to share it, or even that it would be possible for me to do so. Perhaps I should obtain permission before I said anything to anyone else. But from whom?

I opened a packet of a new variety of cabbage and read the label: *Sow March to October. Transplant to just below 1st leaves. Treat as annual. Stake and fleece to avoid white cabbage butterflies.* I began sprinking them on the surface of the compost. Suddenly a wave of desolation overwhelmed me. Suppose he didn't turn up for the bicycle ride, and I never saw him again?

CHAPTER TWO

FREE-WHEELING

I DID not sleep very well on that Saturday night. Normally the sound of the Old Time dance music from the Village Hall does not keep me awake. This time the electric keyboard and the thump, thump, thump of the drums seemed to be bringing the Hokey-Pokey and other favourites right into our bedroom. But my mind was also not easy.

In part this arose from a kind of ineffectively suppressed excitement. But my conscience was also troubled because I had failed to say anything about Benson to my family. After 'Auld Lang Syne' I hoped to drop off more readily. I repeated a number of times some words from Coleridge's 'Ancient Mariner' that I had found effective on such occasions:

> 'Oh sleep it is a gentle thing,
> Beloved from pole to pole!
> To Mary Queen the praise be given!
> She sent the blessed sleep from Heaven,
> That slid into my soul.'

But to little avail. I heard the village clock strike twelve, and then one. I sensed that Angela had woken, and was keeping a vigil of my wakefulness. She said nothing but her breathing was that of one who was awake, but carefully counterfeiting the sound of a sleeper.

I must have eventually dropped off. I do not recall the clock striking three, but I awoke again at 5 am.

Rather than toss and turn I crept downstairs in my dressing gown, and went to my study. At such times I usually find that the best way of inducing calm is to do some routine household administrative work. I organised some bills for payment, wrote several post-dated cheques and put them in envelopes marked 'for posting in several days time'. I looked through my income tax file bearing in mind that the end of the financial year was approaching. I made some notes on what needed to be done. I wrote a short letter to my building society requesting details of the interest that I had paid during the previous year.

At six o'clock I let the cats out through the back door of the kitchen and into the courtyard, then went back upstairs and dressed in the bathroom so as not to wake Angela.

I then crossed to the barn to collect two pairs of bicycle clips and put these into my jacket pocket. As I returned to the house I noticed the morning for the first time. It was soft and grey and gentle, the kind of day that does not get the holiday makers going early, but which I liked to think was understood by the true countryman who could see that a sunny morning was promised later on.

On returning to my study I read through the lessons for the day as they were set out in the Anglican lectionary—these would not be used at the 8 o'clock Communion Services. I also read the short biographies of the saints for the day in the Penguin *Dictionary of Saints*. As it was a Sunday none of them would be actually commemorated this year in church on their day.

St Chrodegang it seems was a French medieval bishop who, in the eighth century, helped continue the reform of the Church of the Franks. This had been begun by St Boniface who had led the great mission from Britain to Northern Europe. St Chrodegang promoted the Benedictine rule in monasteries in his own and neighbouring dioceses, and wrote fluently in Latin It would be good if I could write Latin fluently I reflected. Even at University, when I was supposedly a reasonable scholar, I had never found writing in Latin easy.

St Colette was the daughter of a carpenter in Ghent in the late 14th century. She had a vision of St Francis who charged her with seeking to reform the Poor Clares, the srict order of enclosed nuns founded by St Francis' loyal friend and supporter, St Clare. St Colette persuaded the Papal authorities to allow her to promote this reform. There was resistance within some of the existing Poor Clare communities— this did not seem surprising— but by the time of her death St Colette had managed to found seventeen convents of her strict observance, some of which survive to this day.

I have always been amazed how some individuals of quite humble origins have been endowed with such powerful personalities that they can persuade a large number of others to leave the world and embrace such strict ways of life, or just to follow them. Of course it is God's work, but what amazing people He finds to implement His mission.

The last saint, St Cyneburga, was one of those shadowy Anglo-Saxon female royal saints. After being married to a Northumbrian prince she went on to rule over a convent in Northamptonshire. My book does not tell what happened to her husband, but I imagined that he was killed in battle like so many Anglo-Saxon royals. The men fought. And the women prayed!

As I casually turned over the pages of my Prayer Book my eyes found a psalm which made me briefly examine my conscience. 'Wherewithal shall a young man cleanse his way; even by ruling himself after thy word. With my whole heart have I sought thee: O let me not go wrong out of thy commandments.'

I could no longer be called young. Would I ever be able to develop a stronger will so as to be able to resist what I knew to be wrong?

I looked at my watch. It was now 7.15 am. I could go in search of the bicycle soon. I had been deliberately avoiding taking up the Benson biography, but now the temptation was too great. The book opened immediately at Benson's photograph at the beginning of Volume 1. It was in black and white and it was a head and shoulders portrait. His fine fair hair was cut quite short and swept across his forehead in a strong line. His clerical collar went right round his neck above a plain dark jacket with high front buttons. The lips were full, with a pronounced bow on the upper. His face looked out questioningly.

I closed the book and set out for George Wigsell's house. True to form he was in his backgarden adjusting the gears when I arrived.

"I'm not sure that my friend will be able to master all those gears."

"They're very simple. You just need to be sure to stop pedalling when you change. That's all there is to it. What's he been used to riding? A Penny Farthing?" He laughed and twinkled as he spoke.

"I'm not sure. You see, although he's young, he is rather old-fashioned in his tastes and experience. He's a priest, you see."

"Most of the ones I know are ready to jump on the latest bandwagon, whatever it is, or wherever it's going!"

Not wishing to encourage further speculation I thanked him profusely and wheeled the bicycle back down the side of the house, and out of the gate. When I got on to the road I mounted it a little unsteadily.

"Mind you don't fall off," shouted George after me. He was laughing a little.

I rode the bicycle straight to the church and managed to park it without being seen behind a little group of shrubs and small trees. This hid the untidy compost area where the grass cuttings from churchyard mowing, and the dead flowers gathered up from the graves, were finally laid to rest. This little concealed heap of decaying vegetation always seemed to me a more telling reminder of mortality than the graves themselves.

I returned to the house to collect Angela for the 8 am service. As she was used to my early rising she did not ask me what I had been up to. Her mother did not normally get up for the early service.

As we entered the church I remembered for the first time for several days that it was Lent. There were no flowers on stands in front of the Rood Screen. Benson had not mentioned Lent. Was this significant?

While the Vicar quietly said the 'Our Father' to himself I looked up at the East Window beyond the Rood Screen and the Chancel. I knew the details by heart. From where we sat in our pew I could see Sir Ninian Comper's complex design in the East Window apppearing as a great blue Omega. 'Be still and know that I am God.' The crucified Christ on the Rood Screen high above me was said to be modelled on one of the Kemsing squires as a young man. This was the image of Jesus Christ who had really been crucified and had given us the prayer which the Vicar was softly intoning. It was He who mediated between me and the ineffable beyond. Above the Omega of the East Window was the hand of God pointing down with His index finger to the Dove.

My eyes lingered on the screen. The light from the south window caught the gold on Christ's loin cloth. Gold perhaps because his sacrifice is our hope. His Blessed Mother, Mary, and St John stood on either side of him watching him suffer. Beneath them lay the two dragons of sin, crushed but still snarling. I was glad to see the four winged cherubims standing alongside them like policemen on their golden wheels. In case Our Lady and St John had any trouble, I decided.

"...lead us not into temptation, but deliver us from evil..." Christ on the Rood Screen seemed so young. The carver had shown him without a beard. It seemed to make him even more poignant. I knew that Comper in his old age had worried that the youth and gentleness of his Christ at Kemsing was not right, but at this moment I felt that his young visionary image was perfect.

The voice was now intoning the prayer for the Queen..."We humbly beseech thee so to dispose and govern the heart of Elizabeth, thy servant, our Queen and Governor, that, in all her thoughts, words, and works, she may ever seek thy honour and glory, and study to preserve thy people committed to her charge, in wealth, peace and Godliness..."

What a curious thing is the Anglican Church. Below the rood figures were the arms of King Edward VII. Perhaps this King's private life was not much worse than several of the Renaissance popes, but it did seem a trifle odd for King Edward to have been Head of the Anglican Church. I had even heard a rumour that he became a Roman Catholic on his deathbed— perhaps he felt this was the best way to be fully repentant. His predecessor, Henry VIII, had founded the Church after he too had had complicated relations with women.

What would it be like to be a lay person and Head of a Church? Did a British monarch for instance feel any different in Scotland when, instead of being Head of the Church of England, an episcopal church, he or she was part of the Church of Scotland, a presbyterian church?

Another larger Coat of Arms was on the wall of the North Aisle. The Vicar and Churchwardens had put this up in 1721 to proclaim Kemsing's loyalty to King George I and the Hanoverian succession, which by implication repudiated the Catholic House of Stuart and the Old Pretender.

I glanced up at a window depicting St Edith near the main entrance. She was wearing a crown. This seemed odd. She had sucessfully resisted pressure from the nobles of England to accept the Crown after the murder of her brother.

We parishioners this morning did not look a noble lot in our tweedy jackets, camel overcoats and mackintoshes.

We stood for the Gospel. The text was about the various temptations in the wilderness of that Young Man hanging up there on the cross above us. The devil showed Him all the kingdoms of the world and the glory of them. I looked up at all the gold leaf in the Sanctuary and the great gold baldichino high above the altar. The reredos behind the altar showed a mediaeval king and his nobles unashamedly singing the praise of God at Mass. On the floor of the choir before the altar lay a brass of Benson's Vicar, Skarratt, in liturgical vestments, holding the host and chalice. Christ's temptation was to become a powerful earthly ruler and give homage to the devil. Surely all the beauty in this church was being offered to God alone?

I noticed that my wife was saying the Creed. I added my voice. The sound of the congregation seemed thin, as though the great truths for which the saints and martyrs had died were fading away. Was it surprising that those in the congregation were unsure of what they believed? Many of their present bishops and theological advisers now qualified every clause in this great statement of belief, or re-interpreted it.

Great statements of the creed were depicted in the windows of St Mary's Church: the Annunciation to the Blessed Virgin Mary of our Lord's forthcoming birth by the Angel Gabriel, the Crucifixion, the Entombment, the Resurrection.

How real were these events to those around me? Was it just the beauty which brought them here, or habit? Had it dawned on them that what was depicted was true, and not just a fairy story that might help some people feel better?

"Ye that do truly and earnestly repent ye of your sins..." The sin which I wished to confess now was that of not praying hard enough for the gift of real faith. During the absolution I found myself saying, 'O Lord, increase my faith.' A moment later I gripped the front of the pew tightly, conscious that I did not want too much faith in case it should disturb the peaceful moderate world of my spiritual life.

The sunlight suddenly came pouring in from the South window. A cloud had evidently been swept aside in the sky outside. The Vicar urged us to lift up our hearts, and reminded us that it was our bounden duty. My heart beat a little faster and my voice sounded louder than I intended. "Holy, holy, holy, Lord God of Hosts, heaven and earth are full of thy glory; glory be to Thee, O Lord Most High."

The whole congregation seemed washed in pale gold. The hair of the elderly woman in the pew in front of us seemed on fire with splendour.

We knelt for the prayer of humble access and the consecration. Quite suddenly I felt terribly alone and empty of grace. I kept saying to myself: 'Now He is coming,' but a voice kept saying, 'Are you sure?'

'But He promised, He promised,' I repeated.

The Church was silent. The sunlight had gone. There was a sudden chill. What were we all doing in this old lofty building so early in the morning? Involuntarily I moved my kneeler nearer to Angela's. I pressed my eyes tight.

The shuffling began. The congregation was making its way up the central aisle through the rood screen to the altar steps. In the background I could just hear the Vicar quietly saying: "The Body of our Lord Jesus Christ which was given for thee, preserve thy body and soul unto everlasting life. Take and eat this in remembrance that Christ died for thee, and feed on him in thy heart by faith with thanksgiving."

The strange thing is that I remember nothing of going up to receive Communion myself. It is as if the memory of it was deliberately taken from me. Indeed I have no recollection of the final blessing, or of handing in the copy of the Prayer Book to the sidesman as I left.

One thing convinces me that I did take Communion like everyone else, apart from the fact that Angela would have said something to me about it if I had not, is that I distinctly remember the state of the Vestry. After receiving Communion the congregation always went back to their seats through the vestry and not back down the central aisle. The vestry was on this occasion more untidy than usual with spare surpluses, choir robes and hangers scattered on the floor, and the area under the steps leading to the organ loft was in a fine disorder of vases, dust pans, cloths and buckets.

Angela and I were at the lych gate.

"I think that I will go for a short walk across the recreation ground," I said. "Don't wait for me for breakfast. I will come back and snatch something later on the wing before starting on some of the pruning. I just might call on Jim to see whether he has managed to decipher any of those churchyard inscriptions that I have found so difficult. He has told me that if you photograph them in a certain light it is easier to reocognise the letters."

Jim was the principal local historian with whom I worked on some of my research.

She smiled. "Are you sure you wont need a coat? It's a bit chilly still when the sun goes behind the clouds."

"I think I'll be all right."

I watched her as she set off down Church Lane. I turned left and went into the recreation ground. I had not been honest about what I was doing. I looked at my watch. A bit more than three quarters of an hour before the *rendez-vous*. In defence of my failure to say something I told myself that I was not sure that it would be right to involve those closest to me in something which might well turn out to be rather strange. It would, I argued, be easier to do so once everything had become clearer.

I walked briskly over the vast open space of the recreation ground. The Common Field, as it was known, had been given to the village by one of the squires of St Clere, the large estate which was adjacent to the village. It was one of these squires, when young, who had been the model for Christ on the rood screen. Huddled close to the gate through which you entered the field there were some children's swings.

Most of the field was mown grass but there were several copses of trees and a few speciment trees to give interest. These had been carefully selected as typical of this part of Kent. Some hundreds of yards away, on slightly rising ground, was the cricket pavillion and the village tennis courts. The wide space always seemed to me to be a fine setting for some great historical pageant, or tournament. It was a splendid benefaction.

My thoughts turned to other great benefactors of communities such as the churches, religious orders and monasteries, which had, in the past, provided so many hospitals, nursing homes, alms houses, orphanages, and schools for the young of every condition and ability.

Was it really better for ordinary people now that most of these services were provided by the State or the local authority? Was the care of the modern institutions better? Of course the medicine and the technology were better. But were the staff more dedicated?

I was going through all this in my mind while sitting on a bench. From there I sometimes used to watch the Kemsing cricket team play against clubs from other villages.

When I arrived at exactly a quarter to ten he was already there sitting on a seat in the Church's memorial rose garden. He was reading what I took to be his breviary.

"How charitable and loyal of you to come," he said, looking up smiling, but without the penetrating gaze. "And what a glorious morning. Do sit down for a few moments while I finish my office."

I sat down beside him in silence.

I peeped sideways at the book. It was bound in black leather, but seemed rather worn along the spine. There were silk ribbons hanging down: red, white, blue, black and green. I noticed that they all had little medals attached to them, but I couldn't discern what they depicted. They were half-hidden in the palm of his firm, brown right hand on which the book was resting. I tried discreetly to glance at the text. I noticed that some of the print was in red. He said nothing, but occasionally looked up from the text, and closed his eyes, as if reflecting on the words. While he was doing this I had a better look at the text, and managed to recognise that it was in Latin as I had suspected it would be.

Quite suddenly he startled me by closing the book with a loud thump. He looked at me sideways. It was that penetrating gaze.

"How's your soul?" He grinned. "And where's the bicycle?"

"I'm not sure. Near the compost heap."

"Have you ever confessed to a priest? And has it got gears?

"No, and I'm not sure I want to start at present. Yes, it has."

"It may not be proper for me to hear your confession. I'll

try to manage with the brakes."

"Why wouldn't it be? You must stop pedalling when you change gears."

"Isn't this fun?" he said. "It's like a bit of *stichomythia* in a Greek classical play. Do you think that we can keep it up?"

"I doubt if I can. I am not very good at keeping two trains of thought going at once."

"I am sure that practice will help. Shall we try it again later on?" He looked at me quizzically? "Have you told your family about me?" Then with the same expression he added, "May I try it out on a hill?"

"Not yet. I am not sure what to say." Nor was I sure that I had told him yet that I had a family, although I may have mentioned Cyprian." You might like to try the hill down from Cotman's Ash."

"Don't they approve of papists? What's the surface like?"

Before I could attempt to respond to either of these questions he sprang to his feet.

"I cannot resist the temptation to look at it any longer. When I was in Rome *bicycling* was one of those things which were said to be not very edifying in a priest. But I don't suppose you would have a superior from the English College in Rome up there at Cotman's Ash!"

He didn't wait for a reply but strode off towards the compost heap which I must have vaguely indicated somehow. He passed the two table tombs.

"Am I getting warm? Be a good fellow and come and put me out of my misery!"

"The very blue of a Venetian painting of Our Blessed Lady's cloak." He was standing gazing in wonder at the bicycle which I had propped up against the low brick wall that with several old yew trees half-hid the compost area. I looked at the bicycle which had been recently resprayed in a rather vivid shade of blue.

"May I wheel it along?" He looked at me, and this was the first time he seemed to show a little shyness.

"Of course," I said.

"I don't think that I should ride it in the church grounds, do you? Definitely not edifying!" He laughed lightly.

He began wheeling it over the lawn, and I followed down the path to the Lych Gate. I went ahead of him and pushed open the gate to let him pass. While thanking me he leaned the bicycle against one of the posts of the Lych Gate.

"I wonder if you would mind wheeling it for a few moments while I have a cigarette. You don't smoke, I know." He dived into his cassock and brought out his packet of Benson & Hedges.

"You needn't worry about the road surface," I said. "It's all tarmac. Cotman's Ash hits the Pilgrims' Way halfway down the hill, but it is less steep from then on."

"Oh, I'm not worried. I tested the brakes briefly on the churchyard lawn as instructed. But you haven't told me whether your family approve of papists." He gazed at me with a slightly amused smile, in between fairly frequent long puffs on his cigarette. Every so often he flicked a piece of ash from the end with his right index finger. After he had done this several times I recalled that Benson's oldest brother A C had mentioned this as one of R H's habits in his *Memories of Hugh*.

While I was wheeling the bicycle we went up the stony lane which runs along the west side of the Common Field and goes up towards the Youth Hostel.

"I don't think my family know many. I am not sure how many Catholics there are in the village at present."

"If you have any doubts about your family's attitude it might be more prudent not to mention me to them until we know where we are."

I was all ready to take him up on this point by asking him where he thought we were at present, when he moved ahead of me sharply and turned left. There in front of us was the Youth Hostel. He paused and surveyed it carefully.

"It used to be the old vicarage," I said.

"I know," he replied.

He looked away so that I could not see his face. I noted

that he did not say, 'I remember.' He said nothing more, but took a few deep puffs on his cigarette. When next I saw his face the expression of his mouth was confusing. The upper lip seemed tender and a trifle sad.

He took his cigarette from his mouth and threw it on the ground, and stubbed it out with his heel. He brushed his fair hair from his eyes as if to see left and right more clearly as we stepped on to the road.

"This must be the Pilgrims' Way to Canterbury."

"Yes. You must watch out along here," I said. "The traffic whips along it."

"Let me wheel the bicycle along now, please."

I passed over the handle bars to him, as we started along the Pilgrims' Way. It was very narrow, with scarcely enough room for two cars to pass each other. Grey-white fluffy balls on straggling strands of last season's travellers' joy sparkled in the morning sun. They made links among the ash, yew, hawthorn and blackthorn of the hedges on either side of the road. Before the Reformation Kemsing's shrine of St Edith was a pious and practical stopping off point for pilgrims on the way to Canterbury. Chaucer's pilgrims would have certainly passed this very spot.

"Have you ever been on a pilgrimage?" He spoke abruptly. By now I was becoming used to his sudden questions. Before I could reply a car whizzed past, well in excess of the speed limit. We both had to flatten ourselves against the hedge on the south side of the route. Very skilfully, I thought, Benson had found a small gap in the hedge in which to shelter the bicycle.

"I've never really found the time," I said, as we got back on to the road. "I'm not sure that I would like to face the traffic on foot on this part of the way to Canterbury. Of course some of it later on is a real footpath and goes through fields, but there is a lot of tarmac as well at times, which means cars! Even on this short stretch you are taking your life in your hands as you can see."

"Oh, there is not really a great deal of point in going to

Canterbury these days, now that the shrine of St Thomas Beckett has been destroyed. It's a fine mediaeval building, of course, and there is some wonderful glass. There are even some interesting tombs and monuments."

I remembered that Benson's father was buried there and that he has his own monument— the first Archbishop of Canterbury to be interred in his Cathedral since the Reformation. The Archbishop's service of burial in 1896 was a national occasion of great solemnity. It took place during a spectacular thunderstorm. Hugh, as the only ordained son, played a small liturgical part by reading the litany.

Benson had paused for reflection.

"Of course there are a few interesting authentic extant old shrines in Britain but I think an Englishman's first choice for a pilgrimage must be Rome itself."

I did not comment, but simply followed him as he wheeled the bicycle. I noticed that his cassock had now a spot of oil on it from the bicycle's chain. I am not sure that the bicycle clips, which I had failed to give him, would have been of any use.

"Have you ever thought how different the two royal Henrys' reactions to the deaths of their Chancellors were?"

I must have looked blank for he said.

"Henry II and Henry VIII, I mean. After the murder of St Thomas Beckett, Henry II submitted himself to the monks of St Augustine's Abbey at Canterbury to be publicly flogged—he had come to accept that he was in some way responsible for the saint's death. As far as we know Henry VIII never showed the slightest remorse or pity for the death of *his* Chancellor and *close friend* Thomas More. Men of the Middle Ages, no matter how exalted and violent, had a disposition for contrition and repentance. The besetting sin of a renaissance man like Henry VIII was pride, which gets in the way of contrition and repentance."

He looked sternly back at me .

"I told you when we first met that I was dogmatic."

We had now passed the north side of the Common Field

and there was a gap in the hedge with a farm gate. Through this we could look south across the farmer's fields. Last year the rams had been put in with the flock earlier than usual so there was now a large flock of ewes with early new born lambs below us.

Benson and I stood next to each other. The lambs and their mothers were all clearly numbered so that the shepherd could be sure which one, or which pair of twins, belonged to which ewe. Lambs and ewes were calling loudly to each other. I noticed one lamb seeking the udder of a ewe which I could see from its number was not its mother. She sniffed at its hindquarters, then gently pushed it aside before resuming grazing. The rejected lamb skipped off, bleating with renewed vigour in search of its proper mother.

"They are being raised as fat lambs," I said.

"Part of His dominion," he murmured as if to himself. "Scattered but still one flock. We would be better off like them but our will gets in the way," he added almost under his breath.

I wondered whether it would be proper to ask him about animals' souls. Would it be a legitimate question to put to him? He anticipated the point when he said,

"We owe animals honour as part of His creation. But there is always the danger that we honour the creation more than the Creator, and this can lead to idolatry. Look at those ewes and lambs. What could be more nn...noble."

He stammered as if this was his way of emphasizing a word.

"A symbol of the perfect sacrifice. What an honour! We really ought to become like them, and conquer our wills. We might then follow the shepherd trustingly. Yet we humans must not abandon our dominion over them. Only human beings have been entrusted with revelation. In this sense animals are not rational as we are. They do not have souls, and so do not have to make the terrible choices that are a human being's lot, and whose consequences are eternal. Animals are innocent of moral acts."

I nodded at his exposition of the traditional view. But I also knew that there is no scriptural revelation on the issue. I longed to question him on a matter that his biographer had mentioned. In a letter to a friend Benson gave as his opinion that animals which have developed their nature in a moral direction will have a life after death proportionate to their faculties on earth.

We looked across at a small group of lambs. They had formed themselves into a small gang. Oblivious of their destiny, and of their being symbols for Benson, they had begun racing about the field as if pursued by a phantom sheepdog.

Perhaps spurred on by this sudden burst of activity Benson turned to me and said:

"Would you mind if I began my ride now? Isn't Cotman's Ash the first turning up the hill on the left? I'll meet you up on the top before trying out the brakes in earnest on the descent."

I watched him clamber on, hitching up his cassock so as to make ruffles of black around the seat and central bar. Before putting his feet on the pedals he turned round and grinned boyishly.

"Not in the least edifying!" He pushed off, rather unsteadily at first. There was a bit of a breeze now between the hedges of the Pilgrims' Way and some of his cassock billowed out on either side of him.

"It's signposted East Hill," I shouted. Then, fearful of his road sense, I shouted more loudly. "Don't forget the road rule is to ride on the left."

He didn't respond, but pedalling strongly began to put on speed. To my relief he seemed to be sticking to the left of the road. As I jogged along in pursuit I regretted having said nothing about hand-signals.

We had no agreed point of rendez-vous. It is a fairly stiff climb to the top of Cotmans Ash and I was soon puffing a great deal. Historical research and gardening had not kept me very fit. I was quite glad when I found Benson had stopped before he had quite reached the top. He was admiring the view from a little grass verge just before the entrance to a private drive. He looked down towards me.

"It's quite hard work getting up, but what a m...marvellous view. Why you can even glimpse the tower of Seal Church. As you I am sure know, it was built just before Henry VIII's breach with Rome. What a fine balance between crops and grazing in the fields, and of the houses and the barns. I think that I can still see the group of Tudor cottages which were in sight when we were admiring the lambs. I don't mind the glimpses you get of that big road which goes across the valley."

Kemsingites were in the habit of complaining about the noise of the M 26 motorway which divided the valley, especially those who had lived in the village before it was cut through. As an amateur local historian it was some consolation to me that a number of small Roman villas had been located in the valley when the foundations for the motorway were being excavated. The villas had all been reburied after professional archaeologists had done work on their sites. Up here there was a low distinct hum, but the birds around were competing strongly with their song.

"I think I'll free-wheel down the hill." He looked at me mischievously. Before I could say anything he pulled the bicycle back on to the road. Then, to my horror, instead of placing his feet on the pedals he drew them up on to the cross-bar, catching his cassock up beneath his black shoes with his knees tucked up against his chest.

Free-wheeling he certainly was, as he sped off down the hill, gathering speed all the time.

"Watch out for the traffic crossing on the Pilgrims' Way," I shouted. But I doubt if he heard. Nor would he have been able to apply the breaks effectively if he had been able to slow down. I just prayed that no vehicle would be coming along at the moment he crossed. I peered after him holding my breath. I sprinted down the hill after him. Another few seconds and he had passed the crossroads without incident, still gathering speed, with his cassock flying in the breeze behind.

Several black and white cows had come to a fence on the road. They were peering inquisitively at the passing commotion. Benson had now disappeared round a curve in the road beyond the Pilgrims' Way. As I puffed along I wondered whether he would be able to stop, or I would find him and the bicycle in pieces. I turned the bend. Some yards ahead to my left was the entrance to the kennels of the two local hunts. Benson had apparently managed to come to a halt there. He was waving to me triumphantly.

As I came closer I noticed a long skid mark which began about ten feet from where he was standing. Behind him were the substantial galvanised wire entrance gates to the kennels. A huge German Shepherd dog on its hindlegs was barking ferociously.

"What a mavellous ride!" he shouted. "And no damage to the bicycle! Good dog, we're not going to do any harm." The dog kept on barking but less ferociously. As I came up I could see the huntsman coming down the drive from the kennels. I knew him by sight. He had taken over fairly recently, combining hunstman and kennelman. Very occasionally I went out with the hounds but I had not been in the field since he had taken over.

"My friend has just been trying out the brakes on this bicycle." The tone I was aiming for was light-hearted, a little amused, but reassuring. The German Shepherd had stopped barking but the beagles within the kennels now began to give voice.

"I hope that you didn't mind my coming to a halt so abruptly in your entrance," Benson said, as he went up to the gate.

"Not at all." The huntsman smiled indulgently. When I saw the speed you were travelling from the kennels' window I was amazed that you didn't come off."

"The hand-brake works well. Does the beagle on the gate and the sounds within mean you keep a pack of hounds?"

"Yes, we've the Bolebroke Beagle Pack here, and I also look after the West Kent foxhounds."

"How splendid!" He turned to me. "What a privilege to have hunts based in your village!"

"It's not all plain-sailing," said the huntsman. Quite a few people these days are opposed to hunting, even in Kemsing. They think it's cruel to the animals that are hunted. Of course I say, 'Look at the way foxes will take the head off newborn lambs and cause mayhem among our chickens. I find it more difficult to convince them about hunting hares. Unless they are real countrymen they only see them as inoffensive creatures, and don't want to know about the damage that hares can cause to crops."

I could see Benson beginning to look at the huntsman authoritavely. I sensed a short sermon coming on.

"Much of the problem arises because people are confused about the different nature and roles of human beings and animals. They are in our care for our delight. and some of them for our food. That is scriptural. It is certainly our right to hunt some of them and eat those that are palatable. But pleasure in cruelty to them, perhaps especially in the hunting field, is completely abhorrent to anyone who is civilised. Of course if hunting comes between a man and God that would be wrong, quite wrong. But I am sure that would never happen with someone like you." His last remark was said light-heartedly with a slight bow of the head. Then he fixed the huntsman with his penetrating look and smiled.

"Well, not very often Father," the hunstsman said in reply. His blue eyes twinkled in his weather beaten face. I realized then that he was Irish.

"Would you like to see the kennels?" he added with a roguish laugh.

"That would make my heart rejoice."

We were ushered in through the steel-mesh gates, which I knew had been erected to protect the hounds from hunting 'antis'. Benson immediately made friends with the German Shepherd which licked his hand.

We were shown round the kennels. There were many pens of lively eager beagles. Everything was in immaculate order. Benson asked a number of detailed questions about the history of the pack, the country they hunted, the average number of followers at the various meets, and the beagles' diet.

He seemed absolutely delighted with all he saw and heard. We did not see the foxhounds, which the hunstman said would not be back until later. With much thanking, and an invitation to make a return visit, we said our goodbyes.

When we were out on the road, and Benson had resumed control of the bicycle, he said to me:

"They are breeding them rather small. It must make it a little easier for the field to follow on foot since the hounds will not be able to run as fast. I would very much like to go out with them." He looked a little rueful.

"You seem to have made a hit with the huntsman. I am sure that it could be arranged. I will ask one of the Joint Masters who lives in the village if you like."

"My dear fellow, I am sure that they would even agree to allow a papist priest to go out with them if *you* were to ask them. You were such a brilliant success with the bicycle. But I cannot see how I could possibly fit it in because of the P…Pilgrimage." He stammered as he so often did to give the word emphasis.

"What Pilgrimage?" I enquired innocently.

"Where else but to Rome! Perhaps to some other place on the way if it can be fitted in. Naturally I am hoping that you will join me as you have proved so invaluable so far. Now what's the name of that inn along the Heaverham Road? Ah yes, The Chequers."

He drew the gold pocket watch from his cassock and consulted the time.

"Let us go along there for a glass of something while we work out how we will organise our journey. You will need to take some leave from your employment and not fail in your family duties. I can only manage a few days myself."

He stopped wheeling the bicycle and looked at me pentratingly. Then he burst into laughter. It was the first time that I had heard his full laugh. It had a light tenor timbre.

"You look as though I have suggested something improper. I am sure that a pilgrimage is just what you need in all sorts of ways."

I looked back across the fields towards Kemsing; then back at this extraordinary black-cassocked figure who was wheeling the bicycle along beside me.

Of course I knew that he was right. Whatever it involved, and whatever the consequences, I wanted to go.

CHAPTER THREE

SHALL I GO?

SOME of the notes about our conversation at The Chequers were actually jotted down in the first of my Civil Service notebooks while Benson and I were sitting in the garden outside the pub. Our table with its two benches attached was in the sun, and by now it was becoming quite warm. Benson had insisted on buying the first round. Perhaps I was a little surprised the he ordered beer, and pints at that. After wishing each other good health he lit up one of his Benson & Hedges cigarettes.

The first thing we discussed was not the itinerary for the journey, still less whether it was really practical for me to go at all. Benson said that the most important thing to settle was what he called our Rule of Life for the pilgrimage. Without this, he said, we would not be in a suitable frame of mind for our final goal.

"That is why," he pontificated, "so many people feel disappointed in their holidays, and are yet unable to explain why. P…proper p…preparation and keen anticipation are absolutely essential.

"The first point is to ensure a good balance between duties to God, our neighbour and our own spiritual state. Neighbours for us means each other and those people we shall certainly meet on the way. There will be a lot to fit in so we need to commit ourselves to getting up early. Do you have difficulties in doing this like I do? You will have to guard me against slackness in rising. Can we agree on 6.30 am? There is no need to be extreme. Neither of us are monks, and we will be subject to fatigues and trials on the journey. Even Carthusians when they travel, and this is very rare—virtually only to make a new foundation— allow some relaxation of the Rule they observe at home."

He looked at me mischievously. "I know from experience

that 6.30 am in Rome is easy—even at this time of year it is not really cold. I am assuming we will travel by train much of the way. Half-an-hour in our couchette for mental prayer, followed by the Angelus, Prime and Lauds. Softly articulated prayers should be reasonably soothing to those still slumbering or half-awake. Our devotions may have to be a little curtailed if there are others with us.

"Of course we will book separate compartments for the two of us. This will be desirable in itself, but will also give us the opportunity to keep the right balance between our individual spiritual life and spiritual reading, and our responsibilities to those we meet. It will also ensure that we are fresh for our discussions with each other. Over familiarity can take the edge of one's conversation.

"We will breakfast together in the restaurant car. I don't believe in silent breakfasts when travelling— we may meet people during meals who need our help and advice. After breakfast, letters and postcards in our compartment, then we should discuss aspects of the Catechism for an hour, either together, or with anyone else in our compartment. I suspect that you may not be completely proficient in key aspects of the Catechism. Few Anglicans now are.

"I shall include in my luggage the 1889 version of *A Cathechism of Christian Doctrine*, known as the 'Penny Catechism.' It is brief, authoritative and to the point. I suspect that you will come to like the way it is structured in a dialogue form like *stichomythia*.

"We shall then do our private work. I imagine that you will have some civil service commitments—unless we are called on to do one of the corporal acts of mercy. You may also want to carry forward some of your researches on local history"—had I ever mentioned these to him?—"Angelus at noon, perhaps followed by Tierce, Sext and Nones, although not essential— before a late luncheon at 1.15 pm. Have you ever been to Rome?"

I said that I hadn't. I was on the point of adding that I wasn't at all sure that it would be feasible for me to get away, much as I would like to, and that he was basing his Rule for us on a premature assumption. But he was off again.

"Maps and guidebooks for Rome for, say, half and hour after lunch, unless the scenery is particularly diverting. Perhaps even the opportunity for a brief siesta." He smiled across the table and gave me what seemed to be a rather slow wink.

"We ought to do some manual work after lunch. Always difficult on a train. Can you embroider?"

"No, I can't," I said rather stiffly.

"But surely you can darn a sock, or do a simple repair? If you can't, I will teach you. I am working on a new section of my *Danse Macabre*. It is an appliqué tapestry and I shall remember to bring a piece. We might get some help from other passengers. You look doubtful, my dear fellow. I am sure you will find it great fun, and not demeaning to your masculinity. Tea at 4.15 pm in the Restaurant Car, if we should be still on the train, unless it can be served in our compartment. I cannot bear the way that tea in England has been getting earlier and earlier in the afternoon so as to shorten the time available for useful projects in the period after luncheon.

"After 6 pm more private work until 7 pm when we will say a late Angelus, which I will teach you in Latin.. You may wish to join me in the five mysteries of the Rosary after that, before we go to dinner with our fellow passengers at 8 pm. Wouldn't it be fun if we organised one evening meal as a celebration of some past historical event of significance which is often forgotten? I shall bring a book to give us some ideas. Recreation after dinner until 9.30 pm, followed by some spiritual reading. Have you a decent Lives of the Saints? I think we ought perhaps to say our own night prayers and compline and matins by ourselves in silence in our compartments. Examination of conscience would be after lights out in our couchette at say 10.30 pm, although there is always a risk that one falls asleep without doing it properly."

"But" I protested,"you don't seem to realise at all how difficult it is going to be for me to get away. It may well be completely impossible. What can I tell my family or my office?"

"Why the truth, of course. It is spring. Like Chaucer's pilgrims you have decided to go on a pilgrimage, even though it is not yet April. You expect that this will refresh your soul so that you will be able to tackle any work not completed before you go with greater panache on your return. Because of modern means of travel you wont need to be away long."

"But what am I to say about you?"

He looked at me enigmatically.

"You will have to decide that for yourself." There was a pause, then he said abruptly.

"Of course you will have to defend us both if we are attacked on the journey. You see, as a celibate priest in Holy Orders, I try to follow the Counsels, even though they are not binding like the Commandments. In other words, in the event of assault, I would hope to turn the other cheek. But I have an aggressive streak, as you will come to see. You, as a married man with a family, have a duty to defend you own life as their protector. I would hope that you would also defend me."

At that moment he looked so tough and commanding as he faced me squarely over his pint of beer, that I could not imagine anyone threatening any party of people in which he was included.

"I would, of course, do my best," I said, "but I am not, I am afraid, particularly brave or combatative. But surely you don't think our journey will be particularly hazardous."

"Not in the normal way of things," he said abruptly. "But it is prudent to get such points straight in advance, so that there is no chance of a misunderstanding in an emergency."

I got up to get another round of drinks. Benson was writing in a notebook when I returned.

"I am just trying to work out what we should take with us," he said. "We ought to be able to carry everything on our backs if necessary, so that we can do some walking. I have been thinking that it would help us to be recollected if we were to walk a little at the beginning, starting from near the Pilgrims' Way. We could get the train from, say, Tonbridge to the coast, then take the ferry.

"I never skimp on books, so this will mean very few changes of clothing for me. Fortunately it should be a little warmer in Rome. *You* may have to cram in a suit. You don't happen to have a large piece of cloth? Something in green cotton would be ideal."

"What would that be for?" I asked.

"Well, when one is travelling, especially during the period after luncheon, say in Rome, it can get quite warm, even in Spring, and one can feel soporific. It is good to have something sizeable which can be laid out so that one can sit or even lie down wherever one happens to be. A large cloth is wonderful for taking a siesta in the Borghese Gardens or on the Capitoline Hill above the forum. Green or khaki is the best because it blends in with the grass and doesn't show the dirt. It can also be folded lengthways so as to make a sort of cushion for a seat on marble steps. You can thus keep your cassock, or in your case your trousers, reasonably clean."

"I will look out for this essential item." My remark came out as slightly ironic.

"Make sure its big enough for two of us, but will fold up to be quite small." It was clear he wanted to ignore the tone that I had used.

In retrospect it was quite extraordinary that I allowed myself to be drawn into a detailed discussion of what to take on a journey, which in my case was still quite hypothetical, since I had not discussed it with anyone to whom I had responsibilities.

I have the list of what I wrote down in front of me now. It was drafted while Benson and I were talking:

bouillotte for boiling water for tea in trains—plugs into any available shaving point; tea;

string and pegs for hanging out washing;

Swiss army knife;

small shoulder bag to hold maps, guide book, Italian dictionary for when I was on my own;

sunglasses; jacket, pullover, socks, underclothes, sandals, shorts, two pairs of trousers, sun hat; ? suit (for visits to St Peter's?)

famous green cloth!

rosary? (he was insistent).

Benson said he would take charge of most of the books that we would need, but I should bring anything I thought appropriate, bearing in mind that I would have to carry them. I was not to bring a camera.

"Cameras prevent you really seeing what is there. They are completely distracting. If you want to record something pictorially then you should sketch it, even if your ability to draw is poor. Better an inadequate personal effort with pen or pencil than a conventional photograph that other tourists will all take too."

Later I reflected a great deal on why he was so insistent that we should have no camera.

I was still working on the list when he suddenly drew out his pocket watch from his cassock with the appearance of some alarm. He explained that he had to catch a train to London fairly shortly. He intended to walk from where we were to Sevenoaks Railway Station. Would I mind returning the bicycle and thanking George Wigsell profusely on his behalf?

He would write to me this evening to confirm the arrangements for our pilgrimage. He would send the letter by first class post which I should get some time on Monday or first thing on Tuesday at the latest. All the necessary bookings would be made by him. He would also let me know how the trip was to be funded. His last point was that I might like to try a vigil in St Mary's Church the night before we set off.

Before I could ask any further questions he had said a brief goodbye and was heading off at a cracking pace down

Watery Lane. It must be a good six miles or so to Sevenoaks Station.

Sunday lunch at home that day was uncomfortable: just Angela, my mother-in-law and I. It was not a weekend when Cyprian had an *exeat* from boarding school. Our daughter, Perpetua, was staying with a friend.

We had spring lamb and roast potatoes. The parsnips were from the garden but were rather woody because it was the end of the season. The only fresh green vegetable was some chard which Angela had been overwintering in the greenhouse. I opened a bottle of wine which I hoped would improve the mood. I said our usual grace:

"*Benedictus, benedicat, per Jesum Christum Dominum nostrum.*"

I asked about progress in the morning's gardening. Angela had been putting compost on the asparagus bed. She said that a lot of sheep manure needed collecting from the fields to add to the compost heap. The raspberries and currants needed potash and then compost. I said I would take care of this. I asked my mother-in-law about the Parish Communion. She reported that the Vicar had preached about the implications of the Brandt Report. The former German Chancellor had said the developed world needed to do much more to help the Third World. The Vicar wanted his parishioners to target their Lenten charitable giving towards those charities providing aid to developing countries.

Angela asked me about my walk. She noted that I had been away a long time. I said that I had been up on the North Downs as it was such a glorious morning. On my way back I had passed by the kennels and the new huntsman had asked me in to see the beagles.

"How were they?" she asked.

"It was all looking very spick and span."

There was a long pause. The sound of three people chewing on roast lamb seemed deafening.

"I think that I might give the lawn a rough cut this afternoon too," I said. "It's been so warm that the grass should have dried up quite nicely. I'll cart some manure up from the field for you after that."

Conversation petered out. My wife served pudding. She had made a tart from some rhubarb that we had forced for early eating. She had also made some custard but did not take any herself. I am sure that it was obvious that there was something on my mind. But I could see that Angela had decided not to ask me about it. My mother-in-law got a bit of lamb stuck in a tooth and went upstairs to her flat to deal with this. Angela said that her mother could be excused helping with the washing-up. We had always refused to have a dishwasher.

Angela and I washed up in almost complete silence. As usual she prepared a tissane of Lemon Verbena. We sat side by side on the sofa in the drawing room. One cat was lying on an old cashmere pullover next to the central heating radiator. This was beneath the bay window which looked out into the courtyard. A little afternoon sun was coming in through the high west window. I found that I had lost the will to say what I had been preparing. All I said was:

"Well, I had better start doing the lawn while the sun lasts."

I went out to the barn to collect the mower, then took it out on to the lawn and tried to start it. It was reluctant to get going. My neglect of it during the winter seemed to have made it mope. No one liked it if someone was too pre-occupied to pay due attention, not even mechanical things. I sat on a seat to clean the spark-plug as a first step. But I soon found myself rehearsing the dialogue which I had not had with Angela when the moment had presented itself a few minutes before.

"I've been thinking that I've been feeling awfully stale in my office work, and I don't feel that I have as much zest as usual for the garden. I am sure you have noticed that. It occurs to me that before the gardening commitments get heavier as the spring rushes on it might be a good idea if I had a short break. I would go on my own as it would not be easy to get someone at short notie to stay with your mother. I am not much company at present anyway.

I imagined Angela looking at me inscrutably. In my mind's eye she seemed to be getting herself into a comfortable position ready for a longish speech from me. I did not envisage her saying anything at this point.

"Actually I thought that I might go on a sort of pilgrimage." I looked down self-consciously at the spark plug which I was scrubbing with a wire brush as if to avert meeting her gaze.

"Nothing organised. Just a private pilgrimage, a sort of..." Her response would be abrupt, I imagined

"Where to?"

"I thought of going to Rome actually. Just for a few days, and I would do it very cheaply, so that it wouldn't eat into our budget for our summer holiday." We had already booked a cottage in Wales, the same one that we had been to the previous year.

Her reply, as I envisaged, was quite simple.

"Of course you must go. Mother has commented that you are looking a trifle overwrought." This was one of her mother's favourite words when someone was off-colour.

"When would you be going?"

"I thought perhaps later this week, if the necessary arrangements can be made quickly, and I can persuade my boss and colleagues that I can be spared."

"Are you planning to go with anyone?" I imagined her penetrating gaze at this point.Then I felt that in my struggle with my conscience I would fail and say something awkward like. "Not really at this stage."

I knew that such a reply would be evasive and unworthy. Yet I was sure she would not press me. She would simply ask me to let her have a list of things I would need for the journey. She would want to be sure that I had all the right proprietary items from the chemist that I would need in Rome.

I replaced the spark-plug and tried the pull start of the mower. It kicked into life. It seemed a good omen.

As I mowed I knew that I could not go down this route

with Angela. If I could not tell her what was on my mind and what I was thinking of really doing perhaps I should not go at all. The whole business was just too odd. I had not really solved the issue of what was really happening. Benson talked of danger. Could he be giving me some kind of warning?

I resolved to say nothing to the family and wait for Benson's letter. If it really came! Depending on what it said I could make my decison, and reply one way or the other, provided he gave me an address. I wondered if he would do that, and if so where it would be. How would he address a letter to me?

Sunday evening was uneventful but less tense. Having resolved not to make a decision about the journey yet, and to say nothing, I was able to engage in reasonably normal conversation at supper. My mother-in-law retired to her flat to watch the snooker on television. Angela and I listened to a tape of a Bruckner symphony.

But again I did not sleep well. One dream I remember.

I was on a vast plain. It seemed at first to be the American West. Over the rising ground of sand dotted with scrubby juniper trees there came towards me a wide phalanx of Catholic priests all riding abreast on bicycles—rather like a gang of Californian 'Hells Angels.' Except that they were all grinning as they swept past, their cassocks flying behind them in the wind. As they passed I stepped to one side. One flapping figure, trailing a little at the rear, rather oddly, seemed not to be on a bicycle at all. He was riding pillion on the back of a motor cycle.

The country side now looked more like 'the vasty fields of France.' I seemed to be caught up in a scene from Robert Bresson's film of George Bernanos' haunting novel, *Journal d'un Curé de Campagne*. As I was looking forward to further developments I woke up.

But as I dressed in the morning for the office I could not stop myself from thinking about the Bernanos novel. The last words that the young priest had said when dying were: "*Tout est grace.*" Everything is grace. Could it really be true?

CHAPTER FOUR

AN ORDER FROM ABOVE

ANOTHER extraordinary event. When I arrived at the Treasury on Monday morning there was a message for me to look in on my boss. After opening my steel security cabinet and positioning the files on my desk I locked my door and set off to his room. This was on the floor below. A narrow strip of red linoleum, like an economical version of a red carpet—very Treasury I used to think—ran alongside the offices on this floor to indicate, without great subtlety, that one was in the territory of the more exalted members of the Department.

"Good morning Bridge. Have a good weekend? Surnames between colleagues were the norm. "I've inconvenient news. Gilmore has fallen ill. He was due to attend a rather dull co-ordinating meeting of EC officials. You may well be aware of what this is all about. The meeting is at official level to prepare an agreed line for Ministers to consider at a Council Meeting some time soon. We need to agree a line so that our Ministers are not all over the place when they meet the Americans, the Nordics, and developing countries. They are to discuss tariff reductions and trade-dumping complaints, and the lead-up to the Uruguay Round.

"I would like you to go to stand in for Gilmore. Get hold of the papers as soon as you can. I'm afraid that the meeting is on Friday afternoon. Awkward for the week-end. Another boring element is that for some reason EC coordination is not to be in Brussels as usual but in Rome. I have no doubt that the Italian representative has some personal reason for wangling this. Or perhaps the Commision official in the Secretariat wants a weekend with a *petite amie* in Rome. Have you got much on in the next day or two?'

I noticed that he had the Departmental leave schedule in front of him. He continued:

"I see that you have not taken your full complement of leave. You have just put down two weeks in June. To sweeten the pill of being sent off at short notice you might like to have a day or two's leave in Rome before the meeting, or to make your way there in a civilised way. Are there any points that you would like to raise with me now about the meeting? Or you may prefer to have a word when you have read the papers. I have got quite a lot on this morning."

It was clear that the interview was over. I took the hint and prepared to leave. At the door I said:

"I am sure that I will be able to manage. I will try to fix up my travel arrangements as soon as I can, then leave a message with your secretary when I am going off. I *would* like a day or so extra in Rome. I'll only drop in for briefing if it seems necessary."

"Thank you very much. I am much relieved. I hope that whatever Gilmore has isn't catching."

That was all. I returned to my room, closed the door, and sat down at my desk.

Surely Benson could not be involved in this puzzling turn of events. If I was to be in Rome on Friday afternoon, I need not make firm travel arrangements yet. I could wait to see whether I got a letter from Benson and see what it contained.

If there was no letter, or, if there was but I was still unsure about going with him, I could then book through the Office to go by plane either on Thursday evening or catch the first flight to Rome on Friday morning. Feeling rather as if I was being filmed by some sort of hidden cine-camera I made my way back along the circular corridor. I walked carefully keeping my shoes always on the red linoleum. It was as if I feared that some unseen problem might occur if I stepped off it for an instant. My destination was Gilmore's office on the floor above to locate the papers for the meeting. Having collected these I spent the rest of the day briefing colleagues on my own work which they might need to tackle while I was away.

It was on my return from the office that evening that I found Benson's letter. It had been posted first class late on Sunday evening and had been delivered at home during the day. I noted that the envelope had a sketchy address and no postcode. However I knew that our postman, Jim, who was a good friend, would have taken care to ensure that any handwritten personal letter got through to me quickly.

The letter was lying on a little Victorian table in the dining room where Angela usually left any mail for me. All the other letters for me were bills. I knew that the unfamilair handwriting would have made it the subject of curiosity. Angela was in the kitchen and my mother-in-law was presumably up in her flat. I picked the letter up and smelt it surreptitiously. There was a fain aromatic smell. Was it incense or scented tobacco?

I took the letter upstairs to our bedroom where I normally went to change when I came home from the office. I sat down on our bed. I did not want to damage the envelope. As I had no paper-knife to hand I used one of Angela's nail files to slit it open. But before taking the letter out I studied the handwriting. My name and the address had been written in black ink. The script seemed Victorian to me. The word 'Esquire', which had been added after my name, was written out in full. The address was simply our house name and Kemsing.

There were three pieces of Crown Octavo writing paper within. The paper was plain and good quality, but without an embossed address. It read

The Travellers' Club
Pall Mall
London

My dear Bridge

Many thanks for arrranging the bicycle. As you could see I enjoyed my ride very much. I hope that your friend did not find it the worse for wear. I need more practice at changing gears! I am sure you will have thanked your friend handsomely for his kindness.

I have made our bookings to go out to Rome. We shall be taking the ferry from Dover to Calais. I find that the Railway Company stops the train from London to Dover at Tonbridge so I suggest that we embark there.

I thought we might walk to Tonbridge from Kemsing. I estimate that this will take us about six hours on foot. It will help set the mood for the journey, wear in the new shoes that I will have, and also get us used to coping with our luggage. We might go through Shipbourne which is high and breezy.

The train for Dover leaves Tonbridge at 3.15 pm. We should therefore set off at about 7 am in order to cover the ground and allow time for luncheon. And also for some surprises. I am planning one or two *en route* for you. You might wish to do the same for me. God will doubtless produce others. He usually does. We will want to have a little time to savour these before we have to catch the train at Tonbridge.

I have made a booking by telephone with a small *pensione* in Rome where you can stay for several days. How marvellous of God to have enabled the telephone to be used for this purpose. In view of my clerical status it would seem better if I were to stay in a religious community nearby, which I will do. A *pensione*/hotel seems better for you. We need to be careful what you are exposed to at this stage. As long as we stick to our Rule everything should go well.

Because of the timings of trains we will also need to spend the first night in Paris. I have therefore also booked you in at a small Hotel on the Left Bank. I have chosen the Hotel des Marronniers in the rue Jacob since it is very near the house of a religious community where I will lay my head.

I have one or two ideas for what we might do during our day in Paris. Religion in France, which you will know used to be known as the elder daughter of the Church, seems to be going through a bad patch. The secularist philosophers and anti-clericals have done quite a lot of temporary damage. But there are some bright spots.

I have been thinking much about your wife and mother-in-law in your absence. I hope that you don't mind but I have arranged to send them a rosary each. Don't be alarmed. They wont arrive until after we have left. I tried to get ones that are reasonably tasteful. I hope they like little mysteries. You can explain later what it is all about when you return. I have included a brief note with each simply saying: 'From a friend of Bernard and a sincere admirer.' I thought it best to say the same on each card as they are bound to compare notes! They might read too much significance into any slight variance.

Now about financing the Pilgrimage. I find that I am unusually flush with funds so there is no need to worry about the train fare and accommodation as I will cover these. We will need some money for food on the train, *en route*, and in Rome. The *pensione* will only do a little collation rather than what we English think of as a proper breakfast. If you can bring £120 I think that this will cover meals, local transport, entrance to museums, devotional purchases and allow something for charitable giving.

I suggest that we meet outside The Chequers in Heaverham at 6.45 am. on Wednesday 7 March 1983. I have added the year as I sometimes get moments of doubt on this point.

As a Civil Servant I am sure that you will not forget to bring your passport. I am assuming that you will be there on time. If you have not arrived by say 7 am I will set off on my own. I will assume that some circumstance has intervened.

Yours in Domino

Hugh Benson

The text of this letter, which I managed to copy into this notebook before the original was unfortunately lost, amuses and touches me now. But as I sat in our bedroom on first reading it through I had a sudden renewed attack of agitation, that I had not experienced since the previous day.

Was I seriously planning to slip away at very short notice with a person whom I had met two days ago in a Kemsing churchyard, who appeared to be a Roman Catholic priest and writer, but who was long since dead? I seemed to have decided to do this without telling my family or anyone else what I was doing.

Was I perhaps losing touch with reality? I was already guilty of something akin to disloyalty. What would Angela and my mother-in-law think about an unsolicited rosary? I feared that rather than being pleasantly surprised, they would be mystified, and probably rather annoyed and disturbed at this piece of papistry. It would not be Benson who would have to do the subsequent explaining. It would be *me*!

Perhaps I should try to get in touch with him at The Travellers' Club and ask him not to send the rosaries. If he hadn't already done so. It was all very well for him to insinuate himself into the life of someone like myself, who was, I admitted, potentially responsive. But what right had he to involve my family?

I had almost decided to try to contact him, when Angela called me from downstairs to the telephone. I put Benson's letter into my suit breast pocket. Then, without changing, went down to take the call.

It was a friend trying to arrange a meeting of our little local history group for later in the week. My tone was a trifle abrupt, certainly for speaking to someone to whom I was quite close.

"I am afraid I shall be away until at least next weekend at the earliest, possible longer." I then added a little more warmly, "I could probably do any day towards the end of the following week if the others could postpone the meeting till then."

I later reflected that I had involuntarily used the word 'afraid.' There is no doubt that I was somewhat afraid.

I then gave an explanation to Angela who had overheard what I said.

"I was just about to tell you. My boss called me in this morning. Gilmore has fallen ill and he wants me to go instead of him to an EC co-ordinating meeting on Friday. It's in Rome for some reason, not Brussels. To soften me up Walmsley suggested that because I had not taken much leave I might like to have a day or so in Rome before or after the meeting. Perhaps he was hinting that I am getting a bit stale. I would like to do this. I could see a few sites and look at one or two churches. You know that I have always wanted to see Rome. I hope that we will do it together some day. This will be an opportunity for me to get some ideas for our later visit together. I will be setting off early on Wednesday."

Short official meetings abroad were not unusual for me. Angela said she would help me gather together what I needed for the trip. The moment to come clean about Benson had again passed.

Back in my study I decided against trying to contact Benson. Perhaps he was not actually staying at the Travellers' Club, but had just written his letter from there. What would I do if they had never heard of him? I decided that perhaps the best thing would be to write to Angela *en route* telling her everything in the light of any later developments. I would then have had time to reflect better on what it all meant. I sensed that I must not do anything now which might risk putting an abrupt end to what I knew I really wanted to do, despite all my fears and concerns.

I slept better that night and caught my usual train to London in the morning. I briefed several more colleagues on some other issues that might arise on my own work while I was away. I then tried to absorb the papers for the meeting in Rome on Friday. It all looked fairly straightforward. Gilmore had left useful notes on what the other EC delegations were likely to support, and what the UK line should be.

I telephoned a colleague, Harrison, in the Department of Trade and Industry (DTI) who would also be going to the meeting. since the topics concerned both trade and finance. The main issue was the line the European Community should take when the forthcoming negotiations for world trade liberalisation and reduction of tariffs, the so-called Uruguay Round, began formally in a couple of years time. These trade round negotiations which were designed to reduce protectionism, took years to reach fruition. But they had played an important role in promoting growth in the world economy since the first trade round in 1948.

My DTI colleague and I were both in agreement. Together we would seek to persuade delegates of the other EC member states not to allow the European Commission to brief EC Ministers in a way which overplayed the EC's hand. The United States wanted financial services, such as banking and insurance, formally on the Uruguay agenda. France and the EC Commission, which usually supported the French, would like to keep the liberalisation of services off the agenda. They feared such liberalisation would damage European, and particularly French, financial institutions which might not be able to compete with foreign companies. Our line should be to support the American objective discreetly, since the UK was also strong in financial services. But we would need to do this without appearing to be too non-Community minded.

I later spoke to the Office's Travel Section about my trip. I said that I would make my own arrangements for getting to the meeting and would then put in a detailed claim for reimbursement. I explained that I was having a little approved leave in Rome and would only be asking the Office to pay for one night's subsistence before the meeting.

In my own mind I had already decided that I would repay Benson for the cost of the travel and accommodation in Paris and Rome. It was probably reasonable for the Office to reimburse me for the fares, since I was going to Rome on official business, whatever else I might be doing in addition.

I spent lunchtime in a second-hand bookshop in Sackville Street. I was served by a rather elderly man who looked more like a University don than a shop assistant. I said that I was looking for a guide to Rome with an emphasis on Christian sites.

"In that case," he said magisterially, "there is nothing to touch Luff's *A Christian's Guide to Rome*. Although first published in 1967, and some details are now a little out of date, it was still quite the best work available." He added that he had one still in stock. A quick glance told me that it was exactly what I needed. I then took a gamble.

"You don't happen to have any books by Kenelm Henry Digby, the 19th century antiquarian."

He replied with enthusaism.

"I did not realise that I was talking to a kindred spirit. I am also a Digbeian, but I'm afraid we don't have any in at the moment. As you know they are rare and were all published privately. May I suggest that you try The London Library?"

It was interesting that he presumed I was a member, which I was.

"If you don't know Bernard Holland's memoir of Digby you might find it there. A wonderful tribute to one of the great nineteenth century figures whom almost no-one knows of today."

I paid for the Luff guide, made a slight bow to the elderly gentleman, which he reciprocated, and set off to the Library in St James's Square. A quick glance at one of the massive leather bound catalogues showed me where the Digbys were. I walked up the central staircase past the photographs of famous figures in the Library's history. Mr Gladstone, T. S Eliot, and Dame Veronica Wedgwood seemed reassuring.

I looked in at the reading Room on the first floor. Working at some of the tables or asleep in the leather armchairs in front of the open fire were faces, vaguely familiar from the dust-jackets of their books. The Digbys were on a higher floor. I had to walk along the metal flooring which, as usual, give me a mild electric shock from the static electricity as I made contact with the metal shelving where my treasures lay.

In the end I decided to take out Holland's *Memoir of Kenelm Henry Digby*; as suggested by my new acquaintance at the bookshop. It had quite a few expansive long quotes from Digby's writings, which as usual were left by him in their original languages. Digby always assumed that his readers were properly educated, and so had full command of Latin, Greek, French, German, Spanish and Italian. Translation of the quotations was therefore unnecessary. He probably thought it would be patronising to his readers.

I scanned several volumes of Digby's own works—the Library's collection was by no means complete—but decided that I didn't want to risk losing one of these precious works while abroad. But I did stand for some time immersed in Digby's world of medieval pilgrimages. His great *Mores Catholici* in eight volumes was designed to show how Christ's Beatitudes in the Sermon on the Mount were taken so seriously by many Christians in those great Ages of Faith that they went to great lenghs to live their lives according to its principles.

On leaving the Library I took a route back towards the office which led me along Pall Mall. I stopped for a moment on the opposite side of the street from one of those imposing club buildings. They had bold street numbers outside but no brass plate to explain what secret world was housed within.

I realised that I was looking across the traffic towards The Travellers' Club. I stopped. Would Benson be there? While I was considering what I might do, the swing doors of the club flew open. A black-suited Roman Catholic priest emerged at the top of the steps. He was wearing a very wide-brimmed, black, Roman hat of the kind now very rare.

For a moment I thought it was Benson. He was about the same height. But as his head was turned away I could not see enough to be sure. A second later I realised he was a much slighter figure. Then, when I eventually was able to see his face I realised he was an elderly man, although his expression and features were alert and youthful. I had almost made up my mind to cross the road and ask him about Benson when a black London taxi arrived abruptly in front of the club. The priest quickly swung open the passenger door at the back and climbed nimbly in.

I remember thinking to myself that The Travellers' Club must be alive with priests. I had almost decided that I would go in to the club and ask the Hall Porter about Benson when I looked at my watch and saw that it was nearly 2.30 pm. I had a meeting in the Cabinet Office just before 3 pm. I had agreed to attend this before I went on leave. I hurried back across St James' Park.

I was on my way home in the train that evening when I decided I *would* attempt some sort of a vigil before setting out on the pilgrimage. I told myself that it would be easier to do this, rather than attempt to explain to Benson on the morrow that I had not managed it—by now I had decided that it was more likely than not that he would keep the *rendez-vous*—. I did not want him to think that I had fallen at the first hurdle.

Of course there was still a little packing to do but most had been done in the morning, and Angela could be relied on to fill in some of the gaps that I had overlooked. I felt in my pocket for the plain black rosary. I had hurriedly picked this up at a Catholic bookshop near Victoria Station, and had still managed to catch my usual train.

I was rather proud of the fact that I had also located a large piece of dark green cotton sheeting out in my shed. I had saved it some time ago from the underneath of an old bed that my wife and I had discarded when it became too uncomfortable.

One thing I would need to do when I got back to Kemsing this evening was to order a taxi to collect me at home at 6.30 am. Angela and my mother-in-law might well be still asleep—I would get my own breakfast—. But I was not keen to be seen in casual walking clothes as I set out.

At home and in my room I was rather proud of the way I had managed to pack flexibly. My rucksack would fit into my smartish travel bag. And my travel bag would fold up and fit into my rucksack when I was walking as a pilgrim.

My office suit would be reasonably uncrushable in a suit bag in the rucksack. I also put in a small office brief case with my papers for the meeting, and another small shoulder bag. I ordered the taxi and then sat down with the others for supper.

After this I finished off my packing. I then anounced to Angela that I wanted to go over to the church to check some details of several incriptions on its walls before going off to bed for my early start. To get into the church in the evening I needed to obtain the large key to its massive oak door from the Vicar. Again I used 'historical research' as my pretext, and promised to post the key back through the Vicarage letter slot when I had finished.

My notes on my rudimentary vigil are particularly sketchy.

'Very cold, hideous collage, B.V.M. upside down, *The Light Invisible*, strange presence…? *adiuge nobis fidem?*'

To remember and describe spiritual events and subtle changes of mood is usually particularly difficult for me. To do so on the basis of these few phrases is hard, but I have done what I can.

The coldness and deadness of St Mary's Church when I first entered that evening is something that I can still feel as I write. An icy blast of wind struck me as I pushed open the great arch-shaped leather door which led from the Church porch into the nave. Of course it was a cold evening, but the chill seemed to me to have something unnatural about it. I noisily went to the west end and turned on several lights. The light seemed harsh. The colours of the stained glass window were lost against the dark sky outside. The leaded outline of the figures in the windows seemed grotesque.

Strung between a number of interesting memorial tablets were several hideous children's collages apparently illustrating Lenten themes. One, which consisted of a number of badly-executed Arabs made from what looked like cuttings from magazines, was rather inexplicably labelled Ash Wednesday. I decided to select a pew towards the front in the north aisle where these would be out of sight. In order to reach this I had to squeeze past several large display panels on wheels on which were pinned photographs of various projects in the Third World which the parish sponsored. There were also some posters. I have no notes but I am almost certain that these titles included 'God and The Bomb,' 'The authentic Christian witness of those sexually different from us' and 'Women and St Hilda.'

I sat in the third row from the front and drew my overcoat tightly about me. I had brought Mother Julian of Norwich's *Revelation of Divine Love* with me. If I found difficulty in praying I hoped to find inspiration from it. I had also brought Benson's *The Light Invisible*.

Before getting on to my knees I glanced at the kneelers. The decoration on them had been worked by members of the Church's branch of the Mothers' Union. I noticed that three of the five kneelers in my pew were facing the wrong way so that the monogram of the Blessed Virgin Mary, an 'M' with elaborate serifs, was upside down. I got up and put these errant three the right way up. I resisted the temptation to make a reconnaissance of all the kneelers to check their orientation.

As I knelt down, to the right of my line of vision was the pedestal for church flowers, empty for Lent. From the north aisle where I was I could not see the altar. I closed my eyes.

Then nothing. Just the cold. I was so numb that I found I could not even remember all the words of the Lord's Prayer. I found myself alternating between holding my breath for ten to fifteen seconds, then breathing rapidly.

Common sense told me that I should try to read something from one of the books . But I found that I seemed to be without sufficient strength to raise my right hand to grasp the books from where they lay on the pew beside me.

I remember trying to visualise the scene from Benson's novel, *The Light Invisible*, in which a nun prays before the reserved Sacrament. But I could not picture her. The Sacrament was never reserved in St Mary's Church. There was no silver sanctuary lamp, nor a statue of our Lady. The stained glass in which she was depicted could not be seen at night.

I remember thinking: this is not spiritual dryness, this is spiritual paralysis. I was conscious, but my brain seemed incapable of giving any directions to my body. Nor could it seem to visualise or remember anything. I seemed to remain in this state for a very long time, but it was probably no longer than ten minutes.

Suddenly the spell was broken when I sensed that someone else was behind me in the Church. A few seconds later I found that I could move my fingers slightly, and I seemed to be breathing again normally.

I wanted to turn around to see who was behind me, but before I could do so I was interrupted by what seemed to be a kind of prayer. I have no clear recollection of this, except that it seemed to begin with a sort of version of the Lord's Prayer. Each petition in it seemed to be self-contained, more like a whole prayer in itself. The process was very slow and majestic. When it reached the final phrases: 'For thine is the kingdom…' I began to sense that there were even more people behind me. It seemed odd that I had not heard any of them come in. Several of them seemed to be whispering.

My brain was saying 'the power and the glory…', but my ears were straining to hear what the others were muttering behind me. As I listened more intently the strange thing was that the words, which I heard clearly, did not seem to be in English. I cannot remember much that followed except that I recall asking God to increase my ability to respond to grace while on my pilgrimage. I also made a petition to Him for the safety of my family while I was away.

Quite suddenly there was a huge crash. My concentration broke. I turned around abruptly. There at the back of the Church by the main door was the Vicar. For a moment he appeared not to see me. Then weaving his way between the notice boards and the pews he came down in the direction of my pew.

"I just came in to turn the heating up slightly to get the

Church ready for tomorrow's early service." He peered at me intently. "Anything the matter?"

"No," I said, "I was just praying."

He looked slightly embarassed. It was as if I had said something rather odd. It was only then I realised that there was no-one else in the Church. The Vicar went into the vestry. I peered around the Church. Had I simply imagined the others behind me? I thought of waiting until the Vicar re-emerged to ask him whether he had seen any others. Then I thought that this might also seem peculiar and only embarrass him further.

I rose quickly, gathered up my books and left the Church hurriedly. Outside it was a brilliant starry night. The moon lit up the tombstones. I began to move more slowly. If I had imagined that there were people in the Church behind me what about Benson? Had I imagined him too? I told myself firmly that others had certainly seen *him*, and there were those primroses at St Edith's Well.

I remembered the key to the Church. Rather than go back to give it to the Vicar I went down the lane and posted it through the Vicarage letter slot. I paused again in the road outside our house.

I was sure that Benson had not featured at all in my rudimentary prayers in Church. I had not even thought of asking God whether I could have confidence in Benson.

Suddenly there flashed into my mind what those people in the Church behind me had been murmering. It was a brief Latin phrase, *Adiuge nobis fidem.* The fact that I could recall this filled me with a huge surge of optimism, not just about the pilgrimage, but about my life in general. This euphoria continued until I got back into our house.

I was cheerfully clattering about in the kichen making myself a tissane of camomile when I glanced up at the kitchen clock. It was almost midnight. I realised now why I had not seen Angela and her mother. They would certainly be in bed by now and were probably trying to get to sleep against the background of my noisy activity in the kitchen. I moderated my clattering, conscious that I had been thoughtless.

In an ill-directed gesture of reparation I surprised the two cats by giving them a midnight snack of cat biscuits. The younger of the two, a black and white female looked at me quizzically between mouthfuls. Her look suggested that I had committed a small breach of feline etiquette by providing food gratuitously without her prior importunate miaow.

Just before going up to bed I went back to my study. I took out a copy of the Vulgate. I wanted to be sure about the phrase that I seemed to have heard people murmuring in the Church. Yes, there it was. My supposition was right. It did come from St Luke's Gospel.

In Chapter XVII, verse 5 the Apostles are recorded as putting this petition to our Lord just before He goes up to Jerusalem to be crucified. Their plea seemed to me specially touching: *Adiuge nobis fidem*—increase our faith.

CHAPTER FIVE

ON FOOT

I WOKE at 5.45 am after a peaceful and dreamless sleep. Although I had said I would get my own breakfast I saw that Angela was already up and had gone downstairs. I dressed carefully, and checked my luggage. On my way along the passage to the stairs I met my mother-in-law in a dressing gown. She pressed on me a green shetland pullover.

"Please take this little present with you on your trip. I've heard that the evenings in Rome at this time of year can be chilly still."

I kissed her and promised to fit it in somewhere. Downstairs in the dining room I found an envelope next to my place-setting at the table. Opening it I found that it was a card from Angela. She had designed it herself. On the front were some drawings in pen and ink with light washes of water-colour: they showed our house, the garden with its fruit and vegetables, its high brick walls and iron gates. Our two cats were there, and tiny pictures of some of the garden birds that they terrorized.

It was the back which astonished me. On it there was a drawing of a pilgrim with his staff, scrip, and leather water-bottle with a traditional pilgrim's scallop shell on it. Inside Angela had written: With all my love for your trip to Rome. She had added a text of St Walter Raleigh:

> 'Give me my scallop shell of Quiet,
> My Staff of Faith to walk upon,
> My Scrip of Joy, immortal diet,
> My Bottle of Salvation,
> My Gown of Glory, Hope's true Gage.
> And then I'll make my pilgrimage.'

I drank a cup of tea which had already been poured. On impulse I took a piece of toast and honey with me to the garden. I gathered a little tussie-mussie of spring flowers: snowdrops, aconites, crocuses, miniature yellow daffodils, and one or two primroses. Holding them in a little tight bunch I found a rubber band in my suit pocket. When I went upstairs to clean my teeth I left the little bunch in a small pewter jug on her dressing table. On a page torn from the back of my diary I wrote: '*Gratia et Gloria*! I shall write.' I signed myself B. and left the slip of paper next to the jug.

I went and found her in the kitchen and kissed her. I thanked her warmly for the card, but did not comment. The doorbell rang loudly. It was the taxi.

"I'll write to let you know how I'm getting on," I said as I stuffed the shetland pullover into my bag. One more kiss, then I gathered up my bag and went out through the front door.

"I am afraid it is not much of a fare," I said to the taxi-driver. "I am meeting someone at The Chequers at Heaverham, and then we will be walking."

"Well, it got me up on the road early, and it's a lovely morning to be out."

When we had gone about half-way to Heaverham I said to the driver, "Just drop me here. I'll walk the rest on foot." He stopped abruptly.

"All right, guv," he said. "Just give me a couple of quid."

I pressed a five pound note into his hands.

"Keep the change, and wish me luck."

"I certainly will," he called from the driver's window as he drove off.

My bag weighed 35 pounds. I seemed to be able to carry it effortlessly. It would seem lighter when I got everything into the rucksack and it was on my back. The noise of the birds defending their territories in the hedge-rows was deafening. I began to compete with them singing out the liturgy of St James:

'Let all mortal flesh keep silent,
And with fear and trembling stand;
Ponder nothing earthly-minded,
For with blessing in his hand,
Christ our God to earth descendeth,
Our full homage to demand.'

The irony of shouting out loudly to command others to keep silent appealed to me. In the last field before The Chequers some lambs formed themselves into a gang amd rushed at the fence which separated them from the road. They probably thought I was the shepherd bringing the morning hay. The ewes came across too and eyed me reproachfully. Several lambs took advantage of their stationary mothers to get at their udders, kneeling down and butting hard to encourage the milk flow.

I sang out:

'Rank on rank the host of heaven
Spreads its vanguard on the way,
As the Light of light descendeth
From the realms of endless day,
That the powers of hell may vanish
As the darkness clears away.'

There was The Chequers before me. As I was now walking in the centre of the road the Kentish ragstone Georgian facade was in front of me, but I could not not see into the beer-garden where I had planned to meet Benson. It was hidden from the road by a quickthorn hedge. But I had complete certainty that he would be there.

As I came to the end of the hedge I saw a figure in a black cassock slumped in a chair near an iron table at the far end of the garden. He was half-turned away from me, his body facing the early sun. His head seemd to be leaning back and facing upwards in what seemed an unusual posture.

I was about to shout a greeting to him when I noticed

something most curious. There seemed to be a blur of white substance rising up from his head. Suddenly the figure lifted its hands from its lap—I was by now near enough to see this— and he appeared to catch the stream of ectoplasm. It was only then that I realised that the white airy substance was a stream of table-tennis balls. Benson turned and saw me.

"A little too much early morning breeze. I sometimes can keep five balls juggling in the air longer than that, but even a faint breath of wind misdirects the rhythmic puffing from my mouth."

He cupped the balls into his lap and sat up straight as I walked up to him. He then packed the balls into a side pocket of his rucksack beside his chair.

"They're light, of course, which is essential for travelling. I cannot do more than five at a time, usually only four. After I have said Prime and Lauds I often practice a little. It is wonderful for keeping the reflexes in trim and improving concentration. How spendidly on time you are, Bridge. I am so glad the letter got to you."

He was looking at my boots.

"They seem stout and well worn in. I have a new pair of walking shoes from Trickers in Jermyn Street. They seem all right so far. But the true test for walking shoes, as it is for humans, is how they perform when the going gets rough!"

He pulled out his gold pocket-watch from his cassock and glanced at it.

"We must be off and keep to our sch…schedule." He stammered engagingly on the last word. Then he sprang to his feet athletically, seized his capacious blue rucksack and slung it on to his back. Without turning to see if I was ready and following, he set off at a brisk pace, across the car park and down Watery Lane.

I hurriedly opened my bag and repacked it and its contents into the rucksack within. Although I managed to do this quickly he was already out of sight before I set off. I lengthened my stride to catch up. Fortunately he stopped a few hundred yards down the Lane and was consulting one of his books.

"You didn't bring a pilgrim's staff, and nor did I! But we can cut one each near the Iron Age fort at Styants Bottom. You can also post a note to your family at a letter box in the wall at Ightham Mote. I have brought some stamps."

"Have you sent the rosaries ?" I asked.

"I left instructions at a shop near Westminster Cathedral that they should be sent off on Friday. Your family should get your letter before they arrive. They are Portuguese, and much less intimidating than I feared they might be. They are just simple black beads with a small silver crucifix of our Lord and a medallion of our Lady. You managed to get one for yourself I assume."

"Oh yes," I said. I was going to bring it out when he went on:

"What a blessed morning. Do you hear the hounds? I believe the huntsman must be taking them out for exercise."

He was right. As we came to the M 26 Motorway bridge that goes over Watery Lane, the huntsman, in tweed cap and jacket, was coming along behind us with about twelve couple. The hounds were giving voice enthusiastically and sniffing along the grass verges of the lane. The huntsman had a staff which he waved at us in greeting. Every now and then I saw him use it to guide a more individualistically-inclined hound back into the pack. Benson's face glowed with enthusiasm.

"I've been hoping we might see you, Connor, " he called back to him. "It's the next best thing to going out for a day's sport with you. How do you keep them fit in the summer?"

"We usually take them up to Northumberland in July and August. They really enjoy that, and many of the field go too. It keeps them fit as well. By late summer most of our followers are content to let their gardens go at home."

Benson nodded approvingly.

"Mr Bridge and I are going to Rome, Connor."

The huntsman and the pack were now upon us and we were surrounded by hounds. Benson shouted:

"You should go there too sometime."

"I'd love to, Father, but I would have to choose me time," he shouted back as he and the hounds went on ahead of us. Where the road forked he and his pack went right; Benson took off to the left.

"Remind me to send a post card from Rome to the Master of the Hunt. I want to tell him how much I admire the way Connor has the hounds looking. Did you manage a vigil?"

Benson looked across at me challengingly as we walked side by side. His broad grin was radiant in the sunlight.

I explained that I had made an abbreviated effort. I mentioned the Vicar's interuption and the people that I had heard behind me.

"I thought that might happen. That Church has a pious medieval tradition."

"But who were they?"

"Oh, medieval pilgrims, I expect."

"But why didn't I see them?"

"I don't really know. But I expect that would be overdoing it. What about the poor Vicar! He would not know how to react. Most clergy are particularly intimidated by anything at all supernatural. They are inclined to regard such happenings as an implied criticism by God of their faith. What did the pilgrims say?"

"*Adiuge nobis fidem.*" I was careful not to translate.

"Even though most mediaeval pilgrims would be unable read, many ordinary people memorized the Latin of Holy Mass. And they could probably follow the gist of the readings from the Gospel in Latin. And they would hear the same readings throughout Christendom if they went on pilgrimage to Rome, Canterbury, Compostella or Jerusalem. What a huge decline there has been in the ability to memorize since then. Just a lack of serious practice. The rise of the use of the vernacular instead of the historical liturgical languages—Greek, Aramaic and Latin—has important disadvantages. But it is a subject on which some reserve is prudent in conversation with those you meet along the way."

I looked across at him as I adjusted my pack on my back. His blue eyes were scrutinizing my face. I could see that this was not a subject on which he wished to be questioned further. We fell silent. I was conscious of the rustling of Benson's cassock as he strode along beside me. Occasionally he seemd to be humming what seemed to be a fragment of Gregorian chant.

We came down into the small hamlet of Styants Bottom and we were now in more wooded country. Oldbury Hill, the site of an old Iron Age Fort of the Iceni, I knew to be high up on our left, but out of view.

On our right was a clearing which had been given over to young corn. A large flock of lapwings had invaded the field, their crests bobbing up and down as they investigated the earth. Benson went over to the verge and produced a pair of binoculars from his cassock pocket and studied them carefully.

"They must be local birds. It is too early for migrants." He passed me the binoculars. I managed to focus on one of them. I admired its handsome crest. In the sunlight the metallic green and white plumage made a good contrast with the rich chestnut under its tail.

"Have a good look at them. You won't see many birds in Rome. Only cats. Now we must cut our staffs. Blackthorn is probably the best that we can hope to find here."

He crossed to the other side of the road and slipped off his pack. He parked it behind a bush and in a second was running up the hill, gathering up his cassock in his hands. As he came to tree trunks lying prone in his path he hurdled them effortlessly and let out a whoop of delight.

I followed more sedately without taking off my pack. I found him crouched by a thorn tree with a bright red Swiss Army knife in his hand. With the tiny saw-blade extended he was rasping away at a long straight branch.

"I think that we can probably get two reasonably straight staves from this piece of underwood. See, it has been coppiced. Good countrymen can tell the age of a wood by the size of the coppice stools."

Looking up from his sawing he added:

"There is a lot of chestnut in this wood. I have come to accept the view that chestnut is not native, but was probably introduced by the Romans. It is now certainly very widespread in this part of Kent. I like a tall staff. [the branch was now free from the coppice] This one with a V top is ideal. It is easier to tie string to, and for trapping things which are almost out of reach."

He sat down on a log and began to strip off the lateral twigs expertly.

"Have you got your knife? You could finish this off while I cut and trim the other."

I took off my pack and fumbled in the side pockets where I hoped that Angela had stowed my Swiss Army knife. It was there carefully wrapped in a clear plastic bag.

Benson handed me one staff. I noticed that Benson had already notched a small cross just below the V at the top.

"That one is yours. I shall put the saltire cross of St Andrew on mine so that we can tell them apart. Even in a monastery where everyone has embraced voluntary poverty and attachment to possessions, monks often have personally identifiable napkin rings."

He quickly stripped the remaining laterals off the other staff and cut the saltire cross on it.

"I shall rub mine in the earth to darken it a little." He bent down and moved it vigorously back and forth in the muddy earth at the side of the track by which we had ascended. I did the same. Benson then produced a piece of rag from his cassock pocket and wiped both staves.

We were soon back on the road with Benson humming contentedly. He pointed up again to our left.

"Do you know the caves up over the top of the hill? They always seem to me most convincing lairs for primitive man. They command such a wonderful view of the valley below. You could easily observe and prepare yourselves against a hostile attack from below."

I said that I knew them well, and that they were a favourite spot for our children when young. They used to pretend they were ancient Britons defending their camp against the Romans. I think that this was the first time I had given much information about our children.

Benson laughed loudly. "I hope that they realized the importance of putting a sentry at the top of the steep stone steps which are part of the old gateway to the camp."

"Oh yes, I think my son would have always remembered that tactical point."

"We must bring him something ancient and military from Rome."

I thought for a brief moment of my son, and what he would think about his father going off abruptly on a journey to Rome with a Roman Catholic priest of ambiguous provenance. Perhaps I should wait until things were clearer before dropping him a line.

Our staves were making a fine rhythmic thumping as we walked side by side. Benson said brightly:

"We must look out for a couple of metal tops of champagne corks to fix to the bottom of our staves as ferules. Otherwise they won't stay the course."

I thought to myself that it was unlikely that we would find any on our path, but said nothing. I was pleased, however, by the extra impetus that the staff provided. In no time we reached the A25. To my surprise, instead of turning left and taking the footpath along the road, he turned right. Sensing my puzzlement he said:

"You expected me to turn left and then right further on towards The Harrow Inn. I grant you this might seem a more straightforward way towards Tonbridge. But I thought we might have time to call in at Ightham Mote. If we go the way I am suggesting and pass near to St Lawrence Church, we could then walk along bridleways much of the way. We wont have time to visit that Church, though its history is interesting. One of the vicars of Seal did not get along with his parishioners in Seal village so he just built a new church quite nearby in Seal Chart. Then he went to live there. It was his way of starting again with a clean slate."

I said I thought this was a very human reaction. I knew some people who would like to do something similar at certain points in their lives, but they often don't have the will or make the opportunity.

"But sometimes" I added, "they change their jobs, move out of the neighbourhood or emigrate, rather than building a new church!"

Benson followed this up. "Catholic priests sometimes satisfy their craving for a new start by changing spiritual directors. But serious reflection is needed before doing that—to be sure one is not simply running away from God, or one's duty to one's neighbour. Think of poor Francis Thompson and 'The Hound of Heaven'."

On the bridleway the sun came through only intermittently. The path here was still soggy from the winter rains and was muddy where the horses had churned it up. I tried to avoid getting the mud on my moleskin trousers by walking on the edges of the bridleway. Benson simply marched unconcernedly on in the centre of it—I saw that some mud was intermittently flicked up by his staff on to his cassock. We passed a number of ponds on our right. Then there was a high and abrupt incline in front of us with a large number of steps to help the walker ascend. Neither of us said anything as we climbed the steps. We passed the turn off to St Lawrence Church and I glimpsed it through the trees which were not yet in leaf.

We stopped for a break just off the bridleway to look down into a deep ravine where there may have been an old quarry.

Benson sat on a log and lit a cigarette.

"Well," he said, "we seem to be developing a pilgrimage rhythm. It must be about 8.30 am." He checked his pocket watch, but did not confirm that this was the time.

"There is an opportunity now to do our letters, if you are

ready for that. We can post them at Ightham Mote."

I took the green cloth from my rucksack and spread it out on a patch of grass and sat on it with my back against my pack. With a small writing pad on my knee I began a letter to Angela. My notebook has the draft. This is what I wrote:

"My darling sweetheart

Many thanks for all that you did to get me off this morning, and for your beautiful card. It was amazing that you seem to have guessed that I was going on a sort of pilgrimage as well as on office business.

I have not been completely straightforward. I am sure that you have guessed that there was something on my mind. A rather odd thing happened to me last Saturday morning, which I did not tell you about. I met a Roman Catholic priest who called himself Benson. He was in that bit of waste land below the Youth Hostel where you used to excavate for old village bits and pieces. The odd thing is that his appearance was exactly like the photograph of Robert Hugh Benson, who was curate at St Mary's in the 1890s, and who later became a R C priest. I checked this in the biography of Benson I have in my study.

But the really disturbing thing is that this Benson died just before the First World War. I have calculated that if he were alive today he would be about 113, but he seems to be the same age as he is in the photograph in the biography. I am sure that I am not hallucinating as one or two other people in the village saw him as well, unless it is some sort of collective delusion.

You may find all this very peculiar indeed, as I do. But what is even stranger is that I have, in a sort of way that is difficult to describe, fallen under his influence. He suggested to me that I should join him on pilgrimage to Rome. I knew that I really wanted to do this. While I was thinking about this (and of coming clean about it to you) my boss, as I told you, suddenly asked me to go on official business to Rome this week. It seemed to me that the pilgrimage was in some way being organised for me. Very odd indeed!

What you may find hard to understand is that I have felt unable to put leading questions to my pilgrimage companion, although he has confirmed to me that his name is Benson. It may also seem cowardly to you but I am quite frightened of doing anything which might prevent me following the path that seems to have been set for me.

This included saying anything to you, which I was on the point of doing several times. I must also confess that I feel particularly inhibited from asking what his connection is with the Father Robert Hugh Benson who died in 1914. I suppose because I would not know what I might be compelled to think about the world or my sanity if he confirmed that he was one and the same. You know how matter of fact I have always been.

I am reasonably certain that what I have embarked on is not dangerous. You may derive some reassurance from the fact that Benson himself has encouraged me to write this letter to you. He has also told me that he is sending you and your mother rosaries. I told him that I was not sure how you would react! But he seems to want to do something to keep in your good books, and perhaps give you some part in what is happening to me.

I will leave it to your judgment as to whether you say anything about this at this stage to Cyprian and Perpetua or to any friends. I myself would prefer it if you kept things to yourself until I am clearer in my mind what it is all about, and I have written further. I suspect that others would simply think that I was losing touch with reality, or suffering some sort of mid-life crisis. I would not blame you if you thought this too. All that I can say is that I have never felt saner!

My fondest love to you and Mama

Your pilgrim B."

Benson had also been writing while I was at work. He wrote quickly and there were a number of sheets. But he also kept looking up. When I glanced in the direction of his gaze I saw a kestrel more or less at our height but hovering over the centre of the ravine below.

Benson saw that I had seen it.

"Falconry, has it become popular again?"

"Yes," I said. "I've even seen them on the southern slope of the North Downs above Kemsing. They are usually hunting rabbits."

"I am sure you know what patience and persistence is needed to train a bird of prey. Lots of men and women in the Middle Ages apparently had it. And some Arabs have it still. If you are able to train a bird of prey you may almost be able to tackle the harder task of training your own will."

He smiled apologetically, and stubbed out his cigarette.

We pressed on through the woods. The trees had thinned out a little, the sun was higher and the way seemed much less muddy. We soon hit the road again, but crossed it and reached a well-maintained stile. Benson used his staff to pole-vaut over it athletically. I clambered over after him.

We were now in apple orchards. It was too early for blossom but the leaf buds were swelling. Heavily pregnant sheep were grazing the orchard which had been grassed down. Benson was again humming something. This time it appeared to be the Pilgrim's tune from Berlioz's 'Harold in Italy.' I joined in. After a few minutes he said:

"We must put together some words so that we can sing it more robustly. A task for the train."

The footpath left the orchard and went up higher into woods again. There was now much less sun and our humming petered out. For the first time I was conscious of the weight of my pack. Benson must have sensed this for he said reassuringly:

"It is not very much further to Ightham Mote."

After a few more minutes we again began to descend and were back into fields. No sheep this time, just green grass and some new chestnut fencing and strained wire-netting. The home farm was at the end of our path: a collection of typical Kentish buildings, ragstone walls to the first floor, then a tile-hung second floor. The barns were simply longer buildings than the farm-house, with fewer and smaller windows. There was also a clutter of chickens-pens, small sheds and a kennel. The vegetable garden was only partially dug over and the poles for last years' runner beans were still up. A couple of Toulouse geese honked loudly at our approach as we passed along the fence which divided the footpath from the garden. Back on the path we climbed steeply for a few more minutes with some large dark ponds below on our right. Woods pressed in on us on either side.

I think it was these towering trees which made the sight from the top of the hill when we reached the brow of the hill more enchanting. For there below us in a shallow valley lay Ightham Mote. The Kentish ragstone fortified manor rose from wide green lawns and the glittering frame of its surrounding moat.

Just in front of us on the edge of what was now a road was a low stone wall. Benson slid his pack off his back and set it down on the grass verge. Then he clambered on to the wall and sat down, leaning forward and resting his elbows on his knees. He beckoned to me to sit beside him. I said:

"The moat is about thirty feet wide in parts. It is filled from springs in Martin's Wood; the water descends through a series of ponds to the moat and beyond. It eventually reaches the Medway River by a number of streams."

"Do you know the house equally well?" Benson asked. He looked at me penetratingly. For a second I thought that he was annoyed that I knew a little about it. Then he went on:

"I used to know quite a lot about it. I still have some connections as you will see. But my factual knowledge is rather out of date. The imposing gatehouse is 14th century, as is the Main Hall within. A lot of modifications were made in the 16th century. The two roofs of the parts of the building on either side of the towers are of different heights, as you can see."

He suddenly turned around and dived his hand into his pack and produced a booklet and an envelope.

"You may wish to study this little booklet before we go in. It has a ground plan of the rooms, but we wont be able to see them all. I had hoped that we might have already had a discussion of some points in the Catechism—you will recall the timetable of our Rule—, but on reflection a practical demonstration this morning may be more helpful. I shall now leave you for a quarter of an hour, pay a call of nature, post a couple of letters, and make one or two other arrangements. You will find some stamps in this envelope for any letters you wish to send. As I mentioned, the letter-box is set into a wall in the farm-house. It is just in front of the little road that goes down to a small iron gate through which we will enter the manor grounds."

In a moment he had jumped down from the wall and disappeared into the trees on the other side of the road.

The sun was by now quite warm and I sat for about ten minutes soaking it up and trying to compare the scene before me with the plan in the booklet. Once I had mastered it I looked around at Benson's pack.

Suddenly I had an overwhelming desire to look inside it. Although I managed to suppress it almost immediately as completely unworthy——and perhaps disastrous—, I had a sharp battle with my will. Even when I thought I had completely mastered the urge I still found myself thinking what I could say if I was caught looking in one of the rucksack pockets if he were to find me probing. Perhaps I could plausibly explain, I thought, that I was looking for a tape measure to take measurments in the manor house! However in the end my conscience and fear overcame my inquisitiveness.

Instead I put a first class stamp on Angela's letter and addressed it, and picked up my own pack. I left Benson's where it was, then went down to find the post box. It was where Benson had indicated. There was a defiant GR on the red box which was let into the cottage wall. I had posted my letter and was beginning to study the farmhouse when Benson suddenly reappeared from the other side of the building that I was looking at. His pack was again on his back. Evidently he had been back to collect it. He had a couple of letters to post in his left hand. He strode purposefully across to the letter box and thrust them in.

"I hope that the collection times on the box are adhered to," he said, pushing out his jaw determinedly as he turned to me. I responded by saying that I had already posted my letter to Angela.

"I am so gg…glad." he stammered . "I shall write to her myself later in the trip and explain about pilgrimages. But let us have a look at Ightham Mote."

CHAPTER SIX

WHAT HAPPENED AT THE MOTE

WE were soon winding our way down the short steep gravel drive towards the little wrought-iron entrance gate. Every now and then Benson turned his staff over and over like a drum major. Once he even tossed it about four feet into the air and caught it magisterially, turning to grin at me when he had completed the manoeuvre. A slight breeze had now sprung up that was to prove significant later. There appeared to be a little wooden hut like a sentry box on the left of the iron gate. From this a red-faced, bluff-looking middle-aged gentleman emerged. He greeted Benson warmly. It was clear that they were known to each other, even perhaps that he had already just seen him.

"Mr Clement will look after our packs," Benson said to me. "He has also made things ready for us in the house."

I followed Benson through the iron gate and struggled out of my pack. Benson followed Mr Clement into his hut. They were there together for several minutes, then Benson re-emerged with a small bag. Mr Clement then came out and collected my pack and took it into the hut.

"You know your way, Father," boomed out Mr Clement. "Ruby is on duty and is expecting you."

As we approached the stone bridge which crosses the moat and leads to the main entrance beneath the tower, the sun was warming some of the soft grey ragstone at an angle. I remembered a large old cedar tree on the lawn in front of the house from earlier visits.

"I always tell Clement that he must be a descendant of Sir Richard Clement who built the lovely room which later became the New Chapel here. Sir Richard was one of Henry VIII's courtiers when he bought Ightham Mote. I suspect he wanted to pursue the life of a country gentleman. Clement here always strikes me as an ideal country gentleman too, in dress and manner. But I believe he is quite happy as custodian for the American gentleman who has saved the house from ruin."

We stood in front of the tower just before crossing the short, wide bridge over the moat.

"See the small angled slit in the outside wall on the left of the great door. That is for parleying with a stranger before he is admitted. Medieval and renaissance men and women were probably generally more conscious than the present generation of the importance of the Christian virtue of hospitality to strangers. Yet they were prudent enough to make a careful assessment before actually admitting someone that they did not recognise. Being hospitable never meant being incautious.

"If I may continue as your cicerone," continued Benson, "the great nail studded oak door is probably about a hundred years later than the lower part of the tower which dates from the 14th century. The arms above us on the face of the tower are those of the Selby family who acquired the house in 1591 when Shakespeare was just beginning to establish his reputation in London. The Selbys held Ightham Mote for 300 years."

I peered up at the weathered stone shield, trying to decipher its heraldry. It was positioned between the two sets of decorated windows with three lights which marked the second and third storeys of the tower.

"Can you make out the Saracen's head high up there and the motto *Fort et loyal*?" said Benson. "The Selby family had a crusading history before they came to live at Ightham Mote. What do you think of the Crusades?"

"I haven't thought about them very much," I confessed, then added, "I suppose they were an opportunity for younger sons to go out to the East and acquire some land and titles, which they would not have had if they had stayed at home."

"How unimaginative they must have been who taught you history if that is all that comes to the surface now!

Surely they should have explained to you the feelings of so many men who wanted to visit, cherish and protect the places where Almighty God himself had chosen to be born. And where He had lived, died and rose again for us. That was surely their main motive for going. Of course, being fallen human beings, other desires and temptations got in the way, but the overwhelming motive for most crusaders at the beginning was a pious one.

"You will understand all this better," he continued, "from reading that book about Kenelm Digby which you have brought with you. He is one of the few comparatively modern writers with the imagination to allow the men in the great Ages of Faith to speak for themselves. Of course there are lots of books about the lives of medieval men and women. But often these have a whole dimension missing, and that the most important. Few modern scholars seem to have a sympathetic understanding of medieval men's religious aspirations and feelings. And even if they have some understanding of this, they often seem inhibited from trying to explain it to their modern, secular and often sceptical, readers. Digby felt it better just to quote long passages of the writers themselves in the hope that at least some modern readers would sense their spiritual fervour and be inspired by it.

"But as regards the Crusades, and the Selby family's direct experience of them, I wonder whether they became disillusioned when they saw the original crusading spirit diminish, and become corrupted by a love of material and worldly things. Some of the Selbys kept to the Old Religion which I serve. Perhaps they felt that they might be better occupied in serving the Lord in the tabernacle of their chapel here, than in seeking to retain and regain the ground on which His sacred feet had trodden. Especially after the rulers of the Latin Kingdoms of the Holy Land had lost their spiritual fervour."

Benson delivered this historical reflection in front of a large ancient dog kennel in the courtyard of the Manor

House, just outside the great Hall. I hope I have captured the essence of what he said. It was a discursive little homily which covered a number of Benson's ideas about the past. I am fairly sure that the last part which contained a reference to Benson's own priesthood is very close to his exact words.

As we entered the door that led into a sort of vestibule of the Great Hall a plump middle-aged lady of medium height confronted us with a mop. She had long blonde hair streaked with grey flowing freely on to her shoulders. Her spectacles had upswept frames which hinted at a mask for the Venitian Carnival. She had a warm smile.

"Lovely to see you, Father. Everything is ready. Father Scrope has been over from Tonbridge with what you need, and will return to collect everything tomorrow. We have somewhere secure to keep everything overnight. I shall keep a candle burning."

"God bless you, Ruby. You think of everything. This is my friend, Mr Bridge. From Kemsing," he added.

Ruby freed her hand from her mop and shook my hand warmly.

"If I had known that we had someone from Kemsing," she said, "I would have brought over my photographs of the windows in Kemsing Church which show you all the scenes from St Edith's life. My son, who is a clever photographer —he even develops his own prints—did them for me. St Edith has always been a great favourite of mine."

"She has always been one of mine too," said Benson. "I am sure that she was right to prefer her convent at Wilton to the crown of England."

"Oh yes! She is such a grand girl. It is lovely to think that we might meet her in heaven."

"Although she has always been invoked by those with physical trouble with their eyes," said Benson, "I have reason to believe that prayers to her help those who have a spiritual astigmatism as well."

Ruby seemed on the point of leading us to the left into the great Hall when she suddenly raised her mop to chest height and barred our entry.

"Before you go in," she exclaimed I expect Mr Bridge would like to see Sir Winston Churchill's picture of the water-lilies in the moat. Sir Winston was a friend as well as a neighbour of Mr Robinson, our American owner. Mr Robinson bought the Mote in our Queen's coronation year. Sir Winston used to come over quite often to see him and sometimes to paint too." Ruby used her mop as a sort of pointer to indicate the small slightly Monetesque oil painting hanging in the vestibule.

"Of course Sir Winston wasn't really a professional artist," said Ruby, slightly apologetically. "But lots of people think he was quite good for an amateur."

I told her I thought the picture had a certain colourful liveliness. Benson peered at the picture intently but made no comment.

Once we were inside the great Hall Benson boomed out:

"Of course the Hall is not vast like Penshurst or Knole. Just thirty by twenty feet in size but nearly forty feet in height. As you can see the Victorian owner screened off a corner. Perhaps he did it to make it warmer in winter. The Hall is particularly well lit, especially from those five fine perpendicular windows on the west wall which always catch the afternoon sun. Sir Richard Clement put in the glass during the 1520s. Whenever I see these glass windows I have a feeling of *lacrimae rerum*, which catches my throat."

Benson glanced across at me to see whether I knew my Virgil. Then turning to Ruby with her mop, he added, without the least condescension:

"The window always makes me feel a trifle sad, as I expect it does you. You can see, Bridge, on the far left of the centre light, with its crowned royal arms of England, there is a pomegranite. It's that large orange fruit. This was the emblem which Catherine, Henry VIII's first Queen, had as her personal badge. Poor Queen Catherine! Poor England! Such a short time was to elapse from the time when this window was put in to record her honour, and that of her rejection a few years later by King Henry, and of his marriage with Anne Boleyn from nearby Hever Castle. And so England's link with her religious heritage was tragically broken."

Benson turned and looked at me penetratingly. The lids of his blue eyes seemed more hooded than normal.

"Of course," he continued, "we cannot really understand how free will and grace operate, or how God sees history. But as a mere creature I have often found myself meditating on the life of poor Catherine. So far from her native home in Granada. And the pomegrante! Such a poignant symbol of the warm and fruitful Mediterranean world from which she came. Then there is the classical link of the pomegrante with Persephone, and with her unhappy stay in exile wih the King of the Underworld. But poor Catherine, unlike Persephone in the Greek myth, never managed to return to her homeland again, even for a brief visit."

Benson's remarks about Catherine were the more affecting to me when I saw their impression on Ruby.

Benson then turned my attention to the corbels whose grotesque figures appeared to be carrying the weight of the roof of the hall. It was while I was looking up at these that I heard the first sounds of distant singing. Some male voices seemed to be chanting in unison. Benson made no comment but I noticed that he consulted his pocket watch from his cassock.

"We still have several minutes before I take you to the Tudor chapel. Ruby, would you mind telling our friends that we are on our way?"

Ruby propped her mop against the vast stone fireplace. I made a mental note that it was of comparatively recent date, perhaps late nineteenth century.

As soon as Ruby had gone Benson took me down to a crypt. He showed me a small recess that he believed may have been an aumbry to store communion vessels when the crypt was used for religious services, perhaps during the times when Catholicism was illegal.

We then went back to where the main staircase leads up to the first floor. Benson made me rub my hand over the finely carved Saracen's head on the newel post.

"You can see he even has a jewel in his turban," he said. Above the staircase there was a full length portrait of a woman in mourning dress with a young boy at her side.

"That is the famous Dame Dorothy Selby whose tomb you can see in Ightham Church. The story that she gave away the Gunpowder Plot is nonsense. You should meet Father Francis Edwards one day. He will tell you a great deal about that business. Nothing about the story of the plot as it appears in the history books is quite as they say."

The first room that we entered on the floor above was bare apart from a small table on which there was a small iron crucifix. Benson made a little bow. Behind this was an east window of the decorated period. The white walls seemed to have been lime-mortared, and the roof timbers had been exposed to show off the old beams. It was not until we entered the next room that Benson broke his silence.

"This is the Oriel Room, one of the range of family living rooms. It was here that the family would have received those Catholic priests who were travelling all over England in disguise. At that time to receive a Catholic priest in your house was a capital offence. Those who did so knew that if they fell under suspicion they would be tortured to reveal the whereabouts of the priest, and the names of other families that might be harbouring others.

"You see that little window behind you. That is the squint. From there you could see what was happening in the room below that I have just shown you. I imagine that the Blessed Sacrament would have been reserved down-there. It would have been too public and too dangerous in the new Tudor chapel, which I am about to take you to. The intimates of the family would have been able to have glimpses of our Lord, in the form of the Blessed Sacrament, as they went about their daily tasks. Notice how the squint is angled so that there is a clear view of where the altar and tabernacle would have been positioned."

While I was verifying this point I noticed that the chanting of men's voice had ceased. Benson again looked at his pocket watch. Then he motioned me out of the Oriel Room into a narrow room like a corridor. It was well lit from a wall of windows decorated with small coats of arms in stained glass.

Leading the way, Benson turned left at the end. As I followed we seemed to be on the threshold of the 'new' Tudor chapel. In front of me, on either side of it and facing us, was a small group of young men kneeling on the floor in front of a wooden table that seemed to be serving as an altar. The table was immediately to my right. I guessed that these young men had been the source of the chanting, although they were now completely silent. Beyond the young men was a carved wooden screen; and through this about six high stalls. All these were crowded with men and women.

Benson led me down the central aisle past the screen to the back of the chapel where several stools had been placed in the centre of its tiny nave. Ruby and Mr Clement were already seated on two of the stools. Benson beckoned me to sit in the middle on the third. He whispered:

"It is better sitting in the centre of the aisle as you can't see very well from the pews because of the screen and that over-large pulpit. Ruby, will you look after Mr Bridge and explain what we are about?" He left again swiftly by the way we had entered.

Ruby smiled at me and handed me a piece of foolscap-sized card covered in plastic. But she made no attempt to speak. She knelt down on the boarded floor with her face towards the altar. I remember raising my eyes to the wooden barrel vault ceiling at this point. It was painted in chevrons in the Tudor livery colours of green, white and silver—pomegrantes again, with the white rose of York, the red of Lancaster; and the Tudor rose, together with castles of Castile, arrows of Aragon and the *fleurs-de-lys*.

I noticed at this point a very tall young man—I guessed he was about six foot four feet in height and around twenty-six years of age—at the front beyond the rood screen. He got up from his knees and went out the way Benson had just gone. He returned almost immediately carrying six tall candlesticks which he placed reverently on the altar table. He lit them, then went back to his place and resumed kneeling.

I glanced at the sheet which Ruby had given me. It said 'Benediction with the Ciborium'. I now saw through the screen a boy enter from the right side of the altar swinging a smoking censer. He was followed by two more boys, each carrying a lighted candle. All three were wearing long black cassocks and white cottas fringed with lace. They seemed to be about fifteen years of age and were of similar height.

Benson followed. He was dressed in a white surplus with a white silk stole with gold crosses on the ends. He genuflected before the altar and went up to it and placed a white cloth on the altar, then left again. The two boys with the candles took up position on either side of the altar facing it; the boy with the censer stood over to the far right where there was a small table and a brass stand.

Benson entered once more, this time wearing a white silk shawl held by a chain around his shoulders. He was carrying something in his two hands, but it was hidden under the shawl. I assumed that this must be the ciborium. He placed it carefully on the altar. Now that it was uncovered I could see I was right. The boy who had been carrying the censer, which was now on the stand, moved over to Benson and took the shawl from his shoulders and laid it out on the side-table. He then returned to Benson with the censer and an incense boat. Benson spooned some incense into the thurible then, kneeling, raised it up to his face clicking it against its chain, then incensed the ciborium several times.

The young thurifer came to collect the censer. I noticed that he kissed Benson's hand and some sort of disk on the censer chain after taking receipt of it. He kept it in his hands facing the altar and did not return it to its stand.

There was complete silence in the chapel. Ruby pointed to a text on the sheet. It read:

'Lord Jesus, I really believe that you are here; that you see me and you hear me. My Mother Immaculate, St Joseph, my father and lord, my guardian angel, intercede for me.'

It seemed that this was the prayer which was being said in silence. Everything inside the old house seemed suddenly hushed. I could even hear the lapping of the water in the moat, and a little rattling of the windows as the wind outside seemed to have got up.

Then, while we were still kneeling, the chanting began, starting with the tall young men at the front, but soon followed by those with us behind the screen.

'*O salutaris Hostia, quae coeli pandis ostium:*
Bella premunt hostilia, da robur, fer auxilium.'

The articulation of the Latin was soft but firm. I remember noticing that what was so compelling about the chanting was not just the perfection of its pitch and phrasing, but the merging of each voice together so that none was predominant.

The clicking of the censer by the dark-haired boy punctuated the chanting.

"*Uni trinoque Domino sit sempiterna gloria,*
Qui vitam sine termino nobis donet in patria."

The nostalgic longing in the phrasing of the chanting on the last word '*patria*'—in English 'homeland', which seemed to speak of the heaven from which we were all at present still in exile—was almost unbearably sweet.

I have often since then gone over the Latin of this hymn for the service of Benediction with an English translation. Of course like many Anglicans I had been taught to believe in the real Presence of our Lord in the Eucharist. But what this phrase really meant seemed vague. It seemed to be something at best symbolic.

The reverence of this congregation, perhaps especially the young men chanting in front of the screen, seemed quite outside my experience. While I was reflecting, I noticed that those around me were now speaking in unison in English. It seemed to be a prayer for England addressed to the Blessed Virgin Mary to intercede for the Church's separated brethren and unite them into the one true fold. But before I could reflect on the implications of this the Latin chanting began again.

'Tantum ergo Sacramentum
Veneremur cernui,...'

Here I noticed that everyone around me made a profound bow...

'Et antiquum documentum novo cedat ritui;
Praestet fides supplementum sensuum defectui.'

Benson had now taken the censer again and was incensing the ciborium as the Latin chanting continued.

'Genitori, Genitoque laus et jubilatio,
Salus, honor, virtus quoque sit et benedictio:
Procedenti ab utroque compar sit laudatio.'

I now heard Benson himself chant for the first time unaccompanied in Latin:

'Panem de coelo prestisti eis.'

The young men at the front drowned out the rest of the congregation as they sang out: '*Omne delectamentum in se habentem.*'

Benson then chanted a long Latin prayer. He rose, still facing the altar, and moved across to the thurifer who again put the shawl around his choulders. Benson then genuflected towards the ciborium, took it up and turned towards the congregation. The thurifer now knelt with his censer facing the altar. As Benson blessed the congregation with the ciborium held in his hand beneath the shawl, the thurifer incensed towards the ciborium. Click, click, click against the chain.

A little bell rang too while the blessing took place. I was not sure where the sound came from. It was a tinkling, slightly mysterious sound as if it was coming from somewhere far off in the great house. I guessed in fact that it was probably being rung by one of the young men in the front of the chapel, perhaps the tall young man who had lit the candles on the altar at the beginning. But to my mind it seemed like the bell that hangs on the sheep which leads the flock on the high windswept plateaux of Southern France.

The next thing I was conscious of was that Benson was kneeling facing the altar like us. He was now stripped of his shawl and we were all repeating the Divine Praises. This was easy as they were in English and Benson's clear firm voice gave us the words which we simply repeated. It all seemed majestic, and a fitting climax.

I do not recall what happened next. I suppose Benson and the servers and thurifer must have gone out through the linenfold door at the right of the altar, and that the others followed, probably through the door by which Benson and I had first entered.

For my part all I can now recollect is that while I continued to kneel on the boards of the chapel floor I was surprised by wave after wave of indescribable sweetness and strength. Although I have since come to believe that it must have been a kind of spiritual grace, at the time it seemed to me very much like physical ecstacy.

The only thing I could compare it with was the sensation I had as boy when breasting the sea surf. The feelings ebbed and flowed in the same way, reaching great crescendos as happened when I twisted and rose up in the hollow of a wave and caught its power as the wave and I both sped together toward the vast white sandy shore.

Such joy had quite caught me unawares. As in surfing all that seemed necessary was to be ready to catch the great white-crested wave when it came.

I do not know how long I remained kneeling, or how long this state would have continued. All that I later noted was that I became aware of someone touching me on the arm. Looking up I saw Mr Clement. When I got up we were alone in the chapel.

"Ruby has gone to make ready a bite of lunch," he said.

Mr Clement's voice had a soft Kentish accent which made it reassuring. It was quite unlike the accent of someone from Kemsing. Their accent often revealed their family origins in South London.

"Would you like to join us in the courtyard?" Mr Clement added.

I felt quite stiff from kneeling, but followed him towards the back of the chapel. He pointed out a plaque on the wall just before we reached the door.

"As you see, poor Sir Thomas Collyer-Fergusson, who did so much to restore this house and keep it going, lost one of his sons in the First World War."

I saw that the plaque not only recorded his death but also the award of the Victoria Cross for bravery.

"I never knew Sir Thomas, Mr Bridge, or whether his faith and beliefs gave him sufficient resilience to bear the loss of his son. But it must have seemed a long trial as he coped with the damp, the dry rot, the death watch beetle which one has to face if one owns a great old house like Ightham Mote."

Mr Clement took me down some back stairs, and out through what seemed to be a kind of store-room into the courtyard. As we emerged into the bright but breezy cobbled courtyard I saw that Benson and Ruby were already there. Four upright wooden chairs had been set up in a semi-circle near the entrance to the great Hall. A small oak trolley was nearby laden with food. Benson and Ruby were seated and talking, but rose when they saw us. Benson made a rather formal little bow and indicated that Mr Clement and I should sit on the remaining seats. Ruby began to serve the food.

"Because I know that you are rather pressed for time," said Ruby, as she donned a white apron from beneath her serving trolley, "I hope you wont mind if I make up a plate for you and Father. Please leave anything that you don't fancy."

Mr Clement joined Ruby at the trolley and began to serve drinks. Benson interjected:

"I hope you wont mind, Bridge, if in view of Lent we just have some mineral water for lunch. Put a piece of lemon in Mr Bridge's water, Clement, to cheer it up."

Ruby handed each of us a pink plate with a traditional Spode pattern on which were neatly arranged cold fowl, salad, brown bread, cheese and various pickles. Then she took off her apron, put it on the back of her chair and sat down too.

Benson looked at each one of us in turn, rather as if he was the leader of a string quartet and was getting us ready to play. Then he said:

" I will use a grace of the English poet, Alcuin. It may have at one time been inscribed in a monastic refectory. I will give it in Latin first then in an English translation:

'Qui de rore dapes dedit et de petra bibendum,
Qui convertit aquas liquidas in vina Falerna,
Qui siccis pelagi pedibus superambulat undas,
Augeat ipse suis familis sua dona benignus.'

'May the one who gave a banquet of dew from heaven, and drink from the rock, and who changed clear water into vintage wine, and walked dry shod on the waves of a sea, increase his gifts to his servants, as is his kindly way.'

We all murmered, “Amen”, then tucked into our food on the plates on our laps. To my surprise the bird was goose, extraordinarily flavoursome and succulent. The cheese was smoked, and there were some pickled onions. I was just beginning to tackle this with gusto as it seemed a long time since breakfast when Benson spoke again.

“I hope that you will not mind combining the satisfaction of your physical hunger with something spiritual as well. Mr Clement would like to read us something which he believes is apt for our adventure.”

Mr Clement then produced a small black book from his jacket pocket.

“It is just a short prayer from the English missal which is sometimes used for those who go on a pilgrimage.”

He laid down his plate on the ground beside him, set the book on his lap and put on a pair of spectacles. He began to read in his firm clear Kentish voice which resonated a little around the walls of the courtyard.

> ‘O God, who didst bring Abraham thy servant out of Ur of the Chaldees, and didst preserve him unharmed in all the ways of his pilgrimage: we beseech thee, that thou wouldest voushsafe to protect these thy servants; be unto them, O Lord, a support in setting out, a comfort by the way, a shadow in the heat, a shelter from the rain and cold; a chariot in weariness, protection in adversity, a staff in slippery places, and a haven in shipwreck; that thou, being their leader, they may prosperously reach the place whither they go, and at length return to their house in safety.”

All three of us said “Amen” through our munching. Then there was silence. Everyone seemed to be relishing their food, especially Benson. I was too, but my head was also buzzing with questions on the subject of the service of Benediction. Did it happen often? Was the American owner of the house present? Would it have taken place even if Benson and I had not come? Why weren’t the altar servers at school on Wednesday morning? In the event all I said was:

"Will the young men who were chanting in the service get some lunch?"

Benson gave me his usual penetrating look with his blue eyes.

"Oh yes, they will certainly have a light meal on their way back to their places of employment. It is charitable to be concerned about them, but there is really no need. We for our part need to be concerned about our timetable if we are to be sure of catching our train." He drew out his pocket watch and checked the time.

"Ruby, I thank you for a superb luncheon and you, Clement, for your service with the bottle. And for all the other services that you have done for us. We shall keep you in our prayers on the pilgrimage and in Rome. There is no need to come with us to collect our paraphernalia from the lodge at the gate."

Benson rose quickly and deposited his plate on the trolley, then walked over to where Ruby was seated as if to shake her hand. But she frustrated this manoeuvre by getting up suddenly and, going over to the trolley, bent down and picked up her handbag where it lay on the ground. She fished into it and brought out something with a flourish.

"Father, I would like you to take this little shell with you on your journey. There is one for Mr Bridge too. I brought them from Compostella in Spain."

The shells she presented were two medium-sized pinkish white scallop shells, the traditional kind that you see worn by pilgrims in pictures.

"Father, I thought that you might be able to use yours for an ashtray on the train. I am not sure what Mr Bridge might use his for if he doesn't smoke." She turned to me.

"Perhaps you could use it for holding your shaving soap. Would you find a use like that for it?" she said.

She smiled shyly, then lowered her eyes, brushing her long, grey-blonde hair away from her ruddy face.

"I don't want you to take them if you think they will not be of use. Mr Clement told me that you had a lot to carry."

While Benson and I were thanking her profusely for this addition to our equipment and confirming their practical utility, Richard Clement also sought a part in our pilgrimage.

But it was not a gift but a request. He explained that it was unlikely that he would ever be able to go to Rome. Could we therefore take something from Ightham Mote and leave it there for him? He then produced three acorns from the pocket of his jacket. "There is," he said, "some kind of garden, I understand, on the Capitoline Hill in Rome, above the old Roman forum. H V Morton, the travel writer, tells a good story about picknicking there surrounded by cats. I wonder if you might plant these there. I think that six inches of depth would be about right. Of course, they may not grow, and even if they do the gardeners may not like to have English oak trees there. But then again they might."

Benson said that we would be pleased to carry out the commission faithfully, and slipped the acorns into his cassock. The breeze which had been growing stronger during our lunch made his cassock billow as he did so. He dived back into his cassock a second time. At first I thought it was his pocket watch that he had brought out but as I looked more closely it was another sort of instrument.

"I will just test the wind with this anemometer," he said, moving over in the direction of the main gateway, apparently to get a better reading.

"The strength of the wind is coming along well," he said, turning back towards me, but without giving any explanation as to why this should be of interest to us, or why a more forceful wind was desirable. He then turned and waved to Ruby and Richard Clement. As they waved back their hands and faces caught the sunlight against the dark oak door of the arched entrance to the Great Hall.

We collected our packs, and slung them on our backs. Then, with our staves in our hands, we set out once more on our way. It looked at my watch. It was about 11.45 am.

CHAPTER SEVEN

A FAVOURABLE WIND

I NOTICED that Benson was striding out in a very determined fashion. I suspected that he thought that we might be running a little behind schedule. Our route began up a footpath along the side of the manor, and then through a field gate into what was clearly a bridleway. There were low mixed hedges on either side of the way. Beyond there were arable fields, and to our left two oast houses to remind us that we were in Kent. There were some large old oak trees in the fields and in the distance some stands of poplars and one or two clumps of Scotch pines.

For a long time neither of us spoke. I was still feeling strongly elated by the service of Benediction and the hospitality at lunch. I had little desire to break the silence. Even the pack on my back seemed strangely lightened. I was now less inclined to concern myself with the relationship between Benson and Ruby and Richard Clement. As to the presence of the young men, and the boys who served at the service, I was still puzzled about them, but somehow the beauty of their chanting and the boys' devotion seemed more significant than who they were and why they were there.

There was a a tinge of green in the arable where some of the young wheat was beginning to push through. There were even some leaf buds on a few of the thorns in the laid hedges which divided the fields. Every now and then there were some wood anenomes at the foot of the hedge.

I looked across at Benson as we srode along side by side. His chin was jutting out determinedly as if he was seeking to emphasize the quicker pace he was setting. But the expression on the rest of his face seemed to have a serenity that I could not remember seeing before. It was then that I noticed his hands. They were holding black beads against his cassock. Of course I reflected, he must be saying the rosary.

I felt a strange momentary embarassment, as if I had caught him doing something slightly improper. Then, reflecting that this feeling simply arose from a primitive but deep-seated Protestant reflex, I sought to suppress the feeling and concentrate on the scenery. The terrain was undulating and the path went up and down with it. Some fields had some sheep but there were no lambs here yet.

But I was not entirely successful in my resolution. I found myself slyly glancing back at Benson to see if he was moving his lips as he tolled his beads. After a couple of quick glances I concluded that his prominent bottom lip was motionless. After what seemed about a quarter of an hour I saw him put his rosary back in a little leather purse. I was surprised by the snap this made before he slipped it back into his cassock. We had reached the top of an incline, and there in front of us was a view of the upper storey of a handsome house in the distance. It must be Fairlawn, I thought, the great house of Shipbourne.

"The glorious mysteries are said on a Wednesday as well as on Sunday," said Benson. "It always makes me so happy when I find myself saying them on a glorious breezy day like today."

His whole face was filled with the same boyish innocence and enthusiasm and joy that he had shown on his bicycle ride.

"I shall need to give you a few hints on the rosary before I let you further into its mysteries. Many people never get into the swing of saying it at all. But once you do, you may need to ration yourself, especially when you are doing a lot of hiking."

I rather expected him to launch into a further discourse on the rosary, but he abruptly changed the subject. We had remained standing in front of a gate with the view of Fairlawn beyond.

"Bridge, I want to know how you understand the passage

in Chapter 6 of St John's Gospel which occurs after the feeding of the multitude?"

I must have looked completely blank. Benson came to my aid.

"In the St James' Bible version, which will be the one with which you will be familiar, the important verses are:

> 'Verily, verily I say into you, except ye eat the flesh of the Son of man, and drink his blood, ye have no life in you. Whoso eateth my flesh and drinketh my blood hath eternal life; and I will rise him up at the last day. For my flesh is meat indeed, and my blood is drink indeed. He that eateth my flesh and drinketh my blood, dwelleth in me, and I in him.'

"Now the issue is," and he turned to look me squarely in the face, "whether our Lord here is speaking figuratively. Of course our Lord often *did* speak figuratively: for instance when He refers to Himself as a shepherd over a flock, or says He is the vine and his followers are the branches. In Jewish tradition the use of metaphor to make an important point was well understood and was often used by the prophets that came before our Lord."

His blue eyes seemed to search mine. "But was our Lord really doing this here? Was He speaking metaphorically? The idea of eating human flesh or drinking blood of any kind was particularly abhorrent to Jews. It is clear from the context that the Jews who were listening to our Lord in the synogogue at Capernaum realised that he was not speaking metaphorically *here*, although they will have heard him do so *before*. 'How can this man give us his flesh to eat?' they are reported to have said. The Gospel here also records the reaction of many who had previously been sympathetic to our Lord: 'This is a hard saying; who can hear it?' Our Lord did not then go on to explain that He was speaking metaphorically, which would have been the natural thing to do, if He was. Instead Sacred Scripture records that many of his disciples went back and no more walked with him. Then He turned to the twelve and asked them: 'Will ye also go away?' And St Peter makes his great affirmation: 'Lord to whom shall we go? Thou has the words of eternal life.' "

I was amazed to find myself saying, in response to this scriptural explanation:

"But this passage also helps with an understanding of our Lord's words at the Last Supper."

"Exactly," said Benson. "The inner core of the twelve disciples were therefore fully prepared by what they would hear at the synogogue at Capernaum for the Institution of the Eucharist at the Last Supper. It was then our Lord said to them: 'Take eat; this is my body. And he took the cup, and gave thanks, and gave it to them saying, 'Drink ye all of this; For this is my blood of the New Testament, which is shed for many for the remission of sins.' "

"I suppose I have usually thought of receiving Holy Communion as something essentially spiritual," I said.

"Catholics are always well aware of the body, and should always be grateful for the physical world in general. We have never been afraid of painting pictures or making sculptures of everything in the physical world: of humans, creatures and nature. In some other religions the world of the spirit, the world of the spoken word, are good, but the physical world is sometimes held to be evil and a cause of corruption. But how could this be for us Catholics when our God really became a tiny human being in the womb of our Blessed Lady? How could we then ever be iconoclasts!

"Of course the physical world is not always comfortable or pleasant. He Himself suffered real agonizing physical pain when He was scourged at the pillar and nailed to the Cross. But this suffering as a human was all done for us, His creatures. So God is not just an all powerful disembodied spirit, as the Jews and Muslims believe. He truly became a man and so is both our brother and father.

"It is therefore easily understandable to us that He would wish to leave with us something real, physical and tangible of Himself in the Blessed Sacrament of His Body and Blood. What we have is His Real Presence under the appearance of bread and wine. The technical word, 'transubstantiation', is simply a useful and rather late philosophical way of explaining what Catholics have always believed since they were told about it by our Lord himself, as Sacred Scripture records. The touch and taste remain the same, but the substance is changed into the Body, Blood, Soul and Divinity of our Lord.

"I hope that you can see better now why we feel such reverence for what has been consecrated by a priest. Our Lord was really there in a physical way when I blessed you with His Sacred Body in the ciborium at Benediction before luncheon. Of course He is also here with us now too, but since humans are very much physical creatures, unlike angels, it is particularly consoling to be able, at appropriate times, to have a physical embodiment of God with us. And because It is what It is, the reverence that we show towards It is not idolatry, as some of our separated brethren think, but just another beautiful way for us creatures to give homage to our Maker and Redeemer.

"I have said much more than I wanted to say today. Catechism should have been over by 10.30 am according to our Rule! *Mea maxima culpa*! Everything will, I hope, be a little more routine when we are on the trains. If the wind keeps up, as it seems to be, you will soon be presented with something else physical."

We set off again. The route had now became a footpath, the Greensand Way. We passed a fine horse-chestnut on our left, still not in bud. I noticed that some poplars on our right had impressive round clumps of mistletoe. We reached another view on high ground looking across to Shipbourne Church. The descent took us past a small stream from the Fairlawn Estate with a little waterfall. The Shipbourne Sports field was on our left. The path rose again as we went up towards the Church.

I was expecting Benson to say something about the

Church, as he had done when we were at Ightham Mote. Perhaps he felt he had been heavy-handed. I knew a little of the history of the Church at Shipbourne and wondered if it would be welcome if I said something.

The original chapel, I recalled, had belonged to the Knights Hospitallers. At the Reformation this had been confiscated by Henry VIII. He rewarded one of his supporters, a member of the Vane family, with the church and its lands. The Vane family's gratitude to Royalty did not, however, survive the Civil War, and Sir Henry Vane signed the death warrant of Charles I. At the Restoration of Charles II, he paid for his disloyalty with his life.

But the family survived at Fairlawn. A later member of the family became Lord Barnard who built the first new church at Shipbourne in 1792. But it was the Cazalet family, who acquired the estate later, that built the present Anglican Church. This rather splendid example of Gothic revival, dedicated to St Giles, was the one we were now approaching.

I thought Benson might go into the Church. Instead he led me through the graveyard and around to the left and stood outside the front entrance. From there, looking down the short entrance drive, I could see part of Shipbourne Common. I looked over at Benson. He again was saying something to himself, but he was also looking out keenly across the Common as his lips moved. He must have decided to voice what he had previously been saying to himself. For the concluding words were now clear:

'And the Word was made flesh and dwelt among us. Hail Mary full of grace, the Lord is with thee. Blessed art thou among women, and Blessed is the fruit of thy womb, Jesus. Holy Mary Mother of God, pray for us sinners now and at the hour of our death.

Pray for us, O Holy Mother of God. That we may be made worthy of the promises of Christ.

Pour forth, we beseech Thee, O Lord, Thy grace into our

hearts, that we, to whom the incarnation of Christ, Thy Son, was made known by the message of an angel may by His Passion and Cross be brought to the glory of His Resurrection, through the same Christ our Lord. Amen. May the divine assistance be always with us, and may the souls of the faithful departed through the mercy of God, rest in peace. Amen.'

After making the sign of the Cross, Benson looked over at me. "I was late in reciting the Angelus. I try to do it at noon. In future you might prompt me if I am distracted. I must teach you it in English. And in Latin. You will recall it was part of our Rule."

I looked at my watch. It was now 12.40 pm. There was quite a stiff breeze. Benson looked pleased and took out his anemometer and studied it.

"The wind seems about right. Let us go out on to the Common. But be careful crossing the Tonbridge Road in front of you as there seems to be a lot of traffic."

Shipbourne Common is a large space of a number of acres in extent. It runs in a westerly direction away from St Giles Church. It is mostly laid out to grass with a few specimen trees. Upper Green Road bisects it. The road has a wooden bus shelter and red telephone box on its right, not far from the Tonbridge Road. The Common rises upwards away from the Church. It was just possible to see the tops of a few houses on the far side of the Common, and the tall wire fencing around some tennis courts.

Benson's eyes seemed to be concentrating on a large oak tree almost at the top of the rise on the far side of the Common to the left. Suddenly I saw what I am sure Benson had been waiting for. High up in the sky there were three of them. Two to the left of the oak tree and one to the right. They were flying a good many feet above the top of the oak tree.

"Come on," shouted Benson as he started to run, seeming to make light of his pack.

I adjusted the pack on my back, and set off in pursuit.

But I could not match Benson's speed. About half way towards the oak tree I stopped, rather breathless. Benson was now quite a way in front, and was nearing the oak tree.

I wanted to identify what I was seeing. Yes, they were certainly large box kites, soaring upwards, and then sometimes suddenly downwards, or sideways, as they caught the currents of the wind now blowing strongly. It wasn't quite a March gale, but it was clearly just the right strength for kite-flying. I peered up at the kites. They were oblong and colourful; and were covered with designs on the various panels that formed the boxes which gave them their lift. Right on the top of the ridge of the common I could now see their handlers. They seemed to be teenage boys. Benson had reached the oak tree. I resumed my run. When I was about twenty yards from him he called out to me:

"They're the original Lawrence Hargreaves box kite designs, Bridge, which I have flown. When you get nearer you will be able to see the wonderful symbols painted on the panels."

As I reached the oak tree, I found Benson flushed with excitement. He had taken off his pack, and and was standing with his cassock flapping wildly in the wind. He was staring up at the kites as they rose and plunged down in what seemed to be acrobatic stunts. I strained to see the designs but found them rather difficult to decipher because of the speed with which they were moving. At a distance the colours of what was depicted on the sides and bottom of these flying oblongs seemed to be heraldic tinctures, on a white background. Technically argent, in heraldry, I thought.

"Can you make out any of the symbols yet?" asked Benson excitedly.

The kite to the right of the oak tree seemed to be hovering for a moment and I stared hard at it. It looked like a shield on the bottom panel. On this two feet appeared at the top end of the panel and two hands at the bottom, with what looked like a heart in the middle. There was something black in the middle of the heart. The hands and feet and heart were red (perhaps heraldically sanguine, but outlined in black—sable?).

The kite made a sudden dive catching a down draft and I could see that the design was repeated on the sides as well. I glanced over at the other kites. Their designs were different from the one on the right, and distinct too from each other. They looked more complicated. On the bottom of one there seemed to be a ladder with what seemed to be a long lance lying at an angle over it making a sort of saltire cross. On the other was what looked like a circlet or crown surrounding what seemed to be three large nails.

Benson shouted to me: "Do you recognise what is depicted on the kites? We will see everything better when the boys bring them down. You know we are in Lent," he called out, as if to give me a hint.

But my attention had now turned to the handlers who had moved down from the furthest point of the Common towards us. Yes, I was now almost certain. They were the three boys who had been serving at Benediction at Ightham Mote. My eyes moved down to the ground on the other side of the oak tree. There on the grass lay three bicycles and three capacious ruck sacks.

"Come on, Bridge, I've given you a good clue," Benson called into the wind.

I looked again at the kite held by the dark-haired boy on my right. I was sure he was the thurifer. He was holding the kite steady. Inspiration struck.

"The one on the right has the badge of the five wounds," I shouted.

"B…brilliant!" Benson stammered as he shouted triuphantly. "What about the others?"

I looked left. Yes, on one was the was the crown of thorns and on the other was the ladder and the lance used at the Crucifixion of our Lord.

"I can't see what is on the sides very well, but I think from what I can see that the other two must have some of the Symbols of the Passion."

"Grace upon grace," shouted Benson. You are right. You will see the boys' wonderful handiwork when they bring them down."

Benson and I had been moving around to follow the paths of the kites in the sky. We now moved back to the oak tree. There we sat down with our backs against it and watched the display. I had not even taken off my pack.

The boys were amazingly skilled. At times one seemed to direct his kite towards that of another so that I feared that they would become entangled. But then he seemed to pull hard and catch an upward draft which took his kite soaring away from the other again. Every now and then I managed to decipher one of the panels on the sides of the kites on the left of the oak tree. There was certainly the cock, which crowed for St Peter, the Veil of Veronica, the Holy Sponge on its Long Reed, with which our Lord was given vinegar on the Crosss. I could also make out the Hammer, the Nails and the Pincers. I even thought I saw what was a pot for the spices at our Lord's embalming.

Benson turned to me. "I will want to say something about the Atonement later. But it seemed to me in Lent, after being consoled by our Lord's presence at Benediction, we needed reminding in detail of His sacrifice for us and how terrible it really was. The symbols of the Passion and Five Wounds are the traditional ways of bringing it home to us, and the boys have done this perfectly."

I noticed that the kites seemed to be gradually being lowered. The display was about to end. The boys were now about twenty five yards from us winding their reels and bringing the kites in. Despite the strength of the wind they seemed to be able to avoid any sudden down draft that would crash land them on the ground.

They came across to us hugging the great box kites to their chests triumphantly. Their hair was tousled by the wind and their faces flushed and ruddy. They placed the kites carefully on the ground about two yards from us, but were careful to tether them to iron spikes which they took from their packs and pushed firmly into the grass sward. Benson and I stood up and went over to greet the boys and study the kites. In the distance the clock of St Giles' Church struck one o'clock.

"I would like to present all three of you formally to my friend, Mr Bridge. He was with us at Benediction, as you know. This is Gregory, who was the thurifer. And this is Ambrose who carried one of the lights, and Jerome who carried the other."

"I was quite amazed by the display," I said. "Your skill is fantastic. I will want to have a closer look at the kites in a moment, and ask you about yourselves. But first I want to say how extraordinary it is that you got here on your bicycles from Ightham Mote and had time to get ready this show for us."

Gregory brushed his dark hair away from his face then grinned and said.

"Oh we do this quite often in Lent. And we go almost everywhere on our bikes. But we have different kites for Epiphany. Jerome's kite has the box of gold as its symbol—he represents Melchior—. Ambrose has an elaborate bowl for the myrrh as Balthasar. As Caspar I have a sort of censer for the frankincense. The symbols are repeated on all sides of the kite. Their design is a similar arrangement to that of the five wounds that you have seen. You can see that the design for this is repeated on all my panels. But each of the panels on Ambrose's and Jerome's kites for Lent have different symbols of the Passion. For the Epiphany display last January, which we did in the early evening, we even had someone to accompany our display with fireworks."

While Gregory was explaining this to me I noticed something unusual. While all the three boys were wearing jeans and trainers like most boys of their age, on their dark green rugby shirts a badge had been sewn on to the pocket. Again it was a shield with the symbol of the five wounds: our Lord's two hands were at the top of the badge, His two feet at the bottom—each had a single wound—; and there was a red heart in the centre with the three nails and the wound of the spear also shown. I must have been staring at their shirts rather obtrusively for Gregory said:

"The Five Wounds is the badge of our Club. We're the Knights of the Kite."

Ambrose who had fair hair and dark-blue eyes chipped in:

"We do displays like this in the winter and early spring. Then we take part in competitions and stunt flying with a few other kite clubs in the summer. Of course we use different kinds of kites for the contests."

Jerome, who had short cropped hair, and a slightly intimidating set to his jaw and eyes, added:

"We also do some kite fighting in the summer with a couple of select rival clubs, such as the Hildenborough Heavenlies, so it's not all display. But we don't put knives on the tails of our fighting kites as some of the Japanese do. For if you do that, and successfully cut another kite's cord, the owner will probably lose it forever in the stratosphere if it's a windy day!"

He grinned at the thought of this, but then lowered his gaze to the box kites behind him on the ground. "Would you like us to show you them in more detail?"

Benson and I moved over to the kites and stood over them. The boys formed a semi-circle on the other side. The kites were wonderfully crafted when seen close up.

"As we have become more experienced we have found it best to make them of cambric," said Ambrose. "They are hand sewn on to the thin bamboo struts, which hold it in shape. They are light and rigid, yet not so inflexible that they might snap when there is a strong wind. My sister tried to help with the sewing but could not seem to stretch the fabric tight enough, whether from lack of strength or skill I don't know. We do all the heraldic painting of the symbols ourselves. Each of us specialises in certain heraldic tinctures. We have some books to help us with designs, but have committee meetings to reach final decisions. We don't follow what we see in books slavishly. These kites here are the second versions of the Symbols of the Passion and Five Wounds."

Close up the painting on the cloth was meticulous, with the symbols in their gorgeous colours beautifully positioned on each panel. I remember thinking that much of this was often missed when the kites were flying high.

As if in answer to my thought Jerome said: "It's a bit like some of the stone or wooden carving high up in medieval cathedrals. They were often never seen except by the original craftsmen. There were no binoculars then. Until we bring the kites down a lot of people can't really see what we're getting at. But God of course can see them!"

I turned to look at Benson. He was smiling benevolently on us all. But it was only for a moment, then his expression changed and the mischievous look came into his eyes.

"I wonder if one of you boys would let me have the use of a bicycle for a few minutes."

Gregory got up immediately. "Of course, Father. Where do you want to go?"

"O just round and about—over and around the Common."

Benson and Gregory moved over to the bicycles and Gregory lifted up his for inspection. Benson eyed it eagerly, and pulled his cassock up higher above his calves. He overlapped the surplus material over his belt, and got on. To my surprise and relief then Benson rode off cautiously over the grass with Gregory running along beside him. They reached the road which crosses the Common and went off down towards St Giles' Church. Gregory seemed to have decided it would be wise to go with him to monitor what happened.

The three of us left sat down by the oak tree. I had finally taken off my pack and sat with my back against the tree. Jerome lay prone on the grass supporting himself on his elbows. Ambrose knelt and rested his behind on his haunches with his legs splayed out to either side behind him. I remember sitting like this playing cards for hours when I was Ambrose's age. Jerome had picked up a piece of twig and was chewing it.

"What I would really like to know," I began, "is how you are here now and earlier were over at Ightham Mote this morning instead of being at school on a Wednesday."

"Well," said Ambrose, "you perhaps need to know a little more about us. We are at an Anglican public school in Tonbridge. We all do Latin together, although Jerome and I, unlike Gregory, are really specially interested in the sciences. Our Latin master, Mr Easton, is a Catholic like us, and we see him almost every Sunday at Holy Mass. All three of us serve at our local church, and he knows that we are sometimes in demand for other services as well, and that these are occasionally outside the parish.

"We are, I suppose, favourites of his because we are reasonably hard-working. In class Mr Easton is broadening our study of Latin wih some work on medieval poets as well as the usual Classical texts. We' re working at present on a collection of medieval poems and prose in an edition by Helen Waddell. If we make a case to Mr Easton he will let us go off occasionally to do a service, provided that there is a good deal of Latin. We get away with it with the other boys because all three of us are quite useful in the rugby team. On our return from these occasions Mr Easton makes us bring the Latin texts of the prayers, psalms and antiphons and translate them for him. Even worse, sometimes, if some of the texts are in English, he requires us to put them into Latin. Today we were allowed out after roll call this morning but we need to be back at achool at 2.30 this afternoon."

"He seems a fairly decent sort of bloke," I said. "But tell me more about the Knights of the Kite."

Jerome spat out his stick and looked up at me. He now looked rather older than fifteen which was my earlier guess. The musculature on the arms on which he was resting was well-developed. His serious expression revealed his level of commitment.

"We are all about the same age, although Gregory is almost two months older. All three of us will be sixteen in the summer term. We formed the Club when we all three of us were nearly thirteen. We got on well together, and liked the idea of doing something unusual which got us out of doors. As I said we all play rugby, but we wanted a joint hobby we could organise ourselves. We had quite a romantic idea of chivalry and all that then, so it was understandable that at the age of thirteen we would want to call ourselves knights. At first we thought we would bring some boys from other schools into the Club. The three of us are all serious Catholics like the others in our families. But we found that the boys of our age at the state-funded Catholic schools tended to have stopped going regularly to Holy Mass as they got to our age. We could see the potential for conflict with our objectives. We wanted to do something which would express our faith visually, but also gives us a chance to exercise our skill and compete with others. We found there were one or two other boys' kite clubs in the area— this Common is a popular venue for kiting. Since we have taken up kites it has become more popular and there are now quite a few clubs. But we are the only ones that do these symbolic displays, as well as the stunt work, and the occasional competitive fight. We have refined our rules over the last three years. And we have managed to survive as a small group of three without falling out too much and beating each other over the head." He grinned.

Ambrose, who was of a more slender build, pushed back his blonde hair from his eyes, and chipped in: "Last year we did have one difficult patch of about three weeks."

Jerome responded quickly: "Ambrose is referring to something I really regret. The Club had a commitment to do a display for a parish event. It was on a Saturday. My parents had invited some friends of theirs over on that day. They have a very pretty daughter that I knew slightly and I wanted to get to know better. I knew she was coming too. They were staying to supper and of course I would see her then. But I decided that this was not enough— I wanted to spend the whole day with her—so I rang Gregory to say that I couldn't make the Club display. I was quite abrupt and didn't explain why. Gregory was polite but I could tell that he felt badly let down, as was understandable. It was the first time that any of us in the Club had pulled out of anything. At home on the day when the family friends and their daughter came I was moody— real adolescent stuff— and the girl was not impressed. I got more and more miserable as the day progressed. I was really quite glad when they had all gone home.

"Neither Gregory nor Ambrose made any attempt to contact me for some days. I started to worry that they might try to find someone else for the Club. But I was too proud to get in touch myself. In the end it was Gregory who rang *me* to see how I was. I told him everything, and said how sorry I was to have let the Club down. I said I would never do it again. He was absolutely great and said we could all go on as before. He probably wont tell you but Gregory is seriously wondering whether he might have a vocation for the priesthood. We are all of us interested in higher things!"

He laughed as he said this, and his eyes sparkled as he continued. "But I, being, shall I say, rather more physical and earthy, am hoping to go into the airforce. That is if I can get the right grades in the sciences. I am already in the air cadets. Ambrose wants to go one better and be an astronomer. I have told him that if I can eventually get selected from the air force to be an astronaut, he can watch me in space through the telescope that he already has in his garden!"

Both boys laughed this time. As he was completing his story, Gregory returned without Benson. He did not say anything. Perhaps he saw that we were in a serious conversation and did not want to butt in. He just went over to his rucksack, pulled out what looked like some photocopies and sat down on the grass to look through them. I glanced over at him enquiringly, seeing him perhaps in a new light, but said nothing. But Gregory seemed to sense my glance and called across:

"It's just some Latin poems for this afternoon's lesson. Mostly Alcuin. I am sorry not to be sociable. I'm really rather behind."

The other two, perhaps now more conscious of the approaching return to school, leapt up from the ground athletically and went over to the kites. They began to take off some of the struts which held the sides apart so that each kite became almost two dimensional. Then with great care Ambrose and Jerome slid the kites into oblong plastic bags and inserted the resulting large parcels into their packs. Because of their length, the wrapped kites still protruded about a foot above the top of their packs. I noticed that Jerome had also dismantled and packed up Gregory's Five Wounds' kite as well as his own.

While I was watching Benson reappeared riding the bicycle across the Common, rather expertly I thought this time. He looked pleased and flushed when he parked it against the oak tree.

"I was beginning to be concerned that we might not have quite enough time to walk to Tonbridge and be there for the train which departs at 3.15. So I thought I would see whether there was an alternative, and have a jolly little spin on the bicycle at the same time. Our Lord clearly wants us to be flexible in our pilgrimage arrangements for I find there is a bus to Tonbridge that leaves from over there at that bus shelter at 14.29. The timetable says it arrives at the Railway Station at 14.45. This should give us plenty of time since I already have our train tickets. The boys will have to leave before then so as to get back to school. It will be a chance for us to get back into the swing of our Rule in that fine wooden bus shelter. Can you see it on the side of the road which crosses the Common? Once Gregory has finished his Latin I believe that the boys will be off."

Gregory evidently heard this and got up. Moving over to Benson he said:

"It was a privilege for all three of us to have served for you at Benediction, Father, Do remember us Kites during your pilgrimage to the Eternal City. I hope to get there myself one day."

"May the Lord reward you for all that you do for Him and His Church, said Benson rather formally. "Mr Bridge and I will certainly keep you all in our prayers on our way."

He went over briskly to each boy in turn. I heard him say quietly "Keep the Faith" as he gripped their hands. To each one he added his name: Gregory, Ambrose and Jerome.

I followed Benson's lead. As I shook their hand I simply said: "Many thanks for everything, and best wishes for your future." I also made this personal by giving each boy his Christian name. I seemed to have a lump in my throat. I suppose because I now knew a little of their history, faith and ambitions. But perhaps also because I was just a middle-aged man who had been privileged to glimpse the fervour and energy of youth, and had been made to confront his own past lost opportunities.

By the time I had completed my farewells Benson had already shouldered his pack and was striding out energetically across the Common towards the bus shelter. I gathered up my pack, waved a final farewell to the boys and set off after him.

By the time I arrived at the bus shelter Benson had already set his mark on this quite capacious public wooden structure. He was sitting on the wooden seat. His pack was carefully stowed in one corner. Beside him on the seat he had carefully laid out some maps and what seemed like various guide books and pamphlets. There was just enough space for me to sit down on the seat, but not for anyone else who might come.

"Welcome to the Map Room," he said smiling.

Just then we heard the two o'clock chime from St Giles.

"We are now right on schedule for the map work.There is a little under half an hour before our bus arrives if the driver keeps to the timetable. I thought we might think about our stay in Paris tonight and tomorrow. We shall arrive in Paris rather late on the train from Calais. It gets into the Gare du Nord." He pointed to this on the map. "I considered whether we might walk from the station to your hotel on the left bank and my lodgings. But it would inconvenience your hotelier and my religious community if someone had to wait up for us. As you can see from this map that there is a direct Metro from the Gare du Nord to Saint Germain-des-Prés. This would be convenient for us both. But as we are on pilgrimage you may prefer to hump your pack across Paris. I will leave it for you to decide."

I could see that it would be better to go along with the Benson plan and said so. He looked pleased and a little relieved. Then he turned his attention to the brochures and pamphlets beside us on the seat.

"Of course the obvious thing would be for us to go tomorrow to Notre Dame and hear Holy Mass there. But I am not sure if Holy Mass is quite right for you at this point. It might be better to have as our main task, during the short time we have in Paris, to make progress with some saints. There are two churches not far from where we will be staying that might be useful for this. Perhaps there may be some awkwardness for you. I just don't know. In the back of the Church of England Book of Common Prayer you will be familiar with the Thirty-Nine Articles of Religion. I am sure you know Article XXII."

Here he pulled out of his cassock pocket a tiny book, quite the smallest that I had ever seen being actually used. He opened it up and read from what looked like one of the last few pages:

> 'The Romish Doctrine concerning Purgatory, Pardons, Worshipping and Adoration, as well of Images as of reliques, and also invocation of Saints is a fond thing vainly invented, and grounded upon no warrant of Scripture, but rather repugnant to the Word of God.'

I confessed that I was not really familiar with this Article although I may have read it long ago. I didn't think that much of what it contained was now believed or accepted by many modern Anglicans. But I supposed that it must still be the official line of the Church of England on these matters.

Those seeking ordination as Anglican clergy would probably have to subscribe to the Articles of Religion at some point.

"Do you pray to any saints, despite the strictures in the Thirty-Nine Articles?" he asked, scrutinizing me closely? "Who is your patron saint, and are you in regular touch with your guardian angel?"

"I don't do so regularly," I stammered. "As Anglicans we tend to assume a more direct relationship with God and our Lord Jesus Christ, without the need for someone to intervene on our behalf. Very occasionally I have lit a candle before the statue of a saint abroad. I remember doing so before a statue of St Thérèse of Lisieux. I probably said something to her, although I can't really remember. I suppose my patron saint is St Bernard, but I have never tried to be in touch with him. As a Cistercian monk I am not sure how much he would be interested in hearing from someone like me. I don't think I have ever said anything to a guardian angel."

"Well, our tradition is that those in heaven, while contemplating God and praising him, also continue to show care for those still on earth, and are likely to understand our needs, even if their life on earth was very different from ours. Since they are in His presence they can help us reach out to God, and are in a position to intercede for us. Of course we can be in direct touch with our Lord but there are times when it may seem to us more appropriate—perhaps more humble on our part—to approach God through the intercession of one of His close friends who are with Him in heaven. Remember too that Holy Scripture makes clear that everyone has a guardian angel. This heavenly spirit has the specific task of helping us along the way while on earth. It is well worthwhile getting to know our guardian angel. And when you meet a human being for the first time it is polite to try to remember to greet the guardian angel too. Of course I have already greeted yours!"

I said that I would try to get in touch with some saints and my guardian angel. But I would be shy about doing this since I had neglected them for so many years. Benson reassured me that as saints or angels they would not have worldly sentiments such as resentment at being neglected!

While I was giving this undertaking and receiving this assurance two middle-aged women entered the bus shelter. Benson and I rose from the seat and Benson swept up the maps and pamphlets and went over to the corner of the shed and put them back in his rucksack. Then, turning back to the ladies, he made a small bow and motioned to them to sit on the seat. They thanked him profusely and sat down spreading themselves over the entire seat.

Benson then left the bus shelter. I watched him through the dooway as he went out on to the Common and lit a cigarette. Standing by the door I put a question to the ladies:

"Did you see the kite display just now?" I suppose I was still seeking confirmation that others could see what I had witnessed.

"We have just come from the other side of the village. I didn't see anything. Did you, Madge?"

"Not today, I didn't. But they fly them kites here a lot, especially at the weekend. It's quite popular here at Shipbourne. There's a shop where you can buy kites in Tonbridge. Are you and your vicar friend going shopping?"

"No," I replied, "we're going on a pilgrimage to Rome. We'll be catching a train from Tonbridge."

"Beryl's been to Rome," said Madge, "haven't you dear?"

"As you've already been," I said, "may I ask how you liked it?"

"Well, I'm not really religious," said Beryl, "but I loved Rome, although I'm not too keen on all them ruins. We went to St Peter's of course and I loved that—so grand. What a lovely view there is from that terrace. I was so pleased to find a toilet right up there on the roof too—there aren't many public ones in Rome. We went into the Sixteen Chapel, of course, and we even saw the Pope in the square in front of St Peter's. He was a long way off on a dais, but he has a clear voice. Of course he 'as to use a microphone, I know that. There was a huge crowd of people from all over the world in the square. The Pope even said some words to us in English. He seems to know a lot of languages. I got talking to some Australians from Sydney who seemed very nice. They were Roman Catholics so they knew what to do. At one point they held up some rosaries for the Pope to bless which he did. In fact he blessed a whole lot when thousands in the crowd all held them up at once. I would have quite liked to have had one and have got it blessed. The ones them Australians had were real nice. I don't suppose it would matter my not being a Catholic and not religious. But I didn't have one, so that was that.

"I was *very* impressed by the ceiling of the Sixteen Chapel. Fancy the chap who painted it having to lie on 'is back for all them years to do it. I couldn't lie like that for five minutes with my lumbago, even with a cushion. But I did think that the ceiling looked rather dark and needed a good clean. I suppose it had got dirty with all them candles burning there for years."

Beryl had just completed giving us her Roman impressions when Benson returned. He gathered up his pack immediately and put it on his back. Once it was adjusted he said:

"If the bus is on time it should be here very soon. I am going to stand outside so that the driver doesn't go past thinking that there's no one waiting."

The two ladies and I decided to follow. No sooner had we all mustered outside than the bus appeared.

"I was hoping that it might be a double-decker so that we could sit at the front on top. But that was not to be," said Benson, as an ordinary bus pulled up. Madge and Beryl got in and sat towards the back of the bus.

"Two singles to Tonbridge," said Benson, pulling a wallet out of his cassock.

CHAPTER EIGHT

NEEDLE-WORK AND WEIGHT-TRAINING

WE sat together in the third seat from the front. I had the window seat. We left our packs in a small luggage corall near the entrance. I tried to pay Benson for my bus ticket, but he said that he had undertaken to cover the fares to Rome, and this extra bus trip was his idea.

Soon after the bus set off he got up again and went to his pack. He returned with something in a small bag of white sheeting. He rested the bag on his knee and then pulled out a piece of material. It was an oblong of coarse cloth—canvas or hessian, I thought,—on which several figures in coloured material had been pinned.

"I am extending a Dance of Death frieze," he said. "Did you bring any socks to mend or other repairs?"

"I have something at the bottom of my pack," I replied. "But I wonder if I might just watch you as we wont be long on the bus. I will keep my mending for the train."

"I shouldn't encourage you to be slack, but if I can interest you in this appliqué work you might find it entertaining, and it may turn out for the best. I am sewing these two figures on to this panel. If we have time on the rest of our journey I have some material for others. What do you think this one represents?"

I looked at the piece of cloth which Benson had laid out across his knee for me to scrutinise. There were two figures which were of different fabrics and they were both pinned to the canvas. It was a sort of appliqué work. One of the figures was a man in a dark suit wearing a black bowler hat. He had a vivid white wing colour and dark blue tie. He was carrying what seemed to be a large briefcase. This was a brilliant brick red. He had a rolled black umbrella on his arm. Walking behind him was another figure that seemed to be a skeleton wearing a long white robe. This figure carried a sword which he had above his head as if he was about to strike the figure in the bowler hat. The bowler-hatted man seemed unaware of what was about to happen to him.

While I was studying this Benson had threaded a needle and was beginning to sew the bowler hat on to the canvas. As he sewed with very fine stitches he took the pins out as they became no longer needed and put them on to a small pincushion. Before I could respond to Benson's invitation to interpret what it was all about I heard Madge and Beryl talking behind us.

"Can you see what that vicar is doing?" said Madge.

"I would say that he's sewing something," said Beryl.

"I think you're right. I wonder what it is."

They were making some effort to keep their voices down so as not to seem rude, but they both had penetrating voices so what they said cut through the noise of the bus' engine. I wondered if Benson, who seemed preoccupied with the meticulous work that he was doing, had heard them. A few moments later he stabbed his needle into the canvas, got to his feet and went towards the back of the bus where they were sitting. I heard him say:

"You seem interested in what I am doing. Do either of you sew, embroider or do tapestry? I am working on a long frieze in appliqué. It is an extension of a work called the Dance of Death."

"That sounds a bit depressing to me," said Madge.

"Well, in a way it is," said Benson "The whole frieze shows lots of important people in a long procession looking rather pleased with themselves. I am just working on a small piece of it now. You can come here and see what I am doing if you like. What you won't see is another bit of the frieze which shows the funeral of Death himself. I hope someone has taught you about eternal life—our life after death."

"You went to Sunday Sxhool, didn't you Beryl, like me? But I don't think that we heard much about eternal life.

They probably thought the death angle wasn't a suitable thing to talk to children about. They mostly told us about Jesus loving us, if I remember right. What I couldn't understand then was why, if He loves us, He lets us all die and be in pain. Once I got to secondary school of course we never went to church so I suppose I never got to know whether that got explained later, like in one of them TV sequels."

"I know that Jesus died on Good Friday," I heard Beryl say, rather sententiously. "And they say He came back to life, and then went up to heaven. I hope you don't mind me saying this, Vicar, but I've always found that story a bit far-fetched."

"Most people thought like you all those years ago too, Beryl," said Benson, "except those who were Jesus' friends. But they were absolutely certain that this had happened. His close friends were convinced that they had seen him, and several of them even touched him after He had risen from His grave. Many important people told Jesus' friends to stop repeating this story. But his friends knew it was true that he had come back to life after He had been crucified, and was quite dead in His tomb. So they simply refused to keep silent. Many of Jesus' followers were imprisoned, tortured and killed. But no matter how hard they tried, the authorities could not stop people from believing. There were just too many who really knew what had happened.

"The Church today is made up of people who have accepted this story as it was passed on down the ages. They have heard it from parents and friends whom they can trust. Not long after Jesus went up to heaven the Church, as the followers of Jesus began to call themselves, collected together the best stories about Jesus. These are the Gospels of the Holy Bible. This was useful when those who had actually known Jesus were all dead. But most of the time His early followers were busy telling everyone they met about the things that Jeus had taught, and how they might all go to heaven and live with Him there if they believed in Him, and did what He had told them. That means you

Beryl and Madge." Benson dropped his voice then said:

"But I rather think that you didn't want me to explain all this now. What you were really interested in was the tapestry that I am doing. It will be easier I think if I bring it here to you so that you can see what I'm doing. Then you can advise me."

Benson returned to his seat, apologised for deserting me to talk to the two ladies, then went straight back to their seat carrying his piece of work. I moved over into the aisle seat, in the hope of hearing their conversation better.

I heard Madge say: "Your sewing is very neat—such tiny stiches. I can hardly see where you join the pieces that make the figures on to the background."

"I am so gratified by your compliment," said Benson rather formally. "As you can see it's really appliqué work. I cannot do real tapestry. The pieces for the figures and their clothing are cut out and then backed with tissue paper—I use a wheat starch paste to attach the paper. It is most useful that I can take the panels for the figures around with me and then sew them on to the background when I have a little time. I will sew this whole piece, when I have completed it, on to the rest of the frieze. You notice that I don't put fine cord around the edge of each piece after I have attached it to the background. Real professionals do that in appliqué work. I think it would make the figures less striking here. What do you think of the two figures that I am working on at present? I hope you will be completely honest."

"The man in the bowler hat seems to me to be rather pleased with himself," said Madge. "I am not sure if he is meant to be a City-type like a banker or an old-fashioned politician."

"I cannot make up my mind either,"said Benson. "But I am glad that you think that he looks pleased with himself. That's what I wanted to suggest. Most of the other figures in the frieze are like that. That is why they are unprepared for death. The figure behind the one in the bowler hat is a kind of skeleton with a tailcoat. In the rest of the frieze—I haven't that with me now—behind each important person, such as a king, a soldier, a pope and a cardinal, among the others, there is a skeleton dressed in robes. The idea is to remind everyone, no matter how important, that you never know when your time may come so you need to be prepared for death. Rich and important people are more likely to think that they will live forever, and that death only applies to the ordinary people of this world, and not to them. I hope that you can recognise what the skeleton behind the banker or politician is carrying."

"It looks to me like a pair of old-fashioned weighing scales," said Beryl.

"You are quite right." Benson sounded triumphant. "The skelton has the scales because bankers in the City and poli-icians weigh up in their minds the money they have made, or the taxes that they have raised from the people. Well, that's where I've got to so far. I must let you get on with your conversation with each other and return to my friend."

He must have left them abruptly because I did not hear any further response from them. While Benson was away I had got out the file for my meeting in Rome, rather than my mending. But I had been too caught up in Benson's conversation with his new friends to make much headway with the office brief. Benson got past me and sat down down by the window without a word. He resumed his fine sewing around the bowler hat. Through the bus window I noticed that we were already near the outskirts of Tonbridge.

Benson was using a tiny steel thimble for his work. His concentration seemed total. I remember thinking of a remark attributed to Napoleon: 'When I am brushing my hair I think of nothing other than brushing my hair.' Of course, I thought, Napoleon would not have needed to spend much time brushing his hair. As can be seen from his portraits he had so little.

Madge and Beryl were talking, but they had now lowered their voices so that I could not quite catch what they were saying over the noise of the engine. The bus now had to stop and start quite often as there was more traffic and the occasional pedestrian crossing. A few minutes more and Benson consulted his pocket watch.

"I shall put this away now," he said folding up his piece of work in its white bag and gathering together his sewing kit in a small leather case. He left the two items on his lap and looked out of the window. I got up to take my file back to my rucksack. Since Benson was in the inside seat I wondered if I might offer to take his two items and put them into his rucksack. But I felt inhibited from making the offer: Perhaps he would not wish me to look inside his pack to put the items away. When I came back to my seat Benson was already standing. He went past me to put his stuff way. When he was back in his seat he turned to me and said:

"Shall we postpone our discussion of the Atonement?"

I said that this was all right by me. He smiled at me for the first time since we had been on the bus.

"I am not sure how eager you are for this!"

"Sometimes I seem to understand more when I see something, or hear others talking, than when I have something explained to me directly."

"I had noticed that," said Benson. "But I still think it is important that you are given some clear points, and have a chance to ask questions. Oh, we seem to be almost there so there is no time anyway."

The two ladies had got up. So did Benson. I stood up and moved into the aisle. Benson swept passed me in his cassock, thanked the driver, and got off the bus first. Apart from the two ladies there were only a few other passengers most of whom who had got on after us. When I alighted Benson was standing outside the bus at the door. When the two ladies appeared he helped each of them off in turn. They looked surprised but delighted. I could see him fumbling for something in his cassock.

"I would like both of you to take one of these as a little gift," he said. He put something into their hands, but I could not see what it was.

"That's most kind of you," said Beryl, "but what is it?'

She and Madge then opened their hands and looked at what seemed to be a round ring about the size of a large English coin. On the edge of it were a number of quite small globular knobs. There also seemed to be a sort of cross on the top."

"It's a rosary ring," said Benson.

"It's beautifully made, like your sewing. There is even a little figure on the cross," said Madge. "Did you make it?"

"I am afraid not. But I have blessed it. Of course unfortunately it hasn't been blessed by the Pope." He grinned. "If one of us was to see you on our return you might receive one which His Holiness had blessed. But I thought it better to give you one now in case I don't see you again. You might like it just to keep with you in your purse. It is less bulky that a full rosary, and there are no beads to fall off if they get caught in something. If you are curious about what we Catholics do with it you might call in some day at our Church in Tonbridge."

I could see that he had focussed his gaze on Beryl as he added: "They might be able to tell you about Jesus' resurrection and eternal life, and the rest of the story, if ever you wanted to know more."

Without saying goodbye, he bent down, seized his pack, threaded one arm through the strap and swung it forcefully on to his back. Then, motioning to me to follow him, he got ready to cross the road to the Railway Station. On the other side he turned back for an instant to where the two ladies were still standing looking over at us. He waved very briefly and shyly. They both waived back energetically.

We were in good time for the train. Benson checked the tickets at the booking office and we went through the barrier on to the platform. There were about a dozen or so people waiting for the train by then. Most of them were sitting down on seats. A young couple with their suitcases at their feet were standing talking outside the Waiting Room.

A little beyond them was a tall young man on his own. He must have been about twenty-five, a lot over six feet in height, perhaps six foot three, I thought. He had dark curly hair cut very short, and a tanned face which suggested that he worked out of doors or was recently back from a holiday in the sun. He was very well built without any hint of the slight corpulence which young men of his age often have through spending their leisure in the pub. He had on a pair of khaki trousers—it looked like they were made of canvas—, and a short leather jacket over a black tee shirt. There was a little designer stubble on his chin, and he had a single small gold ear-ring in the lobe of his left ear.

His face was sufficiently striking-looking, I thought, for him to find work as a model for a men's clothing catalogue. But his expression as he studied what seemed to be the sports page of a national tabloid suggested that this would not be something that he would ever contemplate doing.

I concluded that he had not been abroad to ski or to catch the sun in the West Indies or South Africa, but that he probably worked in the building trade. There was intelligence in his expression which gave me the idea that he probably had a trade qualification. The dark curly hair suggested he might have some Mediterranean blood in him, or that some of the his family came from Eastern Europe.

While I was looking over those on the platform, and was making a study of this young man in particular, Benson had taken up a booklet from his pack. It was the guide book to St Germain-des-Prés in Paris. He was evidently doing some preparatory work for tomorrow. As if sensing my glance Benson said:

"This Church is in the student quarter of Paris. It will be a good place for us to see some young people and acquire an idea of where France is likely to be heading in the next decade or so. It will be interesting to see what they have been doing there in Lent, and what are their preparations for Easter."

"Do you expect any surprises?" As I said this, I noticed

that my intonation might suggest that I was probing whether Benson's ability to organise events extended across the Channel.

"I always welcome surprises," he replied, "but only sometimes expect them. If I expect them they are not really surprises, although they often turn out in a way that I had not expected. And that is usually stimulating. Other people's reaction are often the main surprise!"

I was about to ask him about what he thought of my reactions this morning, but the train pulled into the station. One of the carriage doors was right in front of us. Benson opened the door but then stood aside and motioned to the young couple with their luggage to get in before us. The train had a corridor along one side of each carriage. Each compartment had six seats.

We were travelling standard class. Benson preceded me into the train. He walked along the corridor passing several compartments which were full, or had only one spare seat. Finally he found one which had only one passenger, a middle-aged man in a dark suit who was studying what looked like an office file. He was sitting facing the engine in the seat next to the door. Benson and I took the two window seats facing each other and managed with some difficulty to stow our packs in the luggage rack above our heads.

The train had just started to move when another passenger opened the door of the compartment and entered. As I looked up I saw that it was the young man that I had observed on the platform. In his left hand he had a medium sized tote bag of the kind which footballers might use to take their kit to an away match, or for a weekend break. In his right hand he had what looked like a heavy duty plastic case with wheels.

Benson rose and offered to help the young man find a space to store his luggage in the rack above. He moved his own pack a few inches along to make a little more room. The young man smiled and swung his tote bag up on to the rack. There was just enough room.

"I reckon this one's too hefty to be stowed," the young man said. "I'll leave it next to me legs. I 'ope it's not in the way. I don't want it to lob on anyone's feet."

He had a pleasant English voice; the accent seemed South London in origin but I guessed that he might have been at school in Kent. He sat in the middle seat on Benson's side, and so I had a good view across at him from my seat. The businessman was on my side with the spare seat between us.

The young man drew the sports pages that he had been reading on the platform from his leather jacket. Yet I noticed he was not really concentrating. He looked out of the window. His face, which when I had first seen it looked so strong and confident, now seemed rather sad. I looked away. I was just about to go to my pack to find something to read when Benson said to the young man:

"We two are going to Paris tonight, and then tomorrow night on to Rome. Where are you going?"

"I'm going to Paris too, to stay with a mate. I 'aven't been there before. Me mate's a painter and decorator and he's been asked to do some work for an English bloke. It seems this bloke prefers to 'ave an English guy working for 'im so 'e can tell 'im what 'e wants. Like so there's no language issue. Me mate says there's enough space where 'e's livin' for me to kip down. What's Paris like, Father?"

It was clear that the young man realized Benson was a Catholic priest.

Benson laughed.

"Paris is full of French people. You wont find many who will want to speak to you in English. And Parisians are known for being rude, not just to foreigners, but to people from other parts of France. And even other Parisians too! But they seem to have respect for those who look like they're sporting. So I suspect you'll be treated decently."

"Me and me mate used to play football together. 'e's about me size. I think 'e knows a bit of French as 'e's got to get the stuff for decorating from the local shops. 'e said 'e'll meet me at the Paris Railway Station so I should be OK."

He suddenly looked rather vulnerable. Benson took his pocket watch out of his cassock and looked at the time. It was the first time that I had a good view of it. It was gold, and had Roman numerals of the traditional kind. I noticed that the young man was looking across at it too. Benson put it away again and said to me with his most engaging grin:

"It's not really yet tea-time according to our timetable but I am sure that we would all like a cup of tea. My dear Bridge, I wonder whether you might be kind enough to get four cups of tea from the buffet car that I noticed further along towards the front of the train?" Without waiting for my reply he drew out his wallet and gave me several notes.

"I rather think that should be enough," he said.

The businessman next to me said it was kind of Benson to offer him a cup of tea too, but he was getting off soon so he needn't be included. On leaving the compartment, as I was closing the glass door, I noticed that Benson had produced a map, and that he and the young man were looking over it together. It's probably a map of Paris, I thought.

It was quite a long train and the buffet car was some way from our compartment. For a few moments I remembered feeling just a trifle annoyed that Benson seemed to have quickly taken this young man up and had sent me off to get the tea. After all Benson had invited me to go on a pilgrimage with him!

But I quickly suppressed this thought. It was really rather ridiculous to feel like that. After all Benson was a priest and his vocation was to have a care for everyone he met along the way. He had already taken a great deal of trouble over me and had introduced me to what was already a most interesting adventure.

He was clearly hoping to make me take religion more seriously. This should mean, I reasoned, my developing a closer relationship with our Lord, his Blessed mother and the saints, rather than remaining dependent on human friendship of the kind that I seemed to be developing with Benson.

There was a long queue in the buffet car so I had plenty of time for further contemplation.

Out of the blue the idea came to me. As I was on a pilgrimage I might say something to our Lord's mother. This was the title I gave her. I had never attempted anything like this before, or even thought of doing so. I wondered how to start. Would it be helpful if I could visualize her? I tried to think of all the medieval or Renaissance paintings that I knew and liked. But when an image came into my mind it didn't seem to help me think what I should say.

In the end I just said under my breath rather quickly: "Hello my Lady, I'm an Englishman, Bernard Bridge, as you know. You will also be aware that I haven't spoken to you so far. I am sorry for that. I hope that you wont mind me starting now. Would you please help me on my pilgrimage—I'm rather confused? Please also intercede for my family at home, and keep them safe. Sorry to be so abrupt. Good bye for now."

That was all I managed. I made a note of this little speech later in the day and have found the text in my notebook. I had used the word 'intercede' but I wasn't quite sure what I intended by this.

I was not expecting any kind of reply. Nor did I believe that I would receive any kind of confirmation that my message had got through.

By now I had got to the head of the queue and managed to get a pot of tea and three plastic cups with the usual cartons of milk and packets of sugar. I bought three scones and butter with my own money. I carried the tray carefully back through the corridor towards our compartment. When I was nearly there a phrase suddenly came to me like a catch in the throat. It was rather as if I had coughed up a tiny piece of phlegm. The phrase was: 'Launch out into the deep.' Just that.

When I opened the glass door of our compartment Benson and the young man were still sitting next to each other as they had been when I left them studying the map.

But the map had gone. I sensed that they had ceased talking some time before I returned. The young man was now staring out of the train window. He looked a little uncomfortable. Benson had a small black book on his lap but he was looking towards the luggage rack above as if he was trying to understand something which puzzled him.

"Sorry I took so long," I said. "There was a long queue. I have brought a scone each to sustain us." I set the tray on what was now a spare seat. The train had stopped at a station while I was queuing and I guessed that the businessman had got off. I poured the tea and handed each of my companions a scone. "There is milk in these cartons and sugar. I suggest that you do your own." Benson had his black without sugar.

The young man took some milk and stirred in two packets of sugar. "Thanks," he said. That was all.

Benson said: "Many thanks for coming to our aid. We needed a cup of tea. The scone is delicious."

Nothing else. There was a long silence. I tried to think of a topic for conversation but nothing seemed quite right. The young man went back to looking out of the window. Benson now took up the book that was in his lap and began to read. After a couple of minutes he got up and said:

"I am trying to concentrate on some psalms in *lectio continua*. I think I might do better if I walked up and down the corridor of the train. I hope you will both excuse me."

He opened the glass door of the compartment and was gone. The young man turned his gaze from the scenery out of the window to the door and watched him go. I turned to him and said:

"My priest friend likes to follow a fairly tight personal routine during most of the day. But of course he is always willing to break out of this if he might be able to help someone."

The young man looked at me. The face which I had first thought strong and conventionally handsome now looked nervous, almost shifty. I noticed that he seemed to be frowning and that his eyebrows almost met over the bridge of his nose.

"Did the map Father showed you help? Was he able to give you any useful advice?"

The young man looked away from me, and I wondered whether he would reply. It occurred to me that their conversation had ended awkwardly. He suddenly said:

"It wasn't just Paris we talked about. It was London too." He paused. Then continued:

"Everything, really. I'm not sure I should 'ave said what I did. I've also been a bloody idiot. I reckon now I don't really want to go to Paris to stay with me mate. I 'aven't even enough cash to pay me way when I get there. And I'm missing me girl friend and kids. But I couldn't stand the way she always wanted to tell me what to do. She always 'ad to know exactly where I was all the time. See that case of mine that's too heavy to put up in the rack. Can yer guess what's in it?"

I said I couldn't.

"It's a travelling weight-training set. It weighs no more than 15 kilo all up. It's not an Olympic set like I use at the gym. Anyway she doesn't like me using it at 'ome. Or going to the gym either! She says she likes me just the way I is, without building meself up more. She thinks I must be doing weight-training to pull other women. There *are* a few that go to the gym, right. But that's not why I do it. Natch, I wanna look good on the beach in the summer, but it's more the discipline. OK? It's to prove to meself that I can do something and stick at it which a lot of other guys can't. She can't see that. I'm real bad at tellin' 'er things. You know what I mean. She has a big mouth and can always find a way of winning if we argue. I get good wages as a qualified plumber, more than many of me mates. But she did better at school and she earns more than me in 'er office job. A few days ago we 'ad a row. The next day me mate called me from Paris. Would I like a few days away? I must say I jumped at it. 'e knows that she aint thrilled about me weight-training so 'e said, 'Why not bring yer weights?' So that's what I done.

"I told some of this to Father, which may 'ave been not on. Being a priest 'e aint much of a clue about living with a girl, like me and you. You're married aint yer? Father asked about me little boy and girl. Damien's five and 'annah's two. Yer know I almost choked up when I told 'im about them. 'e really didn't need 'im to tell me they'd be missing their Dad. I think Fran will be missing me too. She's the jealous sort and she'll be wonderin' what I'm gettin' up to. The trouble is that she doesn't really want me as I is. She wants to change me. Yet deep down I really wanna make things work at 'ome. But I just mess up. That Father's a real good bloke, I can tell. But things just went wrong with 'im too. I can't explain…"

There was a catch in his voice as he concluded lamely. He looked away out of the window again so that I could not see his expression. I said:

"I've left my wife behind, so we are sort of in the same boat."

"But yer didn't have a row and walk out, did yer?"

"No, but I wasn't completely honest about what I was doing or who I was going with. But I've tried to make amends by writing her a letter. Perhaps *you* could write to your girl too."

"I'm no good at writin'. I just 'ate it even when I've got to do an invoice for me work. I reckon I'm an idiot. I know I've got to do it to get me money. Fran sometimes 'elps with invoices but she can be real picky about me grammar and spelling and stuff."

"I could help you with a letter if you would like."

"P'r'aps later," he said. "I'm too mad with meself and with 'er to think about it now."

Without looking at me again he put his hand into the inside pocket of his leather jacket and pulled out the sports pages of his paper again which had been tightly folded. It was clear he did not want to continue the conversation.

I got up and fished out Holland's *Memoir of Kenelm Henry Digby* from my pack. But I couldn't concentrate. My companion didn't seem to be absorbed in his paper either. I had an idea.

"Look," I said, "I just want to help you. I can see that you're not a happy bunny." I regretted this phrase as soon as I said it. "When I went to get the tea I saw that there was an empty compartment in the carriage before the buffet car. I wonder if it might help if you went along there and did some weight-training. It might relieve your feelings. You could pull down the blind on the glass door, and I don't think that you would be disturbed."

He looked up from his paper and across at me. His dark eyes seemed a little moist, but at the same time there was an element of calculation in his glance. He did not reply for a moment. I wondered if he would just ignore me and go back to his paper. But after a long pause he said:

"You might 'ave somethin'. I'll take me stuff and see what's possible. To tell yer the truth I'm nervous about seeing Father when 'e comes back."

He got up quickly, took down and shouldered his tote bag and gripped the case of weights firmly in his right hand. With his left he opened the compartment door. Before closing it he turned and said with a shy faint smile:

"Thanks. Cheers!" .

As he had taken his bag as well as wheeling away his case of weights, it seemed clear that he did not intend to return. I went back to reading about Digby, but could not stop myself speculating on what had happened between him and Benson which had upset him.

I looked at my watch. It was 4.15 pm. We would be in Dover Western Dock quite soon. Benson seemed to be taking a long time over his Psalms. If he was walking up and down the train corridor it was surprising that I had not seen him pass our compartment door. I considered going to look for him but decided that I should not interrupt unless I had a plausible reason.

Several more minutes passed and I was starting to feel a little anxious about getting organised to get off the train when Benson finally arrived. He was still reading his psalter when he came in and did not look at me. I noticed that there were several coloured velvet ribbons hanging down from the book. He closed it up and sat down in his seat. Then he turned to me.

"Would you be kind enough to let me know what time your watch has? Looking out of the window just now I believed that we're almost there. If my guess is right the train is on time."

My watch says that it's 4.28 pm," I said.

"Perfect," said Benson. "Where's Sebastian?"

I was interested that Benson knew his name.

"There was an empty compartment in the carriage before the buffet car. I suggested he might like to use it for his weight-training. I discovered that he had weights in that heavy case of his, and was keen on weight-training. He rather jumped at the idea. He took his bag as well, so I wonder if we'll see him again."

"That is an interesting question. I will pray that we do. It will be a matter of will for Sebastian."

He gave me a mysterious smile, and began to collect up several items which he had left on the seat and get his pack ready to leave the train. I did the same.

A few minutes later we were on the station platform. We were unable to see any sign of Sebastian. We got ourselves over to the Dock where the British Rail ferry was waiting. As we were approaching the ticket office Benson handed me my ferry ticket.

"I suggest that you go through control now and show your passport and complete the formalities. I have one or two things to do before boarding. Shall we meet in the passenger lounge on the ferry?"

Before I could reply he had disappeared into the crowd. Passengers were now assembling with their luggage outside the ticket office.

It was at that moment that a thought struck me? What would Benson's passport be like? Could it really have as his date of birth 18th November 1871 which was when he was born? Would it be an old passport or had he somehow been able to obtain a new one? Was he even now finding some way of avoiding passport control?

The rather informal queue I was in moved rapidly, and I was quickly processed. There was only a short delay before we were allowed to go on board. On the quay I looked carefully around. There was no sign of Benson. The stiff breeze that there had been during the afternoon, which had helped with the kite display, had continued. I smelt the sea air as I walked up the gang-way to go on board. The sky had become darker now. I remembered thinking that it was still only March.

CHAPTER NINE

A SURPRISING CONFESSION

I MADE my way to the passenger lounge. There were only a few people there so far and I managed to find a seat with a good view of the sea. Despite my puzzlement over Benson and his passport, and the strange and inconclusive encounter on the train with the young man Sebastian, I felt excited to be going abroad, and on a pilgrimage.

I thought of Digby's travels to pilgrim sites all over Europe in the years after the end of the Napoleonic Wars. He often used to sleep rough, under hedges or in barns. My own appetite for physical and spiritual adventure was undiminished, but I was not sure how well I would do if I was denied some of the basic comforts.

The tone of the vessel's engine altered so that it seemed as if we were now moving off. The lounge was beginning to fill up. Still no sign of Benson. Could he have missed the boat while doing 'the one or two things' he said he would be doing? Ten minutes passed. At last, to my great relief he appeared. He no longer had his pack.

"Did you notice the name of the vessel as you came aboard," he said as he sat in the seat next to mine. "I had rather hoped that this might be the one."

"I'm sorry, but as you will have already become aware, I am not always very observant."

"It's the MV St Anselm. Some of British Rail's newer vessels have been given saints' names. Isn't it interesting that the company authorities have been so inspired? And it fits in well with our promised discussion of the atonement. I wonder if you know that St Anselm puzzled over the matter in his *Cur Deus Homo*—Why did God become man? Of course to some people, and perhaps they are specially blessed, the fact that our Lord so loved us that He was prepared to die for us is quite enough for them to love Him in return. They do not want to trouble themselves about those matters which they regard as unnecessarily theological.

"But for anyone who has been given by God a spirit of enquiry, or who may be called to proclaim the Christian Faith to others—as the Gospel calls us all to do—, or who finds himself having to defend its coherence to someone enquiring about it, a question might well be: 'why should God have sent his Son into the world to be crucified for us?' What do *you* think it is all about?"

I reflected a moment, then said: "I suppose various passages in the Old Testament suggest that some sacrifice was always necessary to bring the people of Israel back into a right relationship with God. I recall that in the history of Israel the priests offered a bloody sacrifice in the Temple. Evidently original sin, or the predispostion to sin that all men seem to have, needs to be paid for in some way in order that human beings are reconciled with God. The New Testament is full of passages that relate the Sacrifice of our Lord at Calvary to the earlier sacrifices made in the Old Testament."

"Yes, but why couldn't a loving God just forgive us, without needing to send His Son to suffer a cruel death? Is the idea of the Blessed Trinity threatened by the idea of the Loving Father sending His only Son to die on the Cross?"

I reflected a little, then said: "Having given us free will God knew that we might very well follow our own way and neglect God for whose love we were created. If He just forgave us, as He seems sometimes to have done with the people of Israel when they went astray, it might perhaps have suggested that breaking the divine law and hence our relationship with God was not a serious matter with consequences. The dilemma for God must have been either to let us all die without redemption, which would have put an end to the purpose for which the human race was created, or else He would need to find some way of redeeming us, bringing us back to Him. There must be a penalty for sin for *us*, since it clearly had consequences for *God* in that it broke our relationship with him."

"That seems right," said Benson. "But why did God feel He should become a human being and die for us Himself?"

"I suppose because only by becoming a human—and being incarnate as a man as the Son, or Second Person of the Trinity—and experiencing human weaknesses and temptations could He really fittingly pay the price of the sins that separate God from us. This supreme act would be likely to affect the human race profoundly since, by it, Gods' true love for us, his creatures, would be revealed."

Benson added: "You didn't take up the point about the doctrine of the Trinity. But in my view it doesn't threaten this, since God is not imposing a cruel death on another 'god' or divine being, but He is Himself doing this in order to free us from our sins and from death. Moreover those who accept this gift, and live according to His precepts, can hope to live with Him for ever. No other religion gives as beautiful and convincing picture of the Divine Creator of the Universe, a God of Love and Compassion. Of course it also gives us an inkling of how to understand the suffering of the innocent in this life, when we see our Innocent God suffering in human form."

Although we had been talking to each other quite quietly side by side I noticed that several people in chairs near us in the lounge had begun to listen. Benson looked across at them and smiled. He got to his feet and I thought that he was going to go over to them, but instead he said to me:

"I think that we have cleared our minds sufficently on this topic for the moment. Would you mind excusing me for a short while? As we were boarding I managed to catch up with that young man Sebastian whom we met on the train. He asked me if I could see him at 6.15 pm English time. I see that the lounge clock is already on French time and that I must leave now if I am to be sure of not being late. I would hope to be back for the Angelus before we arrive at Calais."

He strode away to the main door of the lounge, looking a most imposing figure with his head held high and his cassock sweeping along in his wake. It reminded me of what a friend from the Foreign Office had once said to me:

'Arab rulers,' he said. 'in their native desert countries always look imposing and dominating in their flowing sheikly robes, even when short in stature. That's why it is so disillusioning to call on one of these Arab aristocrats of the desert in his holiday house in Mayfair, and see him attired in a dark business-suit made-to-measure by his Lebanese tailor in Beirut.' In the same way Benson's clerical cassock suited him perfectly. I noticed that many eyes followed him as he left, and not just those who had been listening in on the latter part of our discussion.

And what about Sebastian? He apparently left our compartment because he felt uncomfortable. It seemed that he had had some sort of disagreement or misunderstanding with Benson. I wondered if he had really done any weight-training in that empty carriage that I had identified for him. Now Benson and he had met again and Sebastian had made an appointment. Clearly this was a private meeting or Benson would have just suggested that he join us both in the lounge. Had Benson gone to look for him when we had arrived at the station?

I caught myself out being slightly envious of Sebastian, and a little troubled by Benson's private meeting with him. After all I had agreed to go on a pilgrimage with Benson. I suppose I had expected that the emphasis would be always on me. But Benson seemed ready to turn his attention to anyone else he met on the way. A few seconds later I again realised how ridiculous and mean-spirited such a thought was. Benson was a priest. He needed to be ready to fulfil his vocation when the need arose. For goodness sake, Bridge, I said to myself, you are going on a pilgrimage with most of your expenses being paid by another, and Benson, whoever he is, has already done a great deal which you have found fascinating and, yes, I had to confess, challenging.

I turned back to the *Memoir of Kenelm Henry Digby*. I read again a passage that had struck me forcefully when I had skimmed the book earlier. Digby's huge number of books in both prose and verse—he even wrote his autobiography in rhyming couplets—were in large part designed to revive the principles of loyalty and generosity which seemed to him lacking in much of British society in the years after the end of the Napoleonic Wars. They seemed to be lacking still!

His *Broadstone of Honour* was his attempt to raise the moral sights of British Society in the grip of Regency frivolity, depravity and decadence. The ideal was that of medieval chivalry. The four volumes had made some impact, and there were fruits in the Young England movement. The young Disraeli had been a member of this. Indeed the book's influence can even be detected in the ideals of the Boy Scout Movement many years later.

But the eight volumes of *Mores Catholici* and the four volumes of *Compitum*, all published privately over many years between 1832 and 1845, were too discursive, too erudite and yes, too Catholic, to have any impact on the prevailing common sense utilitarianism of the time. This spirit of the age was foreign to all that Digby valued and admired. His writings were a heroic attempt to demonstrate that, despite their human failings, medieval men and women still held to the ideals of the Beatitudes as proclaimed by our Lord in the Sermon on the Mount. They often even managed to live by them too. Digby was interested in bringing back this generous spirit, not just in reviving the trappings of medievalism in tournaments and Gothic architecture, as others had done.

With my interest in family history I was particularly struck by Digby's portrait of an old squire of Sawston Hall outside Cambridge. This figure was a contemporary of many of the dead who interested me in Kemsing churchyard. After Digby had become a Catholic, he did historical research for his writings at Cambridge where there was no Catholic Church. He used to keep a horse and ride over on Sunday to hear Mass at a private chapel. Major Huddleston, the squire of this recusant Catholic house with its own chapel, in due course became Digby's friend.

Digby's portrait of Huddleston in verse in *Little Low Bushes*, a volume of Digby's poems, portrays the ideal of the noble Christian that he found so often in the manuscripts of medieval society, but rarely among his contemporaries.

Huddleston was learned, but never pedantic, accustomed to people sniping at his Faith, but never embittered by it. He always assumed that those who vilified his Church were simply unaware of the true facts, rather than malicious or bigoted. Straightforward, sweet and simple in his manner with others—'like lads in the street,' Digby says—Huddleston had no airs and graces. Although firm in his own faith he was always patient and tolerant with those who had a different view. To Digby Huddleston was a kind of scholarly gentleman saint. The ideal appealed strongly to me too, as I reflected how far I was from being like Huddleston. Would this pilgrimage help me do better?

I read on. Bernard Holland had a chapter on Digby's time in Paris which seemed relevant to our visit there tonight and tomorrow. Before he married, Digby spent some time in the St Germain area where we would be staying while he was working on the *Broadstone of Honour*. After he married Jane Dillon in 1833 they had apartments in the 8th arrondissement near the residence of the Archbishops of Paris.

His wife, Jane, was the youngest daughter of a rich Irish family. It was her personal wealth that enabled Digby to write without the need to earn his living by other means. One of her relations, '*le Beau Dillon*', was one of the so-called 'wild geese', young Irish men whose Catholicism prevented them from being officers in the British army. They therefore joined the armies in Catholic countries on the Continent. '*Le Beau Dillon*' had commanded a French company for royalist France, and was put to death at the French Revolution. But his widow, who had once been French ambassadress in Florence, was still alive when the Digbys lived in Paris in the 1830s, and they used to visit her.

Kenelm and Jane—she spoke French to perfection, and was vivacious and charming—entertained often in Paris. They got to know many of the great men of that high point of intellectual, political and artistic society in the years after the restoration of the monarchy that followed Napoleon's final defeat. Chateaubriand, Montelambert, Lacordaire, Ozanam, Lamartine, Sainte-Beauve, Michelet and Madame Swetchine were all part of their circle.

Digby, I read, even used to go on conversational walks in the old forest of St Germain with Monsignor Affrée, later

Archbishop of Paris, who was murdered by the mob in 1848.

I was far away in the world of Digby's early nineteenth century French and English society when I suddenly found that Benson had returned and was sitting next to me. He had a very small leather bag with him that I had not seen before.

"I am glad to see you absorbed in Digby. We will have a chance to think more about him in Paris, but it is most useful to do some homework before we arrive. Please forgive me for deserting you. I was called to perform the first of the seven spiritual works of mercy. I see you have *A Catechism of Christian Doctrine* to hand as well as the book on Digby. You will see this one is the first of Number 322."

I opened up the little booklet which I had put beside me but had failed even to open. I looked up the reference: The first of the seven spiritual works of mercy is: 'to convert the sinner.'

Benson looked at me with a smile and said:

"Of course I am not able to say what Sebastian told me at his confession. As you know what is said in confession cannot be revealed in any circumstances to another. It was fortunate that we were able to find somewhere where we would not be disturbed. There is a relatively isolated spot near the lifeboats, which seemed acceptable to us both. Incidentally I hope we won't need the lifeboats on this voyage as they look as though they need a good clean. Let us hope this lack of care would not be reflected in their seaworthiness.

"My little bag here contains my stole and all that I need to hear confessions. Incidentally I will not need to trouble you for the time again since my pocket watch has now been restored to me.

"Sebastian told me that you had offered to help him write to the mother of his children. I believe he may wish to avail himself of this opportunity when we catch the train to Paris. I have suggested that we share a compartment. He told me he would now like some reconciliation with Frances and that he had it in mind to suggest that they marry. But no doubt you will learn all about that. Now I think we should say the Angelus so that we are ready when we dock at Calais."

Of course I wanted to ask Benson some detailed questions about this revelation about Sebastian. Had he really stolen Benson's pocket watch and then returned it? I remembered thinking it a little odd that Benson had asked me for the time after Sebastian had left our compartment. What had made the young man change his mind and seek out Benson for confession?

But I had no time for speculation for Benson was now handing me a small sheet of card with some text and what looked like an etching of our Lady and the Angel Gabriel.

"This is the Latin text of the Angelus with an English translation opposite. This may help you with the sense, although you may well be able to follow the Latin without difficulty. Your part is to respond with the Latin words where they are preceded by a capital R in red.

"As you will see the Angelus recalls to us the marvel of the Incarnation of our Lord. It is easy to forget this unique feature of our Faith during the trials and excitements of life. It serves to remind us that the God who created the Universe and all that is, became a man out of love for us human creatures. Later we ask Him for grace and plead his Passion to God so that we may also be resurrected to life eternal like Him. The Angelus is also a devotion in which we ask for eternal rest for the faithful departed. This helps us remember regularly our family and friends who have passed from this life.

"It is considered good practice to say the Angelus at 6 am, noon and 6 pm. But while on pilgrimage I suggest that we should try and say it together sometime during the middle of the day and in the evening. If you are awake at 6 am you might like to say it also before or on rising."

I looked about the lounge which was now quite crowded. Some passengers were already gathering together their belongings. Benson spoke quite quietly but firmly in a clear voice. He pronounced the Latin with the usual Italian softening of the consonant 'c' before 'i' and 'e', and with the Italian long vowels. I was familiar with this from recordings of medieval and renaissance religous music.

'*Angelus Domini nuntiavit Mariae.*'

'*Et concepit de Spirito Santo.*' I was pleased that I had remembered to soften the 'c' in '*concepit*'.

'*Ave Maria, gratia plena, Dominus tecum; benedicta tu in mulieribus, et benedictus fructus ventris tui Jesus. Sancta Maria, mater Dei, ora pro nobis peccatoribus, nunc et in hora mortis nostrae.*'

Benson paused and reflected. I looked at the last words in English on the sheet. 'Holy Mary, mother of God, pray for us sinners now and at the hour of our death.'

If our Lord was really God when incarnate as a man then Mary was indeed the Mother of God. It was easy to see then why Catholics felt such devotion to one chosen for such a role by God. And what about the hour of our death? And of my own death?

'*Ecce ancilla Domini,*' continued Benson.

I managed to respond: '*Fiat mihi secundum verbum tuum.*'

This was the famous '*fiat*' of our Lady which was the beginning of the redemption of human beings. Our Lady's amazing 'yes'—let it happen to me according to your word, that is as you, O God, will it to be—. What would have happened if our Lady had said 'no'? It didn't bear thinking about.

Benson was repeating the *Ave Maria* versicle now. My memory brought back to me an occasion at the cinema. I think it was the first time that I heard some of these words in Latin. It was the opening of Visconti's film, *Il Gattopardo.* The resident family priest was saying the angelus in the family chapel of the great Sicilian aristocratic family of the Prince of Lampedusa. The hot Sicilian wind was billowing in through the chapel window as the Prince and his large family and servants knelt before the Blessed Sacrament.

The film told the story of the end of the dominance of the old aristocratic families in Sicily after the *Risorgimento*, and their accommodation with the new order. But in its final moments it hinted at the persistence of the Faith when the Prince of Lampedusa confronts the prospect of his own death.

What would my death be like? Would I be alone? Would Angela die before me, or would I die before her? Would I live to see my children grow up? Would I ever have any grand-children? Where would I be then in my religion? Would I still be a Christian? Would I have lost my faith? Would I be a Catholic? Would this strange current adventure turn out to be some kind of shadow play with a happy ending? Or without one?

Benson too seemed to be meditating with his eyes cast down. He continued: "*Et verbum caro factum est.*"

I read from the card: "*Et habitavit in nobis.*"

The translation said: 'And dwelt among us.' How real was the incarnation of our Lord on earth to me? I had never been to the Holy Land so I could not really envisage the places where He walked on earth as those who had been on pilgrimage there would surely be able to do. Perhaps our Lord's presence in the Blessed Sacrament should be enough.

Benson was continuing with the two prayers, the prayer for grace for ourselves, and that for the faithful departed with which the Angelus concludes. I followed the Latin text and responded 'Amen' as required by the sheet. Were my parents, who had little religion, among the 'faithful departed'? I had never really considered whether they might be in Purgatory nor what, if anything, I, or anyone else could, or should do about that.

When I roused myself from my meditation Benson looked at me in a friendly business-like way.

"I hope that you were able to follow this. Please excuse me now while I go and collect my pack from Left Luggage below."

While he was away an old man came across to me and said:

"I could see that you and your priest friend were praying the Angelus together in Latin. Would you mind if I said something?"

He stood in front of me looking apologetic. He had longish white hair and was wearing an anorak and corduroy trousers.

"I have always tried to say the Angelus in Latin at least once a day. My wife and I used to say it togther in the evening when I came home from work. But she died some years ago so now I say it on my own. When I say it I remember her specially among the faithful departed. I have come to believe that she is doing the same where she has gone. But I am not very learned so I don't know if there is the Angelus in Purgatory or Heaven. My wife and I met when we were still at school. She died just before our fiftieth wedding anniversary. Such a shame, I thought. Not that it was a perfect marriage by any means. We had our ups and downs like most couples. I went off the rails once or twice but your vows hold you together, and the Blessed Sacrament. I am not sure our young understand this yet. It seems to me more difficult for them these days when both of them work, as most now seem to do. Of course they have lots more possessions than we had when we were first married. But I'm not sure that they're happier. But you don't want to hear all this about me and my family. All I wanted to say was how much pleasure it gave me to see you both saying the Angelus in Latin. Please tell your priest friend this. I always like to say something encouraging to priests. They do so much for us and they have to make so many sacrifices for their vocation."

I rose and shook his hand warmly. "Of course I will tell Father Benson what you said. I am sure he will be pleased. We are going on a pilgrimage to Rome and will include you in our prayers. What is the name of you and your wife?

He looked enormously pleased. There was a slight catch in his voice as he said:

"Francis and Teresa Baker." I made a note of this as he went back towards his seat. He had been sitting quite near us and this had enabled him to understand that we were saying the Angelus in Latin. But he did not resume his seat. He just picked up his small bag and went out through the lounge entrance.

An announcement over the ship's tannoy system informed passengers that we were due to dock in Calais in ten minutes. Benson returned with his pack and I was able to recount my conversation with the old man.

Benson looked delighted. He said that it was important not to be intimidated by secularists and those hostile to religion from expressing one's faith in public spaces. There was growing pressure to move the Faith off the streets and from public buildings and confine it to churches and the privacy of the home. Even in private houses some hostesses in polite society often saw it as their duty to ensure that their guests kept off the topic of religion. This was partly because the British were in fact very bad at discussing it in a civilised way; and it was made worse by lack of practice. All this needed to be resisted firmly. How edifying it was to find an old man persisting in saying the Angelus regularly in Latin. He hoped that Francis Baker, whom we should of course remember in our prayers with his wife Teresa, would be a little consoled by us too.

We shouldered our packs and went below to where a queue was forming near the doorway opposite where the gangway would be placed when we docked. I looked for Sebastian but did not see him.

In fact I have no recollection at all of getting off the ferry. My notebook simply says it was dark when we disembarked and that we made our way to the Calais Railway Station. This is the first appreciable gap in my record and I have been unable to add to the record from memory. We must have gone through some form of passport control and customs but it made no impression. Were we just waived through because it was time for the officers' supper and we'd arrived at a change of shift?

I think that Benson and I were together when we and the other passengers passed through these formalities, but I cannot be certain. I was now so used to Benson that I forgot about the issue of his passport, which had so preoccupied me earlier. We were on the platform at Calais station waiting for the Paris train when I briefly thought of it again. By this time the potential for awkwardness had not been realized. Since Benson would not be staying at an hotel while we were in Paris or Rome, I assumed there would be no need for him to show his passport there. But what about the train journey from France into Italy?

The tallest man on the platform was standing underneath one of the station lamps. It was Sebastian. He turned and saw us, then smiling broadly strode towards us making light work of his tote bag and the suitcase with wheels which contained his weights.

"Hello again, Father." He grinned broadly as he put down his luggage next to ours. "Good to see you again, Mr Bridge. I did manage a few minutes weight-training in the empty carriage. So thanks for that. But I didn't do me full routine as there were some things on me mind as Father knows. I 'ope I've now got some issues sorted. I got a snack on the ferry and that's done me a power of good."

"I hope Bridge and I will also be able to get something to eat in a restaurant car on the train," said Benson. "It seems a long time since luncheon. I will just use the time before the train is due to get a French newspaper. It's as well to know if their Government has fallen again. I will leave all my goods of this world in the capable hands of the two of you. I think I saw that the Tabac is on another platform. I will probably stop and have a cigarette too, so as not to blow smoke in your eyes."

I felt both embarrassed and rather curious to be left alone with Sebastian. Yet he looked open and friendly. There was no ghost of that sad and slightly shifty look that had marked his face on the Tonbridge/Dover train.

"Would it be OK if we sat on that seat behind us?" he said. We moved all the luggage there and arranged ourselves side by side. He leant forward and put his head in his hands for a moment, gave a big sigh and then sat up and faced me.

"Since we're going off to Paris together I thought I'd tell you a bit too. There's a lot of other terrible stuff about me. But that's really only for a priest in confession. What I want to tell yer is some stuff I'd tell a mate."

He paused to see what effect this offer to open up was having on me. I hope I looked reassuring because I felt strangely privileged.

"You see I'd like to take up yer offer of help to write a letter to me girl, Frances. I'm useless at putting me feelings on paper. It's better if yer know a bit more about me if you're going to 'elp. I know I'll 'ave to say it all again to me mate in Paris when I see 'im!"

I promised to keep everything to myself, but to listen carefully I think I must have done so. When I came to put an account of the conversation in my notebook later that evening his words seem to have come back to me easily. I suppose my office training in making notes of meetings helped.

"Well, yer see," he began, "I really didn't 'ave enough cash to pay me way in Paris with me mate. I left in such an 'urry. I didn't wanna take anything from me and Frances' joint account as we'd 'ad that bust-up. I was up to the limit with me bank coz I bought them travelling weights and stuff. So I was skint. When I see Father bring out that gold pocket watch I just couldn't stop meself from thinking of nicking it. I know a bit about these things and I could see that it was a gold 'alf-'unter. Do yer know how much they're worth? A good one should make over a grand, perhaps up to two if it's a bit special. I was a sorta tear away as a lad, even though I was an altar boy. So I'm quite good at pickin' pockets. Me mates at school used to say I was the Artful Dodger."

He laughed awkwardly. "I only got caught once. But the young copper was a decent bloke. He simply cautioned me and told me Mum. She gave me a really good belting, even though she was just a little thing. I was already well over six foot two then and 'adn't reached me limit.. But I knew she was right. I could never 'it a woman, let alone me Mum. Anyway it must 'ave done the trick. I gave up thieving. It was a bit easier for me like than givin' up sex and ciggies!"

He grinned, then continued.

"I still do magic tricks for me kids. Making things appear and disappear. But I really thought I'd given up nicking other guys' stuff for good. I'd a steady job I liked. I was really proud of being a dad. I loved Damien and 'annah to bits and 'ad a steady girl who seemed to love me a lot. No problems! What more did I need? But then came that bust-up with Fran. When I saw Father's 'unter and thought how short of the readies I'd be in Paris with me mate, I just got sucked in again. Father and I were looking at a map of Paris together and it was real easy to get it off 'im. But I knew straight after I done it that I had bombed big time. When yer think about it there was no way that I c'd shift 'is watch in Paris. Me mate would just think I was a wally. Then Father was someone I c'd real respect, — unlike me own Dad who 'ad just nicked off—. Father seemed a bit old school when I first met 'im, but I liked that—some of the best plumbers are old school in the way they do things. And yer know something, Father worked out what was in me head about me and Fran and the kids. When me and you were on our own together in the compartment after I nicked 'is 'unter I was real embarrassed. It was great of you to tell me about the empty compartment where I c'd do me weights. It gave me a chance to clear me 'ead and think what I's gonna do. Yer wont believe this but when I was on me own and had stripped down to do a couple of sets I suddenly felt that I was meant to nick Father's watch. By then I knew I 'ad to give it back. I was also pretty sure 'e wouldn't turn me in, being a priest and all that. And I knew what I really wanted was to talk to 'im about me life and what I was doing with it, and ask 'is help. But I 'ad to say I was sorry *first*, and get back to where I was. As I put on all the weights in the kit for me last big routine I felt sure I'd struck lucky, him being a priest and all that. I guess you can tell I was brought up Catholic—I reckon it always shows—. But I'd not been to confession since before I was confirmed when I's fourteen. But deep down I always knew that things would be better if I could get all the stuff I done since then off me chest. I reached the end of me work out. I knew this was a chance and there was no way it'd come again…ever. I just mustn't blow it. Well you can see that it worked out OK for me. I know it's not just 'im that's forgiven me, but that Big One too."

He paused after the effort of bringing all this out, and then turned to me and said: "I don't think yer're Catholic, are yer?"

He looked at me searchingly. In the station light I noticed how serious his dark eyes were. It was almost like Benson's look. It was I who broke eye contact. I was looking right away from his gaze when I said:

"No, but I'm going on a pilgrimage with Father Benson to find out more about it, and I'll just see what comes next."

"I'm just an ordinary bloke," he continued, as if to soften his direct personal remark. "I left school at sixteen so I never learned much. I've never read a book right through, and can't do what you'd call real writin'. You seem from another world. OK, I was at a Catholic school, and not just the local comp. But I didn't pick up much there—about the Faith— or anything of real use.

"There was only one teacher I respected and he was sacked after six months. They said 'e was too strict, and wouldn't let us follow our own interests. But we didn't really have any interest in school work—just football, beer, telly and girls. That teacher didn't hold with telling us young geezers we were good at something when we were rubbish. The powers that be in the school thought this made us feel failures. That guy was just too honest for 'em. There were too many women teachers in the school anyway— they hadn't a clue how to control us young guys. The lads used to compete to see who could go the furthest to make 'em go red. Me mate Jim used to ask any that were decent-looking for a shag if she came over to look at his work."

"I learnt most of me Faith from me Mum and the priest at our Church. He was a real good bloke. When he said Mass or spoke to me I could tell 'e was sincere. Priests give up a lot to take on what they do,— not just sex and all that—Just seeing them every week in that sacristy place made you feel the pressure they 'ave to take. It's like being a punch-bag in the gym. Funny thing! Yer know I never minded being a server. It wasn't just getting the kit on and swinging the incense. I knew I was doing something special. I was quite a big lad, so I could handle any of me mates who tried to take the mickey. I'm not much of a Catholic— you know that—, but deep down I wouldn't be anything else. It'll always work for me, if I give it a chance and ask 'im. I'm sure it'd work fer you too. You'd be more use than me if yer were Catholic because you've got more up top."

I turned to face him. Now he looked away, as if embarassed by all that he had said. But it had already printed itself vividly on me. He continued:

"I don't usually say much. You know I can't remember ever saying as much before to anyone in one go."

CHAPTER TEN

BLOOD ON THE CASSOCK

THERE was a rapid announcement on the tannoy in French. My French is passable enough for international meetings, but this was rather distorted. It seemed to say that the train for Paris was about to arrive. Fortunately Benson appeared immediately still smoking a cigarette and carrying a newspaper. I wondered if he had been watching us and had waited until we had finished our talk.

He picked up his pack and moved it nearer the edge of the platform. Sebastian and I assembled our luggage alongside his. Benson still had his pilgrim staff, but I must have left mine on the Dover train or on the ferry. The empty train pulled in. It was oldish rolling stock. Benson and I had reserved seats but we found that the other seats in the compartment were without reservations. So there was plenty of room for Sebastian, his tote bag and his case of weights. After stowing our luggage Benson produced three plastic cups which he put on a little shelf near the window seat that he had taken. It was now dark outside, apart from the lights of the outskirts of Calais, as we sped on our way. With some ceremony Benson fished in the side pocket of his pack and produced a small bottle and his Swiss Army knife.

"I managed to find a half bottle of champagne at the duty free on the ferry. I thought we might celebrate in a small way our safe arrival in France."

He carefully cut around the foil with the knife, and then skilfully pushed off the cork. It made a pleasing pop and he quickly poured the fizzy contents into the three small plastic cups. I noted that it was Moet et Chandon.

"My toast is to your holiday in Paris, Sebastian, and a safe and happy return to your family. And to our pilgrimage, Bridge, to the Eternal City. As it is the Feast of St Thomas

Aquinas today in my old breviary, let us also drink to him too. More than perhaps anyone else he was given the grace to produce a comprehensive summary of the Christian mysteries. And these remain broadly an authentic statement of our Church's doctrine roday. I am not sure if you know this story about him. After a personal revelation from God on the 6th of December 1272, he dictated no more of his great writings. For he said that all that he had written, compared to what he had seen in his vision, was like so much straw. So you see, Sebastian, you may not need a lot of book learning to get to know God better than either of *us*.

He raised his glass again to Sebastian.

"Nonetheless, especially for your benefit, Bridge, and to improve your Latin, I thought that I would read to both of you the Collect for the Feast of St Thomas Aquinas which is the one used at Vespers on this his feast day. It is quite short so don't be alarmed. I will offer you, Sebastian, a free translation of my own at the end, but I hope that you Bridge will not really need this!

'*Deus, qui Ecclesiam tuam, beati Thomæ Confessoris tui mira eruditione clarificas, et sancta operatione fœcundas: da nobis quæsumus, et quæ docuit, intellectu conspicere, et quæ egit, imitatione complere. Per Dominum nostrum Jesum Christum, Amen*

O God, who, by the wonderful learning of the blessed Thomas, your Confessor, makes your Church shine brightly and be fruitful by its holy influence, give us we beg you the ability to grasp with our minds what he taught, and so by imitating his example bring to fruition what he achieved. Amen.'

"You can see both of you what the challenge is for us. Here is a great saint who was given grace by Almighty God to understand and make a summary of what God had revealed to us in Holy Scripture and the tradition of the Church. If we have the ability to understand his teaching—and we are to ask God to increase our ability to understand it if we find this difficult—we are to put it into practice in our own lives, and pass what we have grasped of his teaching on to others. Easier said than done, you both will say. But that's the ideal we're to strive for. Now I'm not living up to my ideals or my rule of life for I haven't yet said Vespers. And you both have a letter to write, I believe. I can advise you as a celibate priest on the teachings of the Church on marriage and its nature as a Sacrament. But as to letters between husbands and wives or gentlemen and their ladies, that is best left to laymen. I will walk the corridors again on my own and keep you both in my prayers. You have important work to do. I will also locate the dining car, and call to collect you, Bridge, for our meal a little later. Perhaps, Sebastian you might like a cognac and cigar after your labours." He grinned his infectious grin. "I will try to persuade someone to let me bring these to you."

He swept out. Sebastian and I looked at each other and smiled conspiratorially.

"When I's first an altar boy," began Sebastian, "I remember we 'ad Mass in Latin. I's taught by the priest to reply in Latin. The sound of what Father was saying just now came back. Yer may not believe this but I c'd even make out a couple of words like 'Deus' and 'Dominum.' The nuns at primary school taught us a bit o' Latin. Some priests used to gabble through the old Mass at knots. Even guys who knew Latin real well told me they couldn't always get it. But me priest never gabbled. 'e never seemed rushed. Yer know a funny thing. I really believed 'im when 'e said to me once that what we was doing together was the most wonderful thing in the world—just making our Lord there for everyone. 'Just think of that,' 'e used to say. But coz lots of them guys didn't get what 'e was saying it may have been right to have some stuff in English. I dunno. But it's sure lost mystery. I stopped going to Mass soon after them changes. Perhaps it was now all too easy. Boys like a challenge. Mass seemed to become a more girly thing. The music was terrible—a really bad try at what they thought us kids liked. But I can't say that I stopped going just because of all that. Girls, football and beer seemed more important. Although I was nicking things a bit Mum didn't know at first. She just was real pleased I didn't do drugs. Never 'ave."

He was sitting opposite me while he said all this. He suddenly stood up right in front of me to stretch up to his full height. He put his hands on his hips as if in challenge, but then bowed his head and looking down at me and said very quietly:

"On the level, Mr Bridge, do yer think I can make it?"

For some reason I said very quietly in reply:

"I think so Seb. Youv'e more chance than me. Please call me Bernard."

He sat down again and said:

"Don't say things like that about yourself. I know you're trying to 'elp me but it don't seem right to say that."

"Shall we have a go at the letter?" I said. "Father Benșon will want to know how we've got on when he comes back."

"OK, do yer mind if I have a roll up? It 'elps calm me down?"

"Fine by me, if it's fine by you," I said, thinking of his weight-training.

I produced some sheets of foolscap paper and a writing pad and envelope from my pack. I also had a couple of biros. Sebastian took out a little pack of cigarette papers and a plastic pouch of tobacco and expertly rolled a thin cigarette.

"I think we had better start with some ideas and then do a draft," I said. "Once you're happy with that, you can copy it out on to some sheets of this writing paper and it can be posted in Paris. I've even got some French stamps. I always seem to need a few when I travel on business. But it's got to be *your* letter, and in the words you'd use. If not, she wont buy into it."

"I'm worried she won't buy into it anyway." He had now lit up. "Do yer really think I can handle what I wanna say in a letter?"

"Just tell me in your own words what's in your head and I'll have a go."

I thought of saying to Sebastian that most medieval barons couldn't read or write and that they used to have scribes like me to write letters for them. In my day I remembered a boy at school—now on the list of the world's richest people—who could hardly read or write at the age of sixteen. But he always found a small scholarly boy to write his school essays for him while he dictated what he wanted to say. I decided not to mention this story. It would have sounded patronizing.

"Well," he said, "I first wanna say that I miss 'er and am aching to hold 'er again real close."

He paused as if he was thinking of saying something more intimate then thought better of it.

"Would you want to say that you were sorry about the row?" I asked.

"Yes, that I'm real sorry I walked out and was bloody rude. Could yer also put in the letter that I feel now I blew it when there was so much goin' for us."

"Do you want to say that you hope she will have you back and that she will forgive you?"

"Yeah, I think so. But deep inside I've got to tell yer I still feel mad at 'er that she didn't treat me with…like… more respect. She should 'ave tried to understand me as a bloke. But she'd no brothers, I s'pose. Anyway it's no use banging on about this, I know. We'll never make it if I think like that. I know I've got to be big enough to earn 'er respect — and it's not a matter of having the physique, I guess. And I can't get it just by asking 'er for it, can I?"

"What about the kids?" I said.

"Just write how much I miss 'em and want to hug 'em." He paused. His eyes looked misty and his lips were moist. Then he blurted out rapidly: "Yer know I want them to have a real dad they can look up to, and not a quitter. I don't want 'em to 'ave to tell their friends that their dad's done a runner, or have to make up stories about 'im like I used to do about me own dad. Our little kids need the two of us together. I reckon that it'll stop 'em going off the rails later."

He seemed to be actually speaking to her now for he no longer seemed to be dictating to me. Then he added: "Fran, we owe it to 'em."

Although I was used to making notes I had found it a big

challenge to get down what he was saying. I was affected by his story and that made being accurate all the harder.

"Are you going to come clean about your idea of getting married?" I said after I had finished a lot of scribbling.

"Yeah, I think so. Do yer think I c'd say that I've 'ad some time to think, being away and all that. And I've met a couple of guys who know what makes me tick. I now feel big enough to take advice. P'r'aps I could put it like this: 'I think we can make a go of it and I promise yer, darling, that I'll really try— yer know something: I would like yer to marry me. Yes, I've said it. WILL YER MARRY ME?' Would it be OK if I then said: 'I wish I c'd see yer face when yer read this. P'r'aps yer'll tear me letter up. But I'll light a candle in a church in Paris like yer do when yer're worried'."

"Won't she be thinking about friends who've married and it hasn't worked out?" I felt I should add a cautionary note.

"I don't think it'll only be that with 'er. We're both scared we'll lose out somehow if we tie the knot. But p'r'aps yer right and she'll think like yer said. Could I say: 'we've lots of mates who've got into it with vows and stuff and then it's all gone pear-shaped. But I'm sure we can do better. Yer know how competitive I am, darlin'? She knows about that for sure!"

"What about getting in now with some rules for when you're married. I think you should come clean in the letter so she's got time to think about it."

"Yeah, that's a good one. C'd I say something like? 'If yer can go along with what I'm thinking we'll need to work out how to get things straight before we jump in together. Yer'll want time to keep up with with yer girl friends. A bloke isn't a bloke without seein' 'is mates and doing the things that make 'im what 'e is.' Yer can guess, Mr Bridge, I'm thinking of weight-training, tinkering with the car, the football, and beer with me mates. But I'm not sure I should say this in me letter. I c'd say it to 'er face when I see 'er. That's if she's still on side. P'r'aps I should say that I'll want us to do lots together with the kids— I'm real keen anyway to do boys' stuff with Damien. But she might like it if I said that we sh'd find the time to do some things on our own like. Just the two of us. Perhaps 'er Mum would 'elp out. There's one other thing I wanna come clean about. I hope it wont put 'er off. I want us to get prop'ly married—in a church. She was brought up Catholic. But like me she's not been to Mass since she was a kid. But I know she still likes to go in a church sometimes—she knows how to make the sign of the cross, and goes down on one knee when she should."

He paused and looked at me to see how I was reacting. Then he continued: "I used to think it wouldn't be right to ask a priest to marry us 'aving kids already? What do yer think?"

"I'm sure a good priest will want to help you. If you make your vows in church it should be as beautiful for you both as it was for us when we got married. You may not believe this but you and Fran are certain to get extra strength from the ceremony to help you keep your vows."

"That's what I think. So let's go for it in the letter. He sat back in his seat while I finished making notes, then he scrutinized me carefully as I looked up. For the first time he looked authoritative as he said: " 'ave I missed nothing? Yer've written a fantastic lot. Yer wouldn't believe 'ow slow I'm in writin'. It'll take me all night just to copy."

"I think we can make something of it," I said. "My handwriting is so terrible that I will print it all out for you so it will be easier to follow. If you give me a bit of time now, I'll let you have something for you to check over."

I was not sure how well he could read handwriting. Printing seemed the best way of helping him. I hoped my explanation would not seem to belittle him. He took up the sports pages and seemed to concentrate. I tried hard to catch his turn of phrase, his expressions, his shortening of words and his wayward grammar. I hoped he would modify what I wrote to give it more of his voice. But I couldn't be sure that his seeming greater confidence would continue when he picked up a biro and was faced with a blank sheet of paper. I rather hoped he might decide to spell words as he was used to doing, rather than just slavishly copying my attempts at his usage. But

I thought it better not to say anything to encourage this in case it too seemed patronizing.

I worked away at the challenge. It proved rather more difficult than producing a draft of a Cabinet Office meeting. But after about twenty minutes I thought I had produced some kind of a reasonable effort for him to scrutinize. But just as I was handing it over Benson burst in. He had reserved a table in the restaurant car and said we should proceed there immediately.

"Sebastian is looking through the draft of our joint effort to Frances so it is a good moment to leave him to it."

"If it seems O K," I said to Sebastian, "just write it out on the writing paper. If you get stuck we can work on it when I get back from having something to eat."

Benson interjected with a big open smile: "We shall remember the cognac and cigar if I can persuade someone to help."

As we left and I was closing the glass door of the compartment I noticed that Sebastian had taken off his leather jacket. He was now stripped to his black tee sheet which showed off the results of his weight training. It was as if he had decided to apply the same committed preparation to his emotional task as he applied to his exercise routine.

When we got the restaurant car it was obvious that Benson had already made a friend of our waiter. He spoke to him in English.

"This is Raphaele from Verona. The French Railways are clever enough to seek out the world's best waiters who of course come from Italy. This is my friend, Mr Bridge. He is going to Rome with me. We wont, alas, be calling at Verona. St Zeno's Basilica is one of the finest in Italy."

Raphaele grinned at us, showing perfect white teeth. He was of medium-height and well-proportioned, filling the French Railway uniform to perfection. His black shoes had been beautifully polished. I noticed that he had already put a smoked salmon starter on thin brown bread for each of us in our place.

"I hope you like smoked salmon, Bridge. I thought it would be good to get our teeth into something straight away. I have assumed that you are as hungry as I am. But I haven't been so imperious as to order your main course, you will be pleased to learn."

Raphaele handed me a menu. Benson took the wine list from him.

"My inclination is for meat so we should have red wine, unless you want to go on with fish. I tend to leave that till Friday."

I scanned the menu and chose a rabbit dish which we seldom have at home. Benson chose the venison. I thought that he would reveal himself as a connoisseur of wine, but he simply ordered a carafe of the French Railway house red once he knew my order. Raphaele made a note and went on to another table. The restaurant was almost full so I assumed that we would have a long wait. Benson said a Latin grace quite loudly and set to on his smoked salmon. I had noticed he had eaten quickly at lunch and he did the same with the smoked salmon. I remembered from the Martindale biography that the speed at which Benson ate was well known. I was only halfway through the large platter of smoked salmon when he suddenly said:

"A correspondent of mine has written to say that he uses the word 'Church' to describe a good number of organization that he believes deserve that name: the various Eastern churches, some of which he says outrank Rome, the Roman Catholics, the Anglicans, the Church of Scotland—as you will guess he is a Scot—and a range of vigorous Protestant bodies. What do you, Bb...Bridge, think 'the Church' is?"

I hesitated before replying then said slowly:

"I suppose I have been used to thinking a bit like your correspondent. In other words I thought that the Church was a kind of generalization, perhaps even something mystical which is all embracing. But now I'm not sure I was right. As Anglicans we recite the Creed every Sunday. So I say 'I believe in the Holy Catholick Church'. But I haven't really thought deeply about what that means. Many Anglicans tend to think that what they believe is something entirely between themselves and God. In other words everyone should find out what is best for themselves and then seek to live up to it. They are distrustful of an ecclesiastical authority telling them what they should or shouldn't believe. It doesn't seem quite British. 'Britons never, never never shall be slaves'. But on the Church, if pressed, I would say that the Anglican Church is a continuaton of the Catholic Church. An Anglican priest said to me once that it was the original church in England, without the abuses that Rome had added in the period leading up to the Reformation.

"But I wouldn't go as far as your correspondent in saying that some Protestant sects and the Church of Scotland, with its Calvinist theology, are really part of this generalized church. The Church seems to me to imply some sort of continuity in its nature and structure with the past, rather than an abrupt break, and then reliance on scripture alone. But I confess I am muddled about where the Roman Catholic Church and the Eastern churches fit into this strange concept of mine."

I resumed eating my smoked salmon. Benson had finished. He now pushed his chair slightly away from the table and leaned back. Then he treated me to the following:

"The real issue is authority. It was this too for the high priests, Pharisees and scribes when they asked our Lord: 'By what authority do you teach?' They could not accept that He really was the Son of God, the Christ, the Messiah who had been foretold in their scriptures. Even when they saw His miracles many said He'd received power from the devil. But the whole of Christianity is based on the fact that what Jesus said was the truth. He really was the Son of God. It was this claim which led to His crucifixion. And it was His resurrection and the appearances to His disciples afterwards that convinced them that He was not just the greatest of the prophets, but God, the second person of the Trinity. Of course those who had heard stories of His birth, been present at His baptism by John, been witnesses to the transfiguration or seen Him walking on the lake knew that He was extraordinarily favoured by God, more perhaps than any other prophet in Jewish history. But the trial and crucifixion were bewildering. Yet afterwards there were the resurrection appearances. The link between the Institution of the Eucharist and the Sacrifice of Calvary came to be understood in the light of scripture. And it was confirmed by our Lord Himself on the road to Emmaus. All that was needed was the appearance of the Third Person of the Trinity, the Holy Ghost at Pentecost to transform the small band of fishermen, minor officials and ordinary men and women into that visible Church that is now in every corner of the world."

By now I had finished my smoked salmon and Raphaele had brought us our main course. I said:

"I see all that clearly enough. But I suppose the issue for me is: Did our Lord really found a Church or should we just be content to discover His teaching from the Bible and apply it ourselves. And if He did found a Church, how can we be sure that the Church of Rome is what He had in mind? And what about the other Eastern churches which your correpondent mentioned, some of which are at least as old as the Church of Rome?"

"There are two aspects to the question of whether our Lord wanted to found a Church: the logical and the historical. If Jesus Christ our Lord really was God, the second Person of the Trinity, is it likely that He would become man and teach a band of disciples about His Father and Himself and what was needed for their salvation, and then return to His Father leaving each of them individually to pass on His teaching as best he could? Surely as Almighty God He would want this to be passed on correctly? And with His understanding of the consequences of man being granted freedom of will, He would know that disagreements about His teaching and nature would arise almost immediately. How would these be settled? If we examine the Gospels, the Acts of the Apostles and the letters of St Paul, St Peter, St James and St Jude, as they have come down to us, we find that the texts clearly support the idea that He did intend to create an institution that would preserve His teaching. You might find it useful to look through the New Testament with an open mind to see whether you can identify these texts. I think I can remember the important ones as they appear in the Authorized Version of the New Testment. From St Matthew there is:

'All power is given unto Me in heaven and in earth. Go ye therefore and teach all nations...teaching them to observe all things whatsoever I have commanded you: and, lo, I am with you always, even unto the end of the world.'

From St Mark:

'Go ye into all the world, and preach the gospel to every creature. He that believeth and is baptised shall be saved: but he that believeth not shall be condemned.'

Benson paused to see whether I was really listening. He seemed satisfied and then continued:

"From St Luke:

'Behold I send the promise of My Father upon you: but tarry ye in the city of Jerusalem until ye be endued with power from on high.'

And finally from St John:

'As My Father hath sent Me, even so I send you. And when He had said this He breathed on them and saith unto them: Receive ye the Holy Ghost. Whose soever sins ye remit they are remitted unto them and whose soever sins ye retain they are retained.'

"And r...remember that an institutional Church existed right from the b...beginning. There was an almost immediate collective decision needed to replace one of the twelve after Judas had betrayed our Lord. And to create deacons to deal with the practical matters of the care of the widows. The first Council of the Church had to decide how to deal with the Gentiles, who were keen to enter what was clearly now seen as an institutional Church. Did they need to be circumcised and obey all aspects of Jewish law? It was St Peter who was given a vision from God that convinced him that no food should now be considered unclean, and this enabled him to see that there were no legalistic barriers any more to the reception of pagans into the Church."

Benson had been choosing his words carefully. He had not always spoken directly to me, only glancing at me now and then to check if he was holding my attention. He now seemed to relax.

"Of course, it is a great blessing that there is now so much that we can eat and enjoy. I doubt if I could cope easily with a kosher regime. But I have probably said enough for one evening on the subject of the Church. I shall leave the question of the authority of the Church of Rome for another time. You probably ought to return to see how Sebastian is doing with his letter. I will settle the bill here. I will stretch my legs and perhaps call at the buffet car to try out their coffee. I shall come and join you both ere long. But I will give you a little time to make progress on the matter which is outside my competence."

"You must let me pay for our dinner tomorrow night on the train to Rome," I said.

"That would be most gracious of you."

I smiled slightly cheekily at Benson and added: "Perhaps it would not be quite right if you were paying for dinner tomorrow night when you intend to put me right about the Petrine claims."

Benson grinned back: "I quite see your point, Bridge. But we might discuss the Petrine claims at breakfast tomorrow. I have another idea for a topic at dinner."

When I got back to our compartment I found Sebastian had made more progress than I had expected. He greeted me warmly and I sat down beside him. I explained that Father Benson would join us later with cognac and cigars. Between the two of us lay a couple of sheets of writing paper that he had obviously screwed up as unsatisfactory in some way. My notes were there too. But there seemed to be some pages of the letter which had survived and were on the small shelf beside him.

"I reckon I've got along OK. But I'm having a 'ell of a job, Bernard, with the end. Would yer like to see 'ow I've got on so far."

He looked at me shyly. I was touched that he had called me Bernard. The humility registering on his face made a remarkable contrast with his massive physical presence which seemed to be bursting out from his tee shirt and jeans. He passed me the pages of his letter.

His handwriting was unformed, almost that of a child. There was quite a bit of crossing out and amendment, which gave it a genuine look. A great deal of what he had said to me, or I had suggested, was included. The grammar, and even some of the spelling, I noted with approval, were very much his own. There was plenty of personal endearment. I could not imagine myself letting someone else see this sort of thing if the letter was one of mine to Angela. The main points about the need for his children to have a permanent father at home was there, the proposal of marriage, and the idea that both Frances and himself should have space for themselves for their own interests. The proposal for a church wedding was also in.

When I looked across at him, he was clearly waiting nervously for my reaction. I was completely won over. I said: "Of course women are often unpredictable, but I cannot believe that Fran will not take up what you're offering. I don't think you need add much. Perhaps just something which recalls some moment or event which you know that both of you treasure."

Sebastian looked relieved as I handed the letter back to him. He immediately took up his biro and started to write something on the last page. I decided to leave it at that and got up and took my notebook out of my pack. It was a chance to make notes on the days events while they were fresh.

We both worked silently. Occasionally, as I looked up to recall something, I noticed that Sebastian was also doing some further corrections to an earlier part of the letter. It was while we were at work that I realized that the train was slowing down. A few minutes later I glanced out of the window and saw we were going through the outskirts of a town. It must be Amiens, I thought to myself. I was right. This was confirmed by the station signs as the train came into the station.

There seemed to be a huge crowd on the platform as we

were arriving. I was intrigued. When the train came to a halt the crowd was very noisy indeed. Sebastian looked up from his letter, opened the window and looked out.

"It looks like a football team and their supporters," he said. "A lot of 'em look as if they've 'ad too many."

There was much shouting and some raucous singing. Carriage doors were banging so it was clear that they were piling into the train. The corridors were soon teeming with this unruly mob. A good number looked in through our glass door but did not come in. Either they wanted a compartment for themselves or they may have sized up Sebastian and decided not to impose themselves on us. In fact as the train moved off after the kerfuffle, they seemed to have chosen compartments that were quite a way from ours. But we could still hear them shouting. Occasionally there was some some singing but we were able to go back to our literary efforts.

After about a quarter of an hour Sebastian suddenly said:

"What do yer think Father's got up to?"

Before I could reply Benson's face appeared at the carriage window. He looked flushed and excited. His hands were full with a bottle, some paper cups and a small box. Sebastian got up to open the door and relieve him of the bottle, paper cups and box. As he came into the compartment I could see that the top of the right sleeve of his cassock had a jagged tear in it and that there was a large dark wet stain round it. Sebastian clearly saw this too as he took delivery of the cognac and other items. There was little doubt that it was blood. Before we could say anything Benson blurted out:

"As you can see I've had an encounter with a fellow traveller. He was a member of the football team of the Cercle Athlétique de Paris. I was in the buffet car where I acquired the cognac and cigars when I decided to sit down at one of the few small tables and have a coffee. Soon after that the train got into Amiens. A large number of the team and supporters invaded the buffet car. Most of them had clearly had a lot to drink already, but they rather impatiently began shouting for more drinks to the two men running the buffet. Eventually most of them managed to get a glass and I was thinking that they were calming down when one of the team, a tough looking young man about my height, with a shaven head and some tatoos on his arms, lurched across to me with a drink in his hand. He made as if to offer it to me. I explained in my best French that I was well satisfied with my coffee and was taking a bottle of cognac back to drink with my friends. This refusal to drink seemed to anger him and he began to thrust the glass towards my face. I rose to confront him. He then made what I understood to be a generalised allegation about priests having perverted sexual interests in children. I managed to find adequate French to say that all priests were bound to follow our Lord in loving children. And this meant guarding their innocence. If some priests failed in this matter this was damnable. My own sins were many. But this was not one of them.

"The buffet car had by now become very quiet, and everyone was looking at us. My interlocutor suddenly broke the tumbler in his right hand against the edge of my table which I was now standing beside, and made as if to thrust the jagged remaining half at my face. From past experience I knew that I could have floored him, expecially as he was the worse for drink. I was very tempted to do so. But fortunately our Lord's grace saved my clerical vows, and I did not resist his provocative force with my own. What I did do was make a feint to one side.

"Then came a complete surprise. As I took my evasive action another member of the team, though a soccer player, made a fine rugby tackle from behind my assaillant and brought him down crashing on to the floor. Unfortunately as he was falling the jagged glass was still in his hand and it caught the sleeve of my cassock and made the tear you see in it. The broken glass also slashed through my shirt and cut the top of my arm. Hence the blood. I managed a few words of thanks to my defender, remembered to leave a modest tip for the overstressed young man at the bar who had brought me my coffee, and had arranged the cognac and cigars, and successfully extricated myself from the confusion. As I was leaving the car I managed to recover a little composure. I turned back and faced the crowded buffet car and called out: '*Vive le Cercle Athlétique de Paris! Vive l'Angleterre! Vive la France!*' I was gratified that there were a few modest cheers in response."

I was amazed by the way Benson had handled this nasty and dangerous incident. I recalled that he had said I should defend him if needed, but I had not been there to help in his hour of need. I suspect that I would have probably just had a blue funk if I had been there. Sebastian, however, looked extremely angry.

"Why don't the three of us go back there and sort 'em out?"

"I have every confidence in your ability in a brawl, Sebastian," said Benson, "but the mood of the team has clearly turned against my poor assaillant. It is he who may be in need of our prayers, which I shall surely offer on his behalf. But now prudence suggests that my wound should be dressed. My little first aid kit may be inadequate for what is needed."

Without further ado Benson unbuttoned his cassock at the front and stepped out of it. Underneath he had on a pair of black trousers and black cotton clerical shirt. The top of one sleeve was gashed like his cassock and had more blood on it even than the cassock. Benson rolled up his sleeve. There was a jagged two-inch gash on his bicep. It was still oozing blood.

Sebastian's mood changed abruptly. He sprang up, opened his tote bag and produced a bottle of mineral water. Then he rooted around in his bag again and found a sponge bag with soap, cotton wool, a tube of Savlon, scissors, and various size packs of sticking plaster.

"When we was in our gang it was me who did the repair jobs after somebody got cut up. So I'm in me element." He grinned. "That bicep, Father, looks to me as though it's 'ad some work-outs in the gym."

Benson had now sat down and Sebastian was carefully swabbing the wound with the cotton wool, wet from the bottled water.

"I think we're in luck. It's not really as deep as I'd guessed." said Sebastian. "No need for me to sew yer up with stitches, as I've done a few times. Yer know something? I don't reckon there's any bits of glass in it. "

After some deft work on the wound his dark eyes looked critically at his professional handy work and rubbed some Savlon into the gash.

"I think I've got a piece of sticking plaster big enough to cover it all. But I think I'd better secure the plaster. It'll very likely go on bleedin' a bit. I didn't pack a bandage, but I bought some cotton handkchiefs before I left. I'll use 'em 'ere."

He went back to his tote bag and located them still in their cellophane wrapper. He tore them methodically into strips.

"I must correct you, Sebastian" said Benson, wincing a little but with a smile. "Any development of my bicep dates from school: rowing, and left back in the rugger team. Perhaps it has been sustained a little by more recent tennis and swimming. But I've not been to a gymnasium since school."

Sebastian grinned as he worked. He had now fixed the sticking plaster and was wrapping Benson's arm with the strips of the handkerchiefs. His powerful hands then fixed everything in place with some safety pins.

"It's not too tight, is it?" Sebastian enquired. Benson nodded approval. Sebastian added: "I don't think she'll come off. It'll stop the bleedin' gettin' on everything else. There's a bit on yer priest's collar but it's low down and wont show when yer put yer cassock back on."

I made myself busy pouring out the cognacs. But I could not stop myself from looking up to take in the sight of these two figures, both in black shirts with their arms bare, sitting next to each other. One had expertly, almost tenderly, been binding the wound of the other. And he was the one who only a few hours earlier had slid his hand into the pocket of the other and lifted his pocket watch.

I handed round the cognacs which were fulsomely welcomed. Benson sipped his reflectively while using some of the remains of the bottled water and some soap to get the blood off his cassock and shirt.

"I don't think I'll bother repairing my shirt at present," said Benson, "but I will make an effort with my cassock—it's the only one I have with me. I have some black thread with my Dance of Death. But I shall smoke my cigar first."

Sebastian put his leather jacket back on and repacked his first-aid items. He then took up the letter, put it into the envelope and carefully sealed and addressed it. He said nothing. I found the right French stamp in my wallet and handed it to him. He took it, mouthed a thank you and lit his cigar. Benson lit up too. I am not really a great cigar lover, but I felt the need to be part of our little group, so I lit mine. Benson got up suddenly and brought up out from his pack the pilgrimage shell which Ruby had given us to use as an ashtray.

We were just beginning to relax when two figures appeared outside the glass door of our compartment. One was a huge, dark fellow—almost as tall as Sebastian, I thought. He was wearing a blazer, white shirt and tie and dark trousers.The other was about the size of Benson. The smaller one had a shaven head and tattoos on his muscley arms. This one was wearing a football strip: blue shorts and a white football shirt with the sleeves rolled up. The tall, more-authoritative figure stared through the glass at us. He was either sizing us up, or making sure we were those he was wanting. The three of us got on to our feet quickly. Sebastian squared up and growled to us: "It looks like some of their team are comin' to take us on."

But he was wrong. The tall, dark fellow slid back the door and seemed to push the smaller stocky one into our compartment first. This one then stood just inside the door looking down at his feet. His shoulders were slumped inside his football shirt. I noted the logo on the pocket: 'CAP CHARENTON.'

The tall man then came in and stood beside him filling out the doorway as if to block our exit. Yet it was clear from his body language, and that of the young man, that they were not here for a fight. He addressed Benson in French.

"Monsieur le Curé, voici le membre de notre equipe que vous reconnaissez. Il m'a accompagné per s'excuser formellement, de sa part et de la part du Cercle Athlétique de Paris Charenton. Sa conduite envers vous et son insulte à votre réputation et à celle de la profession sacerdotale sont tout-à-fait inexcusables."

It was clear to me that this was the team captain, and that he was seeking to make amends with an apology. Benson looked the captain calmly in the eye weighing up his words. But he made no reply. All eyes now turned on to the shorter young man. I realized that he must have been Benson's actual assailant. The lad continued to stare at his football boots. The captain was frowning, and seemed on the point of saying something to prompt him.

Then, quite suddenly, the young man, without looking up, took a step forward towards Benson. I feared a further attack. But the young man just knelt down at Benson's feet with his head still bowed. He spread out his hands on the compartment floor. Benson looked down at him for a few seconds. Then he put out his right arm, and carefully placed his hand on the young man's shaven head. Benson's right shirt-sleeve was still rolled up making visible Sebastian's make-shift handkerchief bandages, red from Benson's blood.

In a clear voice Benson then said a few words in Latin. I was so surprised at this turn of events that I did not follow his words. It was clear to all that he was giving the young man his priestly blessing.

The incident lasted no more than a few seconds, then Benson bent down and grasped the young man's tattooed arms and pulled him up gently to his feet. Then he took his right hand and shook it firmly. The poor fellow had at last raised his eyes and was looking at Benson for the first time. After a short pause they then momentarily embraced French style.

The young man still said nothing, but put his hand into the breast pocket of his football jersey. I wondered what he was fumbling for. He produced a small black and white object made of cloth and handed it to Benson, who took it with a look of childish pleasure. Then, holding it between his thumb and forefinger he raised it high for us to see. It was a tiny black and white penguin. Benson then brought it slowly to his lips and kissed it.

I observed the young man's lower lip trembling and that his eyes were moist. The team captain briefly explained in French that the penguin was the mascot of their football team. There was a pause after this. None of us clearly could find anything more to say. The captain then wished us all good evening and a pleasant stay in Paris. He then opened our compartment door. He was clearly expecting his young team mate to precede him through it. But after a moment's hesitation, the young fellow went back to Benson, and looking him straight in the eye—I noted that they were almost exactly the same height—he said just one word in a low voice: '*Merci*.'

This time it was he who put out his right hand to Benson who took it and shook it warmly. Then, remembering his manners, he shook hands in the French way, first with Sebastian and then with me. A moment later our encounter with the *Cercle Athlétique de Paris Charenton* was over.

The three of us sat down in silence.

"Blimey," said Sebastian. "W'd yer believe it?"

"It's most curious." said Benson, "The young man was wearing trousers and a short-sleeved shirt when he attacked me. The captain must have made him change into the team's football strip for his apology. Bridge, we now have someone else to pray for in Rome. I regret not asking him his name."

Benson got up and went to his pack and brought out a sewing kit fom the bag which held his tapestry. He carefully turned his cassock inside out and started to pin together the tear in the sleeve. He was soon working away on the repair. Sebastian relit his cigar. The excitement seemed to have relaxed him. Perhaps the fact that he had finished his letter also helped. When he had finished his cigar he got a professional plumbing magazine out of his tote bag. He seemed to be studying a lot of complicated-looking diagrams.

I went back to my journal. I wondered if I should ask Benson about any points that I could not recall. But everything seemed amazingly clear so I really had no need. In any case I was not sure he would would want to be quizzed. It was a companionable silence, as though all three of us had known each other for years and did not need to make conversation.

A ticket inspector came to check our tickets. He apologised for the rowdiness of the football team. It was typical of teams from Paris, he said. There was never any trouble when the Amiens team went to play away.

The rest of the journey passed without incident. At one point Benson got out his breviary and said compline, but he did not seek to involve Sebastian and me. His repair of his cassock was so neat that you could hardly see where it had been torn. From a distance the only sign now of what had happened was the damp stain. Both Sebastain and I expressed our admiration at his invisible mending skills. He looked very pleased.

When the tannoy announced that we would be soon arriving in Paris I remember that Sebastian asked Benson about churches in Paris. He wondered whether there was one near where he would be staying with his mate. He had told Frances he would light a candle. Benson again got out his map of Paris. He said that St Germain-des-Prés was probably the nearest to the address where he had said his mate was staying. Benson remarked that he had it in mind to take me there too, since it was near where we both were to be.

I noted that it was 10.45 pm when we arrived at the Gare du Nord. We assembled all our luggage in the corridor. Then Benson went back and checked our compartment meticulously. It seemed to me as if he wanted to ensure that there would be no lasting trace of us.

At the exit barrier at the end of the platform Sebastian's friend was there to greet him. He was of the same height and build as Sebastian but with very short blonde hair. He also was wearing khaki canvas trousers, a black tee shirt and black leather jacket. And he had one gold earing in his left ear. It was as though both had settled on a common style.

"'Ow are yer mate?" the friend said, grasping Sebastian's right hand firmly. He took the suitcase on wheels from Sebastian and began to lift it.

"That's me weights, so use the wheels," Sebastian said. Then, turning to us, Sebastian made the introductions.

"I met these two guys on the trip. Father Benson, this is me mate, Gerry. We used to play in the same football team in Tonbridge. And this is Bernard, Gerry. We've 'ad a few adventures on the way that I'll tell yer about later."

"How's Fran?" said Gerry. 'You said you'd 'ad a domestic."

"I've got a letter to post to 'er. It's another story for later."

Benson said he had seen a letter box on the concourse. He took the letter to Frances from Sebastian, and then fished out several letters of his own from his pocket, and went off to post them.

"Where you guys staying?" said Gerry.

"Not far from where you is," said Sebastian. "I've seen where yer place is on a map of Paris Father showed me."

"Would yer like a lift?" Gerry said to me. "I struck lucky. Got parkin' near the Station. I've only a small car. But I reckon us four could just fit in with all yer clobber. Because yer oversized, Seb, you may 'ave to go on the roof with yer weight-lifting gear." He and Sebastian laughed.

When Benson returned I explained that Gerry had offered us a lift. He gladly agreed we should accept, adding:

"You could drop us both at the Hôtel des Marronniers in the rue Jacob. I can easily walk from there to where I'm staying. I can give you directions to rue Jacob, Gerry, once you've crossed the Seine."

It was a tight squeeze but we all got somehow into Gerry's small Citroen. Benson and I were in the back seat, nursing our packs and Benson's staff, so that Sebastian would have more leg room in front. His tote bag and weight lifting case filled most of the boot.

"I 'ope yer weight-lifting stuff don't do me suspension," said Gerry wryly.

It was a fine night in Paris, and rather warmer than Kent. It was a few years since Angela and I had been here on holiday, although I occasionally came for a day on Civil Service business. But I usually saw nothing but the inside of offices.

Benson concentrated on his map which he had rested against the pack on his knee. Gerry was a careful driver and since his apartment was in the same part of Paris where we were to stay it was comparatively easy for Benson to navigate. Gerry and Sebastian talked English club football in the front. I was feeling quite tired, but still got some excitement from the lights of Paris, and from recognizing some of the sights.

Gerry managed to find parking outside the Hôtel des Marronniers. The two young men insisted on carrying our packs into the Hotel lobby for us. We said our farewells there.

Sebastian thanked Benson for all that he had done. He seemed to be on the point of saying something more than just his thanks, but I suspected that Gerry's presence inhibited him. He then turned to me and thanked me for all my help with the letter. I said I hoped it would do the trick. We all then shook hands and the two tall young men went towards the hotel door. But before he went out Sebastian turned and said:

"Perhaps I'll see yer round sometime, in Paris or back 'ome. Yer never know." Then he and Gerry were gone.

Benson waited while I filled in the formalities at the hotel desk. A middle-aged woman was on duty. I completed the hotel form for a resident and she carefully took down my passport details, then gave me a key to a room on the fifth floor. She apologised that there was no lift. Benson's last words to me were:

"If we are to keep to our Rule we should have breakfast together at 7.45 am. There is a Low Mass at 6.30 am where I'm staying. I shall come to you here in time for breakfast. Perhaps you would be kind enough to arrange with the hotel to allow me to join you for this. I believe it may be too cold to have it outside in the hotel's courtyard."

He then bowed to me in the rather formal manner he

had used when we first met, and said good night. Nor did he omit to walk over and wish the lady behind the desk good-night too.

When he had gone, the receptionist said that there would be no problem about Benson joining me for breakfast. She apologised that there was no porter at this time of night. So I humped my pack up the flights of stairs to the fifth floor.

My room was small. There was a double bed, desk and chair, and a wardrobe. It was all in the traditional dark wood of so many small French hotels. I went to the window. There was a fine view of the the rooftops of buildings nearby, and the street lights below. It was very quiet. There was a miniscule ensuite bathroom with a set of spotless white towels.

I tried the bed. It was thankfully firm. As I expected there was a bolster but no pillow. The bedside light worked; above the bed a small wooden crucifix, of traditional style in dark wood. The only picture was a small print of our Lady and the Child Jesus. I thought it might be a Raphael.

I did only mimimal unpacking since I was only staying one night. I found my pyjamas and toileteries quickly in my rucksack. My suit for the European meeting in Rome might benefit from being hung up. I put it on a hanger that I found in the wardrobe.

I located my new rosary and placed it carefully on a small bedside table next to my bed. I also found Benson's card for the Angelus. My notebooks of my encounter with Benson, and of our pilgrimage so far, I put on the desk with the Digby volume, the Catechism and my Bible. I was tired but not sleepy. Too much excitement and stimulation!

Benson had said that we were to discuss the Petrine texts in the New Testament. These I understood indicated St Peter's key role among the disciples during our Lord's life, and after the Resurrection. If our Lord really intended to found a church—and from my conversation earlier with Benson it now seemed likely that He did,—it might be useful to do some homework before our further conversation. I needed to understand the logic that made for continuity between St Peter, a fisherman in Galilee who was one of our Lord's disciples, and the succession of popes in Rome, who Roman Catholics claimed were infallible when they formally pronounced on matters of faith and morals.

I took up my Bible and turned to the New Testament. I decided to skim through the Gospels and Acts of the Apostles to see what I could find that might have some bearing on the matter. St Matthew, right at the beginning of the New Testament, seemed the obvious place to start.

I sat down at the desk. I treated the sacred text as if it were a Ministerial background brief which I had to get to grips with at short notice. My offical work often involved picking up salient points of a report for an oral briefing of a Government Minister who was on his way, at short notice , to answer questions in the House of Commons.

I noted that St Matthew's first four chapters were concerned with the genealogy and birth of our Lord, and of his relationship with St John the Baptist, and then of our Lord's temptation in the wilderness. The last seven chapters covered his entry into Jerusalem on Palm Sunday, his trial, crucifixion, resurrection and commissioning of the disciples. I decided that little of this looked promising territory.

The calling of the disciples was at the end of Chapter Four but I saw that our Lord did not then give Peter any special commission. Chapters on our Lord's teaching and miracles, a visit to his home town, and the disputes with the scribes and Pharisees followed. I concluded that any personal instructions to St Peter were likely to come between Chapters 16 and 21, and began my close reading at the beginning of Chapter 16.

I was much delighted when I very quickly found something that seemed important in Verses 18 and 19. In St Matthew's record St Peter has just answered a question that our Lord has put to His disciples, enquiring who they thought He was. St Peter takes the lead and confesses for the first time that Jesus is the Christ and Son of the Living God. I put in my notebook the two verses which followed:

'And I say also unto thee, That thou art Peter, and upon this rock I will build my church; and the gates of hell shall not prevail against it.

And I will give unto thee the keys of the kingdom of heaven: and whatsoever thou shalt bind on earth shall be bound in heaven: and whatsoever thou shall loose on earth shall be loosed in heaven.'

Of course I must have heard the passage read many times, but I had not really thought about its significance. Two things came to me. The words were recorded by St Matthew. He was one of the first disciples. He would have actually heard what our Lord said. St Matthew seems to be making clear that Peter was somehow selected by Jesus from among them for special authority. This wasn't apparently a role being given to all the disciples. St Matthew, as a well-educated tax-collector, perhaps the best educated of the group, might have been, in worldly terms someone whom our Lord might have wanted to lead the disciples. But St Matthew makes clear that this was not what our Lord intended. Perhaps our Lord foreshadowed St Peter's special status when he called him Peter, the Rock, when they first met. But it was only at this later point that our Lord explained what this would mean in practice.

And the commission was not just an earthly one, to be a leader of the disciples. It was to be a spiritual one as well. For St Peter's decisions, in terms of binding and loosing, whatever that might involve, extended not just to the earthly sphere, but would be effectively ratified in heaven. As I reflected on this, it now seemed an incredibly important commision. Why had I never thought seriously about it before?

I flipped through the other chapters of St Matthew but found nothing more. I now turned to St Mark. I was pleased that it was a comparatively short gospel. I wondered whether there would be anything there at all. St Mark was a later follower, and not a disciple. He was linked with St Paul, but tradition had it that he was also later a part of St

Peter's entourage. I wondered whether St Peter himself would have felt the need to highlight to a young follower a commission of this kind. Mightn't it have seemed arrogant if St Peter had talked about this himself? And not consistent with being a servant of others, as our Lord had stressed? I imagined that St Peter's key role might just be something well understood, but which would not need to be written down by St Mark. Anyway I found no special commission to St Peter mentioned in St Mark's account. The final verse of St Mark's Gospel simply speaks of all the disciples going forth to preach everywhere, after having been commissioned by the Risen Lord following His Resurrection.

I was tiring now, but I felt I should finish off the matter before I saw Benson again in the morning. St Luke's Gospel was longer, and he also wrote the Acts of the Apostles. Again he was a companion of St Paul, and probably never knew our Lord in person.

I have often scoffed at evangelical Christians who seek divine guidance from *The Bible* by simply opening it and reading whatever words their eyes first alight on when the page falls open. But being very weary I did just that with St Luke. My eyes alighted immediately on some verses in the middle of Chapter 22. Our Lord is speaking to Simon Peter and He says:

> '...Satan hath desired to have you, that he may sift you as wheat: But I have prayed for thee, that thy faith fail not: and when thou art converted strengthen thy brethren.'

Surely this too was giving St Peter a leadership role, in particular in regard to the faith of the other disciples? I read on. Immediately St Peter goes on to declare to our Lord that he would being willing to follow him to prison and death. Yet our Lord then prophesies St Peter's threefold betrayal of Himself before the cock crows.

Taken as a whole all this seemed to indicate that our Lord intended that St Peter should have a role in keeping the other disciples on the right path. He conferred this on him, despite His foreknowledge that St Peter, notwithstanding his bravado, would prove himself to be all too human. Did not our Lord's words mean that leadership was important in the Church, but that there would be human failings in that leadership too?

I was pleased with my homework. I decided to keep it open at the passage from St Luke so as to look at it again in the morning. But as I laid it on my bedside table it fell open instead at the last Chapter of St John's Gospel.

I was unable to stop myself from glancing at it. It told of the final encounter of our Lord after His Resurrection with His disciples by the sea of Tiberias. There they had made a miraculous catch of fish, and then encountered Jesus on the shore where He had made breakfast for them. Again it was St Peter who received attention. As if to cancel his threefold betrayal of our Lord at His trial St Peter was asked three times by our Lord whether he loved Him. When he protested his love three times, our Lord gave him the threefold commission: to feed his lambs and sheep.

Surely feeding the sheep must mean passing on the faith to others. And the food would have to be healthy and nourishing. This surely must mean that Peter was to pass it on to his flock, that is the Church, whole and intact. Was Benson a part of this process for me?

I deliberately suppressed a temptation to think any more about all that had happened during this extraordinary day. I had done my best to record this in my journal. I got into my pyjamas and went and cleaned my teeth.

Back on my bed I picked up my rosary. I was very tired. As it was Wednesday, just the Glorious Mysteries. Only one decade perhaps: the first one, the Resurrection, since I seemed to be having some kind of spiritual awakening. I offered the decade for Angela, Mama and our children, and for my poor dead mother and father.

Then I fell asleep.

CHAPTER ELEVEN

DELIVER US FROM EVIL

WHEN I awoke I looked at my watch. It was 6.15 am. I was unable to recall any dreams. Given the events of yesterday that seemed rather surprising.

I remember saying to myself: "I'm really in Paris." I went to the window and pulled back the curtains. It was still quite dark. There were lights on in some of the windows opposite and in the street below. The Benson rule was that we should pray at 6.30 am. Rather self-consciously I said aloud very quietly: "Blessed Lord, I will be properly in touch in quarter of an hour so if you don't mind I'll just reflect a little about yesterday and the day ahead first."

Some of the events of yesterday were clearly carefully planned by Benson: Benediction at Ightham Mote and the kites at Shipbourne. But the two ladies on the bus, the meeting with Sebastian, and the incident with the football team seemed to be surprises to Benson as well. They could not really have been planned by him surely? Did he plan his own first appearence to me, or was that something that he just found himself a part of? I decided that it would probably be unwise to speculate further at this stage. My principle fear remained that I would do something which might cause the pilgrimage to falter prematurely, or end abruptly without a meaningful conclusion. But I was reluctant to speculate on what a meaningful conclusion might be.

Benson had mentioned that our short stay in Paris would be a chance to think about the saints. If I was honest—and it was perhaps time for me to start being so— I was not sure of the utility for us moderns of the intercession of the saints. Who could be more important than the three persons of the Blessed Trinity? Surely Scripture encourages us, I reasoned, to establish a direct connection with God in his three persons. There was no mention as far as I could recall of the need for a saint as intercessor.

I could see how the idea of asking a saint's help might have some appeal in a hierarchical medieval society. At that time you might well often want to have a friend to make representations on your behalf to an important person, a friend at court so to speak.

Yet it did seem clear from the history of the Church that the saints had been invoked throughout the ages and much of this invocation, a least where it had been reported, seemed to have been beneficial. And hadn't I already started tentatively down this road by addressing a few brief words to our Lady as the Mother of God? Of course she was rather a special case as she was so close to her Son. But some of His disciples who are regarded as saints were close to Him on earth too. Later saints only knew Him by faith.

Perhaps the right course for an ordinary fellow like me was just to be pragmatic (very British!) and see what the result of an approach to different saints might be. There could be no harm in that.

It was now 6.30 am and time for me to make an effort to pray. Perhaps my religion so far, and my interest in it, had been just having a hobby that I shared with friends. These included those whom I saw at my church, or with whom I discussed religious matters. Although corporate worship and evangelisation were a part of what we were enjoined to do I was beginning to suspect that there was something that I had been largely missing—what you did when you were completely by yourself, or rather were alone with God.

Some of our Lord's words came to me just then: 'But when thou prayest, enter into thy closet, and when thou hast shut the door, pray to thy Father which is in secret…'

The Lord's Prayer seemed the logical place to start. I knelt down by my bed and rested my arms on it. I said the prayer slowly, trying to focus on the words as though they were new to me. Three aspects came into focus. The prayer reminds us that God is in heaven. But what really did heaven mean to me? How significant was the prospect of heaven and eternal life, and the possibility of a meeting with God in the Blessed Trinity, or in one of His three persons? If I was honest as I ought to be, I did not really think of this very often. With regard to my neighbour, I did not feel that I was particularly prone to acting against my neighbour or resenting him. On the other hand I knew that I had never made a proper examination of conscience. Perhaps I was just complacent. I was not somebody who went out of his way to look for ways of doing good to others. Was I just one of the luke-warm, condemned as I remember in some passage of the Bible?

What about the petition about not being led into temptation? I was not sure that I really wanted this. I had to admit that I quite liked the prospect of temptation. Nor did I mind over much that sometimes I might be unable to resist temptation in its different forms. Was this indelibly staining? Would our Lady, as another human being, although without sin as I recalled the Catholic Church taught, help me gain a real desire to resist temptation? Or was I just like St Augustine who prayed to be made chaste, but not yet?

After the Lord's Prayer I said the Hail Mary. This quite appealed to me as a practical thing to do. I added a few brief words to her. I wondered if I would be granted any response as seemed to have happened when the words, 'Launch out into the deep' came into my mind while I was on the train. At that time in the morning there seemed to be nothing.

I decided to make a big effort to pray about each member of my family, close friends, colleagues at work and the people that I had already met on the pilgimage. I did my best to bring each one to mind in turn, and promised myself that I would make a list of names for future prayer sessions, so that no one would be left out, especially any that had asked me for prayers. I ended with a brief prayer on my own behalf, trying to present myself to our Lord, and our Lady, and to ask for the support of my guardian angel.

When I had finished this rather messy attempt at prayer I got up and went and found in my backpack my copy of Benson's card with the words of the Angelus on it. Then, sitting on my bed I slowly recited the Latin version, trying to bring to mind some picture of the events in the life of our Lord and our Lady that they portray. I was quite pleased with my church Latin pronunciation. I looked at my watch. It was a little after 7 am. I had followed Benson's counsel and said the Angelus at about the time he had suggested.

He had also mentioned Prime and Lauds, the monastic hours, but as I did not have any texts for these I told myself that I had no choice but to omit them. Perhaps I should ask Benson for the texts so that I could tackle them on the train the following morning when we would be, I thought with some emotion, in Italy.

"Italy", I repeated to myself. And I was taken straight back to a performance years before of Berlioz's opera, *Les Troyens*. 'Italy' was the commanding word that the god repeatedly intoned when summoning Aeneas from Carthage, and the embrace of Queen Dido. He was being summoned to his destiny in Rome. Then my mind flitted on to the conclusion of Browning's poem 'De Gustibus', where the poet proclaims exultantly:

> Open my heart and you will see
> graved inside of it, Italy.

Rather ungratefully I then thought to myself: Why is Benson having us waste the whole of a precious day of pilgrimage in Paris when we could be spending more time in Rome?

I went into the bathroom to shave. I put my shaving soap in Ruby's charming little scallop shell. From my window it looked like a promising morning. This was enough to make me repent of my momentary childish attitude and focus on getting dressed and ready for breakfast. To save time I repacked my rucksack, remembering to take my suit from the wardrobe. I would clear my room after breakfast and leave my luggage down at the hotel lobby. A small bag was all I needed for today.

Benson was already in the dining room when I got down there just before 7.45 am. He told me that he had already settled my hotel bill and paid for his own breakfast. He had brought his luggage with him, and the receptionist had agreed to keep his with mine during the day. We would return to collect everything before we set out for the Gare de Lyon.

As he took up a warm croissant from the basket on the table Benson launched immediately into the Petrine claims.

"You know the key texts which we Catholics believe support the Petrine claims."

I smiled. "Although I was very tired I managed to look out some last night before going to sleep."

"Wonderful!" Benson grinned. "I hope you are now able to see that the Gospel writers were clear that our Lord had given a special commission to Peter—that of binding and loosing in regard to His church—even though all the disciples were sent out to spread the Gospel. Peter took the lead by preaching at the first Pentecost. As we see from Acts it was also Peter who laid down to the circumcized Jewish followers of our Lord that some of the basic Jewish observances need not be followed by the new converts. This was later ratified by the First Council of the Church at Jerusalem."

"But if Peter had this special Petrine commission," I asked, "why did St Paul withstand him to his face at Antioch when St Peter seemed to avoid eating with the uncircumsized converts in case he might upset the Jewish converts."

"A splendid point from the Epistle of St Paul to the Galatians. It brings two significant matters together. The first is that St Paul, after fourteen years of his apostleship, felt the need to have an important meeting with St Peter when the first of the apostles was on a visitation to the Christians at Antioch.

"There was no doctrinal issue between the two saints. Both he and St Peter agreed that most aspects of the Jewish law and customs need not be adopted by the new pagan converts. That had already been settled by the first Church Council. The only question between them was the tactical one of eating with the pagan converts. We only have St Paul's version of this disagreement, so we do not know if St Peter simply preferred to eat with his Jewish friends there, and that the pagans and St Paul took this to be a social slight to the pagan converts.

"But even if St Paul was right, and St Peter was acting in an over-cautious way which we with hindsight might now find questionable, the Galatian extract helps us understand another point. St Peter,—and his papal successors, and we will come on to this later—was given the power to act where necessary on doctrinal issues. This is the binding and loosing, where the matter is essential for the preservation of the deposit of faith. Yet it is quite possible, that St Peter, being human, may well have acted at times in a way which we may question or even disapprove of.

"In the case in question it may have been a matter of deciding whether the virtue to practice at this point was fortitude or prudence. The subsequent history of the Papacy and St Peter's successors as popes makes these kinds of human choices and failings very clear. Popes are not infallible human beings. But the Church's view has always been that the leader of the Apostles and his successors, the popes, although they use ordinary human reason as a gift from God in considering issues, make decisions on specific questions of doctrine where this is necessary, and their decisions are providentially correct because of the guidance of the Holy Spirit."

" I can follow this, I think," I said, "and I can see that our Lord's commission to Peter is clear from the passages I have read in Scripture. But how can we be sure that the power was *transferable* to his successors as bishops of Rome? Some other bishoprics such as Jerusalem, Antioch and Alexandria seem arguably to have greater importance and hence perhaps precedence as they were founded earlier."

"The first question is still whether God would have left his Church without some means of preserving our Lord's teaching intact. If you admit this, the matter resolves itself into whether any of the other newly founded churches at Jerusalem, Antioch or Alexandria ever claimed to be the arbiter on important questions of doctrine.

"I think you will not find evidence of this. Of course the

bishops of the early churches often disagreed about all sorts of matters, political, and administrative, where pride and human weaknesses could always rear their heads. Yet from very early on it was the Church at Rome which was consulted when there was a need for a ruling on doctrinal issues. Of course, as Cardinal Newman argues in *The Development of Christian Doctrine*, while Christians were of one heart and soul in the early days of the Church, and the teachings of our Lord were known to many still living, there seems to have been few issues to clarify. But later, when the Church was thrown on to its own resources after the end of the apostolic age, local issues of principle were decided by bishops. And when these became contentious in several parts of the Christian world at once this resulted in a need for ecumenical councils and for consulting popes as the true successors of St Peter.

" It is only when disputes arise that the teaching needs clarifying. Thus we have no formal acknowledgment of papal supremacy in the second century, and no cristalization of the doctrine of the Holy Trinity until the fourth century. As in the law, issues are sometimes not clarified until they come to court, so it is with doctrinal issues. The Church only makes a ruling when it needs to, where disagreements are making difficulties for the faithful."

I decided to raise another issue that had previously bothered me.

"Many people outside the Church, and even some, I understand, within, confess to finding the doctrine of papal infallibility, which was after all only proclaimed by the Vatican Council in 1870, hard to swallow."

"I think you need to remember that the Church has a number of sources of infallibility: these are the recognised General Councils of the Church, the unanimous consent of the Church Fathers, the ordinary Magisterium of the Church as it has operated down the ages, and *ex cathedra* definitions of faith and morals made by the Pope.

"In fact, there are very few subjects on which it would be

possible for the Pope to make an infallible decision which had not already been covered by infallible pronouncements through the other routes. That is why such definitions by the Pope are so rare. However, the Vatican Council decided in 1870 that it was important at that point in history to assert the principle, which had in fact received some kind of general acceptance down the ages. The Vatican decree was not intended to create a new practice, and has not done so. At the same time it is an important element in the Church's means of preserving the deposit of Faith, and it clearly flows from our Lord's injunction to Peter to confirm his brethren in the Faith."

I had gone on with my breakfast while Benson was making this argument. He now paused to drink his coffee, which I thought must be cold by now. I took out my notebook and jotted down a few points so that I would be better able to recall what he had been saying.

He smiled winningly. "I expect as a Civil Servant you are able to record the drift of my points. None of them I hope is original—it is important for priests to avoid ss…singularity in theological matters—. As you will see I do not always follow this principle in other matters!"

I could not but smile at this myself, remembering some aspects of his behaviour that he had already exhibited.

Benson continued. "If you would like me to look over your notes could you let me have them this evening? We will have too much on our plates today, as well as keeping to our Rule. It has probably been a rather indigestible breakfast. Not the food, which is of course just right! Yet while a good understanding of the Petrine claims is absolutely vital, it can make for a heavy breakfast!"

I scribbled down a few final words, concluding with the contrast Benson drew between the assertion of the principle of papal infallibility, and the comparative rarity in practice of its use by the popes since it was defined as a dogma.

"And now for the Communion of saints," he said wiping his chin with his napkin. "Once you have completed your toilet, put together what you may want during our day in

Paris, and deposited what is not needed at reception, we can begin to make use of our legs again.

"I shall write some postcards while I wait for you. I plan to suggest to Gregory, our young altar server at Benediction, that he seek out Mr Hilaire Belloc's book, *The Path to Rome*. Gregory tells me he has some aspiration to the sacred ministry. The combination of physical, intellectual and spiritual adventure might appeal to him. When I was his age, I enjoyed being argumentative like Belloc."

When I came down from my room and had deposited my luggage I found that Benson was waiting for me outside the hotel enjoying the morning sunshine. Without saying where we were going he bade me follow him and he set of at a brisk pace along the rue Jacob.

A few minutes later we came to the Church of Saint-Germain-des-Prés. I was also able to see the Café des Deux Magots. I know the Café de Flore was next door to this. I remembered how French intellectuals had gathered here before the war. During the German occupation Sartre and Simone de Beauvoir had almost lived at the Café de Flore, where they were able to write, hardly abandoning it even during air raids.

Would their existentialism, that had made such an appeal to people like me when young, now receive more than a brief footnote in philosophical and literary history? As for their politics, this had led them to support the tyranny of Stalin's Soviet Union. Did its uncompromising brutality and self-assurance appeal to their intellectual authoritarianism? Benson was likely to know nothing of this recent history, nor was it likely to interest him.

As we stood outside the main entrance on the west front beneath the tower, Benson turned and said: "I don't intend to act as a tourist guide for our visit to this church. But I will say a few words before we go in. I am not sure how much you know of the background. It is one of the oldest church foundations in Paris. The Frankish king Childebert put up a church here in the sixth century to house a piece of the true cross, and the tunic of St Vincent of Saragossa of Spain. A large part of the building you now see, including the bell tower, dates from the twelfth century, when it was the church of a Benedictine Abbey. The monks' land and buildings extended over many acres as far as your rue Jacob.

"There were the usual cloisters, dormitories, refectory, stables, outbuildings, gardens, and a magnificent library. The whole area was walled and fortified. The abbey's great intellectual period was from the early 17th century up to the French Revolution. The monks of the Maurist reform achieved an international reputation for intellectual endeavour. There was one enduring masterpiece, *The Literary History of France*.

"At the French revolution more than 300 priests and monks of the abbey were martyred. The library was confiscated, the twin towers of the transept demolished, and the church was turned into a salt-petre store for gun-powder. Not surprisingly an explosion a few years later destroyed much of the church's interior that the revolutionaries had not previously vandalised. As you will know, the Catholic Church became legal again during the reign of Napoleon. After the restoration of the Bourbons, a great period of rebuilding of the church commenced in 1822. This continued throughout much of the 19th century. You will see this in the interior of the church which I suggest we now enter."

I followed him in. He genuflected in the direction of the high altar and then, locating a stoup of holy water, made the sign of the cross. He turned around to me as if to speak but simply sought my hand and touched it lightly with the moist finger which he had dipped into the stoup. Rather self-consciously I made a version of the sign of the cross and bowed in the direction of the altar.

He motioned to me to follow him and we walked up the central aisle. There appeared to be no service. I saw no priest or servers at the main altar. But a good sprinkling of people were scattered about the the church either sitting or kneeling. Benson went beyond the nave into the apse where there was some more seating. Here at the very front before the main altar was a group of about thirty young people. They seemed to be having some sort of communal act of worship of their own. They looked like university students, a mixture of young men and girls, mostly in jeans and pullovers. We sat down in the very back row of the seating in the apse. Benson had left a large gap between us and the young people. He whispered to me as I sat down beside him:

"One of the young men is leading them in some kind of version of the morning office. It's an opportunity for us to have some quiet recollection ourselves. I do not think we should walk about and become a distraction. It might be a chance for you to think about your relations with your son."

Benson's abrupt personal suggestion caught me quite off balance. I had hardly mentioned Cyprian since I had met Benson. My boy was away at boarding-school, and it was, I had to confess, a little disquieting that I could not remember thinking much about him since I had left to go on this pilgrimage. Had Benson somehow divined this? Was it right for him to put this to me in this way? I wanted to say something to Benson—I was not sure what, perhaps something defensive—but he was already kneeling at my side.

Of course, I would send Cyprian a post card from Rome. He was interested in ancient history: a card of the Roman forum would be just the thing. He seemed to be getting on in Latin, but I was not sure that he was enjoying Greek. I knew he was playing quite a bit of sport. Angela had said that we should go and watch him play soccer after half term. I ought to have a meeting with his housemaster sometime to see how the land lay there, and I could probably combine this with a match if I did some telephoning about dates on my return.

But what was Benson driving at? I looked across at him. He was still absorbed in prayer. The young man was still leading the young people in their office. I could not really follow their Latin.

I had not really looked around the church since we had come in. Around the apse there were a number of side chapels dedicated to various saints as you find in many large

Roman Catholic churches. To my left I had a slightly obscured view of one chapel through the wrought iron screen which surrounded the main liturgical space of the apse.

For some reason my eyes focussed on this chapel. I was able to have a sight of someone standing at one of these side altars. The light was good enough and the angle just right for me to see that it was a tall broad-shouldered man with short dark curly hair. I saw him kneel. I knew it was Sebastian.

I gripped Benson's arm excitedly.

"I believe that's Sebastian." I pointed to the figure praying in the chapel.

Benson roused himself slowly from his prayers and looked across to where I was pointing.

"You may well be right," he said after a long pause. "His lodgings are close by."

"Shall I go and check that it is him and have a word?" I asked eagerly.

"I do not think it would be wise to do that at the moment. For him to be in touch with the Blessed Trinity, our Lady, St Joseph and the saints is more important now than anything we can do. The baton has passed from us."

I felt this gentle rebuke keenly. But Benson softened it.

"Once he has completed his prayers—and I am so glad that he is at the chapel of St Joseph—we might see if we can catch him for a second or two. I've written him a short note suggesting someone whom he and his lady might go to in preparation for their marriage. I could let him have it here rather than posting it and save the stamp. We might visit that altar ourselves a little later."

He went back to his devotions. After a few minutes I noticed that the young people's service had drawn to a close. Benson looked up too. Then, without saying anything to me, he rose and went forward. It was clear that he was going to say something.

A few seconds later he was talking earnestly to the young man who had been leading the service. This stocky dark-haired young man was nodding as if in agreement. He then seemed to be telling Benson a long story, getting more and more animated as he spoke. Benson was then presented by him to a young girl, and later to another young man.

The four of them now seemed to be enjoying a joke. Benson was using a lot of gestures. It was clear that they were speaking French. But I could not catch any words until the end when they all seemed to be saying to each other *à bientôt*. A further meeting seemed to be envisaged.

When Benson returned he said:

"I had hoped we might meet up with some French young people to bring us up to date about the state of the Church in France. As so often happens Providence is looking after us in the matter. We are to meet the three I have just become acquainted with for a picnic lunch later. They told me that among their group this morning there were quite a few who were to be baptised as adults here at the Easter Vigil. All these catechumens are children of unbelievers. The young leader explained that their group was under the influence of the writings of Charles Péguy, the French writer responsible for reviving the pilgrimage from Paris to Chartres before the European War. They are part of a wider group planning another revival of the pilgrimage walk to Chartres later this year. This morning's service was a preparation for this, and to support the young people to be baptised at Easter."

"Will we be able to fit this picnic in?" I said. "You said that we had quite a full programme." I suspect that I sounded a little peeved because the focus seemed again to be turning away from me.

"Oh you will I am sure find it useful too, and it will help me get across to you some of the things that I think you need to know. But let us first get acquainted with St Joseph."

We returned to the nave and then followed the aisle to St Joseph's side chapel. I was right. It was Sebastian. And he was still there. He was lighting several candles as we came up. He beamed across the flickering candles as he saw us, and came around and shook our hands warmly.

"I's 'opin' we might all catch up again," he said. "But I

didn't reckon I'd be that lucky. Gerry's gone off to work on 'is boss' flat so I thought I'd just drop in 'ere and light candles. After this Gerry wants me to shop and practice making a fool of meself in French!" He laughed softly, as though it might be disrespectful to make too much noise.

"I have written you a note, Sebastian, which I was going to post," said Benson. "Here it is. It's got a suggestion about who you and Frances might ask to prepare you for marriage. I think you might like him."

"Anyone you recommend, Father, is sure to be OK by us. But what's also been on me mind is yer arm? Father. How's it going? One of them candles is fer you." He pointed to the stand which had about eight candles burning.

"Bless you, Sebastian" said Benson. "Your dressing seemed so comfortable that I haven't felt the need to change it. I'm sure it's healing nicely under the strips of your handkerchiefs."

"That's a real relief, Father. I'm not Red Cross-trained, yer know." He then looked across at me and said:

"Now I'd better let you two guys get on with your pilgrimage while I try me 'and at shoppin' Frenchy-style."

He shook our hands again, then turned and walked slowly down the aisle towards the West door. Far from being dwarfed by the huge Gothic church he seemed taller than ever. We watched him go in silence. Before he left he turned again. I thought he might look back towards us but he simply genuflected towards the High Altar and disappeared. I thought to myself: I hadn't even asked Benson how his arm was.

"Let's begin where Sebastian left off, at St Joseph's altar." Benson was now facing the chapel with his earnest look.

"I wonder if you also think that the key to the welfare of the community and the nation's health is the relationship between parents and their children. That between fathers and sons is specially vital. The absence of a father creates serious difficulties, as we all know. But even where there is a father, he is often in modern societies absent at work much of the time. When he is at home, his time is mostly spent in recreation with the family. Unlike in earlier times when sons from their early years grew up watching at first hand their fathers at work in their trade or profession.

"Today a son rarely sees his father in his working conditions. His place of work is often far away. Even if it is near, a workplace is somewhere where children and young people are not usually welcome. It may also be where many fathers would not perhaps want their sons to see them. The nature of their work may not be something of which they are proud, or their position in the hierarchy may seem belittling, sometimes even humiliating.

"Such sons therefore seldom have the chance to see their fathers deal with others in some of their most significant roles: with clients, fellow workers, with people in authority, and people subordinate to them. A son therefore may never sees his father in all his strengths and weaknesses. He may well come to physical maturity without the moral maturity which seeing his father in every condition would help form. Opportunities for creating a strong and understanding bond are also reduced. Bonds formed in leisure alone are not the same in kind. When this pattern is replicated over an entire community or nation it can make social problems more likely. An important link has not been properly forged.

"Now the relationship between St Joseph and our Lord seems to have something to teach us. Our Lord grew up seeing his foster father at work as a community carpenter. We can assume that before He began His true Father's spiritual mission our Lord followed the family trade. St Luke's Gospel stresses His return to obedience to Our Lady and St Joseph after the worrying three-day absence from them in Jerusalem. You will remember that he was twelve when he was discovered by them in the temple in Jerusalem. The Gospels stress the complete reliability of St Joseph as a husband and father. We see in St Joseph a marvellous example of the cardinal virtues you will have found listed in the *Catechism of Christian Doctrine*: prudence, justice, fortitude and temperance."

"Modern life does not always make it easy for a father to bring up his son where he can absorb naturally his father's virtues while observing him at work to provide for the support of his family. Who better than St Joseph to ask for help in achieving this?

"You indicated that you were not sure about the value of prayers to the saints and seeking their intercession. We can, as you say, ask Almighty God in any of His Three Persons for *direct* help. But isn't there something appealing in seeking the help of someone who was a simple human being like us, but is now in heaven and available to assist? For St Joseph would have had to face similar problems of fatherhood that modern men have to grapple with: the exercize of authority, with its tension between giving guidance and allowing freedom; the revealing of one's weaknesses as well as one's strengths in action before his Son, yet at the same time confident in the filial and paternal bonds of love.

"I expect St Joseph may then have all sorts of advice for you in regard to your son, Cyprian, which you might find valuable at some point. If what I have said has made any impression perhaps you might like to spend a few moments with him. I shall look for somewhere suitable in this lovely church, resonant with the prayers of ages, to say my breviary."

Before I had time to respond he had gone off down the side aisle to the nave. I knelt at the *prie-dieu* where Sebastian had been. Had St Joseph given him advice about Damien and Hannah? Goodness me, the situation in regard to Cyprian and me was surely very different!

Was Benson implying that I had been neglecting Cyprian? I was paying enough for his school fees! The school had a splendid reputation and seemed to turn out fine lads. Many got into the best universities. If he applied himself Cyprian should manage this too. He had been confirmed in the Church of England. The school had seen to that. In my occasional letters I had suggested to him some books he might find interesting and profitable. All of us had been on some good family holidays together, which he seemd to enjoy.

I looked up at the statue of St Joseph. Then I murmured: "St Joseph. It's me, Bernard, here. Sorry to be a bother. As you may know I've already had a word with the one who was your spouse here on earth (Was this a proper way of referring to our Lady?) What do you yourself have to say about Cyprian and me. Have I been neglectful? Am I too self-centred? I'm sure you know all the facts. What would you do if you were me?"

I wished I knew some formal prayer to St Joseph like the Hail Mary. It would help fill in the gaps while I waited. I studied the decor of the chapel. To my surprise there was no statue of St Joseph. But the stained glass window depicted a man holding a baby boy whom I took to be St Joseph.

I waited. Nothing came into my mind. Oh well, I musn't be impatient. At least I've made a start. I lit a candle for Cyprian, and then another for Perpetua, and then one each for Angela and her mother.

While I was considering whether to light two more for my deceased parents Benson returned. I assumed that he came to check how I had got on with St Joseph. But he did not say a word. He simply beckoned me to follow him. After a few yards he stopped at what was a large chapel dedicated to St Francis Xavier. On the wall on the north side of this there was also a mausoleum.

I read an inscription which said that it contained the heart of John Casimir Vasa, former King of Poland. He later seems to have become some kind of Abbot here in the 17th century when St Germain was a monastery .

Benson said that he wanted to focus my attention on St Francis Xavier. However, when he saw that my eyes had been drawn to the mausoleum, he said we should spend a moment on rhis Polish king.

He described the king as a kind of political, military, artistic and religious dilettante. A Vasa ancestor had been King of Sweden and the family still maintained their claims. As a young man he had had some initial success as a military leader in a war with Russia. Later, before he was elected King, he had tried his vocation as a Jesuit. He was even made a cardinal, but found himself unsuited to ecclesiastical life. He resigned to seek election to the Polish throne in succession to his nephew.

"After his election as king he became an important patron of art. But wars with Sweden and Russia dominated his reign which Poland lost. In 1648 he abdicated. As he had no heirs, the kingship passed from his family. He then came on to Paris to resume his vocation as a Jesuit, which he seems to have been able to combine with the office of Abbot of St Germain. How much day to day authority he exercised here in the abbey is unclear. But the monks seem to have wanted to keep a memorial of him, and when his body was returned to Poland for burial they retained his heart for this mausoleum in their Abbey church."

I commented that the struggle between family duty, with its resulting dynastic claims and pressures, and some kind of religious vocation, must have been difficult to resolve.

"I have no prejudice against absolute monarchy as a form of government. If a monarch is imbued with the virtues, his rule can produce political stability. And if he is intelligent and has a sense of vision, he or she is sometimes able to devise imaginative projects for the welfare of his people, that other forms of government sometimes find more difficult to achieve.

"Democracy, in which the population has a say at election time, tends to produce governments that are pragmatic, but often without vision. In times of crisis democratic elections may also give power to demogogues who can successfully appeal to the electorate's emotions. There is no guarantee that such leaders will be imbued with the virtues. Many in the past have not.

"St Francis Xavier," Benson continued, "like King John Casimir, was also a Jesuit, indeed one of the seven founding members of that great company. He never had the family responsibility of kingly rule, but, being of an aristocratic Basque family, there would have been pressures to take up a calling appropriate to his family's position. Instead, after studying at the University of Paris here, he met a fellow student, another Basque, St Ignatius Loyala. St Ignatius had given up his calling as a soldier after a conversion experience, and decided to be a missionary to convert Muslims. But he realized that he first needed to study so as to be able to argue Christianity's case. Francis Xavier recognized in his friend Ignatius the same longing to bring souls to our Lord. After all, Bridge, that is what we are all commissioned to do by our Lord at the end of St Matthew's Gospel."

Benson thrust out his chin as I noticed that he did when he wanted to emphasise a point.

"Now St Francis was probably the most important missionary of the Faith since St Paul. The young company of ten at first considered their vocation to be to restore the Muslim world to Christianity. You will know that Islam is nothing other than a kind of Christian heresy. Intellectual ly it became stunted within the confines of the Old Testament. It never blossomed with the vigour of the Gospel of love in the New Testament. A key aspect is a rejection of the Trinity with its affirmation that one of the three persons, our Lord Jesus Christ, was not just a man, but part of the triune God. Islam combined its rejection of this historic teaching with iconoclasm—the total rejection of images of human beings and animals. This prohibition has always been a part of Judaeism, and was later a source of dispute within Christianity itself not long after the time when Islam was founded by Mohammed. It was this tragic distortion which the young band wished to combat.

"Their great missionary endeavour began when St Francis Xavier, with the rest of the company, assembled at Venice. Their plan was to go to the Holy Land to convert Muslims back to the Christian faith. But God had other ideas. War in that part of the Middle Eastern world at that time made their mission quite impractical. So they took an additional vow of loyalty to the Pope, and put themselves completely at his disposal.

"The Pope and the King of Portugal considered that a place for their missionary zeal would be Asia. Given its huge population, and growing importance economically, that seems providential. For ten extraordinary years St Francis took the Gospel to Goa, South India, Ceylon, Malacca, the Molucca Islands and the Malay peninsular. He made a promising start in Japan and was just beginning work in China when he died. You might visit his tomb in Goa.

"I have brought you here to his chapel because those wanting to take their religion seriously need to realise that we are all called to pass on the faith. You should ask his help to identify where you are to make your field of missionary endeavour. It is unlikely that as a layman and married man with children, you would be called to the mission field abroad, although life is of course full of surprises. Your opportunities are likely to be among colleagues and friends, or people you meet along the way. Yet St Francis may well help you recognise possibilities, and give you the necessary insight to become a channel of grace for others.

"I will now leave you for a short while with him. I will be sitting on the seat in the garden outside the church where I will do a little private work. Come and join me there when you are ready. There's a little unfinished business in regard to Cyprian. Undoubtedly obstacles may exist to prevent him going to your office to see you in a working context. It seems unlikely that he could shadow you at work to learn how you do things. Instead I wonder whether it might be helpful if you and he went on some journey of a few weeks so that you could really get to know and understand each other."

Without waiting for a reply he left me in the chapel. Cyprian again! Benson seems very focussed on our relationship. I began to wonder why I did not seem to resent this more. I was sure I would have done so if a friend had seemed to be interfering. Could it be something to do with my earlier attempt at prayer to St Joseph? Perhaps it *would* be a good thing to make a journey with Cyprian. But what would the rest of the family think? Anyway I needed to concentrate on the matter in hand. I knelt at the *prie-dieu* in front of St Francis' altar.

My notes here consist of a list of points explaining why any form of proselytizing for Christianity was impossible for me. I find most discussions with others of what I really believe very embarassing. Even if I could bring myself to do it, I did not have the right vocaulary. I could not bear my friends to think me 'holy' or 'pi'. Moreover, any explanation needed to be accurate. But I did not yet have a clear understanding of the Faith myself. Nor a firm idea of what I believed. Even if I had, I would be unable to put it into the kind of language that would be understood by ordinary people. I could not talk as Benson did to the two middle-aged ladies in the bus from Shipbourne to Tonbridge.

Explaining these negative thoughts to St Francis I must have remained at the *prie-dieu* for some time because my notes say that I was stiff in the joints when I finally got up and lit a candle. This one was for me!

One point received no mention in my original notes. I am certain I spent some time thinking about what it must have been like to leave family and friends back in Europe, and go off by sailing ship to the other side of the world. And there live in great poverty and simplicity preaching about our Lord, and knowing that you were committed to die in the mission. Were you, St Francis, I remember saying to him, just too out of my league to take an interest in someone so mediocre as me? The idea of discomfort and disease in a foreign land, and I knew something of Asia and its poverty, made me shudder. What a wimp I was!

Benson was on the seat outside the Church as he had promised. It was now late morning and we said the Angelus together in the sun. I was pleased with my Latin and felt quite buoyant despite my view that I would always be a most inadequate exponent of the Faith. There were a few people about on other seats but they did not seem to notice us. Some mothers had very small children playing in what seemed to be a sand pit.

Benson explained that he had agreed with the French students that we would picnic at the Parc Monceau. We would need to take the Metro. He had seen a shop near the St Germain Metro station. He would go there and buy provisions to take for our picnic. He set off immediately.

I remained on the seat and took out my copy of the Digby Memoir from my small bag. Before looking for the chapter on his time in Paris I gazed about me. The morning seemed to have turned cloudy. It was now not as warm as when we had first arrived at the church. A distinct chill was in the air.

I took out my mother-in-law's pullover from my bag and put it on. I moved to the centre of the seat and lay my bag at my feet. I was just beginning ro read about Digby's visits to Madame Swetchine's salon when two men arrived. They sat down on either side of me on the seat.

"I hope you don't mind, buddy, if we join you," said one of them in English. "This sure is the only seat where there's room for the two of us. The young mums and their kids are like an occupying army on the rest." His accent seemed American but there was something not quite right about it.

I looked from side to side at them. I guessed that they were in their late thirties. One had a shaven head; the other longer hair and a dark drooping moustache like the stars in the film, 'Butch Cassidy and the Sundance Kid.'

"Of course not," I said, trying rather unsuccessfully to conceal my irritation. "I was just filling in time with my book while my companion went to get something for lunch."

They were both wearing tightish jeans which emphasized their paunches. Their trainers looked expensive, like those of teenagers. White tee shirts and dark bomber jackets completed their outfits.

"Yeh," said the shaven head, "we noticed your buddy when we were passing the church. We haven't seen that old clerical gear for ages, have we Lou? All that stuff went out in Montreal finally in the fifties. You would never see a cassock on the streets nowadays."

"Frankie here," said the moustache, "bet me that the guy

was reading his breviary in Latin. I said, 'Lou, no priest would be doing that after Vatican II.' We've got thirty Canadian dollars on it so perhaps you can tell us who's the winner. *Was* he reading a Latin breviary?"

They both turned their round fleshy faces towards me expectantly.

"Yes, his breviary is in Latin," I said crisply. I thought of saying something about Benson's practice, but considered that this might seem inappropriately defensive.

"Wow," said Lou with the moustache." I can't believe anyone today could think that God might prefer a guy to talk to him in Latin! Perhaps your buddy also thinks that the Vulgate translation of *The Bible* is closer to what the Holy Spirit wants us to understand! More than the latest versions translated into modern languages by scholars direct from the Hebrew and Greek!"

There was a slight sneer in his voice which I did not like.

"You must excuse my buddy here," said shaven-headed Frankie. "He thinks everything in the Church needs changing. Persisting with Latin is a symptom of what he thinks is dead wrong. As we're in our street gear you may not have guessed we're both priests. We come over quite often to Paris in the spring to do research on liturgy. Our bishop back in Montreal is interested in some of the early Church liturgies before they got overloaded. The new rite for Mass we use in Quebec in French still needs to be simplified. And livened up if we're going to appeal to young people! Most of them, like us, were brought up on the French student revolt of '68, and Woodstock. There are some interesting ideas floating around here in Paris right now that we might be able to work into the Mass back home. They might give it a bit more sex appeal." He grinned at me. "And besides we like Paris in March, don't we Lou?"

I was on the point of questioning whether changes to the liturgy were really what was needed when Lou spoke across me to his friend.

"You should also tell him that we like to get away when

we can because we're pissed off with aspects of Quebec. Because of what happened three years ago. Our stupid compatriots were fooled by the British provinces and shits like Trudeau to vote down the referendum that should have given us a Free Quebec. But it didn't happen. Frankie and I were active in the *Parti Québécois*. Still are. We even have some comrades here who keep the faith."

I was beginning to feel uncomfortable and to pray that Benson would come back to rescue me, when Frankie looked at me searchingly with a sort of leer.

"What are you getting up to anyway with that priest buddy of yours?"

Trying to suppress rising anger, I blurted out: "Oh, we're on a pilgrimage to Rome?"

"We wouldn't do that, would we, Lou?" said Frankie. "The bishop of Rome is *tout à fait authoritaire* and stuck in the past. The sooner he's just a figurehead and the Church gets into the hands of a democratically-elected episcopal college the better. But I don't get why you're going there. My guess is you're not even a Catholic. Have I got this in one?"

This personal remark was so unexpected that I was quite unable to respond. Seeing that I didn't deny his assertion he pressed home, sensing that he had skewered me.

"I guess you're an Episcopalian —sorry Anglican— like most Brits. If I'm right and you are, I'd just say: 'stay where you are'. Don't get taken in by your priest buddy. He's probably got all sorts of designs on you!"

He leered. "At least you Anglicans seem to be coming round to women priests. Your theology is pretty progressive, right, not stuck in the past with out-dated dogma. We know some Anglican clerics who think like us. They have hopes that the life-style of people like us," he looked across at Lou, "is already tacitly accepted by most of their bishops. It's only a matter of time before acceptance of gay priests is official in the Anglican Church.

"In politics too, the Anglican guys we know seem mostly on the left, unlike most of ours. With the current set-up in

Rome we're light years away from all this in the Catholic Church. But if vocations dry up we can make the case for married priests. It will be the thin end of the wedge, for the other changes us guys want."

Before I could say anything, Lou chimed in:

"Frankie's right. Just stay where you are. Gee, I've suddenly an idea! Why don't you come along with us and pass up the Rome thing. We could help you get a life. We're meeting some nuns this afternoon. They're pretty hot on liturgical dancing. After that we might go off and take in a porno show. We Catholic priests need detailed knowledge of what the punters are on about when they come to us in the confessional."

He gave me a lurid wink. It was this which finally broke the spell. I got up and seized my bag.

"I'm sorry but I'm not finding this one-sided conversation to my taste so I would ask you to excuse me."

I walked away with as much dignity as I could muster, taking the gravel path through the small garden to the gate. I turned left in the direction I knew Benson had taken, and followed the footpath along the Boulevard St Germain. It took me back to a spot directly opposite that part of the garden where the three of us had been sitting.

I knew that it was intended that I should hear and understand one final remark. Lou spoke in English and not in French. His voice was projected in my direction though the little park's iron railings as I walked by.

"I bet you he'll say the rosary for us!" This comment was followed by high-pitched laughter, and what sounded like the two priests slapping their fleshy thighs.

I felt as though I had been physically assaulted. It was much worse than the incident in the train. Everything seemed unreal. I started to wonder if I would ever see Benson again. So it was with huge relief that after a few more yards I sighted him crossing the Boulevard carrying several large plastic bags.

When he reached me he had an air of blissful contentment. I blurted out all that had happened. I held nothing back, including all the insinuations about himself and the

My notes indicate that Benson replied along these lines:

"Provided the priest has been properly ordained and has faculties for celebrating Mass, you as a worshipper can rest assured that your obligation, if you are a Catholic, to hear Holy Mass every Sunday has been fulfilled if you attend a Eucharist celebrated by such a priest. If Holy Mass is conducted irreverently or appears not to be in accordance with the rubrics for the current rite then you are justified in taking this up politely with the priest after the service. Then, if not satisfied with his response, you should have recourse to the priest's bishop. But no matter how scandalous the priest's way of life may be this does not affect the validity of his celebration of Holy Mass. This has always been the Church's position. Of course, saying Mass in a state of unconfessed sin is a grave and terrible thing for the priest himself to have on his conscience. As you know from the Catechism every Catholic has a formal obligation to convert the sinner. In practice this usually means some attempt at fraternal correction of those who are going wrong, whether they be ordained clergy or lay people. But we also need to remember our Lord's injunction about getting rid of any beams in our own eye before tackling the motes in those of others."

We were arriving at Monceau Metro Station as he concluded his remarks. He looked at me sternly as he gathered up his plastic bags and said:

"I hope, as you become more confident in the Faith, and know me better, you will not hesitate to point out my failings."

As we came out of the Metro and were approaching the gate into the park with its huge elaborate dome rotunda on the right Benson turned to me and said:

"Would you be kind enough, Bridge, to buy some wine and mineral water to have with lunch? I think we will be five all told. I considered I had enough to carry with the food. I didn't want to risk a breakage in the Metro. I leave the choices to you. I will look out for our young friends and a place to picnic. I shall try to be as near as I can to the only little kiosk in the Park. Afterwards we can buy hot drinks there. As you walk about the park you may be struck, as I am, by the rather heavy handed symbolism in some of the monuments. The founder of the Park, Philippe d' Orleans, was caught up in 18th century fad for Freemasonry as so many of his class then were. As you will see the garden itself is now very much *à l'anglaise*."

He quickly disappeared through the gateway. I walked along the Boulevard de Courcelles but took some time to find a shop in a side street that would sell me a couple of bottles of cold white wine, some mineral water and plastic cups.

The clouds which had seemed to hang over the Left Bank when I had my encounter with the Canadian priests had now dispersed. It was again a fine spring day as I returned with my purchases. Inside the park I noted how popular it was at lunch time. Yet it was so spacious and well planned as not to feel crowded. The paths of fine gravel were wide and serpentine without many of the straight lines of the traditional French park or garden. The lawns were planted with speciment trees, each on its own so that it was possible to study and appreciate its individual shape.

I noticed one or two lunch-time joggers. There were also a few young children, all well-dressed, some with their mothers, others obviously with nannies or au pairs. A few were clearly in the care of grandparents. I recorded in my notebook that I did not see a single child in jeans. The whole garden was beautifully kept. I had never seen it before but I recalled a painting of it by Monet. The overall effect now seemed more open than I remembered from his picture.

I saw one elderly man raise his hat to an elderly lady, and a young businessman on what looked like a lunch break kiss the hand of an elegant matron. Even the children seemed to be playing in a charming old-fashioned way. One family was playing hide and seek, another group of children were creeping forward in what looked like grand-mother's footsteps. Several small girls, sitting on the wooden seats on the gravel paths, were absorbed in picture books. It was clearly a favourite place of the Parisian *haute bourgeoisie*. I did a rapid perambulation of the park. Dotted about were statues of some French cultural figures: Chopin, Alfred de Musset and Gounod.

I located the kiosk, but could not see Benson. Nearby there was a crowd of small children clustered around one of the seats on the gravel path. It was only when I saw the ping-pong balls being shot into the air that I realized that Benson must be in the midst, though largely hidden from the sight of an approaching observer. As I got closer I could see he was lolling back as I had seen him do at The Chequers in Heaverham. He had rested his head on the back of his seat. From his mouth he was sending a flow of balls into the air, catching them in his mouth and sending them back up again into the air in ectoplasmic-like bursts. As I reached the edge of the circle of children I decided that he had four balls in play.

The young children were completely enchanted at this clerical figure in sombre dress who seemed to be a kind of magician. Of course I had been told not to bring a camera, but this is one of the pictures that I would have most liked to have had. I rather hoped that someone else would take one, but the only two adults who came up to the little group as I approached seemed not to have one either. I reflected that they probably thought taking photographs of this little happening would imply they were too readily impressed by the unusual, and might be viewed as out of keeping with the traditions of the park.

Quite suddenly Benson stopped sending the balls up and caught them all. Two now filled out his cheeks and two were skillfully lodged by him in the hollows of the sockets of his eyes as he lay with his head on the back of the seat. This produced a little laugh from the children. The overall effect was of a strange marionette with a long robe covering its strings that had been laid to rest across the back of the seat.

There followed an enthusiastic but measured little round of applause from the children who looked on in wonder. One of the adults then engaged Benson in conversation briefly. I understood that he was explaining to her that he had only been using four, not five balls as he was rather out of practice. She was then sufficiently authoritative to induce the children to take their leave of their clerical entertainer. Cries of "*Merci, mon pere!*" and "*Merci, Monsieur le Curé!*" came from the children as Benson sat up. Two older little boys stepped forward to the seat and shook Benson's hand with a neat little bow.

As the children and the lady began to walk off down the gravel path I turned to follow them. The procession soon fragmented and the children in ones and twos returned to those who had brought them to the park. I saw that some grandparents near me had already set out some lunch on another seat.

I was feeling hungry too as I walked back to Benson on his seat. He had put away his pingpong balls. It was then I realized that one of the adults who had witnessed the performance was one of the young men from St Germain whom we were due to meet.

"Welcome, Bridge, to the famous Park Monceau. This is François Atanase who organised this morning's service. He lives with his parents over there in an apartment which looks over the park. This is my friend Bernard Bridge."

"*Enchanté*," I said. We shook hands.

"I know that your French is quite good enough for international meetings, Bridge, but I have agreed with François that we will have an English-speaking lunch. He believes that his two companions when they arrive, will be content with that. I remember that you told me, François, that the young lady is studying English literature."

"That is correct, *Monsieur le Curé. Voila*! I now see Bernardette and Yves walking along the path from the other entrance. Excuse me while I go to show them where we are."

He strode off to meet them. Benson busied himself with getting the food from the plastic bags. I proudly produced the green cloth and laid it out behind the seat on the grass which was fortunately reasonably dry. Since the seat faced the gravel path rather than the grass it was not possible to use it as a part of our arrangements for lunch. Its only use was to store our provisions. We would all need to be on the ground around the green cloth.

I produced the wine and the mineral water and borrowed from Benson his Swiss army knife to pull the cork from the wine since I had left mine in my luggage. I found some reasonably flat ground for the plastic cups. Benson had brought several French baguettes which he immediately set about cutting up. He had also bought some paper plates and napkins. These he set out round the edge of the cloth. On the spare paper plates he set out ham, *paté de fois gras*, various sorts of cheese, hard boiled eggs, some olives and fresh fruit. The centre piece was a magnificent glazed apple tart which came from the patisserie with its own paper plate. By the time the three young people arrived Benson was set to play mine host.

François introduced me to his companions, Bernardette, and Yves. Bernadette was a slight very pretty girl with loose flowing dark hair. and long black eyelashes. She was wearing a red corduroy skirt and a white cotton blouse done up to the neck which made her look a little severe. She told me that she had become particularly interested in some Victorian and Edwardian English poets: Coventry Patmore, Francis Thompson and Alice Meynell. She spoke English quite fluently with a slight but charming accent.

Yves said that he was a scientist and hoped eventually to study medicine. He was the least fluent in English. We took up positions around the green cloth. The three young French students all seemed supple and found no difficulty in kneeling on their haunches. Benson did the same with his black coat and cassock carefully arranged behind him over his black shoes. I lay rather awkwardly stretched out on the grass on my side resting my head on my left hand on the edge of the green cloth. Benson invited us to select an assortment of what we wanted on our paper plates. The two young men and Benson took some wine. Bernadette and I had mineral water.

After saying a grace in Latin Benson began by asking

about the pilgrimage to Chartres and how this fitted into their view of the world.

François, pausing from eating, responded in this way:

"Monsier le Curé and Monsieur Bridge, I would like explain you all this. I hope my comrades will not protest if I say you something about my family first."

He took a sip of wine and, with a small gesture of his left hand, asked us the following question:

"Do you know what is a 'Republican marriage'?"

I shook my head. Benson was silent.

"*Alors*, my family are coming from Bas-Poitou, the region of France they now call the Vendée. After the French Revolution and the Terror many people of Bas Poitou wanted to remain Catholic. But the Republican Government had proscribed the Church with its links to Rome and the Holy Father, and had made a new State Religion of Reason. She was a kind of personified daughter of the *Philosophes* of the *Encylopédie*. The Government in Paris had increased taxes in Bas Poitou and their *officiers* came to conscript young men from our region to fight in their army. In 1793 the people in some parts of Bas Poitou took up arms to defend our religion and their independence from Paris.

"The first rebels were simple ordinary men and women, mostly *paysans* as we say. But some young members of important *anciennes familles* in the region joined them. They too were loving our Faith and were loyal to Louis and Marie Antoinette's memory, and to their heirs. Very soon there was a revolt of all classes. Many used to meet in the open air in the woods to hear *La Messe* said by some brave priests who would not accept the new State religion. This rebel army had some great military success against the government forces at first. Some leaders had a gift for good military tactics—how do you say, the war of guerrillas. They were looking for help from Monsieur Pitt's Government in England. But when this arrive, it was too late. The French Government forces were ready for *Les Anglais* when they landed.

"In the end the Government assembled some companies

of *soldats de première force*—what is the phrase *en Anglais* I want, Bernadette?"

"Perhaps 'crack troops'," said Bernadette, smiling.

"Yes, 'crack troop' from Paris. They captured the Catholic strongholds. The rebel army fled north but then they were suffering big defeats. They retreated back to their villages in Bas Poitou. The Paris Government decided on *un politique* of extermination. They massacred almost all the population of the region and devastated the land. Many men, women and *enfants* were burnt sheltering in *les eglises*, or were killed in their houses in the villages.

"There was a guillotine in Nantes to execute the many prisoners. But the numbers were so big that the *officiers* decided: 'It will be quicker to drown them in the Loire.' So they gathered the prisoners by the river and began to tie a man and woman together on to a board, and throw them into the Loire so that they drowned together. Hundred of these were made into pairs in this way and drowned. Most were not married. Many were not even knowing each other to whom they were tied. The *soldats* from Paris called these drownings 'republican marriages'. I learned recently that I descend from a true husband and wife who were drowned bound together like this. My ancestor was a little boy at the time. He had been sent away by his parents to be with his *grandmère* while the terrible events in Nantes were happening."

François had been looking at Benson and me in turn as he struggled with his English, but when he finished he looked down at the green cloth in front of him.

I was on the point of saying how sorry I was about this terrible event. I was also looking for words to ask about the link between this awful story and the Chartres Pilgrimage they were planning. Bernadette seemed to anticipate my question:

"You see, *Monsieur le Curé* and Monsieur Bridge, the story of François' family is just one example of how the leaders of our beloved France have shown the world that hardness of heart that our Lord speaks about. It was not new at the time of the Revolution. Our pilgrimage is a small way of trying to warm French peoples' hearts again. It is also a tiny act of reparation. For so many centuries our rulers have valued the military glory of France above the higher honour of being the elder daughter of the Church. The French people have been complicit too. In their imagination they still revere the Emperor Napoleon and Louis XIV, rather than the earlier and greater Louis IX, our most devout St Louis."

Yves added: "And our artists, writers, architects and musicians, and yes, our scientists too, have glorified man in general or just themselves, instead of God and his creation."

François now looked up and said:

"But it was much worse than that, *mes amis*. Many Bourbon rulers were egoists, without compassion or a sense of reponsibility for those they ruled. But the Revolution made everything much worse. A *la base* there was hatred and envy. The worst was the way it turned *les simples* into pitiless, God-less monsters. It hated the old aristocracy and clergy for who they were, not for what they did as individuals. The Revolution was based on intellectual intolerance and envy, not just of the property of others, but of their intellect and even their moral qualities."

Bernardette chimed in "*Monsieur le Curé* and Monsieur Bridge you see it was an intellectual system without compassion. A *la fin* the revolutionaries also attacked each another. It was a herald of Marxism, because like that it was also based on creating hatred between classes. Charles Péguy, who had revived the pilgrimage to Chartres, could see much of this clearly. He saw the terrible intolerance the Dreyfus affair had revealed. He also feared the growing intolerance of the socialists. Yet he did not live to see much worse things: the collaboration of many *Français* with the Germans who occupied France in the next war, and the complicity of many in the killing of the Jews. Péguy was also fortunate not to witness the nihilism, and self-centredness of existentialism and the barren legacy of Sartre. Nor did Péguy see the terrible degrading of the relations between men and women. *Ma France*, can we bring you back? Is it *trop tard*?" She had closed her eyes as she spoke the last words.

"It is never too late for God's grace," said Benson. " Monsier Bridge and I saw a glimpse of the future of France this morning at San Germain-des-Prés."

"But *Monsieur le Curé*," said Yves." the Cathedral authorities at Chartres have just told us they will not allow our pilgrims to have one of our priests say the Old Mass in the Cathedral."

"That will certainly take some years of pilgrimage to overcome," said Benson. "But they will welcome you in the end. The future is on your side, not theirs. The Church authorities always come to terms with successful spiritual movements that are in love with Holy Church."

Benson paused. Then he turned his light-blue eyes on the three young French students in turn and added:

"Beside your love for the Church, the other great strength that you have is your friendship with each other. Political parties, the nation state, class and racial solidarity, the business firm, the trade union, even local communities, have all been been tried and found wanting in fulfilling men and women. Loyal friendship under God may be the power presently needed for building the kingdom. The isolation of men and women in the great cities, the need to travel or move far from home to find work, have all weakened other institutions. Even the family has been affected. True friendship may be coming into its own. You three may be in the vanguard."

It was clear from the look on the the young students' faces that Benson had understood the secret of their fervour and determination. It was their bond of friendship that was underpinning their spiritual endeavours.

For a few minutes we all ate in silence. Then Yves rose and took orders for coffee, and went off to buy it at the kiosk. Benson took the opportunity to talk to Bernadette.

François then explained to me that his parents had had him baptised François Atanase because these were the names of Charette, the leader of the rebels in the Vendée

Wars. He also agreed that there *was* something providential in his friendship with Bernadette and Yves.

He explained that he himself was a typical member of the French bourgoisie. His father was a prosperous banker. His mother had been at the Sorbonne but had not had a career apart from bringing up the family. Her father was a judge. They lived in a fine apartment which we could just glimpse at the other end of the park.

Bernadette, on the other hand, was a child of the French working class. Her mother was a seamstress who worked from home—"*Oui*, they still exist in Paris and not just in opera—." He laughed a soft laugh. He explained that Bernadette's father worked as a porter on the railways. Yve's parents were both from traditional French aristocratic families. They had a chateau in Normandy which had been in his family for generations. It was only love of the Church, that could have brought together in friendship three young people of such different backgrounds. Their unbreakable solidarity was a rebuke to Marxism! At this point he asked me;

"Monsieur Bridge what are you knowing about Charles Péguy whose pilgrimage we try to revive?"

"Only a very little biographical stuff." I said. "I know he was a journalist, critic, political activist and poet, and died fighting at the beginning of the First World War. I haven't read any of his works."

"One day, you must," said Francois. "There are two things Péguy said which connect with what I was saying to you. I will translate them: 'Love is rarer than genius itself. And friendship is rarer than love.'

"Though it is rare, Bernadette, Yves and I believe we have found it. Peguy was born very poor, like Bernadette. He once said: 'Short of genius a rich man cannot imagine poverty.' So Yves is a genius. All the students from the working class who are to be baptised at St Germain-des-Prés this Easter have chosen Yves, rather than any of the rest of us, as their sponsor when they come into the Church."

Yves returned with the coffee. I studied him carefully as

he handed them around. He was of medium height and wiry looking; with darkish skin; very dark brown hair and dark blue eyes, a prominent nose and strong chin. His colouring made him look Cornish. He smiled shyly as he gave me my coffee as if he had noticed me appraising him.

Benson said: "Bernadette and I have been discussing the consecrated life. As you are already doing much for our Lord and His Church it seems likely that you will all receive inner drawings towards even more heroic action. I would advise being on guard against a subtle form of presumption. It's sometimes hard to distinguish between God's voice and its counterfeit. If it will stand the common light it is good. You have the advantage of being a group of close friends so you will be able to bring into the light of each other's gaze what may seem a particular calling. Avoid being in a hurry. If God means you to do something for Him He will close other doors, and open the one He wishes you to enter. He will beckon you not only by interior feelings but external circumstances too."

It was clear from their faces that the young people well understood what Benson meant. Afterwards when I was recalling the essence of his remarks for my notebook it struck me as relevant to my own situation as well.

The picnic broke up soon after that. Francois, Bernardette and Yves had different study and lecture commitments. As we packed up our picnic things Benson said to me:

"We now have some time to ourselves. I believe that we can manage one more visit before we return to collect our luggage and get to the railway station for our train to Rome. Because you have a trained mind your intellect will need to be satisfied in matters of Faith. A Church not far from St Germain-des-Près may help you in this."

Benson then took me out through the imposing iron gates at the other entrance to the park. The quiet dignified street made a strong contrast with the bustling cosmopolitan streets on the left bank of the city where we were staying.

Our Metro journey back was by another route than the one we came by. Despite a number of changes at correspondences Benson managed to get in a little work on his appliqué tapestry. I was now used to these periods of silent work in Benson's company. I managed to scribble a few notes on the day's events in my notebook.

The Church of St Thomas Aquinas was not far from St Germain-des-Prés in the University quarter of the Left Bank. In contrast with the different architectural styles of San Gernain which reflected its long history, St Thomas Aquinas is all of a piece in the style of the Italian Baroque. The external columns are in classical orders of architecture: six Doric columns mark the three front entrances, and four Ionic columns on the second storey support a triangular pediment.

As we were coming up to the church Benson pointed out a bas-relief above the left entrance.

"You will see that this shows Our Lady giving the rosary to St Dominic. It was St Dominic who played an important part in making this practice popular, although he did not originate it. The original church was dedicated to St Dominic. Soon after he received papal approval for his order in 1216 the Dominicans set up a base in Paris not far from here. St Dominic knew St Francis, but, after seeing the effects of the Albigensian heresy he decided that the Church needed to be able to win the intellectual arguments. It wasn't always sufficient to seek to convert people by showing them the love of God. Some needed intellectual conviction. St Dominic took this need as his mission. What he and St Francis had in common was a commitment to poverty and loyalty to the Church.

"But why is this church now dedicated to St Thomas Aquinas?" I asked.

"This happened after the French Revolution. The Dominicans' church, and the seminary they had established here, were seized by the State at the Revolution. Their leader was guillotined and their property turned into a military museum. I believe the building still actually belongs to the French Ministry of Defence. When the Church was eventually allowed to re-establish worship here it became a parochial church as religious orders were still illegal. It was then re-dedicated to a later Dominican, St Thomas Aquinas.

"You asked why this happened. By this time St Dominic, as the founder of the Dominicans, had become linked in the French public's eyes with the Inquisition. Historically the Dominicans had played an important role in supporting the Inquisition. St Pius V, before he became Pope, was both Inquisitor-General and a Dominican. St Thomas, with his acceptance as a universal teacher, was an alumnus of the University in this quarter of Paris. He may well have been seen as less controversial. But you will see inside they are both honoured. Let us go in, and leave discussion of the Inquisition and other troubling aspects of Church history to later."

As we entered I felt suddenly overwhelmed with joy. I genuflected towards the altar spontaneously myself and not just following a lead from Benson. The baroque interior was bathed in sunlight from the high windows. The church faced north/south, rather than the traditional east/west. A number of clouds seemed to lift from my mind: my concern for my own future, and what my encounter and strange pilgrimage would lead to. I even felt I had overcame my feelings about the disturbing meeting with the French Canadian priests. Even banished was the terrible scene by the banks of the Loire of those 'republican marriages'.

Benson led me down to the front seat on the left hand side of the nave before the stone communion rails. We both knelt. For the first time since I had met and been with Benson I was not conscious of him at all, although he was right beside me. It did not just seem like physical light which was all around me. My mind seemed clearer. Were these two Dominicans part of this? I suddenly felt Benson tap me on the arm. He had never done this before, and it seemed uncharacteristic that he would interrupt anyone at prayer. Was I really praying? He pointed to the cupola above me.

"You can see St Dominic above us with his rosary in his left hand and his right hand pointing up to heaven. St Thomas Aquinas is above us on the other side of the cupola. His eyes are also turned to heaven as he writes his great theological works."

I looked up and read the huge Latin inscription, black letters on gold:

DABIT VERBUM EVANGELIZANTIBUS

'He will give his word to his evangelists. '

"That means you as well as me," said Benson, clearly noticing that I had read the inscription. "But you must now ask St Dominic and St Thomas to give you a sound intellectual understanding of the Faith so that you can be effective."

He resumed his prayer. I closed my eyes and found myself saying fervently: '*Adiuge nos fidem.*'—Increase our faith—, the words of the voices behind me at my vigil. Then in English: 'Increase *my* Faith.' And finally: "St Dominic and St Thomas, am I too late for understanding?"

As if in answer I felt suddenly confident that it wasn't too late. Benson rose beside me.

"I've just one more thing to show you."

He took me around to the right of the church and then along a short narrow corridor. We now entered what was a chapel behind the high altar. It was dominated by a vast painting of St Louis seated on a throne and wearing his kingly crown. The style seemed French pre-Raphaelite. The king was a clean shaven young man. Above him an angel was holding Christ's crown of thorns. On his right was St Thomas offering him a model of the Church, and on his left an angel was presenting him with the chalice and the cross.

Benson whispered:

"St Louis was an exact contemporary and personal friend of St Thomas Aquinas.The king used to have the poor Dominicans of the University to dine with him. Our young French friends long for the days when France will again have a government imbued with the spirit of Christ and his Church, as in the days of St Louis. This has and does still occur, but it is rare, and often very fleeting. The world is truly blessed when it happens. Perhaps someone like you, working in a Protestant country for a hard-headed and perhaps rather cynical government, will receive the grace to open a tiny window of the light of truth occasionally. Shall we ask for St Louis' help?"

He knelt down and I followed. I remember thinking rather prosaically that I could not see how there was any chance of letting light into my co-ordinating EC meeting in Rome! But as I was still feeling suffused with the joy that I experienced when entering the church I was carried along, and began saying a number of traditional prayers, including the Our Father and the Hail Mary. I then made one fervent prayer for each member of my family and several friends in turn, going through a long list.

Benson finally interrupted me. He had pulled out his pocket watch and noted that it was time that we went to collect our luggage. We went back out through the church, genuflected together and soon found ourselves back in the Boulevard St Germain. We parted before we reached St Germain-des-Prés agreeing to meet at the steps leading down to the Metro in half an hour.

I had only gone a few yards when Benson called me back. He then made a little speech in his most endearing manner.

"I hope you will read some St Thomas Aquinas. But I would counsel against plunging straight into his *Summa*. Both he and St Dominic wanted to correct an earlier tendency to set the world of the spirit and of ideas above that of the physical world. A legacy of Platonism. At its worst it led to Manicheism and the Albigensian heresy, that condemned the world as evil. But God, when he created it, saw that it was good. He confirmed his original visionary plan by taking on human flesh as a man. Aristotle was attractive to St Thomas because he committed himself to understanding and describing the physical world. St Thomas's theology sought to encompass everything, both the physical and spiritual world."

He glanced at his watch again and hurried off. When I returned to the hotel a blonde woman at reception handed across a letter. The envelope had been addressed in biro in a large unformed hand I recognised. I sat in a chair at a corner of the reception lobby and hurriedly using my forefinger tore open the envelope. There was a single page inside which read:

Dear Bernard, i cudnt wait. i phoned Frances after lunch and told her wat was in the letter. Wen i asked her strait she sed she would go along with it. so were going to get hiched in church as soon as we can fix it up. i feel grate. tell Father im going to Mass at Notra Dame this evening. Gerry said hed come along too which woz a bit of turn up. Then we'll hav sum drinks and a blow out.

I lit a candle today for you, Bernard—im sure you'll make it.

all the best to you and Father. Seb

PS the lady at the desk must hav liked me. she gave me your home adress so yull get an invite to the wedding. they wudnt do that for me in LONDON!

The receptionist took me to where my luggage was stored. She must have been in her mid-forties: slim, and dressed in a white blouse and black skirt which emphasized her bust and hips. She had a thick gold bracelet on her wrist. Her black shoes had very high heels. Her expression seemed to signal that she took more than just a professional interest in clients. Her blonde hair was shoulder length. She had a habit of pushing it back from her face as she looked you over. It did not surprise me that she had been been susceptible to Sebastian.

She did not mention her breach of the rules on client's personal details, and I didn't raise the matter. I just repacked my rucksack and took my leave.

Benson and I met as planned at the pre-arranged time by the steps leading down to the Metro. We reached the Gare de Lyon without incident. Benson was delighted with my news about Sebastian. It was no surprise, he declared, that Sebastian had been unable to wait before getting in touch with Frances.

CHAPTER TWELVE

SYMPOSIUM ON THE NIGHT TRAIN

I HAD used the Gare de Lyon before so I knew it. But I have no recollection of our arrival there or of finding the platfom. I think the train had already pulled in, and that we found our carriage without difficulty.

Benson had booked us both single compartments. In the corridor of our carriage Benson reminded me of our Rule. This was now time for our private work. He said that he had some letters to write and suggested we meet in his compartment in time for Vespers and the Rosary.

My compartment had two seats facing each other so there was plenty of room for one person. The couchette had not yet been made up. There was a minute wash-basin in one corner and a shaver point so that I would be able to use this to make myself morning tea with my little bouillotte.

I unpacked a few things—toileteries, pyjamas, a shirt for tomorrow. There was nowhere to hang my suit so I laid it out carefully on the spare seat. I would put it on in the morning to be ready for my afternoon meeting. I sat on the seat by the window and took stock.

All that had happened on the pilgrimage and the events leading up to it, such as the Benson 'manifestation'—this seemed an appropriately neutral word to describe his appearance—, and then the various encounters and perfomances like the kite display, the conversations and visits, were all leading me towards the Catholic Church. Should I resist this? Could I? What would be the consequence of completing the pilgrimage and remaining where I had always been in the Church of England? It would certainly mean less explanation to family and friends.

Again, what would *they* think if I decided to make a change at this stage in my life? I wasn't a young man. I knew very few Catholics. Would I ever be able to explain what had been the very strange events which had led to this? Would others think I had 'lost the plot', as a current phrase had it? Did this matter if it was right?

I decided that this was quite enough introspection. What those I had encountered today seemed to have in common was a readiness to act. St Joseph, St Francis Xavier, the French students, the two Dominican saints, could all be seen as practical people of action. St Joseph seems to be one of the most practical people in the Gospels. He seemed to be advising me to take some action with my lad, Cyprian. I would start on this in Rome.

St Francis Xavier took seriously the injunction to go out and preach the Gospel, then went off to the Far East and did just that for the rest of his short life. The students were appalled at what had happened to France over some centuries, and had decided to act. They were seeking to change it by making visible a better way through a revival of the Pilgrimage to Chartres. St Dominic saw that the nature of the Faith was being distorted and misunderstood, and proceeded to correct this through the action of his preaching. St Thomas Aquinas perceived the need for a solidly-based, rational and complete defence of the Faith which covered both the physical and the spiritual world, and set about providing it.

My own practical resolve was to write again to Angela, then cover the latest events in my notebook. I have the draft of my second letter to Angela. This is what I wrote:

My darling sweetheart

I am now on the night train to Rome where I will post this letter. I am not sure how you will take the fact that I am still unable to say more about Father Benson other than that he is a very considerate travelling companion with a wonderful ability to expound the basics of the Church and its Faith down the ages. I have decided that it would not be advantageous to quiz him about himself yet. I shall just wait for him to broach the subject. He occasionally has a look which suggests he might say something, but seems to be held back. I think patience may be best.

We had a service at Ightham Mote soon after I posted my last letter. A simple version of Benediction of the Blassed Sacrament. Father B. took it. There were three teenage boys who served, and two members of the Mote staff, who seemed to know Father B., kindly gave us a light lunch.

Then we walked over to Shipbourne. It was a lovely day but the wind had got up. When we arrived at the Common this helped. The three teenage boys gave us a wonderful display with kites that they had made. Amazingly they had managed to bicycle across from the Mote after the service to get this display ready. They had made their box kites themselves and painted on the covering material some wonderful designs illustrating various Christian symbols. You would have loved the meticulous way they had painted them. They are pupils at Tonbridge School so they went off after lunch for their classes. Apparently they were able to get the morning off because their Latin master lets them do things which involve using Latin. The service at Ightham Mote was mostly in Latin. I was given a crib.

Father B. and I then caught a bus to Tonbridge where we picked up the train to Dover. On the train we got to know a young man in our carriage. It emerged that he had had a row with his lady friend and was going to stay with a chap he used to play football with who was working in Paris. It became clear later that, while I was getting us some tea from the buffet-car, he had picked Father B's pocket and taken his half-hunter gold watch!

While Father B. went off to say his office, the young man, who was called Sebastian, told me all about himself. He didn't exactly confess to me what he had done, but I could see he was troubled. He later moved carriages and I didn't see him again. I assumed that would be the last we saw of him. But apparently Sebastian so regretted what he had done that he returned the watch to Father B. Then, when we were on the ferry to Calais, asked him to hear his confession. It seems that Sebastian had been brought up a

Catholic, but hadn't been to confession since he was a teenager!

This may give you some idea of the effect that Fr. B. has! The young man joined us again in our compartment on the Calais/Paris train. He proved a tower of strength later as Father B. had a rather nasty encounter in the buffet car with a young drunken footballer who got on with the rest of his team at Nantes. Neither Sebastian nor I were there. I was not sure how I would have acquitted myself in the circs., but Sebastian would certainly have done well. He is a tall well-built young man. In fact he showed useful first aid skills with a wound to Father B.'s arm—nasty but not too deep—. The young French footballer later turned up in our compartment with his team captain to apologise to Father B!

Another surprise was that young Sebastian seemed to want to change his life completely and had decided to ask his girl friend, the mother of his two little children, to marry him. You may be surprised to learn that he asked me to help draft a letter to her in which he popped the question. Rather different, darling, from what happened with us!

In Paris Father B. stayed in a religious community but I lodged at a small hotel nearby. Real spring in Paris weather today. Fr B. took me to St Germain-des-Prés this morning. To my surprise Sebastian was also there lighting a candle, but we left him to his prayers. However Father B. slipped him a card with the name of someone to prepare them for marriage—they are to marry in a Catholic Church.

St Germain is right in the student quarter. In fact we met some French students there who were having an informal service. Later on we had a picnic lunch with three of them at the beautiful Parc Monceau. Rather like a London Park in style, but the people there seemed better behaved! No intimidating youths with cans of lager or overweight sunbathers.

The young French students were concerned about the way France has been going over many years—centuries in fact—and had decided that reviving a pilgrimage to Chartres might be a way of getting together a group who think along similar lines. Then later they might perhaps be a kind of leaven in French society. The three lunching with us were all very impressive. All three were of quite different social backgrounds. Their mutual friendship seemed rather moving.

This afternoon we went to another church, St Thomas d'Aquin, which was near my hotel. It has a Dominican intellectual tradition which Fr B. thinks would be good for me.

I've been thinking about Cyprian. Should I be a bit more pro-active with him? On my return, could we go down and see him play a match? We could then try to see his Housemaster to see how things are going. I will send him a card from Rome. I thought he might like something of the Forum.

Well, Fr B. has asked me to join him in his compartment—we have a compartment each—so I should close now. Please give my love to Mama. The pullover has been most useful already. I hope she was not too shocked by Fr B.'s rosary! Nor you! My best love to Perpetua. Tell her I hope she enjoyed her stay with her friend.

Just a thought. The hotel in Paris might be suitable for us if we can arrange a visit. It is most strategically situated.

My fondest love B Stop Press: Seb's girl has said Yes!

I didn't in fact join Benson immediately. When I glanced at my watch there were still some minutes before I was due. I used the time to write up my notebook, adding details that I had failed to mention to Angela. I still felt reticent about including some of the more specifically Catholic aspects. I also left out the details of the attack on Benson, which I felt might be upsetting. I realized that I had also omitted to mention the troubling meeting with the Canadian priests. This was not deliberate but it was perhaps a psychological suppression of something I had found specially unpleasant.

There was a sudden knock on my compartment door. It was the railway official in charge of our carriage. He asked me when I was intending to go for dinner. He would use the time I was away to make ready the *couchette* for the night. I explained that I expected my travelling companion and I would probably have dinner about 8 pm.

He then asked me for my passport. He said he would keep it and present it on my behalf to the Italian authorities at the Italian border. Unless there was a problem I would not need to be woken. When I surrendered my passport I wondered what would happen in Benson's case.

When I joined him in his compartment he seemed particularly buoyant, and this lifted my mood too. He sat me down opposite and handed me a leather bound Vespers Book.

"I have marked the place where we are to begin. It is Vespers for the ferial Office for today, Thursday. As you will see the service mostly consists of psalms. For today we have Psalms 131 to 136. If you can follow my Latin you might like to join in the Gloria and the antiphons at the end of each psalm. Towards the end of the service I will ask you for the book since I don't know the text of the Little Chapter by heart. You will see that it is a short passage from St Paul's letter to the Corinthians. I will try and sing the prescribed short hymn—I hope to be in reasonable voice. The Magnificat and the final prayer and antiphon conclude the service. I thought we would then go straight into the five Joyful Mysteries of the Holy Rosary as it's Thursday. In Latin, now that you are an expert!"— he smiled at me mischievously—, "but we will say the intention for each decade in English."

Without further ado he launched into Vespers.

'*Memento Domine, David...*'

As the Latin poured out of his mouth in beautifully modulated cadences his light blue eyes were raised as if focussing on something in the luggage rack above my head. I began to realise that he was giving an extraordinary exhibition of his memory. I followed the text carefully and every Latin word was exactly as it appeared in the Vespers Book. I was so overawed by this that at first I paid little attention to the text—there was a helpful English translation opposite the Latin in my book, but I did not make use of this during the first psalm. Benson looked down at me when he reached the first *Gloria* and sought with his eyes to bring me in as if he was conducting an orchestra. I managed to make some sort of sound in Latin which approximated to the text. He went straight on to the next short psalm. I followed this better, and was ready for the Gloria and the Antiphon.

Although Benson's voice had a musical quality his Latin enunciation was always clear. I was completely held by the text. The last psalm was '*Super flumina Babylonia*' 'by the waters of Babylon we sat down and wept as we remembered Sion.' Suddenly I was overwhelmed with what I can only describe as spiritual yearning. It was like the feeling of homesickness I remembered as a young boy during my first week away from home at boarding school. Yet it was not a hopeless feeling, just a yearning for a place elsewhere that I wanted badly but knew that I could not then have. Home.

Benson took back the Vespers Book and read the Little Chapter, and then returned it to me. He was now singing the hymn quietly by heart. I recalled his light tenor voice from Benediction, but here, just in front of me, it seemed even sweeter, and not at all incongruous. I was pleased I managed to join in the *Magnificat* and the final Antiphon without breaking the spell.

There was a brief pause when we had finished Vespers. I thought he might say something about it. Instead he simply announced the Joyful Mysteries of the Rosary:

"The First Joyful Mystery: The Annunciation: We offer this for some special friends: Gregory, Ambrose and Jerome of the Knights of the Kite, for Bernadette, Francois, and Yves as they seek to revive the Faith in France beginning with the restoration of the Chartres Pilgrimage, for Clement and Ruby at Ightham Mote, for Francis and Teresa Baker, and for Sebastian and Frances and their forthoming marriage, and their two young children."

He added: "There was a phrase in Vespers that seemed very apt for all of them: '*Ecce—quam bonum, et quam iucundum: habitare fratres in unum.* 'Behold how good and pleasant it is for the brethren to dwell together in unity'.

Benson's Latin continued and I joined in as required. We seemed to get a good rhythm going. I had a little success in visualizing those for whom we were praying, but my attempt to imagine the Annunciation was rather disappointing.

The Second Joyful Mystery, the Visitation, Benson offered for Angela, Cyprian, Perpetua and my mother-in-law. He said he was sure that Our Lady would care for them as she had done for her cousin, Elizabeth. I was glad I had just written to Angela, and would be writing to Cyprian.

Benson said we should offer the Third Joyful Mystery, the Birth of Jesus, for myself, reflecting on the grace I had received so far in my life and in the pilgrimage, and asking that I should be open to new graces as they came. Now, instead of looking in the middle distance between us as he had done during the first two decades, he turned his gaze on me. It was so like the picture in his biography that I felt constrained to look down and not face the directness of his gaze.

Yet I felt buoyed up by the prayer and joined in the responses fervently. I was not sure I ever remembered knowing for certain that I was being specially prayed for.

The mood changed abruptly when Benson said that we should offer the fourth Joyful Mystery, the Presentation of Our Lord in The Temple, for the two Canadian priests I had met this morning. Some words of Vespers had struck him: '*Sacerdotes tui induantur justitiam*'—'Let thy priests be clothed with justice.' From what I had said these young priests were in no way clothed with justice and were likely to do further damage to themselves and others.

"Our Lord makes clear," Benson said, "that the penalty for those to whom great trust is given, and who betray it is grievous. Yet not even grave sinners are completely lost while they live. So regular prayer for them and their victims is a responsibility for *us*."

I did not find this easy. Their final contemptuous remark about praying the rosary still resounded in my head. I was relieved when we reached the Fifth Joyful Mystery. Benson offered this for the conversion of England. "Many Catholics in England," he said, "had always taken Psalm 136, which had been part of this evening's Vespers, to heart. English

Catholics often felt like exiles in their own land. So they could understand the feelings of the Israelites who sat down by the waters of Babylon and wept. They too often felt how hard it was to sing to the Lord the songs of Sion in what for them was sometimes a strange land.

While we were saying this decade I asked myself whether I wanted to be like Catholics, an alien in my own country.

Benson took the Vespers Book from me and returned it to his rucksack. Then he surprised me:

"A rather curious thing happened when the train steward came to discuss making up my *couchette*. He told me that he did not need to check my passport. He was a practising Catholic, he said, and he thought it inappropriate to check the passports of priests. The words he used were: '*absolument incompatibile avec la vôtre profession*.' He said that the fellow on duty tonight in charge of passport control at the Italian frontier took a similar view. He was also a Catholic. Now wasn't that strange?"

He looked at me penetratingly with a slightly amused smile.

"But let us now go and have dinner," he added, without waiting for me to respond.

Before he left the compartment Benson put a little padlock through two metal rings on the top of his pack and pocketed the key in his cassock. Then he picked up a small cardboard box which I had seen beside him on his seat and took this with him to the Restaurant Car. This was already crowded but we managed to find a seat for two. Benson went to have a word with the Head Waiter.

On his return he was without his cardboard box. His boyish enthusiasm was like that before his bike ride in Kemsing. He said rather mysteriously that our meal would be a birthday celebration, although there would be a serious side later when we were having coffee.

I immediately thought that it might be his own birthday. I then remembered that Robert Hugh Benson was born on the 18th of November. I was born in June. I was stumped.

"I promised you some surprises and I have arranged a little

one this evening. By the way, Bridge, I am wondering when you will give me my surprise!"

The Head Waiter himself came over to take our orders. He recommended a beetroot soup, and we both said yes to that. He suggested the roast wild boar, and we both chose that. Benson just asked that we should also have a wide selection of vegetables. The Head Waiter recommended an expensive French red, and Benson said this sounded right. He seemed disappointed we had not taken longer over our selection. He was clearly intrigued by Benson.

When he was out of earshot Benson said a Latin grace. Then he asked me whose birthday I thought it was. I looked blank. He said he would give some hints.

"He's a Scotsman, but he never visited Scotland. He had a brief career as a soldier, then settled in Rome. He used his own money on public works at Frascati, the small town outside Rome known to the ancient Romans as Tusculum. He restored the Cathedral in Frascati, and created a college for the education of priests and select laymen. One of his favourites at the college that he had established, but who never took orders as a priest, later became important in Rome. This favourite was responsible for much of the excavation work in the Roman Forum; he also completed the Piazza del Popolo and the magnificent public park on the Pincio above it. It was this protégé of the one we are to celebrate who also created the Vatican museums as we know them. Who was this Scotsman? You will have an additional glass of wine if you also tell me the name of his important protégé."

"It is clearly the anniversary of the birth of someone who is now dead," I said. "Much of the work of the protégé seems to have been completed in the early 19th century."

"Yes, you are right," said Benson encouragingly.

"His protégé must have been an important minister or official of the popes at that time," I said.

"Correct," said Benson. "But the Scotsman who lived most of his life in Rome, and whose first language was English? Who might that be? A further clue is that he was of noble birth? In fact that is almost an understatement."

An idea came into my mind. "Was he one of the Stuarts?"

"Yes, indeed," said Benson, "but which one?" The Head Waiter had arrived and was pouring our wine.

"Wasn't there one who was an ecclesiastic?" I looked appealingly at Benson.

"Indeed. And I now propose a toast for this anniversary of the birth of Henry Benedict Edward Maria Clement Francis Xavier Stuart, Duke of York and later also known as Henry IX, King of Great Britain. Cardinal Henry Stuart, as he is better known, was born this day in 1725. In opposition to the wishes of his elder brother, Bonnie Prince Charlie, Henry Stuart was ordained priest in 1748 soon after the unsuccessful Jacobite rebellion. His brother was childless and he had hoped that Henry might marry, and that any children would keep alive the hope of a Stuart restoration. But Henry, rather like St Edith of Kemsing, saw the promotion of the kingdom of God as his vocation, rather than the pursuit of earthly rule. Our toast then is to the glorious memory of Cardinal Henry Stuart."

Benson raised his glass and I did likewise. I then confessed that I knew very little about the Cardinal Duke, and did not know the name of his protégé who did so much building work for Rome. As I was speaking the soup arrived.

"The protégé was Ercole Consalvi, later Cardinal Consalvi, who was for two periods Secretary of State to Pius VII. During this Pope's difficulties with Napoleon the Cardinal was Pius VII's strongest supporter and confidant, and went with him into exile. As for Cardinal Stuart, when we go to St Peter's Basilica in Rome, you will see the famous Stuart Monument which portrays him with his father and brother."

"Are you a Jacobite, Father?" I asked. I realized that this was the first time that I had called him Father directly. Was my question too personal? But looking at me with a smile above his wine glass he replied:

"Anyone with a sense of the cardinal virtue of justice will find the Dutch invasion and the usurpation of the throne by

William of Orange repellent. Far from being a 'Glorious Revolution' it remains a terrible stain on the collective conscience of Britons, even if largely unacknowledged. It is one of the incidents in our past, like those which our young French friends regret in their history, which still cries out for penance and reparation. But James II, who had shown he was no coward on land and sea, was right not to stay on and cause the suffering of another Civil War. The Providence of God is often difficult to interpret. But I believe that Henry Stuart was also right to pursue his priestly vocation rather than an unrealistic dream of a Stuart restoration. The title of Henry IX, which made him a Royal Highness and elevated his status in Roman society, gave him and his household some innocent pleasure, although others mocked him for using it. I doubt if he ever seriously thought of pursuing his claim militarily.

"You may find it interesting, as I do, that George IV when still Prince of Wales, made a financial contribution towards the cost of Canova's Stuart monument in St Peter's. A cynic may say the condition for this donation may have been the removal of the Cardinal Duke's tombstone in the Basilica. On this he is proclaimed King Henry IX. Of course the Canova monument represented a suitably flaboyant artistic end to the Jacobite cause, and hence strengthened the position of the House of Hanover, but I also see some generosity of spirit on the part of the Prince Regent."

By now we had both consumed the soup and the wild boar, which was beautifully cooked and tender. Although he was doing so much talking Benson was a rapid eater, and managed talking and eating at the same time. The Head Waiter came and hovered. Benson made a sign, and he disappeared again.

A minute or so later a young waiter came bearing a large silver salver. On this were two plates and a silver jug of cream. On each plate there was what seemed to be a small round cake. They were exquisitely decorated. One of the plates was set down with a flourish in front of Benson and one in front of me. Each cake had a cardinal's hat depicted in red icing at the top. The hat had six strings with tassels, three from each side of the hat; they went round the edge of the cake and continued down the sides of the cake. I had never seen a cardinal's hat but I imagined that the six strings were used to tie the hat on to the head if it was windy! Below the cardinal's hat in the centre of the cake was a crown in gold icing.

"I had them made in London before we left as a little tribute to the Cardinal Duke Th…there's a sh…shop that does this sort of thing near The Travellers' Club. I had intended to include his entire coat of arms, but this would have taken the pastry cook longer than the time which he and I had at our disposal. On reflection I think the simpler design may be better for a cake. It was well packed by the shop, so it has travelled snugly in my rucksack, although I had a few anxious moments."

"They are absolutely charming, and a fitting surprise to crown our celebration of the Cardinal's birthday." My words were tritely conventional, but I believe Benson could see how much pleasure they gave me. Several waiters from other tables came to look at them, and Benson said a few words in French about the cakes' origin in London and the Cardinal Duke. When they had left Benson turned to me:

"I felt that the anniversary of the Cardinal's birth worth recalling. He's an interesting example of someone who thought that he had a fixed destiny—the restoration of the Stuarts to their rightful inheritance, the Crown of England and Scotland—. But God called him to do something different. He was not very intelligent or sophisticated—there are some amusing stories of his naivety—. But he gave his life for the good of those for whom he was responsible, and encouraged the flowering of all the arts in his diocese. Perhaps because the Church encourages us to contemplate the goodness and greatness of God, and the heroic virtues of the saints, we sometimes fail to give thanks for the lives of those who simply carry out their duties conscientiously."

The cake was a sponge and as delicious as decorative.

The Head Waiter himself brought coffee at this point

and two cigars. Benson's face suddenly looked more serious.

"I think that it is now time" he began, "for us to discuss some important shadows over the Church and its history. What do you think about the Inquisition?"

"I haven't thought much about this," I confessed.

"Oh but you must," said Benson. "How can a Divine Institution which we Catholics believe was founded by our Lord, and is infallible in its solemn proclamations on faith and morals, have persecuted heretics so cruelly?"

"I suppose I have just accepted that it was a cruel age and the Church thought it important to protect the faithful from endangering their souls."

"Yes indeed," said Benson. "And we know that the Church authorities in Rome did protest at the severity of the persecution of heretics in Spain by the lay authorities. It is often the laity who are more zealous for the Church than its own bishops. But what about all those burnings under Queen Mary Tudor in England,—the most systematic religious persecution anywhere in Europe. How can that be reconciled with our Lord's Sermon on the Mount?"

"Wasn't the hanging, drawing and quartering of Catholic priests and laity under Queen Elizabeth equally horrific? I remember reading that sometimes the poor men were even disembowelled while still alive, and shown their organs."

"But the cruel behaviour of others cannot be taken as a defence against a charge of barbaric cruelty by rulers loyal to the Bride of Christ, His Church. Of course the way criminals were punished in Tudor and Renaissance times was broadly accepted then, and is now unacceptable. But surely the Church was wrong, terribly wrong, to use such horrific means, even when seeking to combat ideas which it believed would lead members of its flock into spiritual disaster. Was not the right way to seek their return or conversion to the Faith by preaching His word as He had commanded?"

"It does seem so," I admitted.

"Consider the Church under Queen Mary. As a Catholic I admire much that she did to restore England to the

Catholic faith. Protestantism had not really taken a firm root in England, except perhaps in London. The Marian restoration was in many ways popular. The mariage with King Philip of Spain caused political problems, but it was not Philip's religion that upset Englishmen. Historians say that the burnings of heretics turned the tide against Mary. Yet it is becoming clearer that the general public, inured to public executions, were not initially particularly revolted by the burning of heretics. Of course the Protestants understandably made a terrible fuss about them. In due course, during the reign of Elizabeth, they largely won the propaganda war. Englishmen now have an instinctive fear of the papacy. But the historical reality is that by the end of Mary's reign the persecution of heretics had actually turned the tide, and that Catholicism was more firmly established than has previously been understood. In worldly terms the burnings may have been a successful policy.

"But it is interesting to speculate how God viewed the matter. The very success of Marian religious policy through the persecutions and burnings may have been the problem. When this success was followed by the death of Mary, which ended Catholic hopes, and then by the persecution of Catholics in their turn under Elizabeth and James, and the long years when Catholicism was proscribed, may not this have been a divine reminder to the Church of the need to return to our Lord's means of teaching and preserving His Gospel?"

"Yes, that seems very possible," I confessed.

"But there is another question to consider." He drew deeply on his cigar. "Not only can this Divine Institution of the Church be sometimes misguided in its methods and political policies, and yet not receive a bolt from heaven, but its shepherds can be often be wordly, and sometimes evil. The Canadian priests who came to you today, like Job's tempters, are not especially rare. Historians have documented the immoral lives of some notorious popes and their courtiers, as well as bishops, clergy and members of religious congregations. Ordinary Catholics are often challenged by those outside the Church on the immoral or selfish lives of those who outwardly practice our Faith. Why does our Lord allow this? Wouldn't He wish His Church to be always a shining example, and hence easier to defend?"

I reflected for a few moments.

"I suppose it is something to do with our free will. And to remind us that we're after all mere creatures, redeemed yes, but still with a constant struggle within our souls between good and evil. To be confronted by evil in others may be a kind of warning to us. And when we see it in the important and powerful perhaps this should remind us of our Lord's emphasis on simplicity and humility, and of the dangers of pride from any exercise of authority. Might it also be a way of testing our Faith?"

Benson looked at me rather fiercely, jutting out his chin.

"And was your Faith tested by the Canadian priests?"

I looked away from his gaze and lowered my eyes to the table cloth. Then I looked back at him and returned his gaze.

"Yes," I said, and looked down again.

"Sometimes such events may give God the opportunity to bring good out of evil."

"I hope so," I replied.

Benson summoned our waiter for the bill. I suddenly felt very tired. Benson paid, although it was really my turn. He then suggested that we went back to our compartments rather than have a night cap. In the corridor he handed me a small map of Rome, then made clear that it was now time for some spiritual reading on our own. We should say our night prayers separately. Before bidding me goodnight he reminded me that he sometimes found it difficult to wake early. Would I be kind enough to knock on his compartment door at 6.15 am?

My *couchette* was now made up with sheets with the SCNF logo. I got into my pyjamas and sat on the bed. I took out the Catechism without enthusiasm. The page that opened contained numbered paragraphs on the capital sins, the sins against the Holy Spirit and the sins crying out to heaven for vengeance. I had probably commited most of them to some degree. Not wilful murder perhaps, although I had probably several times wished another person dead.

Much of the optimism that I had felt during my pilgrimage seemed to have evaporated. *I* seemed inadequate, *The Church* all too human. What was I doing? And Benson? Who was he? What was he?

By an act of will I got up and found my rosary. I forced myself to spread it out on my lap. I decided on just saying the first sorrowful Mystery, Christ's Agony in the Garden of Gethsemane. I would just offer it for myself.

I said it slowly in English without any feeling or emotion. I tried to imagine our Lord's suffering but my own sudden emptiness seemed to block His out.

At the end I found just a little comfort in meticulously returning the black beads to their little velvet pouch and carefully tying up its drawstring. Then I got into bed and turned out the light. I was immediately more conscious than I had been of the vibrations which passed up through me from the carriage as the wheels sped along the rails. As I drifted off I wondered about the new promised TGV service. It was due to start on new track later in the year over part of the route. Would it provide a gentler ride?

CHAPTER THIRTEEN

A NIGHTMARE AND THEN ROME

JUST as I did not include in my letters to Angela everything that had happened I have seriously thought of omitting from my account what follows. I recorded an earlier dream which had an element of farce about it. I did not find this next dream at all farcical.

The train's rhythm seemed to prevent sound sleep so I was perhaps half asleep and half awake when that barren waste land appeared again. It seemed very like that of my earlier dream. There were the same stunted juniper trees in what seemed a parched landscape. But it then became clear to me that it was not a plain but rather quite a large piece of flattish ground on the top of a hill. There were several outcrops of rock which obstructed my line of vision in several directions.

I was also conscious of some strange singing that seemed to mimic the rhythm of the train. As I listened it was more like caterwauling than singing. I still could not see a sign of anyone. The strange sound continued and in due course I began to see some figures coming from round one of the outcrops. As I watched there appeared a line of figures in single file. I could see that they were all women. They had grey calf-length skirts, white blouses and long grey cardigans. It was their voices that I had heard. As they moved forward in procession they rolled their hips slowly from side to side in time to the music and held their hands above their heads. The line snaked around another outcrop and I thought that they might disappear from view, but I now seemed to have a new vantage point.

I saw them arriving at another part of the little plateau. Here there was a fire. At first this was quite small, but another women, dressed the same as the others but not part of the curious swaying dance, was sitting by the fire feeding it with what looked like branches from the juniper trees. Beside her, on a small rock outcrop, was a basket.

It was when I looked to my left that I saw him. From his size and physical shape he seemed to be a boy about eleven or twelve years of age. He was lying face downwards on another larger outcrop of stone. He was completely naked, with his torso and stomach on the rock and his arms and legs thrust out in front and behind. I stared at him and saw that his arms and legs had been bound with rope. I was unable to see his face because of his position.

But I was certain that it was me.

The discordant chanting of the women continued, but they were some distance from the boy. They seemed unaware of him or of anything else but their strange dance.

Suddenly from behind another outcrop there appeared two men. They were wearing jeans and black tee shirts. I could not really recognise them as they were wearing dark glasses, but I guessed from their flabby shape who they were. They slowly circled the bound boy, but did not go near him. Then one of them walked hurriedly away in the direction of the fire. The other man moved closer to the boy and stared at him. I now saw that the man who had gone towards the fire had picked up a flaming juniper brand from it and was returning to the boy.

"Jesus," I screamed, "they're going to burn me." But no-one noticed my cry.

Suddenly the other man caught sight of his companion's approach with the burning brand, and rushed at him. He started to grapple with him trying to snatch the lighted brand from his hand. The two men fell to the ground in their struggle.

I never saw the outcome of their fight because my focus shifted. The woman by the fire came hurriedly over to where the men had been, seized the smouldering brand from where it had fallen, and went back and replaced it on the fire. Then she resumed her seat on the rock. I then saw that she was tearing up what looked like sheets of paper from her basket. As she tore each sheet I could hear her counting in French before she cast the pieces into the fire. I was surprised to be able to see what was on the sheets. They seemed to be a series of engravings about A4 in size. Each of them was a portrait of a man.

"Quatre-vingt-cinque, quatre vingt-seize, quatre-vingt sette…" she was muttering.

I found I could recognise who was depicted in the engravings. She was burning portraits of the popes. I recall wondering whether she had begun with St Peter and whether she had an engraving of the present Pope. Perhaps, I thought, she would make do with a photograph of him.

I then tried desperately to get back to the place where I had a view of the bound boy, but either he had disappeared or else I was not able to find where he was lying. Nor did I see the two men again. But I could still hear the women wailing as I awoke in a terrible sweat. My heart was pounding. I was frozen with cold and and got up and put on Mama's pullover.

I lay rigid for some time. But eventually I must have drifted off to sleep again for I was woken by a soft knocking at my compartment door. I got up and opened it carefully. It was the man in charge of the carriage with my passport. He welcomed me to Italy.

Although I could remember all the details of my dream, which forms the basis for my record, my mood had totally changed when I was again awake. I felt extraordinarily alive.

I was in Italy! I quickly shaved and recited the Angelus confidently. I was pleased with my Latin. I looked at my watch. It was 6.15 am. I went and knocked on the door of Benson's compartment. There was a soft, sleepy response from within.

"Father, it's me, Bridge. It's 6.15 am. You asked to be woken." Benson emerged briefly in a night shirt and thanked me. He closed the compartment door again.

A strange thought came to me. Would Benson have been

aware of my dream? Although he sometimes seemed to guess what I was thinking it seemed unlikely that he would see into my sub-conscious. Should I tell him my dream, and see if he seemed familiar with it? On reflection I was not sure I wanted to tell him about it.

When I was back in my compartment I recalled our Rule. I should now be saying Prime and Lauds as I had already completed the Angelus. I must ask Benson to let me have a text so that I could do this tomorrow.

I dressed carefully in my suit. Then I made myself a cup of tea, boiling the water in the bouillotte that I plugged into the shaving point above the wash basin. Sitting by the window with my tea I decided to read the Digby Memoir and look out at what I could see of the Italian countryside in the early morning.

It was beginning to be light as I put up the blind and took in the passing scenery. After a few minutes the fellow now in charge of our carriage knocked again quietly. He asked if he could take off the bedding and refashion the compartment for its day use.

He was an Italian. I realized he must have taken over when the train crossed into Italy. I tried out my Italian and asked about the weather. He replied in English, almost without accent, that it promised to be a fine day.

"In Rome?" I asked.

"I believe so," he said, as he started to take off the sheets.

I decided to look at the map of the city which Benson had given me. I was staying in a *pensione* in the Via Serpenti not far from the Roman Forum. My meeting this afternoon was in the Ministero delle Finanze, a sign to me that the Italian authorities saw the forthcoming GATT tariff negotations as a financial as well as a trade and foreign policy matter. My Department at home took the same view. I noted that it was probably too far to walk to the Ministry from my hotel and be on time, assuming Benson had plans for visits during our first morning in Rome. I resolved to take a taxi to the meeting.

I was pleased that I remembered that we had Clement's acorns to plant in the gardens above the Forum. I might find something about the Forum for Cyprian in that area. In our conversation about the Cardinal Duke, Benson had implied that we would be going to St Peter's. I hoped we would do this on Saturday. I would like to get today's meeting out of the way first.

This thought prompted me to get out the file for the meeting, rather than indulging in the Digby Memoir.

I flicked through the papers. The Commission's main objective at the meeting would be to get agreement among Community member states to a line for EC Ministers next week. EC Ministers would soon be meeting their counterparts from the other main countries who were part of the World Trade Organization, the WTO as it was known. The key players were the United States, the Nordic countries, Switzerland, Japan, and some of the developing countries. WTO member states, meeting at ministerial level, would soon be having preliminary talks about the agenda for the forthcoming Uruguay Round of trade negotiations in Geneva.

World trade had already benefitted significantly from earlier trade rounds through member states' mutual reduction of customs duties, and the elimination of many discriminatory trade barriers in manufactured goods. The Uruguay Round was intended to make further reductions, and eliminate barriers in other fields as well.

The United States wanted the new round to extend liberalisation so as to cover services such as banking, insurance and telecommunications. But France was nervous about this, fearing that their banking, insurance and telecommunication industries would be unable to compete with foreign companies if the latter had free access to the French home market.

The UK sympathised with the Americans, because our service industries were also strong. The Commission was always more protectionist, and would be likely to support the French.

My task at this afternoon's meeting was to keep the possibility of services being part of the Uruguay Round still open, without being seen as insufficiently 'community minded', if other member states wanted to oppose this.

My colleague, Gilmore, had produced a useful defensive note on a contentious issue for the UK about London taxis. The technical specification for tendering by manufacturing firms seeking to supply vehicles to be used as London taxis was very detailed indeed. The French were likely to argue that that this precise specification for the traditional London black cab or hackney carriage, with its requirements for ease of access for passengers, height (so that a passenger could keep his hat on!), with seats facing both ways, and a prescribed tight turning circle (essential in some narrow London streets), effectively precluded car manufacturers in continental Europe from tendering for these contracts. Ordinary limousines, manufactured in other countries such as France, Germany and Italy, and used as taxis there, were very different. Retooling to meet the technical requirements for London taxis would not be economic for the vehicle industries in these other countries.

The French representative would probably argue that the authorities in London should allow ordinary saloon cars made by French companies to appear as taxis plying for hire on London streets. They would probably say that the restrictive specification for London taxis was typical of the way the UK behaved in general. We preached liberalisation of trade and opening up of markets, and wanted to include services in the next round of world trade talks. Yet at the same time the United Kindom was ready to use discriminatory specifications in manufactured goods such as taxis, so as to keep foreign companies out of its domestic markets.

Gilmore had provided some robust points to defend the specifications. His note suggested that other cities outside the UK might well benefit from our style of taxi. He highlighted in particular London taxis' excellent safety record.

Gilmore had also produced some useful instances of

French Government departments and local authorities failing to advertise internationally for the supply of manufactured goods for their armed forces, hospitals and schools. They were bound to do this under the existing WTO rules. He also instanced some examples where tenders for certain manufactured goods *had* been advertised internationally by French governmental bodies as required under EC law, but the *deadlines* for submitting tenders had been *so short* that overseas firms were effectively excluded.

After scanning a further background note on UK banking, insurance and telecommunications, I closed the papers. It all seemed reasonably straightforward. Benson had suggested I might produce a surprise for him. The briefing for my meeting did not seem to provide promising material for this!

There was another knock. It was Benson suggesting we went along to breakfast together. In the restaurant car, while we ate fresh rolls and fruit and had some excellent Italian coffee, Benson put forward his suggestions for Rome. On arrival at the railway station we would each get a weekly concession ticket for the buses. which would enable us to get about easily if it was inconvenient to walk, or we were pressed for time.

"We would then go to our respective lodgings," he said. "I hope the *pensione* in the Via Serpenti will prove convenient and agreeable There is a lot to be said for starting a visit to Rome with its pagan origins. I suggest we meet at the Colosseum first, then have a look at the Forum area, and go on up into the Farnese gardens above on the Capitoline Hill. Here we can plant Clement's acorns. I will bring a little picnic lunch that we can have there together. I am sure you will bring the green cloth. I expect that by the time we have eaten and admired the view it will be time for you to go to your meeting.

"If you had not had a meeting, I would have suggested an afternoon visit to the catacombs, the vast subterranean burial ground of early Christians in Rome. A number of the first popes and some of the martyrs were buried there originally, although many were later brought back into Rome itself and reinterred in various churches. However, I have learned that a fine English choir that specialises in Gregorian chant and early polyphony has been invited to sing vespers at Santa Maria Maggiore today. This is in the late afternoon, so we might meet there after your meeting. This great church, you will see from your map, is quite near your Ministry. And of course it is a church which every visitor should see. "

He looked across at me as if to assess my readiness to take in some further information. I smiled back hoping that this would be seen as a positive sign.

"Santa Maria Maggiore was originally built" he began, "about forty years after the Edict of Milan. This, as you will know, was the one that granted full religious freedom to Christians. Further important work was done on the church soon after the Council of Ephesus had conferred on our Lady the title of Mother of God in 432 AD. You will notice that the basilica has been much added to, but it still feels like a very early church. To the Romans themselves it is perhaps the best loved of all the four great Roman basilicas.

"If you have a reasonable guide to Rome you might read about the catacombs when you have time. Many people say that seeing them, with their inscriptions, sculptures and paintings, has told them as much about how ordinary early Christians thought about their faith as the writings of the early fathers. They can also give a strong sense of the continuity of the Church as it grew through persecution and fragility into social and political acceptance. And they should help us admire the work of Providence in action.

"After Vespers we dine tonight in Trastevere and save St Peter's Basilica for tomorrow. Does all this seem reasonable?"

I nodded acceptance. Was I too passive in Benson's hands? Yet I really had no ideas of my own that I might put forward as suggestions. What most preoccupied me was how I might feel about what we did, and where this might lead. But this did not seem something I could say to Benson yet.

As I sipped my coffee I looked across at him. There was

an expression on his face that I had never detected before. Momentarily I wondered if Sebastian had ever been a recipient of this look that I can only describe as a look of great compassion. What he then said was unexpected.

"I hope that the fact that we are on our pilgrimage will not prove a distraction to the performance of your official duties at your meeting this afternoon. That would not be a welcome development. I shall offer a special prayer for you for that intention."

"Really that is most kind of you, Father," I replied, "but it is not a critical meeting. Quite routine in fact, and I have a very good brief, which I have already been through."

"That is reassuring," he said. "I would not want your spiritual quest to result in any perceived slackness in the performance of your secular duties. It could be the subject of adverse comments by those who are unsympathetic to the Church, or be used as a way of undermining your position as a Civil Servant."

I could not at that time imagine that this could be a problem. What I myself believed, or the nature of my spiritual life, was surely a private matter which colleagues would either never get to know about, or, if they did, would regard with complete indifference. Later I came to realize that Benson's concern was in some ways justified, although not in precisely the way that he had suggested.

I managed to pay the bill for breakfast this time. Benson thanked me profusely. We returned to our compartments. In the corridor Benson mentioned that he would be saying his office next, and then he had some post cards to write. If I did not mind a companionable silence initially I would be very welcome to join him in his compartment. He would also look through the notes of one of our discussions that I had asked him to vet.

As we passed one or two people making their way along the corridor in the direction of the restaurant car Benson rather embarrased me by saying rather loudly that I might consider whether there were any of the Questions and

Answers in the Catechism where I felt the need for clarification. "Was I sound," he boomed, "on Purgatory, for example and the need for confession to a priest?"

I collected a few books and my notebook from my compartment and joined Benson. His compartment had also been made up for day use, and was in perfect order. He was sitting in the window seat facing the engine, and was already absorbed in his Office. He did not look up when I entered and sat in the seat opposite him.

I began by reading Luff's *A Christian's Guide to Rome* on the catacombs. He dispelled some old myths that the Christians actually lived in them at the time of religious persecution. They were always cemeteries, and the state authorities and the pagan priests officially recognised them as such. Of the seventy odd catacombs about sixty were exclusively Christian; about ten were Jewish and one was of a little known sect. At that time pagan Romans were cremated. I remembered that Caesar had had a funeral pyre. It was Christianity which had a special reverence for the physical mortal remains of loved ones.

The total length of these underground tombs at their various levels has been estimated at 600 miles, but Luff believes this to be something of an exaggeration. The artistic details and inscriptions sounded fascinating. In 1976, when Luff was writing his guide, it was possible to hear Holy Mass there. Was this still possible? That would appeal to me. I wondered why Benson had not proposed an alternative time for us to visit the catacombs. Why could we not go there after visiting St Peter's tomorrow, or on Sunday? And why had Benson not suggested anything at all for Sunday. Surely he would need to hear and perhaps say Mass?

I turned to the Catechism. As I skipped through it I realized that I now seemed to have little difficulty with almost all of the questions and answers. Once you began to suspect, as I now seemed to be doing, that the Catholic Church was truly a continuation of what our Lord had founded, almost everything seemed to fall into place.

In regard to Purgatory, I had always found this a logical and comforting doctrine. Perhaps this was surprising in an Anglican. I recalled so many established church funerals where it was clear to almost everyone in the congregation that the deceased was very imperfect indeed. Some of his misdeeds were even recounted in the personal reflections which had become a key part of funerals these days. These anecdotes often seemed designed to show the deceased as a loveable rogue. I could not remember one example of it being said that someone had confessed and repented of their sins at the last. Yet Anglican clergy always seemed to imply that the deceased was already guaranteed heaven. The only alternative for Anglicans, that he or she might be in hell, was never alluded to.

The doctrine of Purgatory seemed the sensible theological position. There was some telling scriptural support for it too. I suspected that Purgatory got a bad name at the Reformation largely because the Church had allowed abuses to develop whereby periods of time in Purgatory could be shortened through paying for Masses for the dead. The rates for these in some cases had become exhorbitant. Of course, I could accept that a labourer was worthy of his hire, and Mass stipends were an acceptable way of supporting priests as pastors of their flocks. But the financial element could get out of hand, and this had proved a useful target for those who wanted to attack the Church in the past.

With regard to confession to a priest I had been ambivalent, although I could see that putting one's sins into words to another made one take them seriously. And yet it terrified me personally! Even the look of confessionals in Catholic churches seemed to be well—so very Catholic! Yet I had to admit that what I had learned about Sebastian and Benson, and the results of that confession, had made a deep impression on me.

What would I say if I had to make a confession to a priest? I started to day dream about this. While I was doing so Benson closed his breviary and looked at me. I avoided his gaze and asked him if he would mind looking over the notes on one of our earlier conversations as he had promised.

He said he would be pleased to do this. I handed him several pages that I had taken from the notebook which contained the passages in question. I did not think it appropriate for him to have sight of the whole of the notebook.

Benson studied these with his brows furrowed for some time. Then he looked up smiling.

"Y...you seem to have covered the points admirably. It seems to read much better than when I articulated it. The Holy Ghost must have been at work with one or perhaps both of us!"

He grinned his boyish grin. I felt enormously relieved. It was as though I had passed a difficult exam which I had thought I would fail.

"I don't think I have any points about the Catechism," I then said. "You may find this surprising, but I suppose it is because I am beginning to have some conception of what the Catholic Church really is."

Then I surprised myself by adding: "I am also beginning to see how the Church can be at the same time the Bride of Christ and an infallible source of theological and moral doctrine, and yet have leaders, priests, bishops, even popes, who are weak, deeply flawed or malign. I have no doubt that this also applies to the ordinary lay faithful, even those given the grace of conversion."

Benson gave me his sympathetic look, then said:

"I pray that our time in Rome will only confirm your understanding. Perhaps it is now time for me to tackle a piece of my tapestry, as I have now found that I have no more letters or post cards to write this morning. But please interrupt if points on the Catechism do occur to you."

Benson took out his work from his rucksack, and lit a cigarette. He made used of Ruby's scallop shell as his ashtray. I decided it would be companionable to do something with my hands too. I had brought a pair of grey socks with holes in the heels. I fished them out and located a wooden mushroom to provide support for my darn, a needle with a large eye, and some darning wool. I made a start. Benson looked up and smiled rather conspiratorily. I turned the first sock inside out. I knew the principles: running threads first one way across the hole, and then weaving the wool crosswise in and out of the threads that I had first applied. I could see that getting the tension right was the important thing, but found this difficult in practice.

As I worked at my socks I reflected on what had happened since yesterday afternoon. The most striking thing was that for much of the time since then I had been on my own with Benson. This was a contrast with the previous day, when Benson and I seemed to be constantly meeting people. The earlier day had also been full of unexpected events and surprises. Since yesterday the pilgrimage had become more cerebral, although this did not mean that it was without emotional drama. I shuddered as I remembered my most recent dream. Early in the pilgrimage I sometimes felt that Benson was paying more attention to others than to me. The situation was completely different now. I longed to see what would happen in Rome.

I know that the train had stopped at several large stations during the early morning, one of them I remember was Turin, but neither Benson nor I seem to have cause to leave the train. As we had single compartments there was no question of anyone joining us. I noticed a few people pass our compartment, but none bothered to glance our way. Benson continued to work away at his tapestry. I must have drifted off into sleep.

When I awoke, the socks, with their very amateur darning, were on my lap. I looked across for Benson, but he was not where I had last seen him. There was just the tapestry on his seat. I rubbed my eyes and then saw that Benson had moved. He was now kneeling on the compartment floor at the far end of his seat facing towards the back of the train. His head with its tousled butter-coloured hair was resting on his hands.

I felt momentary embarrassment. He was there for what seemed quite a long time. Eventually he got up and returned to his seat. He looked across at me.

"Sometimes it helps my concentration in prayer."

There was a knock on the compartment door. It was our carriage steward.

"Monsignore e Signor Bridge arriveremo a Roma in poco tempo. Il treno sarà in orario come all'epoca di Mussolini!"

He grinned at his little joke. It was often alleged that Mussolini had made Italian trains run on time.

He repeated his announcement to us in American English.

"Monsignor and Mr Bridge we will be arriving in Rome quite soon. The train will be on schedule."

He pronounced 'schedule' American-style with the 'ch' pronounced as a 'k'. He omitted the reference to Mussolini in his English version.

"*Il tempo e perfetto per i turisti,*" he continued "The weather is perfect for tourists. I wish you a good holiday in the Eternal City of Rome!"

He made a little bow and left. We gathered up our belongings and repacked. Benson produced a cardboard box from his tall rucksack. When he opened it I saw that it contained a clerical Roman hat in black beaver fur. As he was putting it on I saw it was lined with white silk. Benson examined the effect in a mirror which was above our seat. He turned to me and said:

"When in Rome do as the Romans. It is known here as a *Capello Romano*."

I wondered to myself how many priests in Rome would wear a hat like that these days.

"It has travelled quite well in this box, don't you think?"

I had to agree that it looked in good shape. It certainly made Benson appear more striking than ever. I was also surprised to see that he still had the pilgrim's staff that he had cut in Seal Chart on our first morning. I noticed that he had managed to fit a top of one of our champagne bottle corks on the bottom of the staff as a ferule. I am not sure where I had left my staff, but I do not think I remember having it after getting off the ferry. Benson also put on a black coat which he wore over his cassock.

My first sight of Rome was the *Stazione di Termini*, its main railway station. As we got off the train we were confronted by a seething mass of people waiting to meet family and friends. A dark woman with a shawl over her head and a baby had ventured to sit among the melée on the platform near our carriage door. She had a small plastic cup in her outstretched hand. Benson managed to find something in his cassock and give it to her as we were shouldering our packs. The woman gave us a big smile and seemed to be thanking us although I couldn't understand her words.

When we came out of the station into bright sunshine Benson had his determined look and immediately led the way across what seemed to be a large square. Here and there there were one or two booths selling newspapers and magazines. On the side of the path along which Benson was leading me several young African men were sitting on the ground with a small selection of wares on a cloth in front of them. The goods seemed to be mostly wooden necklaces, earrings, bracelets covered in beads, and strange amulets. Although we must have seemed unlikely customers for what they were selling they greeted us warmly.

Exhilarated by the realization that I was really at last in Rome, and perhaps by the the chance of some new human contact, I surprised them by trying out a greeting of a few words in Ouolof, the one African language that I knew slightly. They got very excited because they happened to be from Senegal, and their native language was Ouolof. They insisted on making a gift to me as their brother. It was one of the bead bracelets which they said I should take for my wife.

Of course I ended up giving them some lira for it. I thought it unlikely that Angela would ever wear it, but I admired the panache of their strategem, and I was completely won over by their smiles. Both of them revealed sets of perfect white teeth.

Benson stopped while this was going on and gave them a big grin. At this they pointed to themselves, and made signs of the cross, then bowed their heads. Benson obliged with a blessing in Latin above where they were sitting on the ground. They repeated their signs of the cross, and muttered "Amen."

Since over eighty per cent of Senegalese are Muslims it seemed to me highly unlikely that they were Christians, although if they were, they would probably be Catholics.

Benson strode on purposely until he reached a small kiosk. It turned out to be where we were able to buy our weekly ticket for the buses. With this purchase made, Benson turned to me and said:

"Another time when you are in Rome you should explore the area around the railway station, which has a fascinating history. Just before Christianity became legal the Roman Emperor Diocletian had constructed here a vast complex of baths, swimming pools, shopping arcades, and sports grounds; even a library and an art gallery. It covered about twenty-three acres. The tradition is that the work was done by the forced labour of over 10,000 Christian slaves, who were subsequently executed and buried outside Rome. There is perhaps some irony in the fact that two of the buildings now standing amid the remains of the baths are the churches of Santa Maria degli Angeli and San Bernardo. The Museo Nazionale is also built in the ruins and preserves some of the layout of the gardens of the old baths. It has a superb collection of ancient Roman Christian stone coffins. I do not know what his motives were, but Pope Sixtus V is said to have blown up a huge quantity of the remainng walls of the old baths. Perhaps he just liked explosions!" Benson laughed.

We managed to locate a bus that would take us near to the Via Serpenti where I was staying. Benson said that his lodgings were not far from there. Fortunately it seemed to be a quiet time of day so we did not inconvenience other passengers with our large packs. It was only a short walk from the bus stop to my *pensione*. Benson accompanied me there but did not come in. He seemed very cheerful but a little preoccupied. We arranged to meet outside the Colosseum at midday.

Just before he left me to go to his lodgings, he gave me his firm authoritative look and said:

"Make sure, Bridge, you have all the papers with you ready for your meeting. There won't really be time to come back here to collect anything you have forgotten."

As I mounted the stairs to the *pensione* which was on the first floor I wondered why I was not more irritated by Benson's nannying.

The *pensione* seemed more like a private apartment than a business. An elderly gentleman was seated at a table in a large hall furnished with dark furniture. He was polite but distant. He addressed me in passable English. I did not try out my Italian. He checked the details of my passport and I signed in. Then he showed me my room. It was vast. There was a king-size double bed, wardrobe, chest of drawers and small desk. I noticed with pleasure a bedside table with a lamp. My landlord opened some large doors to show me a balcony which looked down on to the Via Serpenti below.

There was no private bathroom. He showed me the bathroom I was to use. It was fortunately directly opposite. It seemed even bigger than the bedroom. I am not sure I remember ever having seen a larger bathroom. The floor was a great expanse of pure white marble. Isolated in the centre of the room was a huge white bath tub with claw feet. There was no shower. Apart from the bath tub there was little else in the room except a cane chair painted white, a small white cupboard and a free standing wooden towel rail. My landlord said I could bathe any time but he would prefer that I did not do so late at night as the plumbing was '*chiassoso*'— he could not recall the English word so he put his hands to his ears to indicate that it was noisy.

Then he left. I looked at my watch. It was 11.15 am. I calculated that I had time for a bath before our *rendez-vous*. I felt pretty dirty after the travelling. I had made do with a brief wash at the hotel in Paris. It seemed appropriate to be clean for whatever was in front of me in Rome.

Before my bath I checked all my papers for the meeting and put them in my briefcase. That would please Benson, I thought.

I had been supplied with a huge bath towel as seemed appropriate for the size of the bathroom, and I was soon comfortably soaking in the bath. I filled it as high as was possible without letting water out through the overflow. As I soaped up I thanked God for the Roman engineers who had designed such an amazing system of aqueducts to furnish Rome with a water supply that allowed for such gigantic baths. I was looking forward to seeing some of the fountains that my map showed to be abundant in the city. Luff's Guide listed forty with specific names. Papal rule in Rome in the past had clearly provided for physical as well as spiritual cleansing!

After dressing I consulted my street map of Rome and planned a route to the Colosseum. I estimated it would take me a quarter of an hour at the most on foot, probably less. But I wanted to be sure of being there on time. I glanced at the Chapter in the Luff Guide and wondered to myself what line Benson would take when introducing me to the ancient pagan ruins of Republican and Imperial Rome.

As I walked down the Via Serpenti in the warm Spring sunshine I felt completely at home, as though I had been coming to Rome for years. Benson was already outside the entrance to the Colosseum when I arrived. He suggested that we first walked across the road to the Ruins of the Temple of Venus and Roma.

"If you are too close to the Colosseum you will not fully appreciate the size of the structure."

When we had mounted the steps to the terrace which is

part of the temple ruins I saw what Benson meant.

"The larger diameter of the Colloseum's oval design is longer than the length of any English Cathedral. You should try to imagine its facade covered in marble with huge statues in the arches. There is an interesting link with our Lord. You will recall that he prophesied to the Jews the destruction of Jerusalem. When this eventually happened in 70 AD a large number of Jewish captives from the war were brought to Rome and put to work on completing this building. As you will know it was a major entertainment venue seating about 50,000. The tradition is that many Christians were martyred here as part of the entertainment programme. On the bill were gladiatorial contests and battle set-pieces, wild beast hunts and even naval battles as the arena could be flooded.

"Even after Christianity had become the official religion of Rome the Church was unable to stop these contests in which men killed each other for the entertainment of the crowd. It was only when an Eastern monk, St Telemachus, threw himself into the arena in protest at the killings, and was stoned to death for his efforts by the infuriated crowds, that public opinion turned, and fights to the death were finally stopped. It is worth reflecting as we go across the road now and walk through the ruins of the Roman forum, how long it took for the Christian idea of the sacredness of human life from conception to natural death took to make headway, both in pagan Rome and elsewhere. Of course the battle is far from over even now in our own age."

After this little introduction Benson led me to the Forum entrance gate in the Via dei Fori Imperiali. We each paid for our own tickets, then Benson turned to me and said:

"I will first take you down on to the Sacred Way, then along it to the Arch of Titus where you will be able to have a view of what was once the centre of the Ancient World in Europe."

He said nothing as we walked along it, allowing me to

reflect by myself on the ruins. My first impression was of a vast park of classical follies: monumental pediments, columns and ruined buildings set in a valley between hills. Everything was bathed in sunlight so that each marble standing construction seemed to caste a shadow. The skyline was pierced with umbrella pines and thin cypresses pointing into the blue.

It was all impressive but indicipherable. When we reached the Arch of Titus Benson beckoned me to follow him beneath it to look up at the inside first. With his pilgrim staff he pointed to what I could see was a seven branched candlestick in what seemed to be a vast procession, beautifully carved in relief in the stone.

"You see depicted here the triumphal procession of the Romans along the Sacred Way after the capture of Jerusalem. The seven-branched candlestick that the sculptor has carved portrays the one which our Lord Himself would have seen in the Temple in Jerusalem before its destruction. It is gratifying to reflect that it is these great temples of pagan Rome, before which the bloody sacrifices were made, that are now in ruins: the temples of Saturn, of Castor and Pollux, of the deified Julius Caesar, of Antoninus and Faustina. All these are now before you and we will pass them. Tomorrow you shall see St Peter's Basilica, and perhaps later the other basilicas and churches of Rome that succeeded the pagan temples."

"I imagine Cyprian will want me to see where Julius Caesar was murdered."

"You will have to disappoint him. For it is now known that the Senators were sitting elsewhere on that fateful Ides of March day. They were not meeting then in the Curia or Senate House which we will see when we return along the Sacred Way. But you shall be able to say that you have been to the spot where Mark Antony read Caesar's will, and gave his famous funeral oration before Caesar was ceremonially cremated in accordance with Roman custom. For it was on that place where the Temple of the deified Caesar was eventually erected. Let us walk back there now to see it."

On our way I asked Benson about the large building on our right which seemd to have more of it intact than most other buildings in the Forum. He told me that it had been planned and partially constructed by the Emperor Maxentius before he was defeated by his rival Constantine at the battle of the Milvian Bridge. He explained that its wonderful vault spanning about seventy-five feet was much studied by Bramante and Michaelangelo when they were drawing up plans in the sixteenth century for St Peter's.

When we reached what little remains of the Temple of Julius Caesar I made a few notes of my impressions for Cyprian. The remains of the altar in front of the temple are supposed to be on the very spot where Caesar was burned on his funeral pyre. Mark Antony would have delivered his speech from a rostrum where the Temple now stands. Caesar's nephew, Augustus, was responsible for building this temple.

Benson gave me plenty of time for my note taking, but showed little interest in it. I noticed that his eyes were fixed on a small round building a little way off towards the Capitoline Hill. When I had finished, regretting a little that I had no camera, Benson ushered me towards this little round building. When we reached it he said:

"Very little of this small Temple of Vesta is original but the idea behind it is of interest. It was probably made in circular form so as to resemble the original round huts of the first inhabitants of Rome. Each household had a fireplace in the centre of their hut. The fires were always kept going for heating and cooking purposes. The cult of Vesta was a cult of the home and in a sense of the family, which was made manifest in a cult of Fire."

He took me on to what he explained was the House of the Vestal Virgins. As we looked at this open space, with its statues of famous Vestal virgins, pleasant simple gardens and fish ponds, Benson said that this was a kind of model for the courtyards of later Christian convents and monastic enclosures. The walls, no longer standing, would have kept out the busy world of the Forum with its politics, public sacrifices to the gods and commercial trading.

"To me," said Benson, "the existence of a college of priestesses in pagan and notoriously licentious Rome—young women who had all taken vows of virginity—has a spark of the divine. Male priests of the Roman period were secular figures doing a state job of appeasing the gods by sacrifices. They were never expected to be celibate or even of high moral standard. You will remember that Julius Caesar, a notorious pursuer of other men's wives, had a period as *Pontifex Maximus*, or High Priest, on his way to the top of the political ladder. Yet these women, whose job it was to keep the sacred flame alight, which Romans believed preserved the good fortune of their city and Empire, made vows which set them apart. In this way perhaps the great monastic tradition of the Catholic Church was mysteriously foreshadowed."

I was intrigued by this thought and added:

"Perhaps some of them eventually became Christians when the new religion began to establish itself in Rome."

Benson smiled mysteriously as if he knew something about this, but did not comment directly on my point. But he did say:

"Vestal Virgins' vows were for thirty years, but what they did in retirement does not seem to be much documented in the written sources."

"All this chimes in well," I added, "with the essential role which women played in the life of our Lord and in that of the early Church."

Benson nodded in what seemed to be agreement, and then said:

"There is much more to see here, and I would like to show you the important church of Ss Cosmas and Damian which is just outside the Forum. The sixth century mosaic of Christ arriving at the Second Coming is a great masterpiece. But we are a little pressed for time and I think we should now go up on to the gardens of the Palatine Hill and have our picnic."

We crossed the courtyard of the Vestals to some steps which led up to a road through what Luff had explained was the basement of the Palace of the Emperor Domitian. The structure above ground has largely disappeared. Benson and I found ourselves in a picturesque spot that he told me was now called the Farnese Gardens. We spread out the green cloth and Benson got out our picnic. There was a large breadstick, butter, salami and rather surprisingly hard boiled eggs which Benson said he had been able to buy near his lodgings. He produced a half bottle of mineral water and some plastic cups.

We sat down together at either end of the green cloth. The sun was now quite hot and Benson loosened his clerical collar but did not take it off. He was sitting with his legs stretched out in front covered by his long coat and cassock. Only his black shoes were visible. He had parked his Capello Romano and his pilgrim staff at his side and was looking down at the view of the Forum laid out before us. In the foreground below, but still in the gardens, I had a glimpse of some lemon trees in large containers which were covered in lemons. I wondered if they were taken inside during the winter months. Benson apologised that we would be unable to get a cup of coffee. The kiosk which was not far from where we were sitting was only open in the summer months.

We had this little part of the gardens to ourselves—that is there were no other humans about. But we had not been there more than a few minutes when several thin Roman cats came and sat at a respectful distance from us and appraised us with a professional eye. In due course others arrived too. In the end there were seven. Benson commented on this with a grin:

"I cannot decide whether they represent the four cardinal and three theological virtues, or the seven capital sins. I had decided that the small pale tawny one represented

Prudence, and was looking to find the other virtues among the rest. But then that rather handsome dark brown male cat appeared who seems to be a strange compound of Pride and Covetousness.

"The small pale cream one, that seems almost still to be a kitten, and is furthest away, looks like she is at the bottom of the pecking order. She might symbolise Hope."

I suggested it might be more charitable to regard the big male cat as a symbol of Fortitude. "Perhaps he is the defender of his small pride from the attacks of other marauding bands of cats. His rather fierce demeanour could easily be mistaken for Pride."

Benson laughed loudly. "You may well be right. It is sometimes easy to judge incorrectly by first impressions." As he said this he lay flat on his back and gazed up into the sky. I spent a little time trying to trace where our route through the forum below had been.

Suddenly Benson rose up on to his elbows .

"I am sure that there is much that I have told you about the Forum which you either knew, or did not wish to know. But there may be other matters that you would have liked to have discussed but were unable to bring into the conversation." He then looked at me with his penetrating look. "And not just about the Forum. Yet they now need to be left over until later if you are to make your appointment."

He sprang up athletically, and pulled out a piece of paper from his small bag and assembled some fragments of meat and crusts from our lunch on it.

"For the cats," he said. " I fear the big male cat will also epitomise Gluttony."

I squeezed the green cloth back into my briefcase. By this time Benson was ready to lead the way back down through the Forum. But before setting off he reached into his black coat and retrieved the acorns and his Swiss Army knife.

"I am glad we did not forget Clement's commission."

The 'we' was generous. I had completely forgotten. He dug a neat little hole about four inches deep with the longest blade a foot of so from where we had been sitting. He then dropped in one of the acorns and replaced the small piece of turf. He then walked about twenty yards behind and did the same with the others.

We then went back down to the Forum the way we had come. But before we left the precincts we had a brief look at the Aemelian Basilica which dates from the early first century. Here was the place at the heart of the city where currency could be traded and exchanged. Benson pointed out the coins which were still fused into the marble pavement after a disastrous fire when Rome was sacked by the Huns in 410 AD.

We were able to find a taxi in the area near the Colosseum, and I managed to use my limited Italian to engage a young driver to take me to the *Ministero delle Finanze*. As I got into the cab Benson shouted after me that he hoped I could meet him at Santa Maria Maggiore by about 5.15 pm. As the taxi-driver sped off with a roar I looked back to see Benson waving to me with his Roman hat.

CHAPTER FOURTEEN

NOT JUST CARDS

A United Kingdom official record of this meeting exists. I prepared and later agreed this with my colleague, Harrison, of the Department of Trade and Industry. It duly records the meeting's conclusions and, as is usual with such records, while not exactly falsifying the discussion, puts a little favourable gloss on the interventions of those who represented the United Kingdom. I later saw the European Commision's official account of the meeting too, which had its own slant.

Only a very little of what follows is in these two official accounts. Perhaps what you will read here is a more accurate account of what happened. But it also includes the changes in my state of mind during the meeting. Although there are some elements almost of farce I would stress that, as international meetings go, it was probably not much more comical than many others.

My swarthy young taxi driver in dark glasses had driven fast and to my mind rather recklessly to the Ministry. But he had got me there without mishap and in good time. The Italian Finance Ministry is in a huge building which spreads out along the Via XX Settembre. It looked to me to have been built in the last part of the 19th century. There seemed little security as I entered. Eventually I located a Ministry information desk and explained who I was and gave details of the meeting I was attending. I was asked to wait and was directed to a capacious armchair. After a few minutes a tall very smart young man in his late thirties wearing an impeccable dark uniform and white gloves came to greet me and take me up a rather grand staircase to where we were to meet. I was about a quarter of an hour early, and my usher explained that some of my colleagues were already there, and that there would be coffee and biscuits.

We entered what seemed to be an ante-room with a high ceiling and much gilt and heavy dark furniture. I think that there were several oil paintings on the wall but I cannot remember looking at them. I was greeted most warmly by my Italian colleague, Farinelli. He was amazed when I told him that I had come to Rome by train. After a few seconds he broke away and went over to a corner to resume talking to our Danish colleague. They seemed to be having a heated discussion.

My UK colleague Harrison from the DTI came up to me. After exchanging pleasantries about our journeys and accommodation he told me that it looked as though the meeting might be late in starting. My Irish colleague, Jim O'Hara, joined us. I get on well with him. When we first met he offered me a useful prompt for remembering his name: "Think Scarlett," he said, pointing to the few ginger hairs on his balding head.

He now pointed towards the Italian and Danish representatives. Their discussion seemed to be getting even more animated. "I wonder whether they will resort to fisticuffs," he said in a stage whisper.

My colleague Harrison said:

"In all my time at EC meetings I've never known a Dane make a fuss about language interpreting for a meeting. Nielsen seems to be saying that if the Italian delegate uses French rather than English, as he has said he intends to do, the Commision is certain to follow suit. Of course the French delegate always uses French. I know that Nielsen has very little French. He has told me that he has already been to meet the simultaneous interpreter who would be putting the speeches and interventions in French into English for the benefit of people like himself without French. Nielsen has discovered that today's interpreter is an Italian and his translation of French into English is completely hopeless for the technical discussion that we are to have."

O'Hara added: "Nielsen —don't you think he looks like an angry troll?—has just told poor Farinelli that he will now insist on speaking Danish at the meeting. He said that it was his right, and that it was up to the Italians, as the hosts for the meeting, to find interpreters to put his Danish into the other languages being used at the meeting. Nielsen has told me that he always wanted today's meeting to be in Brussels."

O'Hara added: "It's a real Tower of Babel. Do you think I should insist on speaking Erse? No-one here would know how poor my Erse is," he added gleefully.

Poor Farinelli, our Italian host, was raising his hands repeatedly in an apologetic way and shrugging his shoulders as he sought to placate Nielsen. Eventually Farinelli disappeared into what seemed to be the next room where we were to meet.

"He's gone on what he knows is a hopeless mission, but he feels he needs to show evidence of trying," said O'Hara cynically. "We should take bets on how long he will give it on the other side of that door before he returns to report that he has been unsuccessful in finding an interpreter. If he can't find a good interpreter to translate French into English for today's meeting, is there any chance he will find interpreters at short notice to translate Danish into English? And of course into French, and into German and into Italian."

"And into Dutch," I added, having just spotted our Dutch colleague coming into the room.

O'Hara turned to look across at the plump, balding Dutchman. Van Groeningen seemed very red-faced and swayed a little before he sat down heavily in a chair well away from our group. He did not look over at us but sat staring at the floor.

"He seems rather the worse for wear," said O'Hara.

At this point the French and German representatives entered together from the Conference room next door with the European Commission representative in tow. This was quite usual. The three of them often had a little pre-meeting to try and agree a joint line to take at EC meetings. This did not always go down well with delegates from other member states excluded from this cabal.

I studied them to see if I could read from their faces how this had gone. It was not always possible for them to reach agreement. Although the small flamboyant Frenchman, Lucet, continually sought to flatter his tall blond German colleague in a rather pointed manner, so as to try to keep the Franco-German motor running Community affairs, this did not always work with Mueller. On this occasion, rather pointedly I thought, Mueller broke from the other two and came across the room and shook hands with me warmly. He did the same with Harrison and O'Hara.

Another immaculately dressed Italian in uniform came across to us at that moment and handed us all coffee from a silver tray. There were also some little almond biscuits, *amarettini*, which I adored.

Mueller spoke beautifully correct English—he had spent several years at an English University, but much of the credit was probably due to his schooling at one of the best gymnasia in Bavaria. He quizzed me earnestly about some tensions within the Thatcher Cabinet which he had read about in yesterday's *Times*. Since I had not seen this I was able to be non-commital which I would have wished to be anyway.

He then launched into a discussion of English football with Harrison. Mueller had become a fan of Manchester United while he was in the UK and Harrison also happened to be a supporter. O'Hara also followed the English game, so all three were soon in an animated discussion of a recent match between Manchester United and Liverpool. My interest in English football was lukewarm yet it was politic to keep my end up. But I kept my eyes on the door into our meeting room, hoping that Farinelli would emerge soon to confess the failure of his quest for interpreters from Danish. I shared O'Hara's view that he would not have even tried. The interesting question to me was how Farinelli would deal with Nielsen, and with the loss of face that this would involve him in as host. Of course I was also concerned that a delayed start might affect my appointment with Benson.

The door opened slightly and Farinelli slid past it into our room. He did not go over to our Danish colleague, but went to speak to the Representative of the Commission. Monsieur Hubert was a plump Belgian of medium height. He was particularly conscious of being from the French speaking part of Belgium and was barely able to conceal his prejudice against Belgium's Flemish speakers. For this reason, he was particularly disliked by our Dutch colleague, Van Groeningen.

Hubert and Farinelli spoke very quietly, glancing nervously at Nielsen. They then summoned our French colleague for moral support. The three of them went over as a kind of delegation to Nielsen. It was immediately clear that he was unmoved by their entreaties. Farinelli then went into the middle of the room and announced in French that despite some technical difficulties the meeting would now begin.

The usher in the white gloves moved over to the double doors which led into the next room and opened them with a flourish. Standing to one side, he gestured towards us all with a smile that showed his perfectly-formed white teeth, and proclaimed loudly:

"*Prego.*" It was clearly his big moment.

There was then a kind of quadrille of precedence to go through the door. Farinelli, Mueller, our French colleague, Lucet, and Hubert were all making calculations. Should Farinelli lead the way as host at the meeting, or should Hubert, as the Commission representative, go first as he would be in the chair for the day. For these meetings the issue of which country held the rotating Community Presidency was ignored. Would Mueller precede Lucet or Lucet Mueller? This sometimes gave a hint as to the current state of Franco-German relations.

In the end Hubert went first. I thought that Mueller and Lucet might collide as they both went through side by side after him, but they managed to squeeze through the double-doors together, although Mueller banged his shoulder against the door post. Farinelli half-turned to the rest of us, making a gesture to follow, then darted through the door himself.

O"Hara and I looked at each other and grinned. We looked around to see what was happening with Nielsen and Van Groeningen. Nielsen was sitting absolutely rigid and staring at the door. Then, quite suddenly he rose, marched up to the door, and went through it determinedly. He did not look at us.

Van Groeningen staggered to his feet, grasped his briefcase and began to walk very slowly towards the door. It was clear as he began to stagger that he would not make it without help. O'Hara and I went over to him. We each took one arm and helped him into the meeting room.

The conference table was vast. It would have accommodated twenty or so representatives. Although Farinelli and the Commission had a couple of support staff and there were Harrison and myself from the UK, the others were all on their own. The delegations' places were labelled in French. We moved Van Groeningen to his seat and sat him down. He thanked us in English and put his briefcase in front of him on the table. But he made no attempt to get out his papers.

I examined the room. At one end there was a huge 19th oil painting of some Italian historical event, perhaps something to do with Garibaldi. Above this there was a kind of mezzanine gallery which was glassed in. I could see that this was where some interpreters were sitting. They had their headphones on ready to begin They would provide simultaneous translation of the speeches relayed to them from the desk microphones in front of us.

Harrison and I sat behind a bronze desk-plate marked *Royaume Uni*. We both started to fiddle with our microphones and headphones. I would probably only need to use the headphones when Mueller spoke in German, as he was sure to do. My German was very weak. I thought to myself,

I can lisen to him either on the English or French channel. Later I might try out the Italian interpreter's version of French into English when the Commission or other francophones spoke.

An agenda was in front of us, but before I had had time to do more than glance at it we were off.

Hubert from the chair began by saying how grateful we all were to our Italian colleague for providing us with such splendid hospitality. He realised that a meeting in Rome was not convenient for everyone, but it was very much in the spirit of building a United Europe that we should meet in other capitals from time to time. Colleagues would need to be patient with some of the technical aspects which would not always be of the kind provided in Brussels. Farinelli looked suitably shame-faced. Hubert looked pleadingly at Nielsen who did not respond. He continued to look straight ahead stoney-faced.

Hubert continued. "Unfortunately our Luxembourg colleague has not been able to come to this meeting, but our Belgian colleague, Monsieur Lambert, has been fully briefed on the Luxembourg position and will also speak for Luxembourg." Lambert, another small plump version of Hubert, nodded in appreciation. "Before we start on the Agenda itself would colleagues wish to make any general introductory remarks?"

This turned out to be a tactical mistake. Nielsen immeditatly got to his feet. Then he lifted his desk microphone, which was on a short stand, and raised it up to his face as if he was about to make a toast. I looked across the table at O'Hara who smirked. He pushed across a piece of paper on which he had sketched an angry-looking troll.

Nielsen spoke for over ten minutes in Danish. I tried all the interpreters channels. There was nothing available on any. As far as I know not one of my colleagues spoke Danish although Mueller, as a conscientious German, appeared to be making an effort. All the rest of us looked bewildered and waited for the end. Nielsen's voice got louder and louder as he reached the end of his peroration.

When he finally stopped there was complete silence. Before sitting down he bowed to us all ironically. Then he turned and looked up at the interpeters' glass box and said very loudly in English:

"On behalf of the Royal Government of Denmark I thank you, gentlemen interpreters, for all your efforts this afternoon, and hope you will be able to translate into French this my message of thanks to you which I have put for your benefit into English. In this way my colleagues around me will understand how grateful I am."

He sat down. I hoped Hubert would quickly move us on to the agenda, but he was too late. Van Groeningen rose unsteadily from his seat. He stared around at us and bellowed:

"I didn't understand a bloody word that troll said, and nor did any of you! The point I want to make is that Dutch banks are the best in the world. Those Yankie bankers learnt everything from us. New York should have remained Dutch and still be called New Amsterdam."

Then he swayed and fell forward on to the microphone on the table in front of him.

Farinelli, red-faced with embarrassment, rose and went to summon the usher with the white gloves. When this immaculate figure came in he looked disdainfully at Van Groeningen. It was apparent at once that he was concerned that he might vomit on his uniform.

O'Hara and I rose together and went and lifted our Dutch colleague from his seat and managed to get him out of the room. Farinelli, with the usher trailing behind, led us towards a lavatory. Van Groeningen was violently sick into a wash basin, then managed to recover a little and was able to thank us for our assistance. He indicated that he wanted to go back to his hotel. O'Hara offered to get him downstairs. The usher, who had remained outside the lavatory, then went down with O'Hara to arrange for a taxi.

I went back to the conference room.

Hubert said Monsieur Van Groningen was ill. We should

continue with the agenda. Nielsen remained in his seat and occasionally shuffled his papers but took no further part in the proceedings. It was baffling that he did not leave too.

There was one further surprise. Without warning Mueller rose and asked the Chairman in French if he too could make some preliminary remarks. He then took up the desk microphone and some notes and started to speak. He was easily the tallest of us— I estimated he was about 6 feet four in height, and well built, with the kind of Aryan features on which Leni Reifenstal's camera would have lingered if he had been at Hitler's Nuremburg rally. Of course he addressed us in German.

I put on the headphones and listened at first to the interpreter translating his words into French. Mueller said that he wanted to make some preliminary observations about the Federal Republic of Germany and its service industries since this was on the agenda for this afternoon's meeting. Like most German civil servants of his rank, Mueller had a doctorate. I feared the worst.

He began by providing a detailed account of the German banking industry and its history. There were endless facts and figures, descriptions of regional banks in each of the German states, reams of statistics about the shareholdings of banks in German companies. Mueller used powerful sweeping gestures with his arms to underline various points.

His oration went on and on. I turned over to the channel of the interpreter putting his German into English. This was even worse. I went back to the French channel. Mueller seemed to be paying no attention to whether anyone was listening. After about five minutes I thought that he was reaching the climax of his peroration. I glanced up at the interpreter behind the glass screen. He too was waving his arms about. I could not tell whether this was in mockery or just his response to the rapid flow of words. The contrast between Mueller's oratory in German and the strange high-pitched Italianate version in French in my earphones made me think I was at a modern opera, hearing a duet between a tenor and a baritone. A slight *rallentando* suggested to me that Mueller might be nearing the end. But I was wrong.

Mueller glanced quickly down at his notes and then began *fortissimo* with renewed energy on a description of the German insurance industry. Facts, figures and percentages poured from him. The interpreter in his glass box waved his hands about more wildly. On and on Mueller went like a rogue railway carriage that had broken loose from the train amd was now unstoppable.

O'Hara had rejoined the meeting and pushed another note across to me. It read: 'The complete history of German telcommunications will follow, starting with a brilliant but obscure German who inspired Marconi.' O'Hara was grinning. But I was no longer in the mood to grin back.

At this point Hubert from the Commisson intervened. I have never been more grateful for a Commision initiative.

"Representatives present were, I could see," he said, "all as fascinated as I was by the insight and useful background which the German representative provided on German service industries. Perhaps Monsieur Mueller could arrange for a paper on the German banking, insurance and telecommunication industries for our benefit. This could then be translated into all community languages and circulated to colleagues so that they could brief their ministers."

Mueller looked down from his great height at tiny Hubert, clearly annoyed at having his flow interrupted.

But before he could speak in protest Lucet, the French representative, asked for the floor. He welcomed the Commission's idea. If Monsieur Mueller's account of the German telecommunications industry was as masterly as his account of banking and insurance he was personally enthusiastic to hear it. But he added slyly that it might be better if representatatives were able to study the matter more closely with a written document in front of them. He was sure his German colleague was right to have already worked on assembling all the facts on German service industries.

He would seek instructions from Paris on producing a parallel background paper on key French service industries.

However, he continued, the Government of France remained very doubtful whether it really was appropriate to include services in the next trade round, especially as countries like the United States, and even some countries in Europe (here he looked across pointedly at me) were often delinquent in the way they complied with the existing trade rules for manufactured goods. But we would come to this when we formally reached this agenda item.

Mueller remained standing during these interventions, looking round for support for continuing his speech. I smiled up at him sympathetically, hoping that he might translate his annoyance at being cut short by Hubert and his French colleague into being more sympathetic later to the UK's stance on services. Receiving no visible indications of support Mueller sat down, but rose again immediately to say that he would of course comply with the Commission's request for a paper.

We now moved at last on to the agenda proper. It had clearly been drawn up by the Commission with French connivance.

The first agenda item was entitled 'Flagrant breaches of the existing Trade Agreement'. It was clearly designed to wrong foot the Americans and the United Kingdom. The Commision tabled a short paper entitled: 'Dumping of certain manufactured goods on the European market'. It described in detail how some US companies were selling their products in Europe *below cost* in order to establish a foothold in European markets. The paper listed a number of examples of the practice. Lucet then added to the Commission's litany of instances. As expected the heat was then turned on the United Kingdom. There was no Commission paper, but Lucet spoke at length about London taxis. He said that the detailed specification in contracts for these was clearly designed to exclude vehicles from mainland Europe.

I spoke using Gilmore's background facts, and then

turned my fire on French public authorities' tactics for excluding foreign competition. I then asked Harrison to give a number of examples which had outraged potential UK tenderers for French Government and local government contracts. He produced a large dossier of letters of complaint, which he proceeded to read very slowly in full.

To my astonishment, Lambert, our little Belgian colleague, usually content to support whatever France wanted, also instanced some examples of French discrimination against would-be Belgian tenderers. Then, for good measure he added an example of a similar nefarious French practice which his Luxembourg colleague had asked to be raised.

Lucet was taken aback and clearly annoyed. He said that if colleagues would give him the examples in writing he would have them investigated when he returned to Paris.

We now moved on to preparation for the Uruguay Round. The Commission made what was clearly a prepared speech in which Hubert indicated that EC Ministers would be well advised to show extreme caution about the possibility of including services in the coming round. There was still much to do in the coverage and compliance of the trade in manufactured goods which were already covered. *Some*—he stressed this word— other areas might be included. But the European Community needed to ensure that other countries, such as the United States, were more meticulous in complying with what was already part of the Agreement. The Commission was not sure that the European Community was ready for a leap forward at this stage.

I then spoke. I said we should approach the possibility of including services with an open mind. There was no reason why we could not pursue some extension of the agreement in manufacturing, an improvement in compliance with existing rules, and cover services as well if it was possible to reach a sensible agreement with other countries. It was unlikely that the United Kingdom Government would wish to close the door on an extension of the Agreement to cover services in advance, even before the Uruguay round began formally. I concluded with a short panegyric of the benefits which the freeing of markets had brought to the world economy since the Second World War. I expected a well-considered extension of coverage to include services would produce further benefits.

To my surprise Mueller said he agreed with the United Kingdom. The fact that he had done some work on German services showed that Germany was ready to look seriously at the possibilities. The EC should at least be ready to enter into dialogue on this question with other countries. Of course Germany would not be willing to favour including services unless the terms were right.

Lucet was clearly further discomforted, and salt poured into his wounds when O'Hara said that he shared the view of his German and UK colleagues. I doubted whether he had had any instructions from Dublin on the issue, but he had an anarchic spirit and just wanted to scupper what he believed had been an attempt at a French/Commission stitch-up.

Poor Hubert was forced to conclude that the meeting was of the view that the possibility of including services in the Uruguay Round should not be ruled out at this stage, and that this would be the Commission's line for EC Ministers.

Lucet said that he was of course ready to accept the feeling of the meeting. But he warned, looking across at me, that his own Ministers might well be more hostile than he was to an extension to services because of the way American companies were currently behaving. The abject failure of the US Government to halt their companies' flagrant dumping was '*scandaleux*'. The French Government might well seek a judicial panel on these US practices.

A few technical issues were on the agenda and I left these to Harrison to handle.

Although I was satisfied with the outcome, my concentration was now faltering. To remain focussed I again tried listening to how the French speakers' points were put into English. But this did not help. I removed my headphones.

Quite suddenly the whole meeting seemed a charade. Unexpectedly the end of Lewis Carroll's *Alice in Wonderland* came into my mind. It was the moment after the Queen of Hearts had shouted for the umpteenth time 'Off with her head!' Alice, now restored to her full size, suddenly says: 'Who cares for you...You're nothing but a pack of cards!'

It was my pilgrimage with Benson that was real. What had been happening here was irrelevant to what really mattered.

The meeting was now breaking up. I told Harrison that I would produce a record, and wished him a good trip home.

By an act of will I managed to say some civil words to my colleagues. I thanked Farinelli for his hospitality, and Mueller for his support over services. I even said I looked forward to his paper. I then shook hand with Lucet and my Belgian colleague, and told Hubert that I looked forward to the Commission's minutes of the meeting.

Nielsen had remained in his seat. I went over to him and said I agreed that the Italian interpreter's English version of French was poor. He looked at me with a stoney face at first, as though I was not there. Then gave me a wan little smile and said in English:

"What a total waste of time. Denmark and the UK should never have joined the European Community." Then he grasped my hand briefly, gathered up his papers and went out.

O'Hara and I went out down the grand stair-case together. He asked me what I was doing this evening.

"I'm meeting a priest friend for Vespers at Santa Maria Maggiore."

He looked at me wistfully. "I used to be an altar boy. But I've sort of lapsed. You see I'm divorced."

I don't ever remember seeing a sadder face.

I wanted to say something, but found I couldn't. Benson would have found the words, I thought, and would have done something too. Why didn't I ask O'Hara to join us? He could only say no. They are not just a pack of cards. They are human beings! They are just lost. Like me.

When we got to the grand entrance O'Hara asked someone to order a taxi. He even offered to drop me off at Santa Maria Maggiore. I could see it was an appeal for company, and not just an attempt to do a good turn. Without thinking I replied briskly:

"Thanks, Jim, but I've decided to walk as it's not too far and I have plenty of time.

I knew as soon as I had said this that I had missed an opportunity. I also remembered that it was Jim O'Hara who had put poor Van Groeningen into a taxi.

I watched O'Hara go out through Ministry doors with an Italian official to look for a taxi. He seemed a little stooped. The top of his balding head, with its wisps of red hair, came just above the broad shoulder of the young Italian. I stood paralysed near the reception desk. For a few moments I had been smug about the results of the meeting. But now I knew that in every other way I had failed.

CHAPTER FIFTEEN

FEELING THE WEIGHT

MY SENSE of failure grew as I walked to Santa Maria Maggiore. I did not just feel that I had let down Jim O'Hara. It seemed to me that I had always put myself before others, even those for whom I was specially responsible like Angela, Cyprian and Perpetua. Only this morning when I was at the Forum I had completely forgetten about my commitment to buy something on the Roman remains for Cyprian. At least I might be able to remedy this if I could find a stall or shop selling this kind of thing on my way.

I was following my street map of Rome, but I was so preoccupied that I did not really notice anything other than the street names. In his letter Sebastian had said rather surprisingly that he thought I could 'make it.' But how could such a fellow, a chance acquaintance, so different from me in background, education and interests, sum me up and have a conviction as to how I might turn out.

Sebastian had told me a great deal about himself, but he knew very little about me. Some phrases from the Book of Revelation came into my mind, although I had to verify the exact text later:

'I know thy works, that thou art neither cold nor hot: I would thou wert cold or hot. So then because thou art lukewarm, and neither cold nor hot, I will spue thee out of my mouth.'

That was me: lukewarm and mediocre in everything. I reached a square where there were stalls selling newspapers and magazines, and some tourist souvenirs of Rome.

I stopped at one and looked through their guides to Rome. I found one entitled *Rome Past and Present—a guide to the Monumental Centre of Ancient Rome*. It had excellent photographs of the Forum and surrounding ancient buildings such as the Colosseum. For each photograph there was also a detailed coloured transparency which you could lay over the present day archaelogical remains, and thus have an artist's and scholar's idea, based on the best historical research, of what the buildings would have looked like in Republican and Imperial Rome. It was the sort of thing that the Italians do so well, and seemed the perfect present for Cyprian.

The purchase lifted my spirits and by the time I reached Santa Maria Maggiore I had managed a very shy thank-you to St Joseph and my guardian angel. I had decided they must have played some part in this find. I was now eager to meet Benson and looking forward to Vespers.

He was there when I arrived, waiting at the top of the steps to the left of the central doorway. I recognised him instantly as he looked impressive in his *Capello Romano*. He greeted me warmly and asked how my meeting had gone. I explained that the UK government would be satisfied with the outcome, but on a personal level I had missed an opportunity to help a colleague. He put his forefinger to his lips and said: "Later". Then he led the way into the Basilica, tucking his hat under his arm.

This time I was ready when he turned to touch my fingers with the holy water from the stoup, and genuflected without feeling self-conscious. Benson led me to a seat in the nave towards the front. The large Church was I thought a little over half-full. The service was due to begin in ten minutes. Benson brought out his Vespers Book. He whispered that, since it was the Friday after the third Sunday in Lent, the Five Wounds of Our Lord would be specially remembered. We should remember in our private prayers the young Knights of the Kite, who had these symbols on the panels of their box-kites.

The light in the church was dim so I was unable to see the famous fourth century mosaics above the Ionic columns on either side of the nave, or those on the arch above the apse. But the gilding of the coiffered ceiling still dazzled. Luff says that the gold used on this was given by Ferdinand and Isabella of Spain and was from the very first consignment of gold from the New World.

I knelt and tried to pray. All my recent dissatisfaction with my life came flooding back. Very troubled I looked up and saw a celebrant wearing a biretta enter, followed by a choir of eight boys and seven men in choir robes. The celebrant genuflected towards the altar. The choir did the same in pairs. I noticed that there was a lectern in the middle of the sanctuary facing the altar. The last man in the choir, who was without a pair, took the place behind the lectern facing the choir. The priest sat in the choir stalls on the left. He and the choir knelt momentarily, then stood in silence.

A short pause followed, then the celebrant began the chant:

"*Deus, in adiutorium meum intende.* [O God come to my help.]"

To which the choir responded:

"*Domine, ad adjuvandum me festina.* [O Lord, make haste to help me.]"

The celebrant led the doxology:

"*Gloria Patri, et Filio, et Spiritui sancto.* [Glory to the Father, and to the Son, and to the Holy Ghost.]"

The choir responded:

"*Sicut erat in principio, et nunc, et semper, et in sæcula sæculorum, Amen.* [As it was in the beginning, is now, and ever shall be, world without end. Amen.]"

It was this longer sentence that gave me a chance to realise that this was no ordinary choir. Their chant mingled boys and men's voices in perfect clarity of diction and sonority.

The cantor intoned the first antiphon, followed by the choir:

"*Laus tibi Domine, Rex æternæ gloriæ.* [Praise to Thee, O Lord, King of everlasting glory.]" Then the first antiphon for the Five Wounds of Our Lord Jesus Christ. "*Vere languores nostros ipsa tulit, et dolore nostros ipse portavit.* [Surely he hath borne our infirmities and carried our sorrows.]"

Benson handed me his book for vespers open at the page so that I could follow. Once the cantor had intoned the beginning of the psalm I watched the choir sit, and each side chanted the verses, first one side, then the other. All of us stood for the *Gloria*, and the celebrant lifted his biretta. I glanced at Benson who was standing transfixed.

The antiphons that followed each psalm were all different. The English crib opposite the Latin of one of them read: 'The Lord hath bound up the wound of his people, and hath healed their sore.' A strange thing happened. This seemed to restore my spirits. At the *Gloria* after the next psalm I stood for the first time feeling confident. The way each antiphon shed light on each psalm seemed some kind of liturgical miracle. My spirits soared. We all stood while the celibrant sang the little chapter. It was from the prophet Isaiah. It spoke of the suffering servant whose mistreatment prefigured the suffering of Christ. For me some words struck home:

"*Christus vulneratus est propter iniquitates nostras*. [He was wounded for our sins.]"

For my sins! For my sins! Somehow—perhaps because the Latin made me concentrate—the words and their meaning struck home for the first time. So as the celebrant concluded his chant I found myself croakily chanting, *Deo gratias*, with the others.

Benson whispered to me that it was apt that an English choir should sing William Byrd's setting of the *Pangue lingua* which was the hymn for today. As a Catholic himself Byrd knew how much his fellow Catholics were suffering under Queen Elizabeth.

A boy treble began in plainchant alone. His pure liquid sound was that of a King's College Cambridge chorister. I knew from gramophone records that Roman trebles such as those from the Sistine Chapel choir always used greater attack. Suddenly the full choir went into parts for the first time. It was like a moment in a beautifully-crafted black and white film, when the Director suddenly launches it into colour. The poliphany was slow and measured, but very sweet. I felt my throat catch and tears come in my eyes. The verses were telling the story of human beings' redemption in reverse— from our Lord's sacrifice on the Cross to His birth to our Lady. The choir moved alternately between plainchant and poliphony. I specially remember a solo tenor who began one verse alone. His voice was so affecting that I sensed those present catching their breath.

The choir continued at a measured pace until the triumphant doxology at the end. At that point I realized that I had never in my life thought about heaven. What might it be like? Could someone like me ever make it? For the first time I realized that it was something I wanted.

The celebrant intoned the collect, and the choir responded. The words pictured us gazing at our Lord on the Cross pierced with the sword, and mourning for Him. The priest intoned a further antiphon and the choir responded with the chant. Then all stood for the *Magnificat*, our Lady's prayer, with each side of the choir responding to each other. The last antiphon was repeated.

Benson whispered to me:

"Today there should also be a collect for St John of God, patron of the sick, and of those caring for them."

The priest chanted '*Oremus*,' and continued with St John's special collect. It spoke of him pleading for us that we might be healed from our sins. The priest chanted *Dominus vobiscum*. But I was no longer following the words of the further exchanges between celebrant and choir.

Quite suddenly it was all over. The priest and choir began processing out. I was already on my knees before they disappeared. It was not faith I was now praying for. Despite everything it seemed to me that this had been granted. But "Jesus," I kept saying,"my sins, my sins! Will I ever get rid of them?"

I covered my head with my hands. A strange idea came to me. If I were to lift my head and turn towards Benson he would be gone. And I would have my sins for ever.

I was too terrified to look. A soft organ voluntary was in

the background, but it was not reassuring. I had read about people praying fervently, but had never experienced this myself till that moment. I kept pleading with our Lady and my guardian angel that Benson should still be there. There was no sign of an answer, no still small voice as in Scripture. So it was with a desperate act of will that I raised my head, opened my eyes and looked left to where he had been sitting.

Yes! He was still there! But he was not saying his prayers as he usually was when I glanced at him when we were beside each other in a church. Instead his piercing blue eyes were fixed on me. And they seemed full of pity.

"You said you wanted to say something before vespers," he whispered. "A tour of the church will have to come later. If you have finished your prayers we might set off to Trastevere now for supper. You can then tell me what it is."

We went by bus. I remember that we both stamped our tickets in the machine when we were inside. We found a seat next to each other and I cradled my office briefcase on my lap. It seemed to me like when I used to hold Perpetua when she was tiny. I remember nothing more of the journey. I was trying to work out what I was going to say to Benson. He did not speak during the journey which seemed unusual.

When we got off it was beginning to be dark. The lights were on in the shops and cafés and this counteracted the evening gloom. However Benson led me very quickly into a very narrow dark side street, which was much less well lit. At first this seemed sinister—you expected a villain might come at you from the shadows. But then I noticed two small shrines let into the house walls, one each on either side of the alley. Both had images of our Lady, one in mosaic; the other was a sculpted half-bust. The niches were protected with glass. Behind this, some small votive candles were burning and tiny vases of artificial flowers.

We had not gone more than a few yards when suddenly, out of the shadows, there appeared a young man coming from the other direction. He was not much more that five feet two in height and very thin. The torn jeans he was wearing looked too big for him. I guessed that without the piece of frayed string at his waist they would have slipped off his narrow hips. There were sandles on his feet. Even in the poor light I could see that the front of his pale shirt was badly stained. On top of the shirt he was wearing a khaki, padded, sleeveless jerkin. But much of the stitching had come undone along the top of one shoulder so this too looked in danger of slipping off. His hair was long, greasy and unkempt, and the wild effect was enhanced by a straggly beard. But it was his eyes, lit up from one of the votive shrines, which demanded attention. They stared at us from the pallid skin of his face. They were wild, pleading and ecstatic, as though he had seen some kind of vision.

He stopped about two yards in front of us. Benson and I also halted abruptly. I could not decide whether the young man was psychologically disturbed, or was wanting to ask us for money. He ignored me, and stepped forward to stand before Benson. Then he raised his two hands, and grasping both Benson's arms looked up into his face. Benson did not flinch or recoil. A second later the young man was kneeling on the pavement at Benson's feet with his eyes lowered.

Benson put his hand on his greasy hair and gave him a blessing, then made the sign of the cross over him. Benson then bent down, raised the young man him to his feet, and embraced him as he had done with the young footballer on the train. The young man gave a beautiful smile and this time I was included in his glance. Benson seemed to press something into his hand but I could not see what it was. The young man then went off in the direction from which we had come. No word had been spoken, and Benson made no comment as we continued on our way.

I am fairly sure that the restaurant which we reached quite quickly was called '*da Americo alla Luna*'. A little later Angela and I tried to find it again but without success. Before we entered Benson turned to me and said:

"One day you must read a life of St Benedict Joseph Labré."

The restaurant was quite small and we were early. The Romans don't usually arrive to dine until rather later. Despite this a few tables had been taken.

Benson had evidently made a reservation. Someone who seemed to be the proprietor escorted us to a table for two in a quiet corner. He was a middle-aged rotund man with a neat little moustache. There were some Italian breadsticks on the table but he quickly brought us some warm rolls covered with a napkin and the menu, then left us to consider.

Very quietly Benson began the angelus. To my surprise I could remember most of the responses and only had one prompt from Benson. After the 'Amen' he said a Latin grace then turned to me and said:

"Well?"

I tried to speak, but nothing came, although he was looking at me with a most gentle and encouraging smile.

"You said that you had missed an opportunity to help a colleague at the end of your meeting."

"Yes," I said. And I turned away from his glance. Then without looking at him I blurted out:

"Father Hugh, I don't understand anything about what is going on. All I seem to be aware of is my feeling of remorse for my past. I don't think I have ever been conscious of others, let alone of God. It's not just Cyprian and Perpetua, Angela and her mother and colleagues. It's everyone. I seem to have been like it since I was a child. I don't think I have been a spectacular sinner—though who am I to judge?—but there have been hundreds of petty acts of betrayal, failure to act or comfort, misuse of my physical gifts. This pilgrimage has helped make me realise all this. I know I want to change... B...but I just don't think I have the will... Do you think that our Lord...or His Church... could do anything with me?"

During this incoherent stammering monologue, as my voice got louder and louder, it was beginning to attract the attention of the other diners. I never once looked at Benson. When I paused, the whole restaurant seemed to go silent. At last I managed to whisper very quietly:

"Father, will you hear my confession?" Then, even more quietly I added: "It's my surprise."

He looked at me firmly, pushing forward his chin as I had seen him do before when he was about to say something serious. His eyes seemed kind but particularly protuberant and hooded as in the photograph in his biography.

"My dear Bridge, you do not know what you are asking. I cannot hear your confession. That is not for me to do."

Then he added, as if to give a little comfort:

"But it is much to your credit that you have asked."

It was a terrible blow. I stammered:

"But Sebastian? You heard his confession!"

"Oh yes. His situation was desperate. He was a lapsed Catholic. We were on the high seas. A faculty from a bishop of a diocese in either England or France to hear confessions was not an option, given the urgency. But your case is quite different, as is our relationship. We are in Rome. The city is full of priests with appropriate faculties."

My eyes filled with tears as I looked at him. He returned my gaze, then said:

"But I will accompany you to your first confession, if you would like that. But I must first ask you now whether you have resolved to be a Catholic."

As I made no reply there was a further probing question:

"Is it not possible that, by taking this decisive step, and abandoning your wife and children where they are, and entering the Church alone, you are not just surrendering to your self-centredness? "

I took a deep breath and replied:

"It may appear so, Father, but surely in spiritual matters you should follow your conscience wherever it leads? I shall pray that they shall follow me in due course into the Church."

"But how will you react if they feel betrayed by your decision, or perhaps worse, are just indifferent to it?"

I stammered: "I shall just pray for the grace to accept this. Perhaps not being allowed to be a channel of grace for them will teach me humility and make me better able to accept the will of God."

He said nothing. Then I added:

"Will you pray for me?"

He smiled at last. Then he stretched his right hand across the table. I raised my hand and grasped his. It was warm and firm. He had shaken my hand when we had first met. The only subsequent times that I had touched him was on the tip of his finger wet with holy water from a stoup.

As he withdrew his hand he said very quietly:

"But surely there are lots of points in the Catechism about which you are unsure?"

"Yes," I said, "there are some. But I now have a firm conviction that the Catholic Church is the Church, and that in due course I will come to understand why it is right about those things on which I am confused or unclear. Someone like me has much to learn."

"And you will never learn everything in this life," he added.

At some point we must have ordered a main course. I am not sure when it came, or what it was that either of us ordered. Because it was a Friday in Lent it was probably fish.

But I do remember the pudding. Benson asked for some sort of meringue and cream confection which was brought to the table by the proprietor with a flourish. Flames were shooting from top of the meringue and the dish. When he placed it on the table before he served it, the brandy seemed to remain alight much longer than with my efforts at home with the Christmas pudding.

Benson also ordered a small bottle of sparkling white wine which he said was to celebrate our pilgrimage. But he did not order cigars. In fact I never saw him smoke in Rome. When the coffee arrived he again began to look more serious. And this is what he said:

"My dear Bernard—and this was the first time he had used my Christian name—you have been an exemplary pilgrim and a stimulating travelling companion. Tomorrow I shall take you to St Peter's. It might be advantageous to be there by nine o'clock before the tourist parties arrive, if you are prepared for an early start. You and I will seek out a confessional where there is a priest who can hear your confession in English. The tour of the great Basilica and the Vatican you will have to do later. I am not sure of my obligations and movements after tomorrow morning. We shall see.

"I don't think it is realistic, or indeed desirable, that you should expect to be received into the Church in Rome, however romantic that might seem to someone like you. You will need to explain everything to Angela, your mother-in-law and Cyprian and Perpetua. Your other relations and friends will need to be informed as well. All this will need careful preparation and handling. As someone used to the world of diplomacy I would expect you to find this easier than some. Remember that even as a catechumen you will be an ambassador for the Church.

"Family and close friends should be at least asked to your reception. You must pray for the grace to accept it if they are unwilling to be there, or promise to come and then fail to appear.

"But I am moving too quickly. I suggest you make a careful plan. First you will need someone to give you formal instruction. There is a priest at The Travellers' Club who will be ready to advise you. I doubt if he gives instruction himself these days, unless you already happened to be one of his friends. You should simply ask one of the porters at the Club's reception desk on the left as you enter. Say you want to see the priest who is resident there. There is only one, and the porter will understand what you want.

"When you meet this priest, there is no need to mention that I suggested you go to him. Better not. Whoever he suggests will be completely sound. Your main task from now on will be to strengthen and consolidate your life of prayer, and get to know our Lord, our Lady, St Joseph and some of the saints who appeal to you. St Bernard himself is quite a fiery saint, but he has his poetic side which he shows in his commentary on the *Song of Songs*. You may find a copy of this at The London Library." (This proved not to be the case. Perhaps it was one of the library's books destroyed in the bombing during the Second World War.)

"As you make progress you will begin to understand why it was important for us not to interrupt Sebastian at prayer at St Joseph's altar in Saint-Germain-des-Prés yesterday. There comes a time when those of us who have had the privilege of being a channel of grace can be a distraction to a serious change of heart and direction. You may well have to face this yourself in due course.

"Now since you are to make your general confession tomorrow I think we should pay the bill and return to our lodgings."

He looked across at the proprietor who I noticed was observing us keenly. Benson mouthed "*Il conto, per favore.*" He must have already made out the bill for he came across quickly with it. We divided the total in half, added a generous tip and each handed over our share. Before we left I went to the lavatory. When I returned Benson was talking animatedly to the proprietor next to a little counter near the way out. Benson handed our host something, but I did not see what it was. With loud "*buona nottes*" we left.

I have no recollection of our walk back to the bus stop, or of the journey across the Tiber, or my return to the *pensione*. For a number of reasons this memory gap later troubled me a good deal. I think it would have been possible for me to see St Peter's floodlit as the bus crossed the bridge over the Tiber, but I remember nothing.

I was concentrating all the time on what I should say when I made my confession. I am not sure if Benson said anything during our return trip. However he did accompany me to the door of my little *pensione*, and said he would call to collect me there again at 8.30 am in the morning. I do not remember if he said anything else. It seems likely that he did. But up till now I have no idea what it was, although I have often tried various devices to stimulate some recollection.

The night porter gave me my key. The inside of my room seemed even vaster than I remembered. I put down my briefcase on the marble floor and lay on the double bed. It seemed like the night before an exam.

I went and got some sheets of foolscap from my briefcase and lay these on the little table. I put a chair in front of it, took out a government biro from my suit pocket and stared at the top blank sheet.

I had decided that I would need to review my whole life. I got up and retrieved the little catechism from my luggage and reread the exacting sentences on confession. I noted again how sacrilegious it was to conceal serious sin. The fact that the Church took the view that children came to the age of reason at about aged seven seemed to indicate that I would not need to go back further than that.

I decided to make some notes. When I had done this I would organise them in two ways: a chronological account and a thematic one. The overall structure would be sins against God, and sins against other creatures, first human persons, living and dead, and then other living things of God's creation.

To my surprise events and ideas came quite easily and I quickly filled both side of several foolscap pages in my untidy almost illegible writing. I did a lot of crossing out and had to insert balloons of additional points and clarifications. I remembered that long ago, when I was a university student, a Catholic friend told me that it was important to be precise in confession and not hide the shameful truth with vague statements. More and more incidents came into my mind and I filled several more foolscap pages before I attempted some organization.

How awful it must be to be a priest and have to listen to this sort of thing regularly. I wondered if priests ever asked you, when a confession seemed unending, like Mueller's speech this afternoon, if you would perhaps like to come back another time! Would that happen to me?

Organizing what I needed to say seemed to take longer

than making the notes. I was now feeling extremely tired but I struggled on. At one point I knelt down beside my bed. Since it was still Friday (but only just, as it was 11.50 pm) I said the first decade of the Sorrowful Mysteries of the Holy Rosary, remembering our Lord's Agony in the Garden of Gethsemene. Then I pleaded for the grace to help me make a good confession.

The preparation seemed to come together after that, and I produced what seemed a reasonably complete draft of what I felt I should confess. I then read it all through, appalled at what I had done, and at how often I had just repeated the same sins. It also struck me how my serious capital sins had hosts of little venial sins grouped about them like acolytes. I made myself read it all through again and tried to assess what degree of sorrow I had for each one, or whether I just wanted to get them out of my system. It seemed to me that if I really intended to amend my life I needed to assess this.

I then considered this great wad of paper. I surely couldn't take this with me into the confessional box. I decided to produce a summary, a sort of *aide-memoire* that would fit into my jacket pocket. I usually tried to do this if I had to make a speech. I found a piece of card among my office papers and started to work on this. It needed to be comprehensive, but limited to a few key words, in order that they would prompt my memory. I made a further draft of this summary and then a fair copy.

What was I now to do with my copious notes? A disturbing thought struck me. Suppose someone else got hold of them. I wondered if I should keep them to read through again in the morning. No. They must go now. I went opposite to my enormous bathroom. In my sponge bag I located a small packet of wax matches. Standing against the wash-basin I lit the first page of notes and let the ash fall into it. Eight matches were needed to burn every page. Then I turned on the tap and washed the fragments of black ash down the plug hole.

I felt much comforted by this. When I returned to my room I put the summary for my confession face downward on my bedside table, and got ready for bed. A little revival of energy enabled me to kneel down and say some prayers of thanksgiving for the events of the day. I also commended each member of my family in turn to the care of our Lady and St Joseph. I then tried to bring to mind each person that I had met on the pilgrimage and all those attending this afternoon's meeting, especially Jim O'Hara. Finally I addressed my Guardian Angel and all three persons of the Blessed Trinity to ask for grace for tomorrow. It was a little schematic but I felt that I had made an effort and this was of comfort.

Just before I turned the light out I read through the words of the Act of Contrition which I would need to use tomorrow in the Confessional. I resolved to repeat them in the morning so that I would know them by heart.

I woke just before 6 am. I was so disoriented at first that I thought I was in a hotel in Brussels and that my EC meeting was later in the day. But my mind soon cleared and I remembered that I was in Rome and that the meeting had already happened.

I had no recollection of any dreams. I turned on the bedside light. Of course I had come to Rome with Benson. We had had a meal together last night. Had I drunk too much? Then it came back to me. I had asked him to hear my confession and he had declined. He was coming this morning to take me to St Peter's so that I could make a general confession there.

Why had I asked him, and why had I then agreed to go to St Peter's with him when he had refused my request? Was it prudent of me? Benson seemed to have taken over my will.

It all came back to me now. Last night I had tried to prepare myself for confession. I had made notes. But I then remembered burning them. I had tried to cover my entire life. Many of the things I had listed I now recalled, and these appalled me. Indeed it seemed strange that the act of writing them down last night had not swamped me with terrible dreams. I noticed the piece of white card that lay face down on my bedside table. Of course, I had also made a short summary. Or had I burnt this too? Perhaps the piece of card on the table was blank. I avoided turning it over.

For the first time since I had met Benson I was not sure I wanted to see him again. Perhaps if I decided that I did not want to go to St Peter's he would become aware of this somehow—he often seemed to be able to discern what was in my mind—. Would he then just fail to keep our appointment this morning? Did I really want this?

Why did I need to make a confession to a priest anyway? Why could I not just confess to God? Even as I thought this, I knew this was wrong. 'Confess your sins to one another.' That was the scriptural text. In my heart I needed the shame of putting everything into words for another, and yes, the certainty that I had been forgiven.

I found myself saying the Angelus. I managed to concentrate till the end. I felt calm but spiritually numb. I asked myself why I had said the Angelus while I was feeling like this. Was our Lady prompting me? Or my Guardian Angel? Or was it just Benson again, or the habit of the Rule of Life for our pilgrimage?

Quite suddenly I got off my bed. Whatever I decided it would be a fresh start. I must shave. I would then have another turn in that huge white bath. Pilgrims should have a ritual bath. But my doubts made me question whether I now qualified as a pilgrim.

I was tempted to wallow in the bath, but I was brisk, and towelled myself dry energetically. A mirror reminded me that gardening was not enough. I needed to go to a gym.

Back in my room everything started to fall into place again. I retrieved my rosary. As it was Saturday it was the Joyful Mysteries. I chose the second Joyful Mystery, the Visitation. This tells of our Lady going to see her cousin, St Elizabeth, when both were expectant mothers. For some reason Benson had turned up to visit *me* in Kemsing.

I said the prayers very slowly. The intention was for myself. By the end I knew for certain that I couldn't pull back now.

I went over to the bedside table and turned over the card. Of course there was my summary. I read it through critically, as though it were a civil service draft. It seemed complete. I would expand on it of course when I was in the confessional. I tried to envisage this. Would I be able to see my confessor's face? Would he be young or old? I rather thought he would be old and venerable. How long would I have to wait in a queue? I reread the words of the Act of Contrition in the Catechism and tested myself on the text. I reckoned that I had scraped a pass.

I looked at my watch. It was 7.15 am. I must dress. What should I wear? Benson would be in clerical dress. Should I be in a suit? No, I thought, I'm on a pilgrimage. I should wear what I had worn during our walk in Kent. I brushed the trousers to get some mud off them, then decided that they were reasonably respectable. I wanted to have a few things with me—map of Rome, Italian dictionary, green cloth, Catechism, but I didn't want to lug a bag or my large pack around. I took the papers for my meeting out of my briefcase and put into this what I thought I would need for the day. Then I went down to breakfast.

I was the first down, but I could smell coffee brewing and a maid was there putting out baskets of bread and fruit on the tables. I took a table for two though I was fairly sure Benson had indicated that he would breakfast at his lodgings. It was a simple continental-style breakfast. But the bread was fresh and had been warmed. There was a wide choice of fruit: oranges and grapefruit, some apples, some small green figs in syrup, and several imported bananas. I was tempted by a single pomegranite but thought it would be difficult to eat without getting the juice all over me and the table-cloth.

The maid brought the coffee which was excellent. I had my confession crib in my jacket pocket so I read it through again. Several more people came in to breakfast and they all greeted me warmly. The dining room was square and not very large, almost cosy. The curtains had been drawn and the outside shutters were open, although the windows were thankfully closed. The interior of the hotel was not kept very warm but it looked like a sunny morning outside.

I felt purposeful when I had finished. Benson would be here at 8.15 am or so. I went back to my room, cleaned my teeth and collected my briefcase. I also took Luff's *The Christian's Guide to Rome* with me, thinking to read about St Peter's in the lobby until Benson arrived.

However, as I entered the lobby I heard loud bursts of laughter. Over in one corner the proprietor, who had seemed rather severe when I arrived, was now in animated conversation in Italian with Benson. They were sitting opposite each other in two chairs by the window. As I arrived they both rose. The manager greeted me warmly and shook my hand. He then went back to the table where he kept his clients' details. Benson smiled his infectious smile which I had not seen for some time. He was in his usual clerical dress. He had left his Roman hat on his chair when he rose. I saw that his pilgrim staff was on the floor beside the chair.

"I hope you did not sit up half the night getting ready for this morning," he said breezily. "Of course it is important and needs to be done as meticulously as possible, but the key thing to remember is that our Lord loves you, and wants you to 'make it' as Sebastian put it in his fresh, vernacular way. I don't think either of us need to be too solemn."

I looked at him anxiously. Should I tell him about my moments of doubt this morning? Would he say that perhaps it was really too soon after all to make my confession? Suddenly I knew that this was a temptation, and I had to tell him. I briefly mentioned how I had felt.

"Oh," he said, laughing. "You must get used to that sort of thing. Those opposed to a fellow's conversion never let up. At least you weren't knocked up by wayward priests at an ungodly hour this morning! The fact that you were able to mention this to me shows that friendly forces are getting the upper hand. Of course we still need to be vigilant. Now let's get on and start to enjoy a Roman early spring morning."

I left the key to my room with the proprietor and we set off. Benson said that we should go by bus so that we would be there in good time. We got off near the beginning of the Via della Conciliazione so as to make, as Benson said, the most of the approach to St Peter's Piazza. He was now wearing his *Capello Romano* and was making full use of his Kentish pilgrim staff.

"This road," Benson told me, "used to be narrower so that you came upon St Peter's Basilica and the great piazza as a surprise. Now that the road has been widened into a processional route you can see your destination from afar. The experience has changed to one of anticipation, instead of surprise. You know I prefer surprises," he added.

He talked amiably about Anglo-Saxon pilgrims, and the saintly founders of religious congregations who had come to Rome to obtain official recognition and approval of their rule. He also mentioned other famous visitors: Byron, Keats, Goethe and Stendhal. I did not follow his remarks with great attention, but he did not seem to mind.

I was enjoying the early morning sun, but I was still apprehensive about what was before me.

Although I was well prepared by books, illustrations and photographs for the vast architectural elipse which forms the first part of the piazza it still made a huge impact. Calling it St Peter's Square gives a completely misleading impression, since the first part is all curves. Benson said there were about 140 saints on the tops of Bernini's grand colonnade which frames the piazza. Some of the most important, he pointed out, had been placed nearest the Basilica itself. The huge obelisk, that I had read had been so difificult to erect, was already casting a shadow in the morning sun. The water shooting up into the air from the fountain on the right— I remembered this was the one designed by Bernini—was sparkling in the sunlight.

"No eels today," said Benson abruptly, and turned to me with a big smile.

He seemed amused that I was nonplussed.

"The water for the fountains," he continued, "comes from Lake Bracciano about forty miles from Rome. After its long journey it supplies the Vatican gardens, then the underground pipes reach these two fountains. Visitors are sometimes disappointed when the fountains are not running. The cause is often eels. They breed in the lake and their tiny fry can get into the pipes, grow, and when they reach here, create blockages. Fortunately not today!

"Bernini saw that the piazza needed fountains to give it life when there are not many people about in this vast theatrical space. You can see that he was right."

At the far end of the piazza I caught sight of what appeared to be little dwarf figures in clerical suits with small bags in their hands. There was not one *Capello Romano!*

"Those are priests who have been granted the privilege of saying Holy Mass at St Peter's," said Benson. "You can see that some of them have a friend or relation with them."

He strode forward as though he was eager to join them. But after a few yards he tossed his pilgrim staff high into the air and caught it expertly as he had done at Ightham Mote.

He turned and looked back at me and grinned. I grinned back. Then we surprised each other by both saying in unison: "Not at all edifying!"

I don't think anyone else saw his feat. His sunny mood on that morning must have made this private boyish end of term prank in front of St Peter's irresistible.

CHAPTER SIXTEEN

IN ST PETER'S

I REMEMBER seeing a television programme about the election of Pope John Paul II, which showed this piazza filled to its capacity with hundreds of thousands of people. It was no surprise then how long it took us to reach the steps of the great Basilica. On the way Benson pointed out the window in the Vatican on the right where it was possible to see His Holiness saying the Angelus at midday if he was in residence. We walked up the vast steps side by side. When we were outside in the portico before the massive doors Benson turned to me and said:

"You no longer have your pilgrim's staff, Bernard. Please, I would like you to take mine."

He made his little bow and handed it to me before I could protest. Then removing his Roman hat he went in. I caught up with him and we genuflected together. I remained kneeling with the staff and my briefcase, awestruck by the size and grandeur. Benson tapped me on the arm and whispered:

"You will want to concentrate on the matter in hand. But I *will* show you one thing to begin with, and then you must greet our Lord."

He led me to the left aisle and stood before a marble monument.

It was Canova's commemoration of the last three Stuart royals. James III, the 'Old Pretender' was on the left in half bust. His two sons, Charles Edward—'Bonnie Prince Charlie'—, and his younger brother, Cardinal Henry Stuart, Duke of York, were looking across at their father.

"Of course, the two marble angels weeping below them are conventional," said Benson. "But, if you are a monarchist, their weeping may move you to add to your prayers for the conversion of England, a prayer for them, and that the British sovereign will once again be a Catholic." He closed his eyes for a second then took off again down the left aisle.

Before reaching the left transept he turned right and went out into the very centre of the huge nave. He halted in a rather military fashion. In front of us was the *Confessio* into which I could look down towards where the tomb of St Peter lies. I could also look up at the bronze *baldacchino* with its twisted columns above the Papal altar. I was able to appreciate for the first time the massive size of Michaelangelo's dome which was flooded with light. And there were the Latin words proclaiming proudly the scriptural message to the world:

TU ES PETRUS ET SUPER HANC PETRAM AEDIFICABO ECCLESIAM MEAM ET TIBI DABO CLAVES REGNI CAELORUM. [Thou art Peter and upon this rock I will build my church, and I will give to thee the keys of the kingdom of heaven.]

Benson let me contemplate all this for a few brief moments, then genuflected and took me on to the bronze statue of St Peter before the last huge column on the right hand side of the nave. He kissed St Peter's foot very solemnly and I followed suit. Then we were off again to what I recognised on entry was the Chapel of the Blessed Sacrament. There were a lot of early worshippers and it was fairly full. We found a spare pew near the back. Another genuflection and we were both at last at rest.

"O Lord, I murmered to myself, "I really believe that you are here, that you see me and you hear me." I remained seated as I said the Lord's Prayer very slowly. I said the Hail Mary too, asking for her help in my confession. I felt calm and strengthened. I was hardly conscious of Benson although I could see that he remained seated beside me.

I knelt briefly, then rose again and murmered:

"I am ready."

He said nothing but led me forward into the right transept where the confessionals were. They were all in dark, panelled wood and quite elaborately carved. Reassuringly Catholic-looking I now thought.

Above each confessional the religious order of the priests hearing confessions was indicated in gold lettering. This morning they all seemed to be Franciscans. Benson spoke briefly to some sort of usher who indicated which confessor was hearing confessions in English. I then joined quite a long queue waiting my turn. Benson stood beside me. In due course we got near the front and were able to sit on seats.

I checked my crib and the words of the Act of Contrition, then knelt and went over in my mind what I wanted to say several times. It did not seem very long before Benson touched my arm gently to indicate that it was my turn. I left my briefcase and the pilgrim staff on the floor in front of my seat.

I remember not looking back at Benson as I went forward. I pushed open the curtain, went inside and drew the curtain behind me. The priest's face was softly lit. He was younger than I had expected, perhaps in his early thirties. He wore a wide purple stole.

I will not record here anything about my general confession. I imagine that many first confessions like mine are similar. It followed the pattern I had expected. I said something about myself and explained that this was my first confession and that I had resolved to receive instruction and become a Catholic.

I then launched into my sins. I did not need to refer to my crib. The priest was gently probing to make sure that everything I needed to say came out. I made my act of contrition and he gave me absolution acting in the person of our Lord and His Church.

My penance consisted of saying a number of prayers, as I had been led to expect. The young priest suggested that, since I was English like himself, I might like to say these in the Gregorian chapel. He told me that, although it was created for a later pope Gregory, and there was also in it a statue of the important missionary pope, Gregory XVI, it was a good place to remember the first great Pope Gregory, the Apostle of the English. I might even ask him to help me discern what my vocation as a Catholic should be.

He gave me directions to this chapel. I said I would offer prayers for him and went on my way.

The Gregorian chapel was crowded. It seemed likely that there was to be a celebration of Holy Mass quite soon. I knelt and very slowly and carefully said the prayers prescribed by my confessor. Then I made a long thanksgiving for my whole life since conception and for the extraordinary grace that I had recently received. In my darker moments before my confession I had imagined that I might feel nothing at all once it was all over. But for me it was not like that. I just felt supremely happy. The huge burden had been taken from my shoulders.

I tried to envisage St Gregory the Great here in Rome selecting the first Roman missionaries for England. What did he think would be the outcome? What did he say to them about their task? So many years later that work was still going on, despite all the setbacks. "I doubt if I'll be much use but let me try," I murmered.

It was only then that I remembered Benson and my briefcase. I made my way back to the confessionals. The queues were even longer. The seats were all taken. Rather embarrassed I walked along the row of penitents before the English confessional. I saw that my briefcase and the pilgrim staff were in front of the seat where I had left them. There was no sign of Benson. Murmering excuses to a handsome young woman in a black mantilla, now seated where I had been, I retrieved the staff and my briefcase.

Inserted into under handle of the briefcase there was an envelope. I put it into my jacket pocket and went out into the vast nave and sat in a pew.

On the front of the envelope was one word: BERNARD. It was not handwritten. It appeared to have been cut out from a printed book or journal, then stuck on the front of the envelope. I tore this open. In it there was a very small piece of paper. This too had been cut of a book. It read:

36. And, when he had said these things, kneeling down, he prayed with them all.

37. And there was much weeping among them all. And, falling on the neck of Paul, they kissed him.

38. Being grieved most of all for the word which he had said, that they should see his face no more.

There was nothing else in the envelope apart from these three verses from the Acts of the Apostles. For a moment I thought of going back to look for Benson. Perhaps he had gone to confession too. But in my heart I knew that this was useless. The text was clear.

If I had not made my confession I would surely have felt abandoned. But that was not how I felt now.

I walked slowly back along the nave. The tourist coaches had started to arrive. The huge basilica was filling up. At that moment I seemed to be almost the only person walking back in the direction of the great entrance door. I made a last genuflection and passed out into the portico.

I went over to the top of the majestic flight of steps and looked down into the piazza, now charged with colour and movement. It was then I noticed a blonde young man in shorts. I decided he was probably a German student. He was standing by himself some distance away to my right, and was also on the edge of the steps. But he was looking back at the door of the Basilica. I felt certain that he had been refused entry because he was wearing shorts. He was rather surreptitiously smoking a cigarette. Clearly he had lit up in frustration. I had a sudden idea. I walked over to him, trying to recall some student German, and said:

"Können Sie mir bitte Feur geben?"

He produced a cigarette lighter, and looked at me expecting me to hold up a cigarette. But instead I withdrew the crib of my sins from my pocket and took his lighter.

I managed to produce a flame instantly and carefully set

alight the piece of cardboard. In a few seconds there was just black ash at my feet. I took a handkerchief from my trouser pocket, wiped the black fragments into it, and rubbed the marble pavement clean. I put my dirty handkerchief back into my pocket. When I got to my feet again I handed the lighter back to the young man with a little Bensonian bow. Then my German unexpectedly failed me so I thanked him in English.

His response was also in English, flawless like Mueller's.

"You Englishmen are full of surprises." He had only a trace of a German accent.

"I am sorry they would not let you in."

"I had been told that the rule about shorts only applied to girls!"

"You must come back. There's a lot to see." Then I added. "And plenty going on too if you're ready for it."

He grinned. "I'm going back to my van right now to put on my jeans."

We shook hands. I walked down the steps in the sunlight with my new pilgrim staff. The bells of St Peter's began to ring. In the distance I heard the other church bells of the great city giving their reply.